THE BLOOD VIER

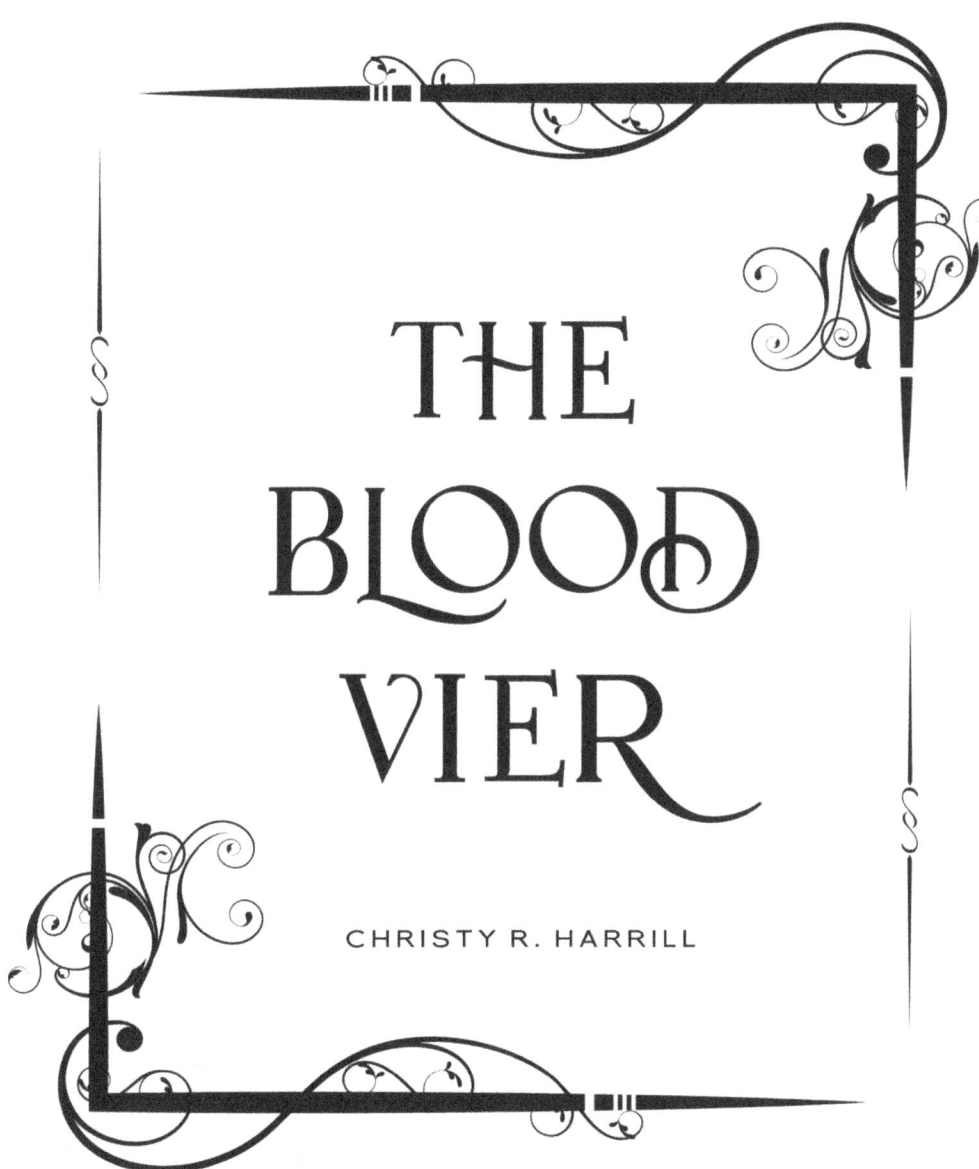

THE BLOOD VIER

CHRISTY R. HARRILL

Rose Hollow Press

This is a work of fiction. Names, characters, places, and incidents either are the product of the author's imagination or are used fictitiously. Any resemblance to actual persons, living or dead, events, or locales is entirely coincidental.

The Blood Vier

Copyright © 2022 by Christy R. Harrill
Dust Jacket Art and Design by Franziska Stern
Hardcase Design by Christy R. Harrill
Map by Christy R. Harrill

Published by Rose Hollow Press, LLC
Oklahoma City, Oklahoma
christyrharrill.com

All rights reserved. No part of this publication may be used or reproduced in any manner whatsoever without the written permission of the publisher except in the case of brief quotations embodied in critical articles or reviews.

Cataloging Data
Harrill, Christy (Christy R.)
The blood vier/ Christy R. Harrill. –First edition.
p. cm. (The Blood Vier series; bk 1)
Summary: After learning she's the key to solving her estranged father's murder, Taryn enters a deadly political game against opposing sovereignties to avenge his death—making her the prime target of assassination for her interference while unraveling secrets and treason threaten to send the kingdom crumbling into ruin.
Library of Congress Control Number: 2022906198
ISBN 979-8-9859243-1-2 (hardback)
ISBN 979-8-9859243-0-5 (paperback)
ISBN 979-8-9859243-2-9 (e-book)
[1. Fantasy. 2. Action and Adventure—Fiction 3. Secrets—Fiction] I. Title

First Edition, September 2022

For there is hope of a tree, if it be cut down,

that it will sprout again,

and that the tender branch thereof

will not cease.

Job 14:7

For Mom

CHAPTER ONE

TARYN

I THOUGHT DEATH would taste bitter, but it was surprisingly sweet. The savor permeated my mouth, growing stronger as Death wrapped his arms around me, paralyzing me with a numbness that chilled every piece of my body. Part of me wanted to escape his grasp and fight my way to freedom; yet another part yearned to melt into his embrace and deliver myself from every sorrow that haunted me in this life.

As Death dragged me into the unknown, my world grew darker, and there was nothing to fill my lungs with. I gasped for air as I struggled against him, but my antics only made his grip tighten. The light was growing dimmer behind me, yet was still within reach, offering me hope. Death clutched at me, desperate to keep his hold as I tried to slip away. I shut my eyes, fear overtaking me. *Not yet*, I whispered.

Death's icy fingers slid over my skin like daggers as he released me from his hold and pushed me back to the warmth of life. I turned to look over my shoulder, to get one last glimpse, but he was already gone. I shivered, the lingering coldness in the air a dark reminder that he would one day return.

My consciousness slowly returned to my body. Each sense awakened like a ray of dawn shooting into the sky, filling the world with color and engulfing it in light. My nose twitched, smelling smoke, and my ears detected the crackling of a small fire. I jolted upright, and an eruption of pain burst inside my head. I quickly fell back with a grimace, gingerly touching my forehead and willing the pain to go away. It swelled within me, the ache growing stronger, blocking everything else from my mind.

A search through my memories grasped for answers but came up short. I could sense them there, lingering at the edges of my clarity, just out of reach. When I managed to touch one, it immediately disintegrated, but then I seized another, and everything suddenly came rushing back like the waves of the ocean. I pieced each muddled recollection together as they shifted into focus—the sharpness of the dagger against my throat, the sickening stench of the thieves, the overwhelming pain as my head smashed against the ground. Clinging to Stryder's neck as he galloped away, and then falling, falling through empty air into the swirling darkness.

My fingers stretched beside me and stroked what felt like the rough fibers of a woolen blanket. I cracked my eyes open, flames licking at my peripheral vision. The star-studded sky was barely visible through the outstretched branches of the trees, their silhouettes woven together like the bars of a cage, imprisoning me. A strange sensation overcame my body. I stiffened as goosebumps traveled up my arm, and the hair on the back of my neck rose. Death may have left me, but I was not alone.

Someone was watching me.

I rotated my head, the forest spinning around me, until I found what I was looking for. Across the fire sat a motionless figure shadowed by the dancing flames. The firelight illuminated his piercing blue eyes. They were fixed on me. And waiting. Waiting for something. Strands of dark hair hung over his forehead, and stubble covered his clenched jaw. Neither of us spoke. Neither moved. I swallowed hard. Fear raced through my body and screamed at me to run, but I didn't move. I held his gaze, my steely eyes refusing to break contact with him.

"If you're looking for money," I said, "I'm afraid I'll have to disappoint you like the others."

The thieves had emptied my saddlebags on the ground in a fit of rage, becoming angrier when they found its contents held little more than the sour cheese and moldy bread I had been rationing. Villages had been sparse out here in the wilderness these past few weeks, and I was fortunate to have what little food I did.

"I'm not looking for money."

His voice was low and steady, spoken with a casualness that implied he possessed all the time in the world to have this conversation. An owl hooted in the distance, the only other noise beyond the crackling flames. I lay there, waiting for an explanation, but he remained quiet. My fingers slowly traveled underneath the blanket in search of a weapon. I craved the security of having something to defend myself with.

My eyes roamed, relaxing as they came to rest on Stryder

grazing several paces away with another horse. Stryder was okay, and with him so close, my chances of escape were rising.

"The horse is fine." The man's gaze had followed mine. "In better shape than you are."

The pain was almost manageable now, but when I sat up on my elbows, my head began to swim.

"I wouldn't get up yet."

I ignored the advice, swaying as I moved into a sitting position, and faced the stranger. The dagger concealed within my boot secretly made its way to my lap, hidden between the folds of my skirt. Without taking my eyes from the stranger, I assessed my surroundings. An escape plan was beginning to form in my mind when another memory resurfaced. This one was of the long-shafted arrows protruding from the thieves' chests—arrows that had not been delivered by my hand. My eyes fell to the longbow lying at the man's side. If he had saved my life, this complicated things. A favor had been granted, and no doubt, he wanted one in return.

That wasn't going to happen.

I had no reason to trust this man and needed to get out of here as quickly as possible. Given my present state, I wouldn't be able to move fast, but if I kicked some of the embers at my feet into the man's eyes, it might give me enough time to reach Stryder and escape.

"Before you run away," the man began, and I blinked, disturbed at his ability to discern my inner thoughts so easily. "You might want to hear what I came to tell you about your father."

Warning bells urgently rang in my mind as every muscle in my body tensed. I tightened my grip on the dagger, a sea of raw emotions flooding my being. Sharp pains shot through my head as I clenched and unclenched my jaw.

"I have no father."

It wasn't exactly a lie.

His gaze fell to the dying fire, and he reached over to grab a stick with his callused hands. As he stoked the fire, the flames momentarily enlarged, illuminating his serious face. He was young, but his authoritative demeanor suggested a knowledge beyond his years. Calmly, he set the stick down and settled his steady gaze on me. "Did Michael Gallows give his ring to the wrong girl, then?"

I sucked in a breath, my fingers involuntarily reaching for the familiar outline of the golden ring on my right hand. The sudden movement gave me away, destroying any hope of indifference. A smile tugged at the corner of the man's mouth, and he chuckled.

"I didn't think so."

Anger rushed through me. Jumping to my feet, I clutched the dagger in front of me, struggling to stay upright. My eyes burned into the man, scared of what he wanted.

"Who are you?" I demanded.

He stood, his eyebrows drawing together, and I squared my shoulders as he rose above me.

"My name is Vladimir, leader of the Kavari." He hesitated for a moment, as if waiting for some kind of recognition.

His rank paralleled the queen's, but it was of no consequence. I would not defer to him no matter who he was.

"And what do you want, *leader of the Kavari*?" I asked mockingly.

"Your father sent me to find you."

An icy chill seeped deep into my bones. He was lying. No

one should know who I was. Who my father was.

"Why does a dead man need to find someone?"

For the first time, his calm demeanor transformed into surprise. Words didn't come at first, as if he couldn't find the right ones to say. "You already know about his death?"

I crossed my arms. It had only been two weeks since I had been informed of my father's death, prompting the immediate departure from my home. With him gone, nothing held me to that small town. I'd been waiting to escape him for years, yet somehow even in death, he still managed to find me. I had barely known my father. Nor had I wanted to know him.

"Why did my father send you to find me?" I asked.

Vladimir's face turned grave. "Because your father was murdered."

My throat tightened, but I kept my emotions in check.
Murdered.

I had only been informed that my father was dead, not that he had been the victim of foul play. I swallowed the lump in my throat, regaining strength. My father meant nothing to me. The revelation of his murder meant nothing to me. I took a step back.

"Whatever happened to my father was his own doing. I'll not have any part of it."

I turned and stumbled toward Stryder like a drunk, the corners of my vision beginning to spin. Stryder gave a low whicker, neck outstretched to greet me. Vladimir's horse grazed nearby, tethered to the ground, and my movements faltered. Stryder stood fully saddled, ready to go except for a quick tightening of the girth, but Vladimir's horse had been untacked for the night. My eyes flicked between the two horses, wondering what the man was playing at.

Footsteps approached from behind, and I inhaled deeply, trying to calm my racing heart. The knife was still in my grasp, and if Vladimir tried anything, I would take him down.

"If you cared so little for your father, why do you still wear his ring?"

My eyes fell to the golden ring encircling my finger. It was impossible to count how many times I had asked myself that same question. When my father had left it behind, all I wanted was to cast it from my sight—just as I had cast him from my sight. Yet every time I tried to get rid of it, I couldn't.

If Vladimir knew who I was, then someone else might too. What if whoever killed my father came for me next? Had the thieves who attacked me known my identity?

My mother and I had never spoken of my father in public. When asked about him, I was instructed to say that he left when I was just a baby. My father never entered the village when he came to visit, and I don't even know that the widow down the road knew about his existence.

I never understood why my mother had been so secretive about him. She insisted it was imperative for our protection; therefore, I had never questioned it. Even after my mother's death, I never spoke of my father to anyone.

I looked out into the darkness surrounding me, and for the first time since leaving my home, the world suddenly felt vast and uninviting. Over the past nineteen years, I'd never traveled farther than the nearest village. I knew nothing of the outside world, and the events that had already transpired frightened me. I had fulfilled my promise to my mother by staying in Navarre until my father bestowed his blessing, but it never came. Upon his death, I packed my meager belongings and set out with nowhere to go and no one to trust. All I had left to hold onto was the hope of finding a trace of my mother's family.

Guilt from the indifference toward my father's death rose within me.

Your father was murdered.

Vladimir's words echoed in my head, twisting around my heart and trying to take root. As much as I tried to harden my heart, the matter vexed me like an itch that wouldn't go away. I might not care for my father, but that didn't mean I was comfortable with allowing him to die without justice. Remorse eroded at my stubbornness, fighting for the upper hand. I placed my hand on Stryder's shoulder to steady myself as my head began pounding harder.

"What happened to my father?" I asked, turning back to Vladimir.

I didn't want to know, but I knew that I needed to.

Vladimir crossed his arms. "Six weeks ago, Michael came to me and said he had stumbled upon information that could be crippling for our country."

"What kind of information?"

"Michael wouldn't tell me, but whatever he'd discovered, it scared him. Three days later, he left the capital and refused to tell me where he was going. My instructions were to meet up with him at Hythe in five days, and that if he didn't show, to go looking for him."

"He never came."

Vladimir shook his head. "Something was wrong. I waited a full day in Hythe before setting off in search of him. The first thing I discovered was a dead Gharridan soldier, thrown off the path with an arrow in his chest. Farther into the woods, I found Michael's frozen body lying in the snow—pierced by his own sword with his throat slit."

I felt the tears at the edges of my vision but held them back. The highest disgrace a Gharridan could suffer was to be taken out of this world by his own weapon.

"There were seven other bodies in that clearing, all burned beyond recognition with no weapons, no identification. Nothing."

I leaned against Stryder's shoulder for support. What had my father done to deserve a death like that?

"Did he send you all this way just to tell me this?"

Vladimir hesitated, his pale eyes determining how best to answer me. "After your father's funeral, I received a missive from a man named Gavil saying he had information about your father's death."

"And what did he say?"

"That he would only give the information to Taryn Gallows."

I frowned. "Why would he insist on giving it to me?"

"Who else besides your father knows of your existence?"

I remained quiet. When I was growing up, there was always a man who brought us money every few months. He never seemed to care about our identity, but carried on as if he was simply following orders. The secretiveness my parents had always enforced led me to believe that no one knew of my existence, but now I wondered if I was wrong.

"Michael insured the information wouldn't fall into the wrong hands by requesting it be passed only to his daughter."

I shook my head in confusion. "How did my father discover this? Did he work for you?"

Something about what I said deeply disturbed Vladimir, and he tilted his head, choosing his next words carefully. "Your father didn't work for me, Taryn. I worked for your father. He led the Kavari before me."

Unease clawed at my stomach, ripping through my gut until I could no longer contain it. I quickly moved away from Vladimir, my head spinning at the implication of his words.

My father had been the most powerful man in Gharridan.

CHAPTER TWO

Taryn

VLADIMIR WATCHED ME with worried eyes. "Do you know—"

"I know who the Kavari are," I snapped.

Everyone did. They were an executive branch of the Gharridan government. Even though the Kavari dealt more with security issues and the Crown oversaw public affairs, no decision or law in the country passed without agreement from both parties.

"If you want to find out who killed your father, I need you to come with me," Vladimir said.

"What if I don't care who killed my father?"

My stomach continued to twist with each word I spoke. I wanted to believe that I didn't care. It made my life easier.

A twig snapped somewhere off in the woods, and we

froze, our eyes drawn to the direction of the intruder. Vladimir's bow was instantly in his hands with an arrow nocked to the string. He motioned for me to mount, and I swayed slightly as I clambered onto Stryder's back.

When he moved to leave, I hesitated to follow. Something else cracked, and as I pictured a stick breaking beneath a heavy boot or the large paw of a wild animal, I quickly decided that I didn't want to face alone whatever was in the woods. Vladimir's horse slowly slipped away from the fire, his hooves plodding quietly across the ground. We picked up speed, meandering uphill through the trees and darkness, as the light from the fire faded behind us.

I cast a look back at the campsite positioned below us and saw three figures, with horses trailing behind them, emerge from the woods into the light of the fire. At the sight of the thieves, my blood ran cold. I steadied myself against Stryder's neck. If our horses had to break into a run, I was unsure if I could keep my seat, but Vladimir was moving forward quickly. Since my chances of evading the pursuing men were higher with an ally, I clutched at Stryder's mane and hurried to keep up with him.

We steadily made our way up the hillside, keeping the horses at a brisk walk, but not breaking into a run. Crashing through the forest only created unnecessary noise. I was angry at myself for letting my guard down in the first place. I'd been watching my back like a hawk to avoid any other travelers ever since leaving home, but my slip of security today had presented them with an opportunity to attack. A lone rider was an easy target. I knew better than to be careless like that.

After breaking out of the trees, we crossed an open plain.

Moonlight illuminated the world, casting long shadows behind us. It was difficult not to look over my shoulder continually, but my ears listened for any unwanted sounds. Even though I'd just awakened, weariness loomed in my consciousness. It had been dusk when the thieves attacked me, and I'd awakened in the dead of night, but I wasn't aware of how much time had passed in between.

"We're not that far from the capital," Vladimir said. "If we can get there quickly, they won't be able to follow us."

I hadn't realized the capital was so close.

I scrunched up my nose. "Who says I'm going with you?"

Vladimir watched me for a moment as if trying to figure out what was going on inside my head. He pulled his horse up and reached into his pocket, digging around for a moment before his hand emerged with something inside.

I looked behind me nervously. The thieves hadn't emerged from the woods yet, but I didn't like the idea of stopping out in the open.

"Vladimir—" My breath caught, eyes riveted on the shiny object in his hands. I reached for it, but he snatched it away.

"Where did you get that?" I demanded.

Vladimir safely tucked it back into his pocket. "Where do you think?"

My eyes lingered on the pocket where my mother's clasp was concealed. It bore her family's insignia, four teardrop leaves with a heavily petaled flower in the center. She had worn it until the day of her death. I remembered her clutching it whenever she was sad, often speaking about how much it reminded her of home. She prized it above any other possession. I thought it had been buried with her, but my father must have taken it.

"If you help me find your father's killer," he continued, "it's yours. Along with your mother's family name."

My eyes shot up. "You're lying."

Vladimir crossed his arms. "When Michael said you'd be unwilling to help, I didn't believe him, but now I'm glad he gave me some collateral."

My eyes flashed. "My father apparently had a lot to say about me. I thought you were here because of Gavil."

Vladimir cringed as if he'd said something he shouldn't have. "That's my business."

I pursed my lips, irritated. Believing this man was the last thing I wanted to do, but I was willing to do anything if it meant getting my mother's clasp and family name. Neither my mother nor my father had ever spoken of where she'd originally come from.

"You can always take your chances with the thieves."

Depending on their skill level, it might not take them long to decipher our trail. I sized Vladimir up, weighing how much I trusted him with how much I wanted that clasp.

"I'll help you, but as soon as we get the information from Gavil, we're through." I studied his face for any deceit. "In exchange for my help, you will hand over what is *rightfully* mine."

Vladimir smiled, reining his horse around.

"Deal."

CHAPTER THREE

Vladimir

SHE WASN'T DOING this for her father.

Anger at her indifference toward his death rose within me, threatening to boil over, but I couldn't let it. I wouldn't be able to get the information from Gavil without her. Until then, I had to remain civil. I had half a mind that she might run away, but I could also see how desperately she wanted that clasp. Distrust blazed in her eyes as we rode. When we stopped for the night, I left my back exposed to the darkness—an act that went against everything within me—and kept my eyes trained on her with a dagger nestled safely in my grasp.

Distrust went both ways.

If she hadn't agreed to the deal, I would have brought her to the capital as a prisoner. It was an endeavor that would have wasted precious time. I'd left the capital in a hurry and without leave. The queen was going to be furious when I got back. The central problem accosting me now, among the many others, was keeping Taryn's identity a secret from here on out.

Her life might depend on it.

The sun woke us at daybreak, and we quickly made our way toward the capital while keeping a close eye on the path behind us. Taryn had no interest in speaking with me, nor did I have any desire to talk with her. She was tactless, displaying no grief or remorse over her father's death. Tolerating the situation was the best I could do at the moment, and the image of Michael's frozen body in the snow was what kept me going.

"How did you find me?"

Her inquisitive voice interrupted my thoughts, and I resisted a groan, subduing myself to the fact that conversation had been inevitable. My face twitched, and I sorted through a few ways to answer her question. *You mean after I went to your father's house and discovered you were gone? Or when your neighbor finally admitted the direction you'd gone, and I had to track a week-old trail through the dense forest?*

Wisdom forced me to keep my mouth shut.

"Your father told me where to find you."

By her expression, I sensed she didn't believe me, but that part, at least, was true. She wasn't ready to know the whole truth, nor did I think I would be able to fulfill it. At least not right now. If she knew I'd promised Michael I'd protect her, she might lose it.

Her father was a touchy subject with her. Every time he was mentioned, I watched her back stiffen—saw her eyes grow cold. Michael hadn't shared much with me about her, but her lack of knowledge about him amazed me. For whatever reason, he had chosen to leave his daughter in the dark regarding his position in Gharridan, but it was actually better that way—for both her and the country.

We stopped for a short break, and I covertly glanced behind us. Taryn hadn't noticed yet, but the thieves were still following us. They weren't likely to have known who she was, but I wasn't willing to take a chance. I'd killed two of their men yesterday; they wouldn't drop the trail that quickly. My throat tightened, noting the sparseness of arrows in my quiver. Our pursuers would go down easily with a sword, but if they had bows, it put us at a disadvantage.

My eyes burned, feeling both the loss of sleep for the past few nights and the weeks of exhaustion on the road. Returning to the capital would not bring much rest. When I had been thrust into the position of leader of the Kavari after Michael's sudden death, I hadn't been prepared.

I'd first met Michael when I was a young boy facing prison or the noose for a crime I had been accused of, and Michael had been summoned to judge the matter due to its unusual circumstances. I was willing to step into the noose and end it all without argument, but Michael saw something in me that no one else did. After speaking with me, he gave me two choices: either I could serve my time in prison or pay for my crime through service to him.

I opted for the latter, and after a year of proving myself, he asked if I would like to become a Kavari. Looking back, I realized that must have been his plan all along. I accepted, and as we trained, Michael became more than a mentor to me. He became the father I'd never had. Shortly after my instatement, he voiced his desire for me to become his successor, but I never imagined that I would have to take on the responsibility so soon.

Only two Kavari were underneath me: Marco and Katherine. If Marco had been anywhere near the capital at the time of Michael's death, I would've insisted that he take my place even though I know he would've refused. Michael had chosen me and me alone for this position.

I snuck a glance at Taryn out of the corner of my eye. She was headstrong and already displayed the stubbornness of her father. The shock of looking into her sparkling green eyes for the first time had left me speechless. They looked so much like Michael's. Her olive skin favored her father too, as did her terribly tangled dark nutmeg brown hair, falling in loose waves around her shoulders.

She caught me staring, and I quickly looked away, angry at her resemblance to a man who had meant so much to so many. Angry at her hatred of him.

I still couldn't believe he'd kept her and his wife a secret all these years. He only told me about her right before he left for Hythe, making me swear to protect her in his absence. After a whispered name and a clasp firmly pressed into my hand, he rode away. That was the last time I ever saw him alive.

"Why did you leave Navarre?" I asked Taryn.

If she had lived there her whole life, then it seemed unusual for her to leave suddenly. Michael had told me she would be there, but it appeared that she had left upon hearing of her father's death. Her departure had added unnecessary time to this venture. To say I was irritated was an understatement.

Taryn refused to look at me.

"I guess you should have asked my father. He already seems to have provided you with a wealth of information."

I ground my teeth together. If I lashed out now, she might rescind her agreement to come to the capital. I needed her to get the information from Gavil, but I wondered if he would go back on his word after less than a minute of speaking to her.

"Regardless, you seemed to be heading somewhere in a hurry."

She turned to me now, expression haughty. "That's my business."

I didn't ask any more questions after that, finding that riding in distrustful silence was easier. It wouldn't be long now. After Taryn obtained the information from Gavil, she could leave, and I would never have to see her again. If Michael had ensured her protection while living in the capital, then so could I.

We returned to the path, and it began weaving in and out through the trees. The numerous bends in the road provided ample places for hiding, and the realization of the danger I'd placed us in only dawned on me when the horsemen burst from the trees.

CHAPTER FOUR

Taryn

AT THE SIGHT of the horses, I wheeled Stryder around to run, but more emerged from the woods behind us, and we were quickly surrounded. My heart pumped rapidly with fear. There were at least ten of them. Vladimir's sword was drawn and held at the ready, but he didn't strike. No one did. With weapons outstretched, they held us hostage inside the barricade of horses.

Vladimir's face was tense, but he did not show any fear. Another horse broke out of the trees and into the barrier, coming to a halt in front of us.

"Put the sword away before your hurt yourself, Vladimir."

Arrogance emanated from the man like a foul odor. He held his head high with authority yet lacked dignity. His hazel eyes bore lazily into us, shafts of sunlight glinting off his golden hair.

Vladimir rolled his eyes and sheathed his sword, but I kept my dagger clutched tightly in my hand.

"What are you doing here?" Tension reigned in Vladimir's voice.

"What am I doing here?" The arrogant man on the white horse repeated Vladimir's question, leaning forward in the saddle and tilting his head. "I'm here because someone doesn't know how to follow orders. The queen wants you back at the capital. *Now*."

Vladimir's back was rigid. "That's where we're going. Right now."

The man smiled sardonically. "Then you won't mind if we escort you."

Vladimir cast a hesitant glance at me.

The man followed his gaze and laughed impetuously. "She's not coming with us. I don't care how much you had to pay her."

The dagger shot out of my hand, hurtling toward the man's insolent face as it prepared to carve its mark. I would've swung my fist instead, but I wasn't close enough. Shouts erupted, and next thing I knew I was being yanked from Stryder's back, shoved against the ground with a sword tipping the hollow of my throat. The creak of bowstrings reverberated, threatening to snap at any moment. I had no doubt that each one was aimed at my heart.

"Lower your weapons," Vladimir ordered.

He dismounted and the press of steel against my neck vanished. I eyed the soldiers warily as I stood to my feet. A trickle of blood ran down my target's cheek and dripped onto his cloak. He wiped at it with his hand, stunned.

"Nice throw," he mumbled, pulling a handkerchief from his pocket. He looked at Vladimir and cleaned his face. "Who's your friend?"

Vladimir's Adam's apple bobbed as his eyes flicked between us. I could've sworn he was about to lie.

"This is Taryn, William."

He didn't want this man to know who I was.

Vladimir's eyes met mine as he moved his horse between me and my target. I wasn't sure if it was for William's protection or mine. "Well done, Taryn. You just tried to assassinate the crown prince of Gharridan."

My stomach plummeted.

Violence against the Crown was considered a high crime.

The crown prince dismissed my actions and looked at me funny. "Just Taryn?"

I was still watching Vladimir's face, noting the slight dip of his head that prompted me to go along with this.

I nodded.

If Vladimir didn't want them to know my name, that was fine with me.

William shrugged, turning his horse up the road. "The queen's expecting you by nightfall."

Nightfall? When Vladimir said that we weren't very far away, I didn't know he'd meant less than two days. My father had lived two weeks' ride away from me, and I had never known. Navarre had always seemed too secluded a town to be in close proximity with somewhere as large as the capital.

The horsemen closed in around us, and Vladimir begrudgingly set off after William. I had no choice but to follow them.

It was the only way to get what I wanted. Even though the air was chilly, Vladimir was sweating, mindlessly rubbing his thumb on the reins. I wondered what he had done to deserve an escort like this. Stryder sidled up next to him.

"What's wrong?" I whispered. Now that the men had lowered their weapons, I was grateful for the extra numbers. The pack of thieves could still be trailing us.

Vladimir's cautious eyes checked for listening ears. "William's going to enter the city through the front gates, but I can't take you that way, and I can't tell him why."

If no one knew who I was, I failed to see why that was a problem.

"I'll be fine," I said.

Vladimir shook his head. "You can't be seen going in."

My throat constricted. There was something Vladimir wasn't telling me, something dangerous that he didn't want me to know. I didn't care much, as long as he delivered on his promise. I stole a glance at his breast pocket, knowing that my mother's clasp was tucked safely inside. Resentment bubbled within me, making me want to rip it away from him. It had never been his to possess in the first place.

Before I could question him, Vladimir rode to the head of the company with William, falling in step beside him. Except for his disregard for others, William didn't act like the crown prince. The simple soldier's uniform he wore didn't differ from the other men around me, and his golden hair was cut the same as theirs. After our initial encounter, I no longer existed to him and seemed of little importance to the men around me. As the day wore on, I was never acknowledged by any of them—something I was grateful for.

The road branched out into the open, and dusk descended from the sky like burning embers smeared across the horizon. Ahead lay the outline of the capital—a sprawling city spread out before the tall towers and turrets of the castle. Never before had I encountered something so massive. My father had described it to me as a young child, and the scene before me laced itself with the words he had painted in my mind to create a beautiful picture.

"Why? So you can disappear again as soon as you're out of our sight?"

Vladimir and William were arguing together quietly, but William's voice carried.

"I might if you could supply me with a valid reason," William said.

Vladimir's expression was earnest as he pleaded with William, but the prince wasn't giving in. When William moved away, Vladimir grabbed his arm and spoke through gritted teeth. I wasn't sure of what he said, but whatever it was caused the thunderclouds in William to explode.

"Continue ahead," William barked at the guards. "We'll meet you there."

Vladimir retained some kind of hold over William that I couldn't quite explain, but between their jabs and arguments, I perceived an underlying sense of brotherhood between the two.

As the other men loped away, Vladimir turned to William. "You didn't have to come with us."

William arched an eyebrow. "And tell the queen what? That you're running late because you were dying to use another entrance? You're not leaving my sight until I've delivered you to my mother."

He led us up a hill as we stuck close to the woods, circling the outer wall while the other guards rode through the main gate.

"I swear, Vladimir, if this is some kind of trick …" William's jaw tightened as he rode ahead.

"What did you say to him?" I asked.

Vladimir smiled. "Just used a little leverage."

Sneaking around this way made me nervous, and I felt like an animal walking into a trap. A trap that contained food and appeared safe, yet it still gave a nagging feeling that something wasn't quite right. Darkness had completely fallen over us, but though I could barely see in front of me, William seemed to know exactly where he was going.

He veered off toward the castle wall and dismounted, moving silently through the night. Vladimir and I dismounted as well, shadowing him as we pressed through the tall grass that parted around each step. William's hands felt along the wall for something, and I struggled closer to see.

Vladimir suddenly brought his horse, Dante, in front of me and blocked William from sight. When I moved to look around him, he cocked his head in warning, and I stopped, realizing that whatever William was searching for was meant for his eyes only.

Faint light filtered out into the darkness, and when Vladimir moved, there was a doorway open in the wall big enough for a large horse to walk through. Dante went through first while I followed, and then William brought up the rear, closing the hidden doorway behind him.

We were inside an orchard, the crisp air carrying the smell of dying leaves and the sweet fragrance of autumn's last fruit.

The torches that lined the castle wall were flickering beyond the rows of trees. I craned my neck back, baffled at the size of the stone towers. From this vantage point, it was nothing more than an impossibly large black mass staged against the moonlight.

Vladimir took both our horses' reins and handed them to William, who accepted them with an exaggerated eye roll. He jabbed his finger at Vladimir.

"Straight to the queen. You owe me."

Vladimir motioned for me to follow him as he crept silently across the lawn. Twigs snapped beneath my feet, which drew irritated glances from him. When we slipped inside the castle through a servant's door, Vladimir took me through empty stairwells and darted back and forth between shadows. Few people passed us, but the hour, as well as his antics, mitigated our chances of being seen. My eyes narrowed as I realized how desperate he was to keep my presence a secret.

Vladimir stopped before a carved door, testing the handle. When it moved beneath his touch, he pulled me inside, quickly shutting the door behind him. The room was dim, moonlight from the windows casting an eerie light around the room. Vladimir strode over to the hearth and struck a flame with the flint. Light seeped into the room, illuminating several pieces of furniture.

"No one should disturb you in here." Vladimir stood and dusted off his trousers. "I'll be back once I've talked with the queen."

My eyes followed him as he moved back toward the door.

"What are you not telling me?" I demanded.

His steps faltered as he turned back. "What do you mean?"

My arms crossed. "If no one knows I exist, then why are you so worried about me being seen?"

He ignored my question, glancing at the hearth. "Don't let the fire die, and don't leave the room."

The door shut before I had time to form another question. I plopped onto the bed, angry. Part of me wanted to throw open the door and leave the room in defiance, but fear warned me that maybe there really was a danger lurking behind these walls. The golden clasp flashed before my eyes, making up my mind. I wasn't going to risk losing that over petty irritation.

With nothing else to do, I began to wear a trail on the floor as I paced back and forth. The bed looked inviting, but I was too anxious for sleep and unwilling to let down my guard again. My stomach was growling, growing louder every minute.

Muttering, I glared at the door. Vladimir was probably enjoying dinner with the queen right now while I stood here with nothing. My eyes flicked around the room. Nothing promised food, but suddenly I wondered if these were Vladimir's rooms. The large wardrobe was intricately carved with an array of swirls and designs that intertwined with one another, and the door popped open easily.

Several dresses colored in muted tones filled the space as well as a pair of women's boots on the floor. I frowned. If this wasn't his room, then whose was it? I looked over my shoulder at the other furniture. No dust lined the surfaces or the floor, and the bed stood freshly made. The writing desk held nothing more than extra ink and a few papers

My steps carried me over to the window, where I found myself staring out through the murky glass. Nothing was discernable; whatever lay outside was a formation of dark shapes among the shifting light.

Worry crept into me uninvited as time continued to tick by, and Vladimir did not return. William had said the queen wasn't pleased with him. Maybe she had arrested him, and he was locked in a prison somewhere, unable to return.

I strode over to the door, fingers hovering over the handle. One quick look down the hallway couldn't hurt. Footsteps echoed from outside the door, and I backed away as my heart began to pound. They came closer, and I took a deep breath. It was probably Vladimir, and if it wasn't, whoever it was would simply continue down the hall.

The footsteps stopped outside the room, and the door opened.

Someone stepped inside.

It was not Vladimir.

CHAPTER FIVE

Vladimir

I HAD NEVER seen the queen so angry.

She leaned forward in her seat, eyes aflame. "Mordakai is not challenging your position as leader of the Kavari, Vladimir. He will be underneath you, yet you continue to argue against my choice without any reasonable explanation. Mordakai has military experience as well as political. His brother is my trusted advisor. Time and time again, he has proven his loyalty and devotion to Gharridan. What, pray tell, is your issue with instating him as a Kavari?"

I would die before I allowed that man to become a Kavari.

I ground my teeth together. The leader of the Kavari decided who joined them. Not the Crown. Queen Adamara knew this, yet she blatantly disregarded it. Kavari were not chosen from the ranks of the military. They were chosen as children, by the leader of the Kavari, and spent years in training before being instated. It was a lifetime commitment, and an honor to serve.

The original reason the Kavari were created was to prevent tyranny by keeping the Crown from obtaining absolute power. Unity within our ranks was imperative. The Kavari needed to think objectively from the Crown, and Mordakai sympathized with it. If he favored with the queen in matters of government, it would undermine our very nature.

I chose my next words carefully. "Your Majesty, with all due respect, I cannot allow Mordakai to be instated as a Kavari. Though he is an excellent warrior, he lacks both the training and the characteristics of a Kavari, and I must remind you that it is the duty of the Kavari, not the Crown, to instate one of their own."

Fury blazed in the queen's eyes. "The Crown would not be choosing the next Kavari, Vladimir, if you were simply doing your job in the first place! While you disappeared into the countryside alone and sneaked back into the capital like a thief in the night, I've been here, fulfilling my duties!" She eyed me knowingly. "You've left me with a country to run on my own ever since Michael's death."

Her words hit hard, causing my temper to flare. Ever since Michael's death, I'd been doing everything in my power to solve his murder.

"Michael was murdered, Vladimir," the queen continued. "When you disappeared, how was I supposed to know that you hadn't befallen the same fate? Michael always left some indication of where he was headed, if not with me, then with the other Kavari. You failed to inform anyone of your whereabouts."

I took a deep breath, trying to calm myself. She wasn't upset because I had left. The Kavari had duties to fulfill outside the capital all the time. She was upset because I'd gone without anyone's knowledge in this time of great uncertainty.

"I am sorry for my carelessness, and I will instate another Kavari," I said. "But only with the *proper* candidate. We don't know who murdered Michael or why, and we need to take the time to ensure the next Kavari is selected carefully."

"Are you implying that you plan to choose a child to be trained up as a Kavari?" the queen demanded. "Years of training are not something that we have time for right now, Vladimir. A killer is still on the loose, which means that we could be facing war. I need assets, and I need assets now—not ten years down the road when you feel your chosen child is ready!"

My mouth opened and quickly shut, unable to conjure a viable response. That was not why I was rejecting Mordakai. She was acting out of fear. There should be no rush in instating a new Kavari, but she saw the decrease in our numbers as a sign of weakness. No law dictated how many Kavari could serve in Gharridan, but the queen had only ever known there to be four, and so four there would be.

"Do you not wish our country to be protected and appear strong to our enemies?" the queen asked.

That was the very reason I denied him.

"The Kavari have not chosen Mordakai, and I will not allow him to join our ranks."

Queen Adamara stood abruptly from her chair, pacing the floor in anger.

"Is it my crown that you want, Vladimir?" Her tone was

accusatory. "Since you seem to know better than I, would you like me to remove myself as sovereign and name you my successor?"

My expression darkened. "My duty is to serve our country, Your Majesty, and to protect it from enemies both without and within. I have no desire to rule it."

"Then stop trying."

I clenched my jaw, her accusations stinging like sharp daggers in my skin. She faced me, eyes boring into me as neither of us budged. The Crown had overstepped its authority. I would not back down to simply keep the peace.

"It is late," she finally said. "I tire talking of this. Since we cannot come to an agreement on this matter, we will bring it before the council tomorrow morning. They will decide what decision most favors Gharridan."

I held in a sigh of relief. At least I would have the council's ear. They were chosen by the citizens of Gharridan, not the queen. Their primary duty was to advise, but when the Crown and the Kavari disagreed, the council cast the deciding vote.

Queen Adamara stopped before me. "If you detest Mordakai that much, I suggest you find a better candidate or come up with a solid reason for your opposition."

I said nothing but held the door as she left the room.

"I gave the approval for you to become the head of the Kavari," she warned. "Don't make me regret that decision."

Guards silently fell into step beside her as she marched down the hall, and I shut the door behind me. It was Michael's approval that mattered. Not hers.

I slid down the cold wall, my face cradled in my hands. I wasn't prepared for this power struggle. The Crown and the

Kavari had clashed many times before, but Michael had always been the one at the forefront of it.

I needed more time.

Without proof, I couldn't explain my inhibitions about Mordakai to the queen or the council. Even with Taryn here, I couldn't get word to Gavil overnight. The council meeting tomorrow would spin into a disaster. I clenched my fists, frustrated, and pushed away from the wall. I was going to have to think of something.

The corridors were empty as I strolled through them, my footsteps echoing along stone halls. Even though I knew the queen was trying to protect the country, she had backed me into a corner with no way out. A glance over my shoulder ensured that no one was following me, and I headed toward Taryn's room. When I reached the door, muffled voices drifted out from inside, and my stomach filled with dread.

CHAPTER SIX

Taryn

HER HAIR WAS shockingly red, almost unnatural, like a cascade of deep red blood flowing down her shoulders in a torrent of waves. Its vibrance was unlike anything I had ever seen before. Her startled green eyes locked on mine, and she wrenched a dagger from her side, surveying the room for any other intruders.

"How did you get in here?" she demanded.

I was still transfixed by her hair, unable to answer.

I realized I didn't even know how to answer.

"What are you doing here?" Her voice grew deadly.

"Vladimir brought me here," I managed, unsure of how much I should share but more concerned by the dagger in her hand.

Her weapon lowered ever so slightly, but I still held no

doubt that she would kill me if need be. When she stepped closer, I backed against the far wall. There was nowhere else to go without jumping out the window.

"Why?" she pressed.

The fire illuminated my face as I stepped closer to the hearth. My dagger was tucked safely in my boot, but I wouldn't be able to get to it before she reached me. For the first time, she looked closely at my face. She hesitated.

"Who are you?"

I swallowed hard. First names surely couldn't do much damage. "Taryn."

Her brows lowered. She stared as if she knew me. "Taryn who?"

The door opened, drawing our attention. I felt relief as Vladimir stepped inside. When he saw us, his face paled.

"Back off, Katherine."

A fire lit in the woman's eyes. "You have a lot of explaining to do."

Vladimir shut the door. "And you were supposed to be in Carna."

"Until you disappeared. Queen Adamara ordered us to stay here until you came back. You left at a bad time, Vladimir."

He took the dagger that was still in Katherine's hand and tossed it onto the bed. "I didn't have a choice, but we have a bigger problem to deal with right now."

"Bigger than you hiding a fugitive in my bedroom?" Katherine shot back.

"The queen wants to instate Mordakai as a Kavari. She's announcing it to the council in the morning."

I had no idea what that meant, but his statement frightened

Katherine.

"But you said—"

Vladimir shot a glance at me. "I don't have proof. That's why she's here. To help me get it."

"Proof of what?" I asked.

They both turned to look at me.

"I'll tell you when I get it," Vladimir explained.

When I started to object, Vladimir patted his pocket with the clasp and gave me a knowing look. My mouth snapped shut. The deeper I got into this situation, the more I despised it.

"What are you going to do?" Katherine asked.

"I don't know." Vladimir shook his head. "But I need her to stay here with you tonight without anyone knowing. No questions asked."

There was a way of communication between them, like they could read each other's minds. I would have guessed siblings, but their features were too starkly contrasted. Vladimir seemed to know that Katherine wouldn't like what he was asking yet knew that she would accept. Katherine crossed her arms and shot me a glare, nodding reluctantly.

Vladimir turned to me. "I'll try to get word to Gavil tonight. Hopefully, we'll be able to speak with him tomorrow."

He quietly slipped into the hall, and an awkward silence hung in the air. I moved over to the thick rug in front of the hearth, preparing to lay down for the night. Katherine retrieved a blanket and threw it at me. I snatched it out of the air and unfolded it. She was still watching me, a strange look on her face.

"Where are you from, Taryn?"

I smiled slightly. "I thought Vladimir said no questions."

My stomach growled, and I glanced at the door, wondering how far I'd have to wander to find food.

"You'd never make it to the kitchen without being seen." Katherine must have heard my stomach.

For a moment, I contemplated asking her to get me something but quickly decided against it. That was what she wanted me to do.

My back was turned to her as I lay down on the rug and pulled my blanket over me. I could feel her eyes boring into my back. I began to understand why Vladimir was so apt to keep me hidden. I'd never given much thought to the resemblance between my father and me, but although she didn't voice it, there was no doubt in my mind that Katherine knew exactly who I was.

CHAPTER SEVEN

Taryn

THE SUDDEN KNOCK at the door startled me, and I dropped the bread I'd been eating. Katherine had been gone when I'd awoken, a tray of food left in her absence, and Vladimir had already been by to inform me he was headed to the council meeting. Both of them would be there now. Sunlight streamed in through the windows, dispersing any shadows that might hide me. I licked my lips nervously as the knock came again.

"Katherine?"

The voice was muffled through the door. Frantically my eyes swept the room in search of a hiding spot, resting on the wardrobe. I unhooked its door as quietly as possible and pulled it shut behind me. The latch clicked, and I angrily bit my lip, realizing that I would be stuck in here until Katherine or

Vladimir returned. My feet balanced awkwardly on the contents lining the bottom of the floor as clothes pressed against my back. The outer door creaked open, and I held my breath, assuring myself that whoever it was would leave as soon as they found the room empty.

I was wrong.

Boots thudded on the stone floor, growing softer when they reached the plush carpet. The intruder ambled from one side of the room to the other without speaking. Knees cracked as someone knelt down, no doubt to look beneath the bed, and my heart hammered within my chest. I silently pulled my dagger from my boot, holding it in front of me. For several painstakingly long moments, I heard nothing except for the pounding of my own heart, but I could still sense someone in the room.

Without warning, the wardrobe doors flung open. I lunged at the intruder, faltering as I realized it was William. The moment of hesitation was all he needed to knock and twist the dagger from my grasp, kicking it out of my reach.

"That's the second time you've tried to kill me with that."

An angry red line still puckered along his cheek, but it was shallow enough not to need stitches.

"What are you doing here?" I demanded.

William laughed. "I knew he wasn't stupid enough to hide you in his own rooms." He motioned toward the door. "Let's go."

I stared at him, thinking he must be crazy. "I'm not leaving this room."

His smirky grin turned sour. "All right, listen. I'll be nice and give you three choices. One, you can come with me willingly. Two, I can force you out at swordpoint, or three, I can throw you over my shoulder, and the entire palace can watch as you kick and scream down the halls."

"I can't leave here."

"Will it be option three, then?"

By his expression, I didn't doubt his words, and I was left without a choice. I crossed my arms. "Where are you taking me?"

"The council meeting."

"Why?"

My questions seemed to irritate him. "Because my mother wants you there."

He held out a hand toward the door, and I tentatively left the room, finding two guards stationed outside. William shut the door behind him, marching down the hall, and I followed unwillingly, wondering why his mother would want me in the council meeting. If she knew I was here, it must be because William had told her.

"So you betrayed Vladimir even though he begged for your secrecy?" I asked.

He frowned, not seeming to appreciate my perception.

"Vladimir's not the only one with leverage."

William pushed ahead of me, and as we hurried through the endless halls and corridors, it was impossible for me to keep track of where we were going or where we had come from. Our path was little more than an endless connection of mazes.

The castle looked different in the daylight. Sunshine streamed in through stained glass windows, illuminating the various tapestries and artwork that lined the walls. Through the glass, I could see the jagged rooftops from the city far below, a vast sea of buildings.

William turned to me abruptly, still keeping step. "In advance, I'm sorry for whatever happens in there. I would prefer not to be involved with this."

Confusion washed over me. "Involved with what?"

William wouldn't meet my eyes. "Vladimir left without word and without leave. It won't fare well with the council if he did it because of a woman."

Understanding dawned on me, and I stumbled with the shock of it. "Wait, you think—" I cut myself off, unable to say the words. "That's *not* why I'm here." My words were vehement and emblazoned with passion.

He stopped before two large double doors. "Then why *are* you here?"

My lips parted, but I couldn't tell him, and I suddenly realized the dilemma. If the queen planned to use this rumor against Vladimir, he couldn't prove his innocence without betraying who I was.

"I'm not going in there," I stated.

I could care less what happened to Vladimir, but I needed my mother's name and clasp, and if Vladimir believed there was a danger of me being discovered, then I didn't want any part of it.

William's hand clamped down on my arm like iron. "Actually, you are."

The doors swung inward, and I couldn't fight him without creating a scene. Light descended from a massive window that filled the ceiling, casting a warm glow over the council members seated in a semicircle at the far end of the room.

At our entrance, we drew the attention of a woman, and I knew without question that it was Queen Adamara. Clothes woven of the finest linen I'd ever seen draped across her body in cascades of royalty with immense detail given to the embroidery and stitching. Her hair, colored with the same luxurious golden shine as William's, was piled elaborately on top of her head with a circlet of silver around it. There was no denying that she was a very beautiful woman. Her sharp yet gentle features would merit the envy of a goddess.

As we approached, her scowling face transformed into one of satisfaction. Vladimir was in a deep argument with one of the men, his back to me. We'd drawn the attention of several other council members, including Katherine's. A trace of fear lined her eyes when she saw me. My mind was racing, trying to come up with a convincing lie, but I couldn't think straight. It would only take a moment to decipher the shallow origins of our deceit. Some of the council members' stares lingered on my face, and I prayed I wasn't close enough for them to recognize any familiarity with my father.

The queen interrupted the men, cutting off Vladimir's argument. "Since we can't currently seem to agree on the next Kavari, I suggest we move onto another issue while the council is gathered."

The focus shifted to the queen as she prepared to speak. Her mannerisms were calm and confident. Not a shred of doubt hovered in her eyes as she obtained complete control over the situation.

"Only a handful of weeks has passed since Vladimir assumed the late Michael Gallows' position as the leader of the Kavari, yet he took it upon himself to vacate the castle without leave and without word. Pray tell, Vladimir, what was so demanding that you could not inform anyone of your absence or whereabouts?"

Vladimir's back stiffened, his head held high. The room grew deathly quiet, like the eerie calm before a massive thunderstorm when the birds don't sing and the squirrels don't chatter.

"It was a matter of urgent business, Your Majesty."

She arched an eyebrow. "If it is urgent business, should not the Crown be alerted lest we be taken by surprise?"

Vladimir remained silent.

Queen Adamara looked beyond Vladimir to me. "Perhaps it has something to do with this young woman here who you were found with on the road and insisted on bringing into the castle discreetly."

The council members shifted uncomfortably in their seats as Vladimir turned and noticed my presence in the room for the first time. His flushed cheeks quickly diminished in color until they were ghastly pale.

"We all have personal lives, Vladimir, but you know as well as I that when you take the oath of Kavari, the country will always come first."

Whispers passed between the council members as suspicion swirled in their calculating eyes.

"Would you care to explain this woman's secret presence, Vladimir?"

He looked back at me with tormented eyes. He couldn't tell them, but if he didn't, he faced dire consequences. Sweat broke out on my brow as he licked his lips, and a light flicked on in his eyes.

"I had hoped for more time," Vladimir began, then hesitated. He was forming sentences one word at a time. "But since you are so concerned with our country's security, and I see the wisdom behind your concern, I suppose that now will do."

The queen's eyes narrowed.

This was not what she had been expecting.

"Yes, I am against Mordakai taking Michael's place as a Kavari," he continued. "I did not disclose my whereabouts because I feared of offering false hope, but my search was successful."

Expectation permeated the room like a strong fragrance, eager for Vladimir's next words.

"I argued against Mordakai's instatement because I have a better choice."

"Who could possibly be a better choice than Mordakai?" the queen asked.

Vladimir turned back to me.

"The daughter of Michael Gallows."

CHAPTER EIGHT

Taryn

EVERY EYE IN the room turned, a sea of shocked faces staring at me. If they hadn't noticed any resemblance before, they were undoubtedly searching for it now. My mouth went dry, and I couldn't move, unable to understand or process what was happening. Queen Adamara's expression outdid all the others. Her surprise at Vladimir's words left her speechless.

"Michael Gallows doesn't have a daughter."

The words came from one of the council members seated next to the queen, his disbelieving eyes boring into me. I inhaled sharply at the startling sight of the man. Something about his appearance simply made me want to vomit. His skin was disturbingly pale, like death had touched him and left him with a ghostly presence. Hair as white as freshly fallen snow swept across his forehead. It was an unnatural color for a man still several years away from turning gray.

"Perhaps you should look again, Zedekiah," Vladimir suggested.

The queen cocked her head, studying me. "Come forward, child."

All I wanted was to flee from the room, but I found my feet obeying the order as I shuffled closer. The scrutiny was terrifying as she surveyed me up and down, her eyes noting my father's ring on my finger. As she perused my face, I caught a flicker of recognition.

"You have your father's devilish green eyes."

Her words hung in the air, an invitation for the other members to soak in the resemblance.

"How old are you?"

"Nineteen."

"Mmm," she mused, watching me like a cat waiting to pounce.

One of the other men shifted in his chair. A jagged scar ran across his dark skin, starting at his forehead and running down across his left eye. He blinked normally, the old wound not seeming to have affected his eyesight.

"The ring was not on Michael's body when it was buried," Scar-eye observed. "How did you come to possess it?"

My eyes flicked between him and the queen. "When he visited several weeks ago, he left it for me."

The pale man scoffed at my words.

"Did he visit you often?" Curiosity ruled the queen's voice.

My own words stuck in my throat.

No.

No, he didn't.

He abandoned me.

"Yes," I answered. "Though the past few years were not as frequent."

The past five years. He had not returned after my mother's death. Not until a few weeks ago, when he had shown up unannounced without explanation or apology. My heart hardened at the remembrance of his abandonment, and I pursed my lips.

The queen appeared dizzy. "I need a respite to ponder this. The council will reconvene in a quarter hour."

The room stirred as people rose from their seats, and I stood there awkwardly, a lone sheep among a pack of wolves. Vladimir caught my eye and moved toward me, but I quickly broke for the door.

I was halfway down the hall before he caught up with me.

"Taryn." He placed a hand on my shoulder.

I jerked away. "Don't touch me!"

My voice lashed out like a whip. I was seething, my chest rapidly rising and falling as anger pumped through it.

"Please, just—"

"I agreed to help you get information from Gavil," I hissed. "Not to be a pawn in your political games!"

Vladimir glanced up and down the hall, our argument drawing attention. Katherine had walked up and with a quick nod of her head stepped into the nearest room. Vladimir pushed me in after her, bolting the door behind us.

"Let me go!" I yelled, moving for the door, but he blocked my path.

"Keep your voice down."

I was shaking now and tried to dart around him again, but

he pushed me back, a wildfire blazing in his eyes.

"I need you to hear me out before you leave this room."

"Are you out of your mind?" Katherine's voice was fearful, her eyes wide.

"I didn't have a choice, Katherine!" Vladimir exploded. "What was I supposed to do? Even if I hadn't told them, they'd still already seen her. It wouldn't have taken them long to figure it out."

I never should have agreed to come here with Vladimir. It was a mistake, no matter how much I wanted my mother's clasp. I was cursed. My father was dead, yet by some sorcery, I was still bound to him.

"Why are you so against this Mordakai becoming a Kavari?" I asked.

I failed to see how I was a better choice. I had no training, no knowledge of the workings of this government, and no desire for the position.

Vladimir leaned back on a dusty table, his jaw clenched, exhaustion hanging heavy in his eyes. "When your father spoke to me before his death, he insinuated that there was a traitor in the palace, but that he couldn't accuse anyone without proof. I believe he found that proof—and was killed for it."

I turned the information over. "And you think Mordakai is the traitor?"

Vladimir's face grew dark. "Your father never trusted Mordakai, and they'd worked together in Gharridan since they were boys. Mordakai has been rising in the military ranks for the past twenty years. He was considered for the role of captain of the guard, but Verone was chosen over him. He didn't take the defeat well. Mordakai has always had a taste for power. When the captain's position was suddenly out of reach, he began aiming for the Kavari.

"As a Kavari, our role is to protect Gharridan from enemies both without and within. Our interests lay in the future of Gharridan, which is why we are given the power of directly allowing or revoking the decisions of the Crown. Though Queen Adamara is the ruler of the country, the Kavari are a means to preserve the balance and keep any ruler from falling into the temptation that comes with absolute power. Instating Mordakai as a Kavari puts him one step closer to attaining the power of making decisions that directly control Gharridan, and if he is involved in treasonous affairs with surrounding nations, it would be catastrophic for our country. Michael's death weakened us, and whoever fulfills the role of the next Kavari will be the tipping point of who controls Gharridan."

"But if you're still in charge, how does that give Mordakai any power?" I asked.

Vladimir gripped the edges of the table, his eyes serious. "Mordakai murdered your father. If he becomes a Kavari, that leaves one person standing between him and the power he desires."

Vladimir.

Mordakai had murdered before. There was no reason he wouldn't do it again. Vladimir may be my father's successor, but if something happened to him, that left the position wide open. Even if Vladimir had already chosen another to replace him, the queen could endorse Mordakai as leader, just as she was endorsing him as a Kavari now.

I sat down. The politics were making my head swim. No one in this country seemed to be in agreement on anything, but now I understood the precariousness of the situation.

"Does Gavil have proof of Mordakai's treachery?"

Lines of stress and uncertainty carved into Vladimir's face. "I don't know, but I can't accuse him without proof. Mordakai is very close to the queen, and though she does what she can for Gharridan, she is easily persuaded. She lacks the wisdom and judgment that her late husband King Roldan possessed."

I closed my eyes, trying to absorb everything he was explaining. "You said that Mordakai started aiming for the Kavari, and you're certain he was part of the plot to kill my father?"

A long look passed between Vladimir and Katherine, questions and answers swirling between them as they seemed to read each other's minds.

"That's what we've suspected." Vladimir's voice was dark. "The man Michael hunted down was one of Mordakai's messengers, and Mordakai was absent from the capital at the time of your father's death."

A twinge of hatred lit inside me for this man seeking to take my father's place, and I was surprised at my sudden desire to destroy him. If I was to have any peace, then my father's murderer needed to come to justice, and here he was within my grasp.

"How is the council even considering me to be a Kavari?" I asked. "I have no training."

"The Kavari are usually chosen and trained at a very young age, picked for their skill." Vladimir glanced at the door behind him. "But just as the crown passes from one generation to the next, the role of Kavari can also be passed down from one generation to another—in this case, from father to daughter."

I shook my head defiantly. "I'm not going to have any part

of this."

"You don't have a choice." Katherine's words shocked me, but there was no malice in her tone. Her earnest, dark green eyes flicked between Vladimir and me. "Mordakai wants a place in the Kavari. He's proven that he's willing to do whatever it takes to get it. Whether you like it or not, Taryn, your father was the leader of the Kavari, which makes you a Blood Vier. You have a claim to the Kavari, and you always will.

"You're a threat to him in more ways than one. If he knows your father came to visit you before his death, he may suspect that your father told you information about him. Set one foot outside the capital, and you're as good as dead."

I stared at her, a cold dread flooding my veins, and in that moment I realized my life would never be the same again. That no matter how hard I tried or how much I fought to get away, I would always be bound to my father. Because of my relation to him, and because of the position he held in our country, I would never be able to escape him. I would be hunted down because of the family I was born into, even if I wanted nothing to do with it.

Both Vladimir's and Katherine's expressions were somber, neither knowing what to say or how to proceed.

"Is that why you brought me here?" I asked. "Because I had a claim to the Kavari?"

"Taryn." Vladimir closed his eyes in frustration. "I didn't know the queen planned to instate Mordakai until last night. I only asked for your help to get the information from Gavil."

His words rang with sincerity, but they offered no consolation or resolution.

There was no way out of this.

"So my choice is to either become a Kavari or die?"

Vladimir, deep in thought, pushed away from the desk and paced slowly around the room. If he was hoping for a solution, there wouldn't be one. Katherine had explained my future very clearly.

"You don't have to become a Kavari," Vladimir said. "But you will need to vie for it."

"What do you mean, vie for it?"

"What we need is more time," Vladimir continued. "If we can get Queen Adamara to agree to a choosing ceremony, there'll be a set amount of time to prepare for it. During that time, we need to get that proof from Gavil, at least enough to get Mordakai convicted so that he will be ineligible to compete."

"How does that keep me from becoming a Kavari?" I asked incredulously.

"Once Mordakai is convicted, you can withdraw your desire to join the Kavari."

He made it sound so easy, yet I doubted it would be that simple.

"You need to write to Marco," Katherine told Vladimir. "He's been in the government longer than either of us. He'll know what to do."

"Who's Marco?" I asked.

"He's a member of the Kavari," Vladimir explained. "He has more experience and should have become our leader, but Michael had already named me successor. He would've received the missive about your father's death by now and should be on his way to the capital as we speak."

Their arguments were thin, the solutions nothing more

than a whispering hope. Gavil might not even have proof, but there was nothing else to go on. I turned away from them, considering the mess I found myself in. Nothing in me wanted to take part in this, but my birthright had stolen my free will.

If I left right now, I would be hunted down and assassinated. Vying for the Kavari was the last thing I wanted, but it was better than being dead. If I went along with this, I would get my mother's clasp and her family name. All of this was based on the assumption that their plans played out perfectly.

"If I comply with these plans, can you guarantee my safety?"

Vladimir let out a long breath. "I can't guarantee anything, but I promise on my life to protect you as much as I can."

He looked to Katherine, and she met his gaze, frowning as she crossed her arms. "As will I."

Vladimir looked at me expectantly. All of this hinged on me agreeing to their plans. Without me, they couldn't move forward or rescue themselves from this predicament. Every voice in my brain was screaming no, to leave here and never look back, but there was another voice, one that was telling me to do what was right. My mother's voice echoed in my head, encouraging me always to make the right choice.

My own conscience echoed my mother's. He had still been my father. He deserved more than this. I wanted to take down the man who murdered my father, and if Mordakai was indeed responsible for my father's death, I didn't want him anywhere near a position of power. No one did.

"I'll do it."

Relief filled both of their eyes.

"Thank you," Vladimir said.

When the council reconvened, there was a new man present. He stood square-shouldered in a military uniform, beard neatly trimmed, hair swept back. As I walked by him, I felt his condescending gaze pass over me.

"Mordakai will be joining us as we make our decision," Queen Adamara began, sitting down in her elegant chair. She lifted her chin as she looked at Vladimir, accusation in her voice as she dared him to contradict her.

"You do understand, *Lord* Vladimir," she said, mocking the term, "that Gharridan appears weak in the wake of Michael Gallows' death. Our country needs protection and to be able to prove that we remain strong. Instating Mordakai, who has proven himself to our country in both actions and words from his years in the military and more recently in the court, can provide both the protection and the strength Gharridan so desperately needs."

The queen paused, passing her gaze to me. "Yet, you would rather instate this girl, whom we know nothing about, and who has no prior involvement in our government. I fail to see what wisdom you seem to be using in this situation, nor do I believe the people will smile on it. You and Michael have always insisted that the Kavari be brought up and trained from a young age. If this is indeed Michael Gallows' daughter, he never revealed her to us. She doubtfully has had any proper training, even if she is of his blood. Though Mordakai may not have been specifically trained to be a Kavari, he has been in military and political training from a young age."

Vladimir's face remained unchanged, his eyes boring into

the queen. "Perhaps the best way to determine who is most suitable as a Kavari would be through a choosing ceremony."

The room fell quiet, small whispers dispersing among the council. Everything depended on having enough time to get the proof. If the queen didn't agree with this, the scheme would fall through.

Queen Adamara remained calm as she considered Vladimir's words. "There has not been a choosing ceremony since Marco was instated over twenty years ago."

"It had its purpose then, and I feel it has its purpose now," Vladimir stated. "Twenty years ago, two eligible young men had been trained to become Kavari. The Crown ruled that Gharridan only had need of one. To prove who was most worthy, they were given the option to vie for the position before the council, Crown, and Kavari."

Feet shifted uncomfortably beneath the table, glances going from Vladimir to the queen, waiting to see which one would speak first. I twiddled my fingers, the importance of this moment weighing on me.

Queen Adamara turned to each of the council members. "Do you all agree that a choosing ceremony is the appropriate action for this situation?"

The room fell silent for a moment before a tumble of nods in confirmation of their support spread around the room. Zedekiah's face was sour, but the queen ignored his apparent distaste.

"A choosing ceremony will take place exactly one month from today," she decided. "The contestants will be evaluated on their skills as they vie, and it will be determined which is more fit to fulfill the role of the Kavari."

Another round of nods circled the room, and the queen stood from her seat. "Council dismissed."

My eyes found Vladimir's as the members dispersed around us.

One month.

I didn't know if that was enough time to gather the proof, but it was all we had.

CHAPTER NINE

Taryn

THE ROOM I was provided wasn't as spacious as Katherine's, but I was glad for it. The cottage I'd occupied with my mother in Navarre had been small. It was what I was used to. The only reason I had stayed there after her death was to keep the promise I had made her. My father had continued to send money, but I wondered if maybe that was out of obligation.

Not wanting to make the same mistake I had made earlier, I made sure the door was securely locked before relaxing onto the bed. After weeks of sleeping on the ground, it felt almost too soft and luxurious. I rolled off the cushions onto a plush floor rug, staring up at the carved ceiling.

After the council meeting, Vladimir had explained to me what would happen over the next few weeks. We had to keep up the ruse that I was vying for the Kavari, which meant I would have to train like one. Vladimir would do what he could and cram into four weeks what took others years to learn. His skepticism was evident as he walked me through each aspect of the intense training, and I didn't say much; just nodded my head. Some things I already knew, which meant the process shouldn't be too difficult. The only thing that concerned me was getting proof of Mordakai's treachery in time.

Vladimir had sent word to Gavil that I was here, but with the speed at which the news of the choosing ceremony and my existence was spreading through the capital, he would probably hear it from someone else first.

I rolled over onto my side and curled my fingers into the fibers of the rug. Why had my father never brought me to the capital? Maybe he'd been ashamed of me and didn't want someone like me joining him in the Kavari. My gaze flicked back to the ceiling. Had my mother ever been here? She'd never mentioned it, so I doubted it was possible, but I was still curious. Why had we hidden away in Navarre my whole life while my father lived here? It didn't make sense.

My mother had always been a bit paranoid, wary of strangers until she was confident they could be trusted. It had taken years for her to have a full conversation with Lidia, the widow next door to us. I smiled, thinking of Lidia. She'd had no one, just like me, so we looked out for each other.

My eyelids grew heavy, the mental exhaustion of the past few days catching up with me. I'd barely slept last night, the day's events weighing on my mind and the unknown frightening me. I thought tonight would be just as difficult, but my eyelids slid shut, and sleep gently lifted me from consciousness.

In the morning, I practically had to jog to keep up with Vladimir's long stride as we sped through the castle halls. His urgency felt unnecessary, but I reminded myself that both he and the country depended on our deception.

"Any news?" I asked, hoping he would catch my meaning without having to explain more. There wasn't a time frame for how long it would take Gavil to get back with us. Vladimir understood my words and shook his head. The sunshine blinded me as we broke out of the castle walls, and I quickly covered my eyes.

"Where are we going?" I asked breathlessly, hoping he might slow down to answer. At this rate, I would wear out before the day even began.

"The training fields."

He'd reached a total of five words now. *Follow me* was the only other phrase he had muttered since yesterday. He was consumed by whatever lay ahead.

"Are you a fast learner?"

"Yes."

"Then I need you to be even faster. The queen has already asked to receive updates on your progress. If she feels you are not improving enough, I fear she may call off the choosing ceremony altogether."

I swallowed.

We were already short on time as it was.

"When did you start your training?" Curiosity overcame me.

Vladimir's steps faltered, my question catching him off

guard. He pushed ahead, glancing over his shoulder. "Twelve years ago."

Vladimir couldn't be more than a handful of years older than myself, yet he had taken on a role fit for someone twice his age. The pressure placed on someone this incredibly young was astounding, and I marveled at his ability to handle it.

As we approached the training fields, the clanging of metal on metal reached our ears, growing louder as we treaded deeper into the sparring fields. Several regiments appeared to be in the middle of practice. One group of young recruits was practicing their blows while an older squadron engaged in an intense field of one-on-one combat.

A particular duel caught my attention as one trainee was pushing his opponent back at an alarming rate. The opponent fell backward, the winner touching the tip of his sword against the hollow of his fallen comrade's throat, and a cheer broke out among the observers. One of the bystanders was the council member with the ghostly pale skin and white hair.

"Vladimir, who is that man?"

His eyes followed mine, darkening when they came to rest upon the sickly figure.

"Zedekiah. Advisor to the queen, and the brother of your competitor, Mordakai."

I followed his eyes as the winner's back turned to reveal his face, and I realized it was Mordakai. My opponent's dark blonde hair and fit frame bore no resemblance to the thin, gangly form of his brother. Mordakai caught sight of us and noticed my stare. He spat on the ground, glaring at me for a moment before returning to his training.

"It would be best to avoid both of them for the time being."

I gratefully accepted his warning.

Vladimir took us into the armory and began scanning the great assortment of swords. I'd never seen so many in my life. The walls were completely covered with them, coming in every shape and size imaginable. The sound of a hammer hitting an anvil came from somewhere close by, the pounding of the steel bringing the promise of more weapons.

I picked up a long sword, testing its weight in my hand. It felt good. Vladimir quickly replaced it with a smaller sword specially crafted for beginners. My displeasure was impossible to hide.

"Vladimir, I don't think—"

"If you're training to become a Kavari, you need to have at least a basic knowledge of sparring, woman or not."

It was not the sparring that I had started to protest, but after cutting me off, he was no longer interested in what I'd been about to say.

A bald man with sunken eyes entered the armory, grimacing as he approached us. A slight limp plagued his left leg, and the worn, leathery skin of his hands was covered in calluses.

"Lord Vladimir," he said.

"Simon." Vladimir indicated me. "This is Taryn Gallows, your new trainee. I need you to teach her everything you possibly can in the next four weeks."

Simon frowned, inspecting me, and no doubt less than thrilled at the prospect of having a woman on the field.

"Are you training for the position of a Kavari?"

My lips parted slightly, wanting to object, but I pursed them and nodded.

He *harrumph*ed and retrieved his sword from nearby. "Then let's get started."

I turned to Vladimir, irritation seeping through me. "Vladimir, this isn't—"

"I'll be back in a few hours."

I clenched my jaw as Vladimir marched away, leaving me alone as I stalked after Simon, dragging my sword along behind me. If Vladimir would simply hear me out, he would understand that trying to teach me how to fight was a waste of time.

We moved to a corner of the field that was sparsely populated. Hungry eyes followed our path, curious about the daughter of Michael Gallows.

Simon began with the appropriate way of handling a sword, demonstrating correct and incorrect methods before starting several basic patterns for sparring, including the stab and cut. I tried to be respectful to Simon as he taught. It wasn't his fault he was stuck with me for a student, but I struggled with being demeaned to the basics. I tried to change my attitude, telling myself that refreshing the basics was good for me. Simon's knowledge on the subject was immense, backed by years of experience, and I surprised myself by chewing on each tidbit of advice he offered.

While Simon watched as I practiced each blow, I found myself sneaking glances toward the other end of the field where Mordakai was still practicing. I realized what a laughingstock I must appear to everyone. Mordakai had been training his entire life for a position like this, yet here was the Kavari, trying to replace Michael with an untrained girl utterly ignorant of the inner workings of her country. While I stood here practicing blocks and thrusts, he took down opponents one at a time.

"Very good, Gallows," Simon grunted. "Keep it up; I'll be back."

I nodded, realizing I'd almost forgotten he was there. My eyes wandered back to Mordakai, wondering if the same stroke that took down his opponent was the one that killed my father. Anger coursed through my veins, distracting me, and my sword swung through empty air.

"Missed the mark there."

I looked up. Prince William was leaning against a post, watching me with one eyebrow raised. He no longer wore the fine clothes of a royal but a simple soldier's uniform. I turned away, ignoring him as I continued with the task Simon had left me with a while ago, practicing my strikes against the wooden block.

Whack!

I pulled the sword back.

"Not very chipper today, are we?"

Whack!

"Or talkative."

I gritted my teeth, sheathing my sword. If William hadn't told the queen about my arrival, none of us would be in this mess. "Is there some way I can be of service to Your Highness, or am I free to continue practicing?"

The words were bitter in my mouth, and I threw him a steely gaze.

William smirked, his arms falling to his sides as he pushed away from the fence. "If you want to beat Mordakai, you're going to have to do better than that."

I broke my stance and turned to him. "You have a habit of

interrupting things. Was the council meeting not enough?"

William's smirk vanished, a twinge of regret in his eyes. "I didn't—"

"I don't care," I snapped.

William unhooked his cloak and let it fall to the ground. "You're the daughter of Michael Gallows. Surely he taught you something beyond the basic strokes."

He unsheathed his sword, letting it hover above the ground in a neutral stance.

"I already have an instructor." I turned away, back toward the block.

"What, afraid you'll lose? Or do I need to take it easy on you?"

He was baiting me, and though I knew I should ignore it, the allegation stung.

"Don't cry when you fail," I warned him. "You might make me feel bad."

William chuckled, his sword still hanging low at his side, but his grip on the handle was focused. I took a deep breath, testing the weight of the sword in my hands. We didn't move for several moments, and I realized since he considered himself the more experienced swordsman, he was expecting the beginner to strike first.

Darting forward, I swung a blow he easily parried, which I followed with a pattern Simon had taught me. The look on William's face hinted at amusement as he easily swept aside each of my blows. His attitude remained passive, like he was simply swatting at an annoying fly dive-bombing him.

"Maybe Vladimir was right to start you with the basics."

William laughed, and I smiled. His own words distracted

him, and that one tiny distraction was all I needed. I lunged, swinging overhead in a flash and then feinting to the right, coming back at him from the opposite side. My speed took him off guard. He caught my blow at the last second, but lost ground and I quickly ate it up. He stumbled backward unprepared, and I began to batter down on him with the most complex series of blows that I knew.

He wasn't laughing anymore.

The clash of steel rang in my ears as each blow was parried. My clumsy movements revealed just how out of practice I was, but the refresher this morning had helped knock off some of the rust. I continued gaining ground, but then he regained control of the fight and started pushing back. I firmly held my ground and played with him, darting in and out, circling him. It became a dance, breaking away and then coming back together.

His sword came bearing down on me, and the force behind the blow jolted my arm as I parried it. William was good. He was very good, and he knew what he was doing. As the crown prince, he would've been training before he was even able to hold a sword.

For a moment, I thought he might be an equal match, but it quickly became apparent that he was more skilled and better practiced than me. I began losing ground at a quickening rate, and became more forceful, fighting back with everything I had. His blows were coming quickly, and I barely had time to block them. Our swords caught, and William pushed out of it. I lost my footing and fell to the ground, William's sword hovering above my throat. Sweat dripped from his brow as he took a step back, pushing the hair out of his eyes, a bewildered look of approval covering his face.

Suddenly Vladimir was there, his icy blue eyes staring down at me in a troubled frown. I rolled to my feet and grabbed my sword, taking several steps away before he blocked my path.

"Michael trained you." He spoke as if stating a fact he didn't want to believe.

I was too out of breath to speak, so I simply nodded.

He stood there for a moment, his face growing darker. "Why?"

A memory flickered across my vision, one that had once been a fond memory, but was now painted in the shadows of hurt. It was shortly after my seventh birthday, and my father had just begun showing me the ways of a sword. I could almost feel the summer heat still beating down on my back as I dropped my sword into the dirt, frustrated.

"Father, why are we doing this? I'm never going to be as good as you, and anyway, I am a lady. Ladies do not fight, and you promised you would always protect me."

A smile twitched at the corner of my father's lips as he knelt in front of me, taking up my sword and placing it gently in my hands. His sparkling green eyes found mine as he squeezed my other hand with his, chuckling.

"Yes, you are a lady, and I promise that until I breathe my last breath, I will protect you with my very life, but there will come a day when I am no longer here to protect you. In my absence, I want to ensure that you will be able to defend yourself from anyone who would wish to cause you harm."

The sun glinted off his hair as he stood and turned once again to face me. "Shall we go again?"

The heat of the sun's rays evaporated into the cold, cloudy sky that loomed overhead as the memory faded away. Vladimir was staring at me, waiting for an answer.

"So that I could defend myself one day when he was gone."

Simon approached wearing a scowl. "I see you didn't find it important to mention your previous training."

"I wasn't asked." I shot Vladimir a pointed look and noticed for the first time that every eye in the field was fixed in our direction. When I turned around to look at them, they all shifted uneasily back to whatever they had been doing before, but there was one gaze that did not turn away. Mordakai's harsh gaze bore into me, a threat burning behind his dark eyes. I stared right back, the same fire burning in mine.

"Not bad." William's voice sounded mildly impressed as he swaggered away.

"Thank you for your time, Simon." Vladimir reached for my sword, handing it back to its master. "Time to go."

Something in Vladimir had changed. What he was displaying was not fear, but I sensed another emotion boiling beneath the surface. I thought he might have appreciated the fact that I already knew how to fight, but the expression on his face was anything but gratitude. I followed him as we moved off the fields, the trainees watching as we marched away and out of sight. Vladimir remained silent and never looked at me. Dread seeped into my veins as I sensed a storm brewing beneath his calm exterior, lightning waiting to strike.

"It would have been helpful to know that Michael was training you, Taryn." He kept his voice dangerously low, still refusing to look at me.

"I tried," I said. "You kept interrupting."

Vladimir growled between gritted teeth.

We'd disappeared behind several trees, and Vladimir suddenly swung around toward me.

"You just put a target on your back. No one knew Michael Gallows had a daughter, and if she wasn't trained, then she couldn't be much of a threat. I left you to train with Simon to show all of them that there was nothing to fear from you. If Mordakai saw how underprepared you were, he wouldn't give you a second thought, but you decided to turn it into a spectacle, which proved to everyone watching that you are now viable competition."

"Don't you want the others to have someone worth rooting for?" I asked.

I understood what he was trying to say, but playing me as a fool threatened to shorten our time.

"Not if you have no intention of vying for it. Mordakai didn't need another reason to hate you more than he already does. No one took you seriously yesterday. The council's agreement was merely a means to pacify me, but with that stunt, you just proved that you're serious about this, which also means that you're in more danger now than you already were."

"But they would have already tried to kill me if I'd left," I said.

"*If* you'd left."

I felt the blood drain from my face at the realization of what I had done, the hatred on Mordakai's face making sense. It would now be necessary for him to outdo me. I wanted to blame William for all of this, but I was the one who had allowed him to provoke me.

"Michael taught you the sword; how good are you with a bow?" Vladimir's mind had already shifted ahead.

I tightened my fingers, remembering the feel of the bow in my hands. "Twice as good as I am with the sword. Even better if I brushed up."

"How have you kept up your skills if you haven't trained with your father in five years?"

I shot him a look. "Before my mother died, she insisted I keep learning. I trained with people in our village."

Vladimir nodded as he moved farther into the woods and studied the earth beneath his feet, stepping more slowly as we went. He stopped abruptly, pointing to a specific spot. "Can you tell me what that is there?"

I surveyed where his finger indicated. "The ground."

Vladimir rolled his eyes. "Excellent observation. Could you tell me what is on the ground?"

I knew what he wanted now. "You just found part of a deer trail."

"So you know how to track?"

His question nearly made me laugh. It was like asking a bird if it knew how to fly. "My mother and I lived far out of town, Vladimir. Most of our food was provided through hunting."

"What all can you track?"

I shrugged. "Deer, rabbit, pheasant, basically whatever can be used as food."

I'd been hunting since I could draw a bowstring. If my father wasn't able to hunt when he was home, he supplied us with more than enough money to buy meat. After my mother's death, I never kept the money for myself but gave some to either Lidia or the poor in our town. Accepting it felt like my father was buying my love. I hunted and grew my own food, sell-ing any surplus in town.

Vladimir's mind was working, searching for something else to test me on. "What's the most dangerous plant?"

"Mors Secunda."

"Why is it so deadly?"

I cocked my head. Weren't all children warned about the deadly red flower? "Because its poison doesn't take effect immediately. As you begin to heal, it causes an infection so strong that it can strike you dead, almost acting as a second death."

Vladimir rose to his feet, a battle warring in his eyes. "You're positive that Michael never mentioned one word to you about who he was?"

We had already discussed this. My father had never said a word. I don't know why he thought my answer might change. Though I knew of the Kavari, I had never suspected my father might be one of them, let alone their leader.

Vladimir eyed me, and I could tell that he didn't quite believe me.

"What?"

There was no denying that I was irritated. He ignored my question and began making his way back to the castle, and I had to hurry to fall in beside him.

"At some point, the queen is going to speak with you. It is good to be honest, but make sure that anything about our agreement is not acknowledged or discussed."

I nodded, although the statement seemed unnecessary. His cold demeanor insinuated a distrust that had not been present before, and it made me question him. He thought I was lying.

I wanted to know why.

CHAPTER TEN

Vladimir

THE MASSIVE TAPESTRY covered nearly an entire wall. The intricacy of its threads wove in and out of one another, an array of tiny details pieced together. On their own, the woven strands were nothing special, but carefully pieced together underneath an expert's eye, they transformed into the masterpiece hanging before me. One could not fully appreciate the tapestry without stepping back to take in the larger picture. My gaze roved over its complexities as I stood with my arms crossed, hands stroking the rough stubble on my chin.

I was too close to the situation at hand. Michael's murder, Taryn's part in this, the unrest in the government; all of these pieces fit together to create a larger picture, but I couldn't see it.

A flash of red caught the corner of my eye, and I realized

that someone was speaking. I turned. Katherine's lips were moving, but I was not taking in a word she was saying. She stopped, looking at me expectantly.

"You didn't hear a word I just said, did you?"

Her lips pursed, a bit of annoyance flashing in her fiery eyes. My face went blank. I had no earthly idea what she had been speaking about, nor how long she had been talking.

Katherine crossed her arms. "What's bothering you?"

My gaze returned to the tapestry, my mind working out the thoughts swirling around inside my head. What little information I possessed continued to lead back to the same conclusion every time, but the answer didn't make any sense.

"You heard what happened on the training fields?" I asked.

"Word travels fast."

My eyes traced over a waterfall woven into the fabric that cascaded into a pool below a mountain.

"Taryn said her father trained her so that she could protect herself."

Her head tilted. "That's not uncommon."

"What's uncommon is that he trained her to the point where she was almost capable of beating William."

Katherine's eyes watched my face as I surveyed where the pool of the waterfall faded into a valley with mountains rising on every side. "She knows how to use a bow," I continued. "I didn't see her shoot, but she said she was good. She can track and hunt. She knows how to survive in the wild. I don't know how well learned she is in matters of politics, though." I hesitated, deep in thought. "Her horse, the black one, he's an Adellaion steed."

Katherine stilled. "How did she get him?"

I forced a laugh out of my throat, not wanting to believe my own words as I turned toward her. "Michael gave him to her."

Katherine's mouth closed, surprise filling her face as she absorbed my words. "You don't just give someone an Adellaion steed."

Silence followed as I turned once again to the tapestry, carefully considering my next words as she searched my face.

"What are you getting at, Vladimir?"

I still didn't want to say it. I didn't want to believe it, but there was no other explanation.

"Michael was preparing her to join the Kavari."

Katherine quickly shook her head. "If she was called, Michael would have brought her here to be properly trained. It's his job as leader to discern the candidates and bring them before the council for consideration."

I shrugged. "That's definitely what he should have done."

"Then why did Michael keep her hidden all these years?"

My face grew more serious. "Why would Michael have a wife and a child and hide them in a remote valley to ensure that no one would ever find out they existed?"

Our eyes met, a million questions passing between them. Katherine was at a loss for words. The entire situation bothered me—had bothered me ever since Michael told me of their existence right before his death. Something wasn't adding up, and I couldn't find the missing piece.

"If Michael kept her hidden, there was a reason," I said. "He'd been carrying a secret with him for years, but I don't think it was just his wife and daughter. It was something else. He took it with him to his grave, and whatever that secret was, it's imperative we discover it because I think it may be foundational to saving our country."

It still bothered me that Michael had instructed Gavil only to give the information to his daughter. If I hadn't been forced to seek her out, the critical information would already be in our grasp. Unless—

I turned to Katherine. "I think Michael wanted Taryn here in the capital."

She frowned. "After all those years hidden away?"

He'd made me swear to protect her. Insisting that the information be passed to her ensured her presence in the capital and my promise being kept.

"What if Michael knew Mordakai would try to infiltrate the Kavari after his death?"

It was a bold assumption, but it fit into the bigger picture.

"Michael would never have allowed that to happen, but the only way to combat it would be with another eligible candidate."

Katherine's eyes narrowed, thoughts swirling behind her eyes. "He knew that Taryn had training."

I nodded. "And that she could invoke the right of a Blood Vier."

"Leaving her his ring gave proof of her heritage."

We stared at each other, piecing it together. Nominating Taryn as Kavari hadn't been an accident. Michael had intended this all along.

CHAPTER ELEVEN

Taryn

THE STABLE YARD sat still and silent in the falling shadows of twilight. No one lingered except for a few stable boys finishing the last evening chores before retiring for the night. They gazed at me as I strode past them into the barns, but I ignored their stares.

Stryder appeared content in his stall, surrounded by a warm bed of hay with food and water readily available. The long weeks on the road had been hard on him. There hadn't really been a point in coming here to check on him other than that I needed an excuse to escape my rooms, but in all honesty, I missed him. After my mother's death, he'd been my source of comfort and security. Stryder hadn't left my sight the last two weeks and being separated all day wasn't easy for me.

Stryder eyed me lazily, noting my presence but disinterestedly returning to his hay. My eyes fell on the saddle and bridle lying in front of his stall as my mind worked. All I would have to do was throw it on, and we could be out of here for good, but my mother's clasp flashed before my eyes. The hunger to find my family was greater than the desire to disentangle myself from the political affairs in which I had become so completely wound.

Of everything I had learned in the last few days, there was one question I couldn't get out of my head: why my father had never told me who he was. It bothered me that my mother had never mentioned it. I suppose it partially explained why my father so seldom came to visit when I was a child. He had been preoccupied with protecting the country in which we lived.

My heart hardened.

That was still no excuse to keep my mother and me hidden away from the rest of the world. Had he been ashamed of us? There was a time when I had wondered if my mother was his mistress, yet I knew in my heart that was not who my mother was to him. I could still recall the pain in his eyes every time he left, the sun glinting off the wedding band encircling my mother's finger, and one last wave as he rode away. I struggled to remember any resentment between them, but I could only ever remember my mother speaking highly of him.

A thought suddenly struck me, bringing me to a halt.

Had I been illegitimate?

The idea bounced around my head. A child of my mother but not my father? It would explain a lot, but I struck down the possibility. Everyone said that I looked so much like my father, and even I could see a tinge of the resemblance.

I made my way back into the shadows of the yard, quickly

moving toward the castle door. Torches lit the way and blazed along the outer wall every few feet. Once I entered the castle, I relied on my memory to get me through the endless corridors. For the most part, I was confident I could find my way back to my rooms without getting lost, but I still hesitated on which direction to go each time the halls diverged.

A shout broke out in the corridor to my right but was quickly cut off. I froze, staring down into the darkness, my ears poised to detect the slightest sound. I hadn't seen anyone besides the guards this evening.

Wisdom told me to continue on my way, but curiosity cared little for such thoughts. Melting into the shadows lining the dimly lit corridor, I slunk along the wall. My skirts swished soundlessly across the stone floor. The very faintest of voices reached my ears, and I walked faster, realizing that the voices seemed to be coming from within the walls.

"—trying to get you to focus. You agreed to this." The man's voice was restrained.

"This is not what I agreed to." My heartbeat quickened as I recognized Mordakai's voice. I pressed my back against a pillar, keeping my body perfectly still. "You didn't tell me that Michael Gallows had a daughter."

"I had no idea she existed! But you're a fool if you think the council will choose her over you!" The unidentified man's voice rose almost to a shout again, the hair on the back of my neck rising as his words echoed quietly off the stone walls.

"Keep your voice down!" Mordakai hissed. "Are you blind? Or did you already forget how the people worshiped at Michael Gallows' feet? They will do the same for his daughter."

"Don't forget that you still have the support of the

Crown."

"I need the support of the Kavari to ensure my position," Mordakai said.

"Then she will be taken care of."

My heart pounded harder in my chest. Mordakai's retort was quiet and unintelligible and carried on for several moments. I strained my ears, but his voice had grown too low to discern.

"If this goes terribly, it will be on you," warned the other man.

Someone spit, then with a voice full of disgust, Mordakai snarled, "We're done."

My eyes widened as the wall itself opened, revealing a hidden door. From its depths emerged a figure with white hair so pale that it shone in the darkness. Zedekiah stormed down the corridor, his muffled footsteps barely noticeable in the night.

My eyes riveted on the spot where the door had vanished once more into the stone wall. I held my breath, waiting for Mordakai to emerge from the place beyond the door, but it remained as solid as the stone it was made with. After a few moments, I tentatively took a step forward out of the shadows.

No sounds of life came from the other side of the wall. Had he gone down a passageway? I squinted as my eyes roved over the wall in search of a door. It should be right here, but as my fingers traveled across the cold stones, they didn't find any cracks or creases in the rock.

I turned back the way I had come, listening to make sure no one was coming. When no sound came, I glanced back at the wall one last time and nearly jumped out of my skin. Mordakai's cold eyes bore into mine as the hidden door silently shut behind him. My heart hammered within my chest as guilt washed over my face. I froze in fear, unable to move.

His steely gaze morphed into a chilling smile.

"Taryn Gallows." He said my name slowly, chewing on it as if he couldn't decide whether he liked the sound of it or not. "It's quite late to be out by yourself. Might I escort you?"

His hand clamped down on my arm, dragging me down the corridor. I stepped blindly, my mind racing. His death grip on my arm didn't loosen, and I floundered beside him helplessly. Did he know I'd just overheard what they had spoken about? We crossed the corridor I had just entered from and continued into the next. A cold sweat trickled down my back as we briskly turned another corner, and he opened a door on his left.

"After you." He snarled and pushed me into the room.

I stumbled into the dimly lit space. A desk lined the far wall with two chairs in front of it. A few papers lay scattered over the desk, but aside from the two torches along the wall, nothing else occupied the room. It felt like a cage. The air grew thick, threatening to suffocate me. The door opened again, and two soldiers entered, guarding both sides of the door.

"Sit." His hand grabbed my shoulder and forced me into the seat. "I insist."

I sat as stiff as a board, my hands clenched into fists at my sides, wondering what he would do to me. Only moments ago, he and his brother had been plotting my death. I didn't glance back at the door. That would show him I was afraid. I kept my eyes pinned on Mordakai and wished that Vladimir were here.

"So you're Taryn Gallows." The accusation rang in his voice as he leaned back against the desk, folding his arms.

"Yes."

He grunted, indifferent to the fact. Heat flared in my chest, and I squared my shoulders as my confidence grew. If he was trying to intimidate me, bringing me here alone at night, I would make sure that I didn't let him.

"Michael never mentioned he had a daughter."

I cocked an eyebrow. "My father kept many secrets."

He lifted one hand, slowly stroking his chin. "Yet I still find it strange. After the beloved Michael Gallows was killed, a stranger shows up claiming to be his daughter, and the same girl desires to take her father's position. A very highly sought-after position, I might add." He paused to watch my expression, which I determinedly kept unreadable. "I feel the queen's council might feel differently about our"—he hesitated—"*predicament*, if they were given that perspective."

He wanted to be in the Kavari, and he was going to do whatever he needed to get there. He'd cleared the board but hadn't been expecting competition.

"I see," I said. "Yet you seem to have had a great interest in the Kavari for a long time, and are suddenly vying for a position that would never have been available to you while my father was still alive."

Mordakai laughed. "I've spent my whole life preparing for this role, not running away from it. I'm the only man in the kingdom fit for the job."

"If you're so confidant you'll become a Kavari, then why do you act threatened?"

His face darkened with anger, but he quickly replaced it with a knowing look. "You surmised I had an interest in Michael's position, yet I find you failed to question the man who actually replaced his role."

If he couldn't get at me, he would go after Vladimir.

"Do you not find it odd, Miss Gallows, that your father went on a mission he told only Vladimir about, and that Vladimir was the one to find the body, with no witnesses to the scene besides himself? He stepped into Michael's role after his death and conjured up a daughter that no one knew about except him, all for the sake of deterring resistance from the people under his command."

I swallowed, taking in his words. They were lies. He was trying to whittle away at my determination, yet I still saw the logic he wove into his words. Vladimir wouldn't lie to me. My surety faltered—but Vladimir was willing to do anything to get what he wanted. It was unsettling, but I realized Mordakai was implying I wasn't Michael's daughter. That small truth chipped away at his argument.

Mordakai must have sensed the war inside my mind because he smiled and lifted his hand to the door. "You may leave now."

I rose slowly from the seat and walked to the door.

"One more thing."

I turned back to him. "Don't forget, Miss Gallows, my loyalty is to my country, and I will do whatever it takes to protect it. If there are those among us who are not loyal to Gharridan, I suggest that they leave this country while they can, and while they are still free to do so."

The door shut behind me, and I hurried back to my rooms, the iciness of his voice chilling me on the way.

CHAPTER TWELVE

Taryn

THE ALLEGATIONS MORDAKAI planted in my mind about Vladimir's untrustworthiness sprouted and grew over the next week. The idea consumed me. Everything about Vladimir became suspicious. His words. His advice. His actions. Mordakai's theory that Vladimir had orchestrated my father's death was logical. Vladimir had reason. He had motive.

But did he possess the desire?

Was he really capable of killing my father?

The thought of my mother's clasp had kept me from analyzing the situation more than I needed to, but maybe I had placed my faith in the wrong person.

I'd kept Mordakai's intimidation to myself, but as we drilled on the history of Gharridan, I decided to finally let it out and gauge his reaction.

"He threatened you?" His blue eyes burned with ire as I relayed the events.

Was he upset that Mordakai had threatened me, or did he fear that Mordakai had said something he shouldn't have?

"Not directly."

I shifted my weight, wincing as the action pulled at my sore muscles. My arms ached from drawing the bowstring, swinging the sword, and anytime I moved, my legs and backside screamed from spending the entire day in the saddle while we practiced tracking. It was the first time I'd ridden since arriving, and I was paying for it.

Vladimir crossed his arms. "Why didn't you tell me this days ago?"

I shrugged.

"You said he came out of the wall?"

I nodded. "I can show you where if you'd like."

Vladimir shook his head. "I'll check it out myself, but you need to stay as far away from there as possible. We don't need you confirming suspicions that you overheard him."

Or maybe Vladimir wanted to ensure that I didn't hear anything more.

"How many secret passages are there?" I asked.

"I don't know."

I frowned. "How do you not know? Aren't you the leader of the Kavari?"

"The secret passageways in this castle are reserved for the royal family. Most people don't even know about them, although I'm sure they suspect. William and the queen know how and where to access them, as does one of the Kavari and the queen's personal guard."

"Well, if you don't know, then who does?"

"Michael knew," he said. "He didn't exactly get to pass the torch, so there are things I should be privy to that I'm not yet. I'll ask William about the tunnels, but I need to be sure my inquiries won't be noticed."

I cocked an eyebrow. "If they're reserved for the royal family and not even you know, how do Mordakai and his brother know?"

Vladimir scowled. "His brother is the advisor to the queen, and Mordakai has always been very good at discovering secrets."

Like when he found out my father had discovered his betrayal.

Or maybe it wasn't Mordakai's betrayal after all.

"Are you as good at keeping secrets as he is at discovering them?" The edge in my voice gave me away.

Vladimir watched me, noting the hostility of my demeanor. "What else did he say?"

Suspicion rang in his voice, and I could tell he knew something was wrong.

I scrutinized his face, searching for deception, but seemed to come back empty. Through every new day of training, Vladimir had remained steady, dependable. My heart told me he was innocent, but the facts pointed otherwise.

"Mordakai had his own suspicions about Michael's murder," I finally answered.

Vladimir took a step closer. "And just what were those suspicions?"

Silence hung between us.

He knew what I meant.

It was written all over his face.

"You think I had something to do with your father's death, don't you?"

I avoided his eyes, Mordakai's words turning over in my mind. *Vladimir was the one to find the body, no witnesses to the scene besides himself.*

"I can't say the thought never crossed my mind," I ventured.

Fear hovered in Vladimir's gaze.

I cleared my throat. "Tell me again how you found him."

Vladimir grew distant, his thoughts taking him elsewhere.

Was it all just an act?

It took him a moment to get the words out. "He was in the clearing with his throat slit, his chest pierced by his own sword. Seven bodies lay around him, completely burned beyond recognition."

"And he told you he was leaving because he found information that was crucial to Gharridan's survival?"

Vladimir's haunted eyes met mine. "He was scared, Taryn. The fear made him rant and rave like a madman, and the words coming out of his mouth were incoherent. He kept saying if 'they' found out he knew, they were going to kill him."

"Why wouldn't he just tell you what he suspected?"

"I don't know. I think he was trying to protect me." When I didn't say anything, his expression grew serious again. "You can believe whatever you want, Taryn. I'm not going to waste my time trying to convince you otherwise. I have better things to do like trying to find evidence against Mordakai, but if he did kill your father, it would make perfect sense for him to pin the murder on me, especially when I showed up with an heir he knew nothing about and complicated matters for him."

No emotion came from Vladimir, only facts. If he had wanted to take my father's place so badly, he had a funny way of showing it. And he was right. I had no doubt that Mordakai would use his theory to bring Vladimir down in order to elevate himself, and if Mordakai was the culprit, he would have thought of this theory early enough to plan it out. Some of the facts might point otherwise, yet my heart told me he was innocent.

One fact was for certain. I hadn't met anyone more tormented over my father's death than Vladimir. His love for Michael was apparent in both action and word, and I didn't understand how the man who abandoned me had managed to stir up such devotion in those who worked for him. The lines of stress across Vladimir's face deepened, and everything in me told me that this role as leader of the Kavari was not one he wanted to fill.

No, it was not Vladimir.

The manner of my father's death proved that by its intent to dishonor and humiliate. The message behind the killing beckoned a darker connotation—this was about more than a mere power struggle. A deeper motive was involved.

"Say that I do believe you," I began. "That doesn't mean that other people will, especially if Mordakai begins to whisper this accusation among the court."

Concern lined Vladimir's face. He was being attacked from all sides. Each day the pressure surrounding him seemed to grow more intense without any signs of decreasing.

I tilted my head. "Which is why we need to get that evidence as quickly as possible. Have you heard from Marco?"

He shook his head. "Not yet, but we should be hearing something any day now."

I gazed out the window, watching the dying rays of the sun stretch out across the sky and hoping that when the light returned, it would bring Marco with it.

CHAPTER THIRTEEN

Taryn

SOMETHING WAS PULLING me away from the blissful darkness in which I slept, and I rolled over, wrapping my blankets tighter. My eyes squinted open as the disturbance repeated itself. Someone was knocking at my door. Fear rushed through me, and I snatched the knife from my side, slinking toward the door suspiciously. I waited, holding my breath, then the knock came again, louder this time.

"Who is it?" I asked quietly.

There was a pause.

"Vladimir."

I opened the door a crack, peeking out and wondering what in the world he was doing here in the middle of the night.

"What's going on?"

"Get dressed. You need to come with me. And quickly."

He glanced over his shoulder. "Meet me down the hall."

I shut the door, my thoughts still fuzzy as I reached for my dress, slipping it over my head and securing it with a belt. My cloak lay over the chair, and I hesitated for a moment before grabbing it and hurrying down the hall looking for Vladimir. He emerged from the shadows like a ghost, placing a finger against his lips as he led the way without any explanation.

The chilly draft blowing through the castle awakened my thoughts, and I wondered why we were secretly sneaking around the castle in the dead of night. He walked briskly, never looking back except for a quick glance to make sure I was following him. Our only companions were the torches burning along the walls and illuminating our path.

We descended into a lower level of what I assumed was the servants' quarters and then back up a staircase until we reached a side door.

"Where are we going?" I whispered.

"Not here." Vladimir reached for the handle, and I placed a hand on his arm.

"I'm not going any farther until I know what's going on."

Vladimir's gaze darted up and down the corridor. "I received a missive from Gavil today. He's in the capital, and he wants to speak with you."

Hope flared in my chest. If we obtained proof of Mordakai's treachery, all of this would be over. We slipped through the door and emerged onto the castle grounds. Several hundred feet to our right lay the main gate. I kept glancing at it as we shifted through the shadows and moved toward the outer wall. Not many soldiers patrolled this area, but I kept stride with Vladimir to keep from falling behind. Vladimir stopped before the wall and began running his hands over the stones. I looked back the way we had come and recognized the same garden of trees from the first night when we'd snuck into the castle.

"I thought you didn't know anything about the secret passageways."

There came a muted sound of grating stone, and then a door swung open in the wall.

"Its an exit. Not a passageway. Michael and I used it all the time."

After we stepped through, I watched as the gate disappeared into the wall, once again hidden from view. We stumbled through the woods in darkness, moving indirectly toward the sleeping capital. Vladimir set a quick pace and appeared to know where he was headed. Twigs snapped beneath my feet. I cringed. He turned with annoyance, placing a finger to his lips. My cheeks were burning as I tried to step more carefully, but walking silently through an unfamiliar forest in the darkness was not as easy as he made it out to be.

The trees thinned, and I peered at the outline of the city up ahead. Darkness clung to the streets, and we spirited through them like shadows in the night. Not a creature stirred; not even guards roamed the streets. We descended deeper and deeper into the city's depths as time stretched on and on. It felt like hours since I had left my room, yet the sky remained black.

The distant sound of laughter trickled to my ears, and a beam of light shone across the street from the tavern, the only building that displayed any sign of life.

"Pull your cloak up," Vladimir said.

I did as he instructed, squinting as the blinding light invaded my eyes. None of the guests in the tavern paid us any attention as we walked along the wall and ascended the staircase to the second floor. The steps creaked beneath my feet, groaning from years of countless patrons climbing them. Doors lined the hallway upstairs, and we padded along the worn rug to the end where Vladimir stopped at the farthest door on the left, giving it three quick raps.

I held my breath, not sure I was ready for whatever was on the other side. Sounds from the noisy tavern below drifted up the stairs, distracting me. My eyes flicked down the hall, fearful that we might have been followed. Vladimir rapped softly on the door again, but only twice this time. Movement drifted from inside as footsteps crossed the room. The door cracked open to reveal a shadowed, apprehensive eye that surveyed us up and down. It lingered on my face, wandering over me suspiciously. I pushed my cloak back. I had nothing to hide.

The eye disappeared, and the opening in the door widened. Vladimir stepped across the threshold, and I followed, casting one more glance over my shoulder to ensure we weren't being watched.

The small room held only a few worn pieces of furniture. A fire crackled along the far wall, the flames beginning to dwindle into embers. My gaze finally came to rest on the man whose eyes still watched me with obvious distrust. Dirt smeared his filthy clothes, the scraggly beard hanging from his chin suggesting he'd been traveling for a while. No identification marked the simple tunic and trousers he wore, but a sword hung from his side. One hand remained firmly planted on the hilt as he looked up warily at Vladimir, who towered over him.

"Do you have proof of her heritage?" The man's voice was pointed but quiet.

This conversation was not to be overheard.

Vladimir indicated my hand, and I raised it, revealing my father's ring. It shone in the light of the flickering flames as the man examined it and then relaxed. He gestured toward two chairs by a lopsided table. Vladimir and I took our seats, and the man sat on the bed.

"When Michael told me he had a daughter, I didn't believe him." His eyes flicked between us. "Yet I was assured that after his death I would hear the name Taryn Gallows."

Vladimir shifted across the table from me, and I glanced from him to the man. There was something I didn't know here. My father couldn't have known I would come forward after his death. If Vladimir hadn't found me when he did, I would already be halfway across Gharridan.

"Why did my father insist you only give the information to me?" I asked.

The man met my eyes with the coldness of his own. "Your father wanted to make sure the information didn't fall into the wrong hands, and that other"—he glanced at Vladimir—"*promises* had been fulfilled."

I gave Vladimir an inquisitive look, about to ask what the man meant by promises.

"Why did Michael come to see you, Gavil?" Vladimir quickly asked.

"Because I found Jarrod Lynch."

For a moment, it was as if the world had stopped, yet the flame's shadows dancing along the walls rejected the notion. Vladimir eased back; his face stricken in surprise. A smug smile spread across Gavil's face, and he crossed his arms, rather pleased with himself.

"It was Jarrod's brother, Randal, actually, if we're being specific," he added.

"Michael looked for him for years and never got close. I only saw him and his brother a few times—it was years ago." Vladimir seemed to drift away to thoughts of another time. "How did you find him?"

The man sucked in his cheeks and lifted his head like a mighty noble. "Pure persistence and determination. I'd been tracking him for the past seven years. It was only a matter of time."

"Who is Jarrod Lynch?" I glanced between them, my frustration growing at being left completely in the dark.

"He's—" Vladimir stopped as if he had forgotten what he was going to say. Gavil laughed knowingly, taking a sip from the mug on the table before he addressed Vladimir's confusion.

"You don't know why Michael was looking for him, do you?" Gavil asked.

Vladimir crossed his arms, staring intently at the far wall and refusing to meet Gavil's eyes.

"Truth is I don't know either." Gavil set the mug down and leaned back. "Michael sent me looking for him years ago, but never told me why. I remembered Jarrod; he was a physician in the city." He shook his head "But something sent him packing, and it's been a horrible time trying to track him down. He's been on the move ever since, sneaking from one city to another. I don't believe he's even in the country right now. Took years, but I finally found a little leverage and arranged a meeting with his brother."

Vladimir leaned forward as I continued to watch the man, anxiously waiting for the information we so desperately needed.

"And?" Vladimir asked.

"He said he would speak with his brother."

There was a pause.

"About ...?" Vladimir urged.

"Michael needed him to testify against someone. Of course, he never told me who, but Michael believes someone committed treason against King Roldan, and he couldn't prove it without Jarrod's testimony."

"Treason against the king?" Vladimir asked.

King Roldan had died years ago.

"The king—Gharridan—there was treason involved somewhere."

"Did he speak with his brother?" Vladimir asked.

Gavil shrugged, "He slipped through my fingers again, but Michael wanted you and his daughter to know what he was doing."

He shifted his weight and bent forward. "That's not the only reason he came to see me, though."

Vladimir and I exchanged a glance.

"What do you mean?" I asked.

"A high document left the capital about a week before he died. When Michael got wind of it, he was able to intercept the letter, but the messenger escaped."

"Who was the messenger?" Vladimir pressed.

"I don't know," Gavil said. "Michael didn't leave me with many details."

"What was in the document?"

Gavil scrutinized our faces before answering. "The terms of a treaty to be fulfilled after the death of Michael Gallows."

My father's murder had been carefully planned out. He was

betrayed by the very country he'd sworn to protect.

"A treaty with who?" Vladimir nearly rose from his seat.

Gavil's eyes flicked to the door, fearful Vladimir's sudden outburst might have drawn attention. When all remained silent, Gavil continued. "A neighboring country. I don't know which one."

"Where is this document, and who signed it?" Vladimir lowered his voice. "Did you see it?"

Gavil shook his head. "He sent it to Marco, but it had the seal of Gharridan on it."

Vladimir's face paled.

"Can't you tell who is responsible by the seal?" I asked. I didn't understand his fear. This sounded like good news to me.

Vladimir looked at me, questions swirling behind his eyes. "Our country has three official sets of seals. The royal seal, the seal of the Kavari, and the seal of Gharridan. All the council members have access to the seal of Gharridan."

"Including Mordakai?"

Vladimir shook his head. "Not directly, but if Mordakai killed Michael to join the Kavari, he would've found a way to get the seal either through force or blackmail. He's personable and familiar with the council members. If Marco has the letter, then we may be able to prove that Mordakai is guilty when he arrives."

"How can you be so sure?" I asked.

Vladimir crossed his arms. "If Michael went to such great lengths to preserve that document, whatever's inside must expose the treaty and incriminate the guilty parties."

I breathed a sigh of relief. The moment when I would be able to pry myself away from this situation was drawing nearer.

It was the first possible hope we'd had of justice for my father's murder.

"How did Michael get the document to Marco?" Vladimir asked.

Gavil's face looked strained. "I don't know; I assume by one of his messengers. My conversation with Michael was very brief, and there wasn't time for specifics."

"Was there anything else he told you?"

"Michael wanted me to warn you to be careful, Vladimir," Gavil said. "If someone wanted the previous leader of the Kavari dead, they'll most likely want you dead as well."

Vladimir's jaw set hard, and we sat in silence for a few moments, pondering this information. He stood, peering out the window's murky glass.

"We need to go. The sun will be rising soon."

We left the inn, the world slowly beginning to wake. I drew my hood back up. People were leaving their houses, setting up shop and starting work for the day. Vladimir remained quiet and thoughtful as we meandered our way back to the castle. Thoughts swirled around in my own mind like the wind carrying autumn leaves through the crisp air.

When my father had come to see me for the last time, he had known he was going to die. The realization pierced me like a knife. I had turned away as he left. I hadn't even said goodbye. He wanted to see me one last time, and I discarded him like an old rag. Guilt washed over me, and I swallowed hard.

By the time we reached the castle gates, the sun had already risen, and we passed through without suspicion. My body ached from tiredness, and I glanced at Vladimir, who looked much worse for the wear.

"You're concerned," I observed.

Vladimir's face was serious. "I am."

"Once Marco arrives with the document, we'll have proof."

"That's not what concerns me."

I cocked my head, confused. "Then what?"

Vladimir walked several more paces. "All the council members have access to that seal. Drafting the terms of a treaty and arranging for a Kavari's death would be no small job and not easy to hide."

I wasn't sure where he was going with this.

"I don't think that Mordakai did this alone. I think he had help from someone, or somewhere else."

CHAPTER FOURTEEN

Taryn

I STOOD BEFORE the door as still as a statue, my eyes riveted on the wood panel separating me from what lay inside. The carpentry was simple. There were no extravagant carvings or painted canvases, just an old wooden door reinforced with steel that lined the edges. The room hadn't been difficult to find. When I asked a servant for directions, a look of sadness crossed her face, and she was kind enough to take me directly there.

My fingers curled around the cold door handle, but my legs remained locked in place, unwilling to move. I didn't know if I was allowed to be here, which was why I'd refrained from asking permission. Ignorance was a valuable ally in this situation. With a shove, I jolted the door open and stepped inside. The breath I'd been holding escaped my lips when, for the very first time, I beheld the place where my father had lived.

Light poured in from the windows at the top of the high arched ceiling, bathing the room in warm light. A grand hearth lay dormant on the far wall with a cushioned chair and a bearskin rug positioned before it. The large bed was still dressed as perfectly as the day it was made. Two tall bookshelves lined a wall, and a writing desk sat on the other. A bottle of ink left open had dried, and three pieces of parchment gave evidence to words that had never been written.

My eyes caught at the small wooden wardrobe, and I moved to open it. A pair of boots lined the bottom. Only a few clothes occupied the hanging space. I took a breath and briefly inhaled my father's scent, tears stinging my eyes. I quickly shut the wardrobe and backed away. The memory of him shouldn't cause me to feel pain. He had left us. He had left *me*.

I perused the room with a new resolve. There had to be something in here to help us, something my father would have left behind. The bookshelves drew my attention, and I meandered over to it. The titles ranged from books on history to several books on herbology and rare plants. My eyes fell to the dust coating the wood in front of the books. It was thick, showing weeks of neglect, yet I noticed that not all the dust was the same height. Only a thin layer lined the places where it appeared books had been removed. I walked over to the desk and, upon closer inspection, found that most of the dust was disturbed.

Someone had searched this room before me.

My eyes shot in every direction expecting the intruder to appear, but all remained as it was. Whoever went through this room had been gone for a while. I returned to the bookshelf, looking for a possible journal, but found nothing. My eyes caught on a well-weathered book, the binding ragged from use, and I gingerly pulled the book out. The title was embossed on the front cover. It was a book of children's tales and legends. I knew it well, for my mother had pulled me into her lap and read me stories from it on those bleak days when all I could think about was missing my father.

My fingers flipped open to the first page, and I blinked. A lock of dark brown hair lay in front of me. My mother's hair. I would know it anywhere. Underneath the lock was a drawing of my mother; her beautiful features perfectly defined as she gazed at some unknown sight. My hands began to shake as I stared at it. Loss, sorrow, and hurt overpowered my mind. I gripped the edges of the book, taking a deep breath to calm myself. Of course he would have it. It wasn't until my mother died that he had stopped coming. I flipped through the rest of the book, instinctively moving toward my favorite story about the dragon and the mouse. My eyes fell on the page adjoining it, a page that had been blank when I was a child, but it was not blank here. It took me a moment to realize the drawing was of me. A daisy arrayed my flowing hair, and a bright smile enveloped every part of my face.

The world tilted as I stared at the drawing, absorbing every line and curve that created the replica of my face. My father must have drawn it from memory. I'd never even seen him draw before. I flipped back and forth between the portraits of my mother and me. Both were executed with incredible attention to detail. Both evoked deep emotional feelings and had been crafted with obvious love. I shook my head, flipping through the rest of the book, but there were no others. A small phrase was scribbled beneath the drawing.

If only to see her smile like this again, for her to understand.

Understand what? He'd known I wasn't happy, but he should have known why. If he had wanted to be a part of my life, he would have tried. Abandonment was not love.

Hot tears stung my eyes as I slammed the book shut, shoving it back onto the shelf and glaring at every object in the room—everything that had kept my father from me. There was nothing here. I was stupid for having thought I would find something.

I stormed across the room, my eyes falling on a triangular object barely peeking out from behind the desk. I stopped, snatching it from its hiding spot. Disappointment weighed down my shoulders as I realized it was simply an empty envelope with a broken seal, cast off indifferently. I set it back down on the desk and froze, eyes fixed on the chipped seal. With trembling fingers, I drew the top of the envelope to the bottom half, bringing the two pieces of the seal back together. Once united, they created four teardrop leaves with a heavily petaled flower in the center. It was my mother's seal. I'd seen it countless times before, never considering it anything special, but here, five years after her death in a place she'd never been—

I frantically searched behind the desk and tore through the drawers for any whisper, any hope of the envelope's previous contents. Beneath the rug, under the bed, behind the wardrobe—but there was nothing here. Hope was fading, but I held onto what little I could as I wondered what had come in the envelope.

I tucked the envelope inside my dress and hurried to the door, ready to hunt down whatever mystery surrounded my mother. I flung open the door, coming face to face with the queen.

She took a step back in surprise, and I felt the guilt rush to my face. We stood there with our eyes locked, questions playing across our faces.

"Miss Gallows," the queen managed, her surprised expression morphing into disapproval.

For a moment, I stood there in shock, unsure if I had done something wrong, then I quickly curtsied before the words rushed out of my mouth. "Your Majesty. I'm sorry, I hadn't been here before. I just wanted to see …" My voice fell, sounding so full of emotion, yet it was only the nerves trying to keep me from relaying everything in one breath.

The queen's face softened, but only slightly. Her eyes remained steady on mine before raising a hand to the guards behind her. "Ensure that this door is locked."

My eyes darted between the guard and the door, and I realized that my mother's picture was now unreachable. I should have grabbed the book before I left. I took a step to leave, but the queen's words caught me before I could escape.

"I would like a word with you, Miss Gallows."

I felt myself nodding as my heart beat faster. The queen's eyes gave nothing away as she continued down the corridor. Dread clutched at me as I followed, not knowing what the conversation might entail. Our paths hadn't crossed since the meeting in the council room, and I hadn't so much as seen her from a distance. The distaste she'd held for me in the council room had been evident from her visible dissatisfaction and accusing eyes, but although she wasn't happy about my presence here, she hadn't completely rejected it.

I took a deep breath, reminding myself I had nothing to

fear. The queen sauntered through the castle with a grace that was both beautiful and deadly, her head held high. I felt like a shadow, forever constrained to fade behind the grandeur of another's existence. My presence was never acknowledged as we strode through the castle corridors and out into the evanescent gardens whose color was diminishing after the first snow. Winter was building like an ominous storm, visible from a distance, but not yet striking the world with its full force.

Queen Adamara ran her pale fingers over a dying rose bush, plucking a shriveled rose from the brittle stem. It twirled in her fingers as she brought it to her face and inhaled its scent before releasing it to join the graveyard of petals encompassing the base of the bush.

"I keep asking myself why you are here," the queen mused, her hands gently caressing a browning leaf. "When Vladimir first brought you in, you had no apparent desire for the Kavari."

I hadn't had any desire. Nor did I now. I had wanted to run from the council room the moment I entered it.

"Yet, you've remained here, vying for a position with them."

Her blue eyes scrutinized me, searching for secrets. "What does Taryn Gallows want? I can't seem to find an answer to that question."

Her stance was patient, yet expectant. I tried to swallow, but my mouth went dry. Sweat prickled on my forehead even though the temperature was near freezing. What did she want to hear? Every part of me wanted to look away, but I refused to show weakness. The queen was not someone I could trust. For all I knew, she had succumbed to advice from the brother of a killer. My words were formed carefully before I answered.

"I want my father's murderer brought to justice."

While this wasn't the entire truth, it was still a portion of it. Yes, I wanted my father's murderer brought to justice, but my reasons were quite selfish.

She cocked her head, a knowing look on her face. "One could not judge you for that." She strolled through the garden at a leisurely pace while I kept step behind her. "I can't help but feel you have the wrong impression of me, Taryn." She paused, watching for my reaction. "That I am heartless, moving on so quickly after your father's death. Make no mistake. I respected your father deeply. His sole concern was for the prosperity and security of his country; his wisdom unfathomable. Your father loved our country, and he will forever be remembered by the great things he did for Gharridan. We, as a country, still feel his loss, and I hope you will accept my condolences."

I blinked, her last sentence taking me off guard.

"Thank you," I managed.

We walked in silence for a few paces, the queen's mind somewhere else. She let out a sigh. "Vladimir is experienced, but he is still young. When Michael named him as his successor, none of us expected him to have to take on that responsibility so soon. He should have had at least another decade of training under Michael. The truth is, I don't believe Vladimir is ready to take on this role, and the immense pressure may have caused him to make some poor decisions."

My heart beat faster as the air between us grew tense, anticipating the queen's next words.

"It would have been better if another more experienced individual had been selected to lead the Kavari until Vladimir was ready."

I remained silent, afraid to speak.

She stopped and gave me a serious look. "Your heritage gives you a claim to the Kavari, Miss Gallows, but you have no experience in the matters of our government. I fail to see how your instatement would bring any kind of security to Gharridan. You are unknown to the people; you have nothing to offer." She started walking again. "Mordakai, on the other hand, has grown up here. He knows our ways, our policies, our diplomacies. He is known among the people and has much to offer Gharridan.

"My advice to you, Taryn, is to walk away. Let Mordakai become the next Kavari. If you still possess the desire to serve as a Kavari, I find no reason for you not to continue training with Vladimir; however, I do think it unwise to put yourself through too much too quickly. You lost your father less than two months ago, and attempting to quickly fill his shoes is too large a task."

Her gaze rested heavily on me, waiting for me to note the meaning of her words. After a moment, she motioned to her guards, indicating that our meeting was over. "I hope you will think over our discussion, Taryn."

I dipped my head then watched as she walked away. A shiver ripped through my body, and I hugged myself, suddenly chilled. She wanted me to back out, which was what I so desperately wanted to do, but that was exactly why I wasn't going to do it. Marco couldn't get here fast enough.

In a sense, I could understand why she despised me. She was simply trying to protect the country she'd safeguarded these many years. Had I been in her position, I might feel the same way.

I strode away, determined to find Vladimir. He'd warned me that the queen would want to speak with me, and I wanted to tell him what had transpired. I stepped through the double doors back into the castle. Someone rushed at me, and I threw out my arms in defense, relaxing as I realized it was Katherine. Her steps were rigid, her pale face strained.

"What—" Before I could form the question, she grabbed my arm and hurried us out of the guard's earshot. Down a deserted corridor, she pulled me behind an alcove, her eyes wide.

I raised my eyebrows in question, unsure if it was safe to speak or not.

She took a deep breath, steadying her shaking hands on my arms. "Gavil is dead."

CHAPTER FIFTEEN

Taryn

THE WORLD AROUND me shrank, growing smaller and smaller till all my focus homed in on Katherine's pernicious statement. Her words left me dumbfounded. "What do you mean he's dead?"

I had seen Gavil with my own eyes, alive and well, less than two days ago. It wasn't possible. It couldn't be possible.

Fear ruled Katherine's eyes. "A man reported someone dragging a body toward the drainage system. Guards found his body—what was left of it—half-buried in the mire. He hadn't been dead for very long, but torture was evident."

I shook my head. If Gavil had been tortured, that could only mean one thing—he had something someone else wanted. *Information* that someone else wanted, and if he was dead—they'd gotten what they'd needed from him.

"The letter." My heart skipped a beat, afraid of her answer.

Katherine shook her head reluctantly. "I don't know, but if Gavil told them that Marco had the letter, then Marco is in extreme danger. Vladimir took an entire squadron of soldiers to try to reach Marco before anyone else and escort him safely here." She trailed off. "But it may already be too late."

That letter was my lifeline. Without it, everything we'd planned would crumble to dust. Without it, there was no way to prove Mordakai was involved with my father's murder, and if Marco didn't make it, I might not have a choice in whether or not I joined the Kavari.

"Katherine, if we don't get the letter—" I cut off, afraid saying the words might make them come true. I started pacing back and forth, worry embedding itself in me.

"Why didn't Vladimir take me with him?"

"He knew you would ask that. Under no circumstances are you to leave the castle alone, per his orders. It's not safe for you out there."

I lifted my own chin. "Yet it's safer here, where a man was murdered within the city walls."

Footsteps approached from the other end of the hall, and Katherine pulled me out of the alcove toward the opposite direction, speaking in a low voice. "We don't need any more eyes on this than we already have. Vladimir rode out under the pretense of making sure Marco arrived safely after what happened to Michael. If you were to go with them, questions might surface that would draw unwanted attention." Katherine looked over her shoulder before her gaze darted down the corridor near the kitchens. "Until he returns, you need to continue your training and proceed as if everything is playing out as it should."

What I needed was to tell Vladimir about my conversation with the queen. I wasn't sure this was something I could share with Katherine. Vladimir appeared to hold a lot of trust in Katherine, considering he confided in her about the letter, but I hardly knew her. I didn't trust her. Not yet.

Vladimir knew how the queen's mind worked. Surely he could discern what her conversation with me had meant, because everything from her words to her demeanor had felt like there was an underlying meaning to what she had told me. It was like she was trying to tell me something without saying it. Was it a threat?

"What if Vladimir doesn't reach Marco in time?" The worry wouldn't leave me.

Katherine pursed her lips together. "He will."

It seemed Katherine's way of dealing with things was to act like nothing could possibly go wrong, but I was starting to wonder if anything could possibly go right.

"Who am I supposed to train with while he's away?" I asked.

"He asked me to help with part of it."

I waited for her to continue, but she didn't. "And the other part?"

She hesitated, biting her lip. "You're not going to like it."

CHAPTER SIXTEEN

VLADIMIR

I COULD HAVE skinned myself alive for letting this happen. Gavil should've had protection when leaving the city. I had taken every precaution not to be followed: meeting in the middle of the night, sneaking out through the side gate, keeping our heads low through town, yet someone had still reached him. Judging by what he looked like, they'd had him for a while before disposing of the body.

I pounded my fist on my thigh in frustration. He shouldn't have even been allowed to leave the city. He knew too much. There were safe houses I could have placed him in. I ran a hand through my hair, trying to sort it out. He hadn't been dead for long when we found him, which meant that we should have time—but we didn't.

The second whoever had created that document found out

where it was, they would have gone after Marco. I'd asked for a dispatch report, but there was no record of anyone leaving. That meant the dispatch rider had either been removed from the records or was not in the army.

After Mordakai's unceremonious meeting with Taryn, I'd had one of my men trailing him, reporting on his whereabouts and affairs. So far, everything had appeared standard. Most of his time was consumed with training for the Kavari, the frequency of which had doubled after Taryn's stunt on the training fields. He'd attended dinners with high officials and advised on situations regarding the state. Every night he had returned to his room, but if he had access to the secret halls of Gharridan, he could slip out without us ever knowing.

If the queen had trusted Zedekiah with that secret, then he must have passed it along to his brother. Zedekiah also needed to be removed from his position. There was no denying he had a talent for strategy and a mind that could sniff out deception a mile away, but his loyalties were unclear. He'd threatened to kill Taryn in order to instate his brother as a Kavari. No, he'd said that he would take care of her, but I had no doubt in my mind that was what he intended. He was so incredibly difficult to read, and I wondered if maybe he was doing what he thought was right for Gharridan by instating his brother. But killing Taryn to do it? That was not like him, nor was it the Gharridan way.

The sun still warmed the sky. We had several hours of daylight left and pushed on at a heavy pace. Our group spread out, scouts surveying the farther edges of the path, but keeping step with us. There was no guarantee he would take the road. He could be anywhere between us and the next hundred miles.

I sat back in the saddle, Taryn on my mind again. There had been no time to tell her, and I worried about her reaction. I knew how much she wanted her mother's clasp and family name, but I didn't know if it was enough to keep her there while everything we'd planned for was slowly falling apart. She was just as stubborn as Michael. The lines on her face replicated his when they curved into a frown. The fire that had lit her eyes when I told her Mordakai was responsible for her father's death was the same that burned in Michael's, and there was also the hurt. She'd been masking it underneath indifference and anger, but as one who knew the craft, I could see it well. I didn't know what ill will she harbored toward her father, but I could see the bitterness slowly destroying her.

Her impulsive reactions were the most frustrating, making it difficult to keep our enemies from reaching her throat. She was unpredictable, a trait that would either save her life or get her killed.

Frustrating as they were, her antics were the least of my worries right now. This was no longer only about Michael's murder. Betrayal lurked deep within the court of Gharridan, and I would never have known until it was too late. Even Michael may not have known until the moment of his death—if he had even known then.

The list of people I trusted was diminishing by the second. Captain Verone and Katherine were the only two I trusted without hesitation. Queen Adamara was unreliable. By trying to protect her country, she was only further endangering it. I knew William could be trusted, but he was also loyal to his mother. Everyone else was a coin toss on who might be a possible traitor. Mordakai could've infiltrated anyone on the council.

Someone was trying to destroy Gharridan. I urged Dante faster, praying the document Marco carried would expose the perpetrator.

CHAPTER SEVENTEEN

Taryn

VLADIMIR WAS RIGHT.
　　I wasn't going to like it.
　　I hated it.

"So let me get this straight." His mocking voice started speaking again, and I clenched my fists. "You're vying to become a Kavari, yet you don't even know who started them."

I slowly closed my eyes, my blood boiling. "Obviously, it would have been a king of Gharridan."

"But—" He held up a finger, and I fought a grimace. "You don't know which one."

I looked down at the history book in front of me for the hundredth time. It was difficult to bite down every retort that came rushing to my lips as I avoided his arrogant eyes. I wasn't going to last until Vladimir came back. He'd already been gone for a week. If it was only the waiting that was torturous, I might have been able to bear it.

"It was my grandfather, actually." William sat on the desk next to mine with a haughty air. He scrutinized my face and tilted his head. "Is this too difficult for you?"

It was the fifth day I'd been forced to endure him. When we were training, at least I could throw my frustration into the force of my sword's blow or the strength behind the draw of a bowstring. In here, surrounded by shelves of books and William's smug expression, one could only internally pound their fist on the table so many times.

I knew William was enjoying this. He'd been enjoying it from day one. No matter what we were doing, he found some way to undermine my abilities and humiliate any attempts. My archery was never precise enough, my tracking never thorough enough, my sparring never calculated enough, and now my knowledge of Gharridan's history wasn't deep enough. There was always something to critique.

"I may not know every specific detail about Gharridan's history." I forced the words out with difficulty. "But I do know the basics of it."

William raised an eyebrow. "Which would be?"

I ground my teeth together, my eyes burning into him. I no longer cared if he could see the frustration in me.

"What do you want to hear? That Gharridan has thrived for hundreds of years among the countries surrounding it, or that it is one of the only countries whose sovereigns have stayed within a single family of nobility since its establishment?" I turned the pages in the book, looking at the endless pages of currently useless information. "I can't name off every single one of your predecessors, but I know King Roldan reigned for twenty-two years before he fell ill, leaving his wife, Queen Adamara, in charge for the last seven years. And—"

I looked up and saw that William's face had darkened. For a moment, I'd forgotten that King Roldan was his father, and from his expression, it must still be a painful topic. The last thing I needed was another reason for him to hate me. My eyes fell back to the book, and I surveyed the map laid out on the pages before me, lowering my eyebrows as I realized something was missing.

"Where's Dalendria?" I asked, puzzled.

"Are you referring to a place or a person?" There was an edge in William's voice.

"It's—" My eyes roamed over the places listed on the map, disappointment clouding over me when I couldn't find it. My mother had talked about it all the time.

William's eyebrows raised expectantly.

"Never mind." Perhaps it was too small a place to show on this map—or was simply a fable she had made up.

William clapped his hands together. "Well, Gallows, your knowledge is quite extensive, which means you'll only look part of a fool next to Mordakai instead of a complete fool. He won't even have to open his mouth to vie for the Kavari. Your ignorance will push him straight to the top."

I slammed the history book shut and jolted to my feet. "If I'm so worthless and headed for failure, then why are you still here? You obviously don't want me to have any part of the Kavari!"

William laughed, spreading his arms wide. "You think I want to be here? Do you *really* think the crown prince of Gharridan wants to spend his days training a hopeless Kavari candidate?" He stepped toward me. "The only reason I'm here, Gallows, is because I owed Vladimir a favor, and this is my way of paying it back."

"Well, it looks like Vladimir got the short end of the deal. If Katherine didn't have other duties to fulfill, he wouldn't even have asked you!"

William stood over me, a smug smile on his face. "Yes, he would have."

His words shocked me, causing my anger to abate.

I hadn't expected him to argue with that.

His smile widened. "You don't even know why, do you?"

I crossed my arms, unsure of where he was going with this, and not sure I wanted to hear it.

William chuckled. "Think about it, Gallows. The only supporters you have here in the capital are Vladimir and Katherine, and she only supports you because Vladimir told her to. It's blatantly obvious to the people and the entire council that the Crown favors Mordakai. My mother would be crazy not to. No official in their right mind would reject a trained, respectable well-known contender such as Mordakai over the daughter of a Kavari—a daughter no one knew existed. Let alone the fact that she has only mediocre training and hardly any knowledge of the government or country she hoped to protect. By having me work with you, out in public, it shows that at least part of the Crown holds some support for you as well."

I wished Katherine had taken the time to explain that to me, but if I'd simply thought for myself, I would've realized Vladimir's underlying purpose in this.

"If the Crown shows support, does that mean that your

mother supports me as well?"

"No." William cursed. "She's as furious as an angry hive of bees that I'm helping you, but she can't do anything about it."

I sat back on the desk. All along, I thought Vladimir had been trying to somehow punish me, but apparently there was a method to his madness.

"Are you saying you don't want Mordakai instated as a Kavari?"

William took the history book from my desk and placed it back on the shelf. "What I'm saying is I want the candidate who has more to bring to the table. But if you don't get this information down and learn it inside and out, you're not going to survive past the first course. This is a game to them, and you need to learn to play it well."

William hadn't said he was for me, but he also hadn't said he was against me. I wasn't sure why his opinion mattered to me, but all the unsatisfying results of my training with him seemed to have served a purpose—to make me better, stronger. I hadn't been giving my all, and I had done so purposefully. It had never been my intention to go through with the vie for the Kavari. Vladimir had promised I wouldn't have to go through with it. But our deception was working, and threats were coming at me from every direction.

Apparently, there were people to whom this did matter. And they were counting on me.

I walked over to the shelf and took another history book from its place, dropping it on the desk. William didn't need to know I had no intention of joining the Kavari. He just needed to think I was willing to fight for it.

"Again."

CHAPTER EIGHTEEN

Vladimir

MARCO WAS GONE.

As we thundered up the hillside, the cold wind searing my skin and the pounding of hooves drumming in my ears, hope was leaving me. When I saw the pattern on the ground, I knew. We were too late. A lone rider's tracks had marked the road. Deep crevices littered the muddy ground where half a dozen horses had emerged from the woods to surround the one. The point where the two sets of tracks met was trampled with hoofprints going in every direction. There had been a struggle. The ambusher's trail carried across to the other side of the road and disappeared into the trees.

"Spread out."

Our squadron expanded from a close unit into an outstretched cavalry line. The tracks were easy to follow, the muddy ground a witness to their crime, but it was beginning to dry. This had happened hours ago. The trees grew thicker, slowing our advance as we had to weave in and out of them. Brush grabbed at my trousers and tore at Dante's mane. My men remained quiet. No one called out. Nothing had been seen.

I gripped the reins tightly in one hand, the other resting on my sword. Whoever killed Gavil shouldn't have been able to find Marco this fast. Dread settled deep in my stomach. At this point, I was only expecting to find a body.

The sound of gentle waves floated through the trees, and my head snapped to the right. Beneath me, Dante charged through the forest, and we broke out onto the bank of a lake that expanded miles in either direction, its crystal blue waters sparkling in the sun.

The waves lapping the shore eroded a deep trench showcasing where a boat had pushed off. Dante's hooves dug into the sand as I pulled him up, my eyes frantically scanning the waters.

The lake lay as quiet as a frosty winter morning. The only sounds that carried across it were the tossing waves and chilly breeze. No boat was in sight. They were already gone. Even if we had a boat of our own, there was no way to know where they had docked on the other side. We wouldn't beat them riding around the lake. There was a reason they'd chosen to cross it. Going around the lake would take days. It was too much time—time that we didn't have. Based on the depth of the impression left in the sand, the boat hadn't been very large. A few hoofprints led back into the trees, indicating that only half of the group had crossed the river.

"Vladimir!"

The shout rang out across the lake, and my eyes shot up. Two soldiers farther down the bank burst from the trees, dragging a man between them. I urged Dante forward, and he sent clods of sand spraying around us as we galloped toward them.

Both spoke at once.

"He was spying in the trees—"

"He tried to run away."

I dismounted, my nose wrinkling at the man's dirty face, his ragged, muddy clothing bearing no identification. He met my eyes, a smug smile stretching across his teeth.

"Lord Vladimir." He spoke with a slight accent, his head dipping into a mock bow.

I crossed my arms, my unwavering gaze revealing nothing. Something was wrong. The man had addressed me by my name. He hadn't been trying to run away—he wanted to be caught. I stepped closer to him.

"Where did they take Marco?" I demanded.

His smile stretched wider. "What does it matter? He'll be dead before you reach him."

I slammed my fist into his stomach, and the man doubled over, sinking to his knees. My voice was venomous as I crouched before him, inches from his face.

"I'm going to ask again. Where did they take Marco?"

The prisoner spat, blood spraying from his mouth. "I don't know."

My eyes narrowed. "Why did you ambush him?"

"He had something they wanted."

"That who wanted?"

"I don't know."

My dagger was at his throat in seconds. "Who?"

The man groaned, straining away from the knife as his gaze bore into me. "All I know is we were hired to work for the man. I never met him. The only thing I was told about our mission was to capture the Kavari."

I stared at him, realizing we would get no information. The truth was in his eyes.

"He's a scurion." I spat.

The thing every military commander feared—a scurion. A soldier left in the dark to everything except specific information that a commander wanted him to know. It kept secrets hidden, and information from reaching the wrong ears.

The man dropped his eyes, looking across the lake. I cocked my head. Whoever killed Gavil had only been hours ahead of us. That was not enough time to hire a band of mercenaries.

"When were you hired?"

The scurion shrugged. "Weeks ago."

They'd planned to capture Marco before even knowing about the letter. He was never meant to return to the capital.

"He comes with us." I mounted, reining Dante around. "We're splitting up. Half of you go around the lake that way," I pointed. "We'll take the other half. Figure out where they ran aground and stay on their trail. Figure out where they're headed."

A maniacal laugh bellowed from the scurion, and I turned back to him.

"He wants the Kavari destroyed." The man coughed. "You're wasting your time with Marco. He's going after the imposter next."

"What imposter?"

The man licked his lips, angling his eyes away from me.

I leaned over Dante's shoulder, and the scurion flinched. "What imposter?"

"The daughter of Michael Gallows," he proclaimed dramatically. "Unless he's already gotten rid of her while you've been away."

His words felt like a punch to the stomach. The world around me seemed to slow; my heartbeat pounded in my ears as my vision blurred. Everything around me faded as the realization of what was going on began to settle in. Finding Gavil's body had been no coincidence. Whoever was behind this had wanted me to go after Marco, wanted me to leave the capital. Had wanted me to leave Taryn unprotected.

"Melvin, with me," I barked, ordering three men to follow with the scurion and the remaining soldiers to continue around the lake.

Dante's ears perked up when I turned him toward home, and with my nod to Melvin, the horses shot forward, racing back through the confines of the forest.

CHAPTER NINETEEN

Taryn

THE RED DOT blurred into distortion as I closed one eye and refocused my aim. The wind blew across my skin, and I measured its weight, calculating its effects on my arrow. A slight creak came from the wood as it arched, my grip firm as the string grew taut. I released the bowstring, feathers tickling my cheek as the arrow shot forward. It flew straight and true, landing with a distant *thud* as it smacked the target. It was a good shot, but I didn't smile. My head swiveled to Katherine for approval.

Her face was unreadable as she moved toward the target, examining the shot, her eyes calculating every tiny detail. Chewing on her lip, she turned back to me.

"Can you shoot that accurately on horseback?"

I knew my aim while mounted was not near what it should

be, but there had never been a necessity for it. Until now, the bow had only been a means for hunting.

I shrugged my shoulders. "Somewhat."

Katherine raised her eyebrows, taking my answer to mean not at all.

"Keep practicing."

She headed toward the stables, and as I nocked my next arrow, I watched the soldiers she passed either throw her a dirty look or ignore her. One muttered under his breath, spitting at her feet. I drew back on the bowstring, eyes focused on the target. It wasn't the first time I had seen this kind of behavior toward her, and it wasn't just from the soldiers. Whenever Katherine came to escort me from one of William's training sessions, he wouldn't even acknowledge her presence. Even some of the servants averted their eyes as she passed. The only person I'd ever seen show her any kind of respect besides Vladimir was Captain Verone.

Thud.

The arrow was straight on target, just as every shot before it had been. Something moved out of the corner of my eye, and I found Mordakai surveying my work. Our eyes briefly met before he turned away. We hadn't spoken since he'd threatened me, but I knew I could always find him lurking somewhere nearby.

I drew another arrow.

Vladimir had been gone for too long.

Thud.

Whether or not he had the letter, he should have been back by now. Both Katherine and William were worried. I could see it in their eyes, in the distant expressions, and the constant glances at the door as if waiting for someone to walk in. I'd asked Katherine if she thought something had happened to Vladimir, and she'd pasted a smile onto her face, assuring me that he was fine and would be back in no time.

I didn't believe a word of it.

The four weeks Queen Adamara had allotted us were almost up, and if he wasn't back soon, I wasn't sure the queen would let us go through with the choosing of the Kavari. I still didn't want to go through with it. Vladimir had said he would get me out of this, but my escape plans were running very thin.

This scheme had swept me so deeply into its deception that I had almost forgotten why I'd come here. It wasn't to be a Kavari, but to find my father's killer, learn my mother's family name, and get her clasp. I pulled the bowstring taut, then slacked off. Was that what I even wanted anymore? In light of everything Gharridan was facing, my own desires suddenly seemed trivial.

Katherine approached, leading both Stryder and her horse, Flicker. I slung the bow over my shoulder, noticing the harsh treatment the soldiers continued to offer her.

"Where do you want me to start?"

Katherine's eyes roamed the training fields, passing over Mordakai.

"Not here," she said in a low voice.

We mounted, and I followed as she and Flicker left the training fields and exited the castle grounds. I hadn't been outside the castle walls since our meeting with Gavil, and the change of scenery was refreshing. After leaving the city by a side gate, we rode toward the river, and as we crossed the bridge, I stared down at its raging waters.

"You should see it in the spring," Katherine said. "The Jidero River grows higher and twice as violent when the mountains shed their snow, but with the way the gorge narrows, it's dangerous year-round. Once you're caught in its frigid waters, it's nearly impossible to get out."

"Is this the only way across?" I asked.

"Within fifty miles. Any enemies would be hard-pressed to attack from the west."

We continued on, and although the air was crisp, I relished in the openness that the lower fields offered. I was used to being out in the open, not confined to the walls of a city or castle. I'd almost forgotten what this freedom felt like.

The sky in the north was dark. No doubt the snows that had begun in the mountains were steadily bringing winter closer to us. Stryder snorted beneath me, and I held him back as he pulled on the reins, wanting to take off as the land stretched before us, tempting him. Katherine pulled Flicker up, scanning the tree line.

"Do you see that mark in the wood there, on that center tree?" she asked.

I squinted, catching a patch on the bark of wood that was a slightly lighter shade than the rest of the tree. "Yes."

"Can you hit it from the top of the hill?"

I looked at the top of the hill, my heart dropping.

It was a long shot.

"Maybe."

Stryder cantered up the hill, and I dropped the reins, gently guiding him into a straight line with my legs. Ever so carefully, I nocked an arrow to the string. Stryder surged into a gallop, and my eye focused on the discolored wood that was now a fuzzy blur in the distance, calculating the pressure of the wind.

I released the arrow with a twang of the string, and it flew straight and true. Until it got closer to the tree, and I realized how off course it was. Picking up the reins, I guided Stryder over to where Katherine was examining my shot.

"Maybe I should have had you aim for the tree line." Katherine's voice was amused. "I'm glad we came out here. Mordakai doesn't need to see this."

Inwardly, I groaned. Katherine had uncovered a weak spot, and we wouldn't be finished here until it was made stronger.

"Let's go again."

By the time I'd provided her with several satisfactory shots, the sun had already begun its descent. Bright streaks of pink, orange, and yellow stretched across the sky, illuminating the world in vibrant colors.

"We need to get back to the city before sundown," Katherine called.

My arms were aching, and I grimaced as I recalled the humiliating tumble I had taken off Stryder after losing my balance when he unexpectedly swerved. The thought of falling into my overly soft bed in the castle was enticing.

I was more than happy to oblige and let my arms rest at my side as we hurried back across the countryside. Katherine was silent, and I couldn't help but ask what I'd been wondering.

"Why are others so disrespectful toward you?"

Katherine arched an eyebrow, seeming surprised. "You mean, why does everyone look down on me like a lesser human being?"

I hesitated, then nodded.

"You know the purpose of the Kavari is to protect Gharridan from enemies both without and within."

Of course. I nodded again.

"Each member of the Kavari is given an individual job unique to the talents they already possess. Marco is a peacekeeper and manager of the different territories within Gharridan. Vladimir oversees Gharridan's military, and Michael was skilled in diplomacy and kept our foreign relations stable, but also oversaw the jobs of the other Kavari. I was entrusted with being a servant to the people of Gharridan, specifically in the area of healing."

Healing? Most towns had their own healer. I'd only been to ours once, but the job seemed very mundane for a Kavari.

"I heal people who possess ailments both physically and mentally."

I looked sidelong at her, thinking I'd missed something. "You're saying you're skilled with herbs?"

Katherine quickly shook her head. "When I say healer, I'm not referring to a traditional healer. I, myself, heal people."

I waited for the grin, the laugh, an indication that it was some sort of joke, but Katherine's face held no hint of deception.

"Like magic?"

Katherine tilted her head. "In a way, I guess, but it's not magic, it—it's something else. Something in my blood that I was born with. When someone is wounded, and I touch them, it's like I can feel the infection, and I draw it out."

I stared at her, not sure I'd heard correctly. The power to heal? I'd never heard of this. It wasn't possible.

She looked at me curiously. "Have you never heard of a Radonaya?"

My blank expression answered her.

"There are not many of us," she explained. "Usually, our hair gives us away. I'm sure you've noticed that my hair is not, shall we say, natural?"

It was true that her hair was the first thing I had noticed about her, but I had nothing to compare it to as I'd never seen anything like it in my life. Its blood-red hue would draw the attention of anyone.

"All Radonaya are born with the gift of healing and the unusual hair. People look at us differently. We're either accepted as a sign of life or rejected as a symbol of death."

"Why would it be a symbol of death?"

Katherine looked at me seriously. "Our gift brings great joy to those it heals, but to those who cannot be healed, our gift becomes a curse. The red color of our hair symbolizes the blood of the people that we could not save."

"If you have the ability to heal, why would anyone treat you with disdain?"

Katherine fell silent. Her tense body sat rigid on Flicker, hands clenching the reins in her fist. "Because," she finally managed, "there was someone I was unable to save, and they never forgave me for it."

Flicker picked up his pace, ending our conversation, but my mind was still reeling with her revelation. If Katherine truly had the ability to heal people, that made her more valuable than almost anyone else in the kingdom. Her attitude indicated that she seemed to disdain her gift, and I wondered who it was she had been unable to save. Why had no one told me about any of this before? The hatred others held toward her didn't make sense. She hadn't been able to save one person, but how many others had she saved?

Stryder's ears pricked forward as the rush of the river grew louder. The sun hadn't quite set, illuminating the world enough to get us back before dark. Stryder suddenly sidestepped, his nostrils flaring in and out.

"It's just the river, boy." I patted his neck and urged him onto the bridge, the clatter of the horses' hooves bouncing off the woods around us. Above us, a branch creaked loudly, and I looked up.

A mass of weight crashed into my back and pulled me from the saddle. Stryder bolted, and I slammed into the wooden bridge, the force of the fall snatching my breath away. Someone was on top of me. The glint of a knife flashed in my vision. It was a tangle of bodies and limbs as I tried to free myself from the perpetrator, the edge of the bridge looming closer. I bit the man's hand, and his roar of anger filled my ears as I watched the knife clatter onto the wood. We both lunged for it, my attacker reaching it first as he rolled over me and toppled over the edge with my arm still firmly clamped in his grasp.

The moment I hit the icy water in the raging river, the current ripped us apart and hurtled me away from the bridge. The weight of the water surrounded me, pushing me beneath it. I fought to get my head above the surface, my limbs growing heavy in the water, and the dead weight of my dress dragging me down. My head broke through the water's churning top, and air rushed into my lungs like a powerful wind. I struggled, looking for the shore, but was met by a hand that shoved my head back underneath the water.

I choked, inhaling liquid as the fist intertwined its fingers in my hair, holding me prisoner beneath the water. I kicked out, but my movements were in slow motion, and I couldn't get enough momentum to do any damage. My elbow met something solid, and his grip loosened, allowing my head to surge up again. I coughed up water, desperately trying to get air into my lungs. Everything was a blur; the river moved too quickly to focus on anything.

The hand found my head once more, and there was no time to cry out before I was underwater again. Panic set in, and I thrashed about underneath the water, my sluggish motions hoping to find a way of escape.

I had to get away.

He was going to kill me.

I scrunched my knees up to my chest, my feet finding the man's body, kicking out at him as hard as I could. His hold on my neck released, and I broke free of the water, gasping for air. Out of the whirling confusion, I saw him propelling toward me, but we were also rapidly approaching a rock. His hand reached out for me. I shoved against the waves, the break in the current separating us. When I looked to see if he was gone, all I got was a brief glimpse of him emerging on the shore. I flailed my arms about, trying to swim to land, but I no longer had control over my body. I was to the water as a feather was to the wind. Wherever it bid me go, I had no choice but to obey.

The river grew more violent as the number of boulders I had to dodge increased. There was nothing I could feel except the swiftness of the river. My entire body went numb, my limbs immovable. An undercurrent sucked me beneath the surface again and held me prisoner longer than it ever had before. I kicked, struck, flailed. I did whatever I could to get away, but the river was my authority. It bent me to its will.

When I finally rose to the surface, my shoulder crashed against a rock, and I cried out, slipping underneath over and over as I bobbed in the water. The shore was just a distant thought now, and the reality of my predicament set in as I struggled to keep my head above the water. There was nothing, *nothing* sweet about this death. It was bitter as wormwood and poisonous as a serpent. The current yanked me below its waves, forcing me farther and farther into the water's depths. No light shone here; no hope resided in the river. There was only twisting, swirling darkness.

Down.

Down.

Down.

Down to a watery grave.

CHAPTER TWENTY

Vladimir

NO ONE WOULD dare strike within the capital, but even as I assured myself, doubt continued to fill me. No one *should* dare strike within, but nor should anyone kill the leader of the Kavari within his own borders. Or kidnap another Kavari.

Unless he's already gotten rid of her while you've been away.

The scurion's words plagued my mind. It was troubling that Mordakai's influence had reached so far without raising the suspicion of anyone else in the capital. Stealth was not usually one of his skills. Mordakai was not one to stop and think through a situation, but rather blunder through it blindly.

Exhaustion weighed heavily on both Melvin and me, the long days in the saddle taking their toll, but we were almost there. We'd pushed ourselves even harder today, and it was already well past dark. I wasn't willing to spend another night out here, completely unaware of what was going on in the capital.

Lights bobbed in the distance along the river's edge.

"What is that?" Melvin asked.

"I don't know."

Dread filled my stomach.

With a kick of my heels, Dante surged forward into the night, galloping across the moonlit barren. My heart hammered within my chest, every nerve in my body warning me that something was horribly wrong.

Don't let it be Taryn.

The lights grew larger as we approached until I recognized them as torchlight. Several shadowy outlines shifted into the forms of horses, and I pulled Dante up, skidding to a halt.

"What's going on?" I demanded.

A grey speckled ghost moved in the night: William's horse, Othello.

"Vladimir?" The strain in William's voice was evident, his expression grave. Silence hung between us in the dark night. Whatever it was, he didn't want to tell me.

"What is it?"

William shifted uncomfortably in his saddle and avoided my gaze, looking toward the river.

I wheeled my horse around.

"William."

He brought his eyes to meet mine, fear emanating from them in the dim light.

"She's gone."

His words ripped through me like a knife to the chest, the scurion's warning ringing in my ears. My tongue suddenly felt heavy, my question struggling to get out.

"What do you mean she's gone?"

"I mean she's gone, Vladimir. Katherine and Taryn were attacked crossing the north bridge. Katherine got away, but Taryn was dragged into the water."

I could feel my heartbeat quickening within my chest as the blood drained from my face, tension growing tight inside me.

"We've been looking since sundown." William glanced away again. "We haven't found the body yet."

The body.

As if there was no hope of life to find.

Dante trotted forward, and I took a torch from one of the guards. "Is this where you've left off?"

"Vladimir—"

My harsh expression cut William off. I knew what he was going to say, and I didn't want to hear it. I wouldn't give up until we found something.

William pointed to the south. "Katherine is still on the other side searching the riverbank. She hasn't found anything either." William hesitated. "We've gone miles. It's been too long, Vladimir. There's no way she—"

"Keep searching until she's found."

Dante and I left them behind and cantered up to the bank. Even in the darkness, the river tore its way through the forest. Its deceitful waters were always on the prowl and ever watchful, never sleeping. They flowed mysteriously, waiting to strangle their next victim.

I should have asked how long she'd been in the water, but I didn't want to know. The temperature of the river was not yet as frigid as it would be in the winter, but it was still cold. She would've had to make it to shore quickly.

I lifted my torch, watching both the bank and waters carefully for any sign of her or her tracks, but the only disturbed sand on the shore was from the hoofprints we were currently making. The air was cold. Even if she had made it out, her clothes would have been drenched, and in the cold night air—

My eyes spotted an indent up ahead, and hope rose within me. I leaned low in the saddle to examine it. They were deer tracks. I sat up, catching William's questioning eyes, and shook my head.

The night lengthened, and we continued on, torches roaming over the bank, my arm nearly numb from holding one for so long. There was no sign. There was nothing. I pulled up Dante, staring ahead into the darkness. The river ran ahead of me, its gurgling a laugh of victory that taunted me. There would be no aftermath to deal with. Michael would rise from the grave and kill me himself for allowing this to happen.

I should never have brought her here, never put her through this. Everything that had happened to her since she'd arrived in the capital was my fault, and now her blood was on my hands.

My shoulders shook with both cold and fear as we traveled up the bank, my tired eyes blearily looking for any sign of hope in the night, but there was nothing.

The river did not deny it.

The elements ensured it.

Taryn was gone.

CHAPTER TWENTY-ONE

TARYN

COLD.

THE SENSATION enveloped my body until no warmth existed in my world. I was left with only a hollow, frozen shell encasing my soul. I wondered if this was death—an endless eternity of cold and pain. Even as I became more aware, I still had no connection with my body. That is, if I was still even in my body. Perhaps my soul had shed itself of my frail human skin.

I reached out with my mind, but there was no one to greet me, no one to pull me back to the warmth of life. I hovered on empty air, completely and utterly alone. No light shone here to brighten the darkness, and my fingers felt without feeling. My feet ran without moving. Surrounding me was simply nothing.

I tried to remember who I was, what I was doing, and

where I had been, but I couldn't. I knew the memories were there, tucked away somewhere, surrounded by a fog that dulled them and slowly ate away at my mind. The sensation of falling overcame me, and I struggled to hold on to the nothing surrounding me, but I found it was easier to simply succumb to the darkness.

CHAPTER TWENTY-TWO

TARYN

I DIDN'T REMEMBER how to open my eyes. Eventually, the cold dissipated, but only because it was overpowered by pain. The pain was everywhere, coursing through my veins, pulsing through my head, emanating from my limbs. I fought to scream and cry out, beg for it to stop, but I couldn't find my voice. It was no longer under my command. Something wrapped tightly around me, and I heard strange noises surrounding me. I struggled to sort through them, slowly making sense of what I figured out were voices.

"I don't know if it will work. I've never tried this before."

"She's going to kill her."

Please, don't kill me, I wanted to say, prepared to beg for my life. I felt myself shaking.

"I will not sit here and do nothing. From what you both are

saying, she's going to die either way. We're going to try."

Try what? Another emotion dispersed through me.

Fear.

I felt myself slipping away as the voices grew muddled again, whatever they'd been saying no longer of any importance to me. Even though the cold had subsided, my life still felt like a flickering candle that could dissolve into smoke at any moment. An uncomfortable pressure landed on my side, and I tried to squirm away from it, but my mind was still not in control of my body.

Warmth emanated from the pressure, flooding throughout my body—then it suddenly turned into a blazing fire. I don't know whether I cried out, but every fiber of my being screamed as the inferno ripped through the organs in my body. Anything was better than this, even being alone in the darkness.

I saw the faces of my father and mother watching from beyond a veil. Their expressions were unclear, but I could tell they were waiting for me. The fire burning inside of me took me back to my childhood, where I was lying in bed, burning with fever. I wasn't even five years old. My mother nursed me, tried to cure me, but the fever continued to have its way. I remembered seeing a red flower, its precious petals crushed to dust.

The heat intensified, and I yelled out, light streaming through each particle of my body. There was no escaping. There was only the feeling of the flames devouring me. The cold and the pain were nothing compared to this, and I realized that this, this must be death.

CHAPTER TWENTY-THREE

Taryn

HARSH SUNLIGHT STREAMED across my eyelids, lifting me away from the encompassing darkness. My eyes fluttered open, squinting as the bright light penetrated them. Once they adjusted to the light, fear gripped me. I possessed no memory of the rough wooden walls surrounding me or the bed on which I was lying. The air smelled damp and clung to me. All I remembered was the stinging cold numbing my body and the torture of the fire burning within me. I shuddered at the memory even though the sensations were gone, and wondered if I would ever forget the feeling.

I swallowed, realizing my mouth was parched, and rolled over, desperate for a drink. Someone was sleeping against the wall, and I cocked my head. Her face stirred memories deep inside me, pushing them back to the surface until they came rushing up all at once.

Water.

Water was everywhere.

It pulled at me, choked me, stole the air from my lungs. But the water wasn't my only enemy. Someone else had been there with me, dragging me into its depths.

Someone had tried to kill me.

I sat up abruptly, the blankets falling around me like a curtain. I realized I was only wearing a shift and ripped the blankets back up, wrapping them tightly around me. The movement woke the woman beside me, and she stood with a start.

"You're awake!"

Katherine crawled into the chair beside the bed, her eyes filling with relief. A dark bruise covered her left brow, and an abrasion stretched across her forehead.

"Are you okay?" I asked.

Her brows lowered in confusion, but the movement must have triggered pain because she touched her fingers to the bruise, a befuddled expression consuming her face. "It's fine, but I'm not the one you should be worried about."

I tried to shift positions, which was when I realized that I ached all over. It felt like I'd been trampled by a horse. My muscles were tense, my body sore, and I grimaced as I stiffly maneuvered into a sitting position.

"How long have I been asleep?"

Katherine wearily leaned back in the chair. "Two days."

Two days? I rubbed my forehead, a headache beginning to set in. While some of the memories were slowly reforming, many were still muddled together.

"Where are we?" I asked, glancing around the room. It wasn't the castle. I knew that much just by looking at the walls, but a tree was the only thing I could see outside the tall window. I didn't understand how I had made it here—how I had made it out of the river.

"An old cabin," Katherine said. "It's just a few miles outside the capital."

The door opened, and Vladimir strode in. Dark circles hung below his eyes, and his shoulders stooped with exhaustion. At the sight of him, Marco and the letter rushed to my mind, flooding me with relief. Vladimir had made it back safely, and his presence meant that he must have the letter.

"You're alive," he said, looking like a tremendous weight had been lifted from his shoulders.

"What do you remember?" Katherine asked.

I sat there for a moment, trying to gather my thoughts. "I remember being attacked, and—and the river. After that, I remember cold, and then a heat that burned me. It doesn't make sense."

They both remained silent, glancing at one another.

"What happened?" I asked.

"We were both attacked." Anxiety hovered in Katherine's voice. "It was an ambush. They were hiding in the trees. I managed to get away, but by the time I did, there was no sign of you. We looked for hours, Taryn; we didn't—we thought—"

"We thought you were dead, Gallows." William sauntered into the room with a cheeky smile and a disheveled head of hair. He crossed his arms, leaning against the back wall. "But here you are."

I thought I'd been dead too.

"What was that heat?" I asked. The memory was shrouded by the pain protruding from it. "It felt like I was on fire."

All their expressions were so vastly different that I didn't know where to look first. William's face clouded over, Katherine went white, and Vladimir looked nervous. They stood there, avoiding eye contact and unwilling to speak.

"What is it?" I asked.

Vladimir spoke first. "Katherine healed you, Taryn."

The Radonaya.

"I'm sorry if it hurt." Katherine stepped forward. "I've never tried to heal something like that before. You were so cold and covered in bruises. There was a gash on your head."

I lifted my fingers to my forehead only to find smooth skin.

"It's gone now," Katherine continued. "I didn't know if I could take the cold from you, but it looks like I did."

The burning had almost been worse than death. If that was what the healing was like, I didn't want to ever feel it again.

"Who attacked us?" I asked.

Vladimir's face grew serious. "I'll give you one guess."

No doubt it was Mordakai, or rather someone hired by Mordakai. He wouldn't be foolish enough to do it himself. Attacking us like that in the daylight had been quite bold of him. I hadn't gotten a good look at my attacker, but the brief glimpses I had didn't trigger any familiarity.

My gaze shot to Vladimir. "Did you find—did you get to Marco?"

His jaw set hard, the expression he wore answering my question.

"We didn't get to Marco in time. Someone else took him.

Took everything."

I fell back against the pillow.

Took everything.

The piece of evidence we'd been hoping to secure all along was out of our reach. Marco was gone. Nothing was left for us to stand on. Nothing was left to keep me from the Kavari.

"What do we do now?" I heard the hint of desperation in my voice as the words came out.

That document had been our only chance. I stared at Vladimir, trying to convey that I wanted to know how he planned to get me out of this situation. Whoever had tried to assassinate me wouldn't stop until they'd succeeded.

Vladimir crossed his arms, shifting as he looked at each of us.

"As of right now, everyone thinks you're dead except for the three of us. The rest of the search party was sent back to the capital. Queen Adamara plans to name Mordakai as a Kavari in two days' time. Without a contender, there is no reason for him to believe that he needs to vie for it. There is also no opponent for him to try and dispose of if that opponent doesn't exist. He thinks he's won, and we need to keep it that way. I propose that you stay here until the ceremony, and at that time, we will bring you before the council to challenge Mordakai's claim to the Kavari."

He didn't have a way out of this for me.

"What if she tries to instate him before then?" Katherine asked.

"He can't be named until both Vladimir and I are present," William put in. "If we're still out looking for your body, my mother will have to wait."

Vladimir knew this was not what I had agreed to. He stood there, watching me and waiting for my reaction.

I could leave right now. There was no need for Mordakai to chase after a dead person. Both the setting and timing were perfect. I glanced at the pocket where Vladimir always kept my mother's clasp hidden, but this was no longer just about getting my mother's clasp. My father's murderer was walking free, preparing to take his place. No justice had been served, and now he had tried to kill me. I fidgeted beneath the blankets, warring with myself.

"Well," I began, my mind made up. "Let's hope your teaching was thorough enough to convince the council and sway them in my favor."

Ever so slightly, Vladimir dipped his head in thanks, relief flashing across his tense expression. I had never given him any reason to believe that I would go through with the choosing ceremony.

"Gather as much strength as you can, and if you are able, we will train what little more we can before the ceremony."

"If I can move by then," I muttered.

I wasn't sure exactly what could be crammed into two more days of training that we hadn't already accomplished, but William and Vladimir left, leaving Katherine and me alone in silence.

"Thank you," I said to Katherine.

She lifted an eyebrow in confusion.

"For saving me," I explained. "It sounds like I wouldn't have made it had you not intervened."

She dipped her head in acceptance, her eyes sincere. "I know that this isn't what you wanted. Thank you. For Michael's sake."

Unsure of how to respond, I simply nodded. I could understand their desire for justice, but I still couldn't wrap my head around Vladimir and Katherine's absolute devotion to my father. He had been their leader, but their connection to him seemed so much more than that.

Katherine left to let me rest, and I looked through the sunlight to the dense woods outside my window. The temptation to run away pulled stronger than ever, but I kept myself rooted. Mordakai had warned me to leave Gharridan while I was still free to do so. It appeared that offer had now expired, and I wanted to see this through. Needed to.

It was time my father's murderer be brought to justice.

CHAPTER TWENTY-FOUR

Taryn

A KNOCK CAME at the door, and Katherine entered, holding a parcel.

"I picked it up for you this morning."

Her mind seemed somewhere else as she handed me the package. I turned it over in my hands, unable to discern its contents. I peeled the paper away and saw cloth folded carefully inside. Gently, I pulled it out, revealing an olive-green dress with brown ties and a white shift. I shot Katherine a questioning look.

"It's for the ceremony."

The dress was not ornate, appearing to be built more for durability, but it was finer than any dress I had ever owned. I pulled on the fabric and found it to be flexible, unlike most stiff tunics.

"It makes it much easier to draw a bow," Katherine explained.

"Thank you." I was surprised at the unexpected gift.

"If you're going to sway the council, it's best to look presentable."

I blinked once, hiding my reaction as I realized the garment had not been merely a thoughtful gesture. I didn't need to look down at my dress to know that it was faded, worn, and about the furthest thing from presentable. Most of the stains were permanent. The hem was frayed, and the cloth behind my elbows and under my arms had grown alarmingly thin. The river had not been kind to the aging cloth either. Fresh tears and rips permeated the fabric, making it look worse than it ever had.

Out of the corner of my eye, I glanced at Katherine's dress, which bore signs of use but was still in far better shape than mine. Mother and I had always worn our clothes until they were nearly rags. Held to my previous standards, my dress still had quite a way to go before it was time to retire it.

Katherine left while I quickly changed. Vladimir had brought me my father's sword yesterday, and I belted it to my waist. The extra weight it added was heavier than expected, and I took a few steps, testing it out.

Katherine stepped back in to examine me, checking to make sure everything was in place as I nervously twisted my fingers. I was ready for this to finally be finished. The past few days of training hadn't accomplished much, and I doubted how successful this was going to be.

"Are you ready?" Katherine asked.

I swallowed, placing a hand on the hilt of my sword, and nodded. Vladimir and William were waiting outside with the horses. I didn't meet their expressions, afraid of the disappointment I might find. I marched directly up to Stryder, put a foot in the stirrup, and swung up into the saddle, grimacing as the movement pained my sore muscles. The others followed suit, and Vladimir took the lead as he began to head back to the capital.

My stomach twisted, my mind running over every piece of information I could think of pertaining to the country of Gharridan. Sweat made my hands slick as I tightly gripped the reins, allowing fear to overpower me. I had no idea what I was walking into. I couldn't do this. If I became a Kavari, there was no backing out—I was tied to this position for life.

"Are you sure you don't know what to expect?" I asked Vladimir.

His mouth set in a hard line, face strained.

"The council is free to ask you whatever questions they choose, or to have you complete whatever task they assign."

I swallowed.

"Everything will be fine, Taryn."

Vladimir's words of assurance were meaningless. He couldn't promise that. He hadn't even been able to keep his promise that I wouldn't have to vie for the Kavari. Ideas bounced around my head, but not one of them included me walking away from this predicament. I felt like a prisoner about to be sold as an indentured servant.

The massive city gates spread wide before us, and we passed through without difficulty. The streets of the capital were quiet with only a few scattered people wandering about their daily errands, but as they recognized us, they stopped to stare, quickly bowing before William. Whispers spread through the town of our presence, and others began to line the street, creating a parade of people for us to ride through.

All I could see was the castle looming above the city, its grand towers reminding me just how minuscule I was in this vast world. As the castle gates loomed closer, sweat slid down my back and from my brow. The guards' stares fixed on me. I was a ghost to them. The girl who had died had now returned.

I dismounted, surrendering Stryder's reins to a stable boy.

"William and I will go in first," Vladimir leaned over and whispered in my ear. "You and Katherine will wait a few minutes before following in after us."

I watched as they disappeared into the castle walls, my throat tightening as fear crept up my spine. Katherine and I held back, counting the seconds ticking by before finally following. The castle corridors seemed longer than before, and my feet grew heavier as my heart pounded within my chest.

"You cannot show fear, Taryn." Katherine kept her gaze fixed straight ahead. "Men can sniff it out like dogs."

I straightened my shoulders. I had agreed to do this, and I would do this. Our footsteps echoed off the stone walls, and we turned the last corner, the throne room's ornate doors growing higher before us. I would go in there with confidence, but I resolved to find a way out of this. My jaw clenched. Time was running out. I could sway the council, but I wasn't sure I wanted to.

My eyes roamed over the elaborate doors as they swung open, and Katherine and I stepped inside. Granite columns twisted into the tall ceiling, lining the pathway to the throne along the checkered floor with tapestries displaying the flag of Gharridan decorating the walls between the columns. Immediately, my eyes were drawn to the throne at the far end of the room. Its high back was carved into the shape of a rearing horse, with intricate detail engraved into the flowing mane and tail.

The queen leaned forward on her throne, watching me. Two soldiers flanked her, and Zedekiah lingered in the shadows to her left while Prince William stood calmly on her right. The council members lined the walls near the throne. Vladimir stood a little lower on the dais, and below him, standing before the council and the queen was Mordakai. He had turned at our entrance, a slight smile touching the corner of his mouth.

My breath grew shallow as everyone's gaze roved over me, their expressions varying from shock to confusion to anger. I looked beyond them to the enormous tapestry that hung behind the throne. Our country's history was sewn into the fabric, weaving together the glorious history of our land to create a masterpiece.

I stopped directly in front of the queen, standing slightly ahead of Mordakai. My head dipped forward as I bent into a curtsy, showing the Crown the proper respect. My eyes came up to meet the queen as I rose and tried to read her perplexed countenance.

"Your Majesty," I began.

"What is this?" the queen demanded. She perused the onlookers with an accusatory glare. "Was I not told that this girl was dead?"

I lifted my chin. "I can assure you that I am very much alive."

"Since you are so *very much alive*," Zedekiah growled, "why have you come before us today?"

I lifted my hand, exposing my father's ring. "I come with the right of a Blood Vier—to claim the Kavari, as the daughter of Michael Gallows."

I hadn't been ready before, but I was ready now. I turned to Mordakai, waiting for his reaction, but his expression only grew more arrogant. The council shifted uncomfortably, and the queen looked down, her face expressionless. My questioning gaze found Vladimir's, but he seemed just as perplexed by the council's response as I did.

Mordakai's cold, dark eyes leered down at me like a hunter who had already cornered their prey. "It's too late for that now."

Everyone in the room seemed to be privy to a crucial piece of information we were missing.

"Did you not state that the choosing of the Kavari would be held in four weeks' time?"

"I did," the queen replied. "Which is why Mordakai was elected by the council this past hour."

Had a feather drifted to the ground, I would have heard it hit the elaborate floor. They could not have held the choosing ceremony without us. Mordakai lifted his head in superiority, and my eyes fell to his hand, resting on the hilt of his sword. The sunlight illuminating the room shone off a freshly molded ring engraved with the mark of the Kavari.

"Your Majesty." Vladimir turned. "It goes against the law of Gharridan to engage in a choosing ceremony without the leader of the Kavari present."

William stepped forward. "He speaks the truth."

The queen's gaze shot from annoyance at William's intrusion to Vladimir. "I find it rather difficult to accomplish anything in this country when the leader of the Kavari is always running off and never in place to fulfill his duties to Gharridan. Taryn was missing, Vladimir, and you were nowhere to be found. You could've been dead, and I wouldn't even have known! In these dangerous times, I need you to inform me about your plans and whereabouts. There was no communication of when you would return, and I was inclined to keep my promise on the date of the choosing ceremony."

"Would you have me endanger more lives by wasting time to return to the capital so I could keep you informed of my intentions?" Vladimir asked. "These precarious times should *give me* the excuse to act quickly and efficiently unless you find yourself mentally incapable of making any decision on your own."

A small gasp echoed off the walls as the throne room sat in stunned silence. I held my breath, shocked at Vladimir's insult. The queen froze and then leaned forward with fire in her eyes.

"What would you have me to do, then? You speak as if I should make every decision, yet anytime I make one without you, it's unacceptable! This choosing ceremony, for example. I made a decision and held to my word on when it would be, yet you are still unsatisfied."

Vladimir's face darkened. "It's unacceptable if it's against the law! This whole ceremony is going against Gharridan law!"

"Then what should I have done, Vladimir?" Queen Adamara asked. "You obviously deem yourself to be higher in wisdom."

Their dispute grew more heated as they shot back and forth at one another, insults and accusations flying from their lips. The room swelled with tension, the nervous council members murmuring as they shifted uneasily in their seats. Arguments broke out as various council members threw support for the Crown and others held their support for the Kavari. The remainder stayed frozen in their chairs, observing the chaos as it broke out and surged among them.

My throat constricted. If there was nothing to vie for, there was no longer any use for me, and we no longer had any time to prove Mordakai's treacherous acts.

Zedekiah signaled something to the guards stationed at the doors as the unrest escalated, and within minutes soldiers began to march in and line the walls. I placed a hand on my sword, unsure of what was going on. The council members who had stayed neutral nervously glanced at one another, but those engaged in arguments hadn't seemed to notice the soldiers' presence.

Behind me, Katherine's face had turned livid. Through it all, the queen remained rigid in her chair, refusing to listen to reason. William's frustration with his mother amplified as she dismissed Vladimir calling her out on her breach of protocol but heeded every word that Zedekiah whispered in her ear. Soldiers tightened the grip on their swords, tensions continuing to mount as the noise in the throne room rose to a crescendo.

"Someone tried to kill me." My voice was loud, but not loud enough, and I nearly screamed the words the second time. "Someone tried to kill me!"

The room fell silent, my voice echoing off the stones.

"Did you not wonder why you were told I was dead?"

I had their attention now, and I swallowed, unsure of how to proceed. "Three days ago, Katherine and I were crossing the Jidero River when we were attacked. Katherine managed to escape her attacker, but I was pulled into the river where I nearly drowned. Hours later, after I lay completely drenched on the bank in the frigid air, Vladimir somehow found me. The reason I did not immediately return to the castle was because it was not safe for me to do so."

The queen's fingers drummed on the arm of her intimidating throne. Her fierce eyes carefully surveyed me as I spoke, and then flicked to something beyond me. "You said Katherine was attacked as well. How do you know this?"

I blinked.

That was not the question I had been expecting. "She told me."

"There are no other witnesses?" The queen's mouth curled into a calculating smile. "My dear, how can you be sure that Katherine was not a part of the attack herself?"

Her words left me speechless, and although they made sense, they were at the same time preposterous. "Your Majesty—"

"You were pulled into the river, Miss Gallows. Do you not find it strange that Katherine did not experience the same fate as you?"

The council members were muttering among themselves again, casting suspicious glances to where Katherine stood behind me. I turned to look at her. Her expression was passive and unreadable, albeit paler. Vladimir's jaw tensed, his eyebrows drawn in controlled anger as he digested the unfolding events.

"When you say that someone in this room wants you dead," the queen said, "I suggest you watch your back carefully."

The council members were growing louder, some standing

to their feet. I couldn't believe they hated Katherine so much that they would be so quick to condemn her. My gaze flicked to Mordakai, but to my surprise, no triumph hung in his eyes.

"If Katherine wanted me dead, then why did she heal me?" My voice filled the hall, hushing the council members to silence. "When Vladimir pulled me out of that river, Katherine used her gift to heal me, and it is the only reason I am able to stand before you today."

My statement did not convince the queen, but she accepted it. "Her gift has always appeared more like a curse. This matter will be looked into, but I'm afraid what's done is done."

My lips parted. What's done is done? There had been an attempted murder, and the queen was quite eager to look the other way. She had the Kavari she wanted. Nothing else was going to bother her.

Mordakai stepped forward with an inquisitive air, head tilting. "If I may, Your Majesty, I believe this warrants more investigation than it is being granted."

I shifted on my feet. What was he doing? My eyes caught Vladimir's, but he was just as perplexed as I was. Mordakai wouldn't be stepping in for us unless he had an ulterior motive.

"You have your position, Mordakai. What is it to you?"

I bristled at her words, questioning for the first time the queen's ability to rule. Dealing with conflict was not her forte. She would rather wait for an issue to disappear all on its own. I'd hardly been around her, yet with each small interaction, her weaknesses were becoming more and more pronounced.

"With all due respect, Your Majesty," Mordakai continued, "I don't feel I can rightfully assume my role as a Kavari under such circumstances. My whereabouts can be vouched for on the day of her attack, but I find it glaringly obvious that the attack was intended to prevent her from vying for the Kavari today."

Shock ruled the majority of the reactions throughout the room as they witnessed Mordakai remove the ring from his finger and place it on the armrest of the queen's throne. Queen Adamara stared at it as if unable to believe what she was seeing, slowly drawing her gaze up to meet Mordakai's.

"You show great character in your willingness to put justice before your own desires." Respect and pride emanated from her words. The queen turned to the council. "Is that not the making of a true Kavari?"

From the look that shadowed his face, this response had not been part of Mordakai's plan, but the queen was twisting it to her own agenda. His actions, unintentional or not, were solidifying his favor with the council. I wouldn't have a dying chance if I vied for the Kavari now.

Mordakai walked down the steps to stand in front of me, his eyes focused intently on mine, as if he was trying to tell me something.

"I suggest another Kavari not be chosen until a thorough investigation has been completed. I find it suspicious that Michael Gallows was murdered, and now there has been an attempt on his daughter's life. It is not right that we proceed with these actions unanswered. The perpetrator should be found, tried, and punished."

Zedekiah leaned over to whisper in the queen's ear briefly, and she shifted on the throne. "It makes me very uncomfortable to leave our country incomplete. I do not like to appear weak to our enemies."

Mordakai turned to the queen. "Your Majesty, it appears

that the enemies are not without, but within our borders. It would be wise to seek them out before they integrate further and weaken our country more than they already have."

The deliberation in the queen's face was evident as she prepared to make her decision. It made no sense for Mordakai to be saying these things. He was practically condemning himself. Her uncertainty shifted between Mordakai and me, calculating.

"Mordakai speaks wisely," the queen finally said. "The choosing ceremony will be postponed until we have found the attacker and any accomplices."

I couldn't believe she had agreed to it, yet the more the queen thought about it, the more firm she became in her decision. Zedekiah scowled behind her, glaring at his brother.

Mordakai's attention remained intent on me as he listened to the queen's pronouncement. Whatever was brewing in his thoughts finally made a connection, a realization that became evident in his countenance. He took a deep breath, his eyes never leaving mine. "There is another matter I should like to discuss before the council."

He paused.

"It pertains to the death of Michael Gallows."

He had everyone's attention now, and my hopes lifted within me. He knew something, something that had given him a sudden change of heart.

He had found my father's killer.

Mordakai hesitated, beginning to turn his head back to the throne as he spoke. "It has come to my attention—"

He gasped, and I blinked, unable to process what transpired before me as a sword emerged from the center of his chest. It disappeared as quickly as it had come, ripping itself from his back. Mordakai's shocked, widened eyes stared lifelessly as he toppled to the ground, a line of blood slowly beginning to drip from his mouth.

I barely saw the flash of silver and wrenched my sword from its sheath to meet the down-coming blow. The clash echoed throughout the throne room, bouncing off the walls and ringing in my ears as I used every ounce of strength to keep the blade from crushing me.

Screams and shouts reverberated off the walls as I heard the sound of swords being drawn, the clatter of steel meeting steel. Blood dripped from the attacking sword, and I struggled underneath its pressure as I slowly lifted my gaze and found myself looking into the pale face of Zedekiah. I pushed away, the shock giving me enough strength to create some distance between him and me. War raged around us, but I refused to take my eyes from him.

It had never been Mordakai.

It had been Zedekiah all along.

"He was your brother!"

Zedekiah shifted the sword in his hands.

"He was a traitor," Zedekiah corrected. "You were never supposed to come out of that river. I should have drowned you myself."

His next blow came so quickly I almost couldn't block it, and he swung another before I had time to recover from the first. He was fast. Faster than anyone I had ever dueled before. The advantage he held solely rested on his speed. I was losing ground as I fought to get the upper hand and keep him from killing me.

Zedekiah feinted, doubling back and knocking my father's

sword from my hands. I felt my back press against the throne room wall, and my breath caught as the cold tip of his sword pressed against the hollow of my throat.

I could see the rest of the throne room beyond him. Zedekiah must have had loyalists planted in the throne room because guards had turned on each other, fighting among themselves. Swords that had moments ago been allied now clashed as foes. Bodies littered the floor; soldiers limped away. One of the renegades rushed at Queen Adamara, but Vladimir blocked his path, and the queen's guards quickly cut him down. They rushed her from the room, fending off impending attackers as Vladimir and Katherine helped to clear the way for her.

Zedekiah's gloating gaze roved over me. He was savoring this moment, balancing the entirety of my life in his hands. A smile twitched at the corner of his mouth.

"You have your father's eyes. I recognize the same pool of fear that dwelled in his eyes—right before I plunged that sword through his heart."

The world grew very cold around me, the air thickening as the movements of everyone in the room slowed, as if time itself was trying to stop.

Right before I plunged that sword through his heart.

Zedekiah's words played over and over in my mind as I beheld Mordakai's body crumpled in a puddle of blood. Everything suddenly made sense. More than anything, Mordakai had wanted to be a Kavari, and more than anything, Zedekiah had needed a Kavari that he could control. Zedekiah couldn't control my father, and he murdered him for it.

I recalled when Mordakai had taken me to his office, informing me that his loyalty was to his country, and he would do whatever it took to protect it. Today, when he laid down the ring of the Kavari, it was because he knew there was a greater threat to his country, and it would never be defeated as long as he bore the title of Kavari.

Zedekiah noticed where my eyes had wandered, had witnessed the realization in them, and his smile grew wider.

"If he'd simply done as he was told, my brother might still be alive. It's a shame, really."

There was no remorse in his voice, only triumph. It fanned the fires of rage building within me.

"Traitor." I ground the words out and flinched as the tip of his sword threatened to break my skin.

Zedekiah raised an eyebrow. "Traitor? You're the one trying to protect a country you care nothing about. It's written all over your face. You didn't come here as a Blood Vier to become a Kavari. You came here for something else."

The room had quieted. I drew in a hopeful breath as the tip of a sword slipped below Zedekiah's chin.

"Drop the sword, Zedekiah. You're outnumbered." Vladimir's voice was deadly, his entire body prepared to end Zedekiah's life with one stroke.

Zedekiah's focus flickered between me and the threat of death as several other soldiers closed in around us. In one swift movement, he slipped from Vladimir's reach, pulling me in front of him as a shield, the sword's edge now pressed against my neck.

I had to tell myself to breathe as he held it tightly against my throat, knowing the slightest slip of his fingers would be the end.

"Stand back," Zedekiah demanded as he began to slowly

retreat.

"Let her go, Zedekiah." Vladimir was advancing at a safe distance, his hands outstretched before him.

The distraction had allowed some of the rogue soldiers to rally behind Zedekiah. My breath grew tighter in my throat as each one passed us, their weapons raised threateningly against anyone who dared follow.

What could have only been minutes felt like hours as I stumbled backward, trying to keep the blade from pressing any harder against my skin. Zedekiah's sword arm continued pressing me backward, his other hand gripping my arm so tightly it nearly went numb.

I didn't understand why he was doing this or what he thought he was going to accomplish. There was no way for them to escape. They would be apprehended before ever reaching the castle gates.

For a moment I thought my vision was growing narrower, until I realized we were entering a tunnel. Panic lit through me, and I squirmed in Zedekiah's grasp, the cold steel pricking at my skin.

I was going to die.

Vladimir had continued to advance. I stared into his pale blue eyes in horror, pleading for help even though I knew none would come. They were the last thing I saw before the door to the tunnel slammed shut, enclosing us in darkness.

CHAPTER TWENTY-FIVE

Vladimir

I'D SEEN ZEDEKIAH'S angry face as he stepped down the dais toward his brother, but by the time I understood what was happening, he'd drawn his sword, and it was too late. When he plunged his blade through Mordakai's heart, shock ruled the throne room. I gaped, unable to believe what was happening before my eyes.

Zedekiah went after Taryn, but his actions had been a signal. The guards turned on each other, and I found myself under attack from all sides. The council members were fleeing the throne room, trying to avoid the bloodshed.

It was Zedekiah—not Mordakai—who was the traitor.

How could I have been wrong? Everything had pointed to Mordakai. His thirst for power and immediate desire to fill Michael's position. Mordakai had threatened Taryn.

I feinted to the right as a soldier bore down on me. I couldn't tell who was friend or foe, and I continuously circled, hammering away at the oncoming blows. Anytime a pathway to Taryn or the queen opened up, another soldier quickly filled it. Several soldiers stormed the dais but were quickly cut down before they reached the queen. Out of the corner of my eye, I saw her personal guard rushing her to safety. Taryn was holding her own against Zedekiah, but she wouldn't last long.

Zedekiah knew.

He had known that Taryn was still alive.

A blade whistled through the air, and I quickly parried it, catching the eye of one of the soldiers involved with searching for Taryn's body. The blade he wielded was not on our side. Fear seized him as I approached, sword raised. My expression turned cold as I struck him down, but within, anger and agony ripped me to shreds.

I had trusted him.

The few remaining rebels were rallied behind Zedekiah. My throat constricted when I saw the tip of his sword pressed into the hollow of Taryn's throat. My steps were quick as I approached and slipped my sword beneath his chin to end the onslaught. But Zedekiah refused to give up. I followed behind him at a safe distance as he forced her away as a hostage. Any closer and I feared he might take her life. There was nowhere for him to go.

Gharridan's men blocked him from reaching the throne room doors. I was so transfixed with the pressure of the blade on Taryn's throat that I failed to figure out his plan in time. A door opened in the wall, and I rushed forward, Taryn's horror-struck expression boring into me before the door crashed shut in my face.

My shoulder slammed into the hidden door, pain shooting through my arm like a lightning bolt, but the door did not budge and vanished back into the wall.

"William!" I bellowed as my foot kicked aimlessly at the stone wall, unable to see the lines of the door any longer. William's fingers were already searching for whatever knob would grant us entrance. My foot connected with the door again in anger. Taryn would be dead as soon as Zedekiah and his men knew they were out of danger. It might already be too late.

Something clicked, and the stones shifted, popping out the secret door. I plunged into the darkness, my steps slowing as I extended my sword out in front of me, trying to determine the way. William's forceful grip yanked me backward before I could move any farther.

"There are stairs, Vladimir."

I let him step in front of me, my heart racing inside my chest. The clink of armor echoed up the stairs as we descended. They knew we were coming, and since we hadn't come across a body, it meant she was still alive. For now.

The air grew damper the deeper we went, suffocating me. It felt like walking through a tunnel at the bottom of the ocean. Eventually, the stairs leveled out onto a flat tunnel, and William broke into a run.

"Keep your hand on the wall!" he yelled back.

The tunnel walls were wet with moisture, and I avoided thinking about what my fingers were touching as they slid over a myriad of different textures. My only thought was to get Taryn back. Alive.

A faint light glowed in the distance and grew brighter as we approached. The ebb of the darkness revealed a separate passageway branching off in another direction.

"Keep going this way."

William was following the faint glow. He knew where the tunnels would let out.

The tunnel dragged on forever, my breathing ragged as my heart pounded in my ears. Fear threatened to take over my body. Sweat poured from me, drenching my clothes. I lowered my hand from the wall as the passage continuously grew brighter, hope rising within me as I saw sunlight streaming in from the tunnel entrance up ahead.

A whinny echoed down the tunnel, and my throat constricted.

They had horses.

William cursed, pushing himself even faster than before as we tore toward the exit. I could see the ivy hanging over the tunnel entrance, and my sword was raised as we charged through it. I squinted as we burst out into the bright sunshine. Most of the men were already mounted. I deflected a sword that bore down upon me, the rider retreating out of reach. As the circling horses interchanged spots, I found Zedekiah, saw the grin on his face as he raised the sword to Taryn's throat.

He'd been waiting for me.

He wanted me to see this.

Above all, he wanted to make sure I knew that I had lost, and he had won. He was too far away, and I would never reach his sword before it took Taryn's life. A yell tore out of my throat as his hand began to move.

That was when the arrow hit his arm.

The sword plummeted from his hand as he lurched backward, and Taryn toppled forward onto the ground. Katherine stood behind me, her bowstring still vibrating when one of the riders drove his horse into her and knocked her to the ground.

I rushed forward, yanking Taryn to safety as Zedekiah scrambled onto the back of a horse, clutching his shoulder. Hoofbeats thundered around us as the horses took off at a gallop, leaving a billowing cloud of dust behind.

"Are you okay?" I asked, grabbing Taryn's shoulders.

A small stream of blood flowed from her neck where the blade had nicked her. Her body trembled as she stared after the riders, anger blazing in her eyes.

"You couldn't have at least made it a fatal shot?" William hovered over Katherine, who pulled herself off the ground.

"I had less than a second to take that shot," Katherine hissed. "It was either wound him or kill both of them."

Taryn's feet pushed off the ground, and she ran through the dust to follow after the men.

"Taryn!" I yelled and chased after her. Her boots pounded against the earth, and I struggled to catch her, grabbing her arm and pulling her back.

"Let me go!" she screamed, wrenching my arm from her grasp and fighting against me.

I grabbed it again, wondering if she'd gone mad. "You'll never catch up to them on foot."

"They can't get away." Tears welled in her eyes as she watched the riders fade into the distance.

"What is it?" Her reaction frightened me.

Her entire face transformed into fierce hatred, a fire burning in her eyes as she watched them disappear. She brought her gaze back to mine, stepping forward.

"He murdered my father."

The words didn't register at first. "What?"

"He admitted it directly to my face. He murdered my father. He tried to drown me in the river and just tried to kill me again!"

I took a step back, her words sinking in.

Zedekiah had killed Michael.

I ran my hands through my hair as I moved back toward the others.

It all made sense now.

As the queen's advisor, Zedekiah would have had access to the seal of Gharridan and to that document. He was trying to advise the queen to rule the country one way, while Michael was advising her to rule it another. He'd known that I wouldn't be controllable, but he also knew that if Michael was dead, then his brother would be able to vie for the Kavari. After Mordakai was instated, it wouldn't be long before Zedekiah would be asking the council to promote Mordakai as leader of the Kavari on the basis he was superior to me.

"I want a company of twenty horsemen ready in the next fifteen minutes."

I would kill Zedekiah myself.

CHAPTER TWENTY-SIX

Taryn

I HELD A cloth against the cut on my neck to make sure the bleeding had stopped. My body shook as I stormed into the stable and slipped into Stryder's stall. I took a shuddering breath, leaning against the wall and covering my face with my hand. My heart still hammered away inside my chest. Tears hovered at the edge of my vision.

I couldn't deal with this right now.

Taking a deep breath, I pushed away from the wall, letting the cloth against my neck fall from my hands. All that mattered was that I was still alive—and that we stop Zedekiah, who was still out running free. My hands tightened into fists as the fear and anxiety coursing through my veins transformed into anger.

I pulled Stryder from the stall and hurriedly threw his tack on before leading him out into the stable yard. The others were almost ready, and I double-checked Stryder's girth.

"What are you doing?"

Vladimir stood behind me with condemning eyes.

"What does it look like?" I buckled the strap and slipped the reins over Stryder's head, preparing to mount.

"You're not coming." His voice was firm.

"Says who?"

I went to swing into the saddle, and he held me back. I jerked out of his reach, causing Stryder to nervously sidestep beside me.

"Taryn—"

"You can't stop me," I said. "I am not a Kavari and am not beholden to you. Zedekiah killed my father, Vladimir. I will not rest until he's dead."

Irritation radiated off Vladimir as he stood there, looking like he was holding back a million different retorts, but after a moment, he walked away, choosing to leave it alone. I climbed up onto Stryder, and the men around me began to mount as well.

I didn't quite know why I was so bent on revenge. It wasn't like I cared for my father, but right now, it felt like my focus on catching Zedekiah was the only thing keeping me together. I gathered the reins in my hands, my fingers itching for vengeance.

Hours passed, and there was still no sign of the perpetrator. The trail Zedekiah and his men had left was fresh and undamaged, but having to go back for horses had cost us precious time. Vladimir rode at the head of the company, keeping the group moving at a steady pace. His eyes fixated on the ground as he followed the groove of hoofprints etched into the dirt. No one spoke a word, but we each kept one hand on a weapon and both eyes on our surroundings.

"We're going to find him, Taryn."

Katherine rode beside me, her face placid. Her words meant to be a comfort, but comfort wasn't what I needed right now. Zedekiah was what I needed. Fire still burned within my chest, a heat that kept me warm as the cold wind tried to rip my cloak from my shoulders.

"I know," I said.

Vladimir suddenly brought the company to a halt, dismounting as his eyes combed the ground. I craned my neck, straining to see what he had found. There was a change in the pattern. I examined the deeply distressed ground imprinted with endless hoofprints overlapping one another and dispersing through the trees.

"What is it?" I wasn't skilled enough to interpret the markings, but the concern lining Vladimir's face indicated he was. Vladimir swept forward through the trampled earth, stopping several paces ahead. His shoulders fell as he turned back to us.

"They parted ways here."

I urged Stryder forward, and my hope faltered. Out of the chaos emerged two sets of tracks, one branching off to the north and the other toward the southwest. It was split evenly—three riders to the left, and three to the right.

The company fell silent, unsurety written across each tired face.

"We're going to have to split up," Vladimir decided, rising to his feet. Determination filled his sour expression as he mounted Dante and reined him around.

Split up? My chest tightened at the thought. Dividing our group would weaken us—but Zedekiah would've known that.

"There's little more than an hour of daylight left," William put in.

Vladimir hesitated. "If we camped here tonight, we could wait to split till morning, but I don't want to lose any more time than we already have. We won't be able to track them in the dark."

Vladimir roved over each face in the group, looking for opposition but finding none. "Melvin, I want you and nine of your men to follow me. The rest will go with you, William. I want you to follow the path to the southwest."

"Katherine—" Vladimir hesitated, his gaze shifting from Katherine to me, to William, and then lingering between the crown prince and the healer. The men shifted uncomfortably on their horses as William's gaze burned into Vladimir, his face stone cold. He made it quite evident that he had no desire for Katherine to travel with his group. I marveled at the animosity that emanated from him whenever Katherine was around.

"I'll go with William."

The words escaped my mouth before I could stop them. I knew firsthand how efficient Vladimir was, and I would much rather continue on with him, but the thought of leaving Katherine to the wolves didn't sit well with me. I would go with William if it kept us from sitting here and arguing over it.

I steered Stryder over to stand by William and Othello, and Katherine's gratitude-filled gaze caught mine.

"When will we meet back up?" I asked.

Vladimir shrugged. "Whenever one of us finds Zedekiah

and drags him back to the capital. Send word as soon as you find anything."

Vladimir reined his horse away without giving me a second glance, our paths dividing. Katherine threw a glance over her shoulder, giving me a nod of reassurance, and I turned to follow William's group, cutting in directly behind him. The moment anything happened, I wanted to be the first to know.

The absence of the other soldiers seemed to put a damper on the men. After our split, they grew eerily quiet. Numbers provided safety, and though Zedekiah had lost most of his rogues, the men had witnessed enough bloodshed to know that this mission involved risk.

As the sun lowered, nervousness and anxiety built within me. William was a good tracker, just nowhere near Vladimir's speed or efficiency. I constantly had to watch my tongue, biting back the impatient words that threatened to pour out every time we had to backtrack, or he missed a sign on the trail. The shadows of the trees were elongating, the light growing dimmer. I stretched my legs out on either side of Stryder, stiff after the many long hours in the saddle.

William suddenly pulled Othello up. "We'll continue in the morning."

My heart dropped within me. There would be no justice tonight.

None of the men spoke to me as we made camp. A few cast wary glances as they passed, but quickly avoided eye contact, almost as if they were afraid. I crossed my arms uncomfortably, realizing I was the only woman in the group. I offered to help but was quickly turned down as the men insisted they had it under control. Beginning to feel like a nuisance, I moved over by Stryder. Staying here all night while Zedekiah still roamed free ate away at me. Daylight needed to return quickly.

I surveyed each of the soldiers around me, wondering if any of them might be in league with Zedekiah. He'd obviously been able to sway some of the soldiers to his side before. I feared some of them might be in our company.

Each soldier wore identical uniforms, giving the charade that they were unified in both thoughts, actions, and allegiance, but I knew underneath each and every one of those identical uniforms was a person who had their own desires and agendas. It was a façade. They did not all hold the same values.

"Vladimir handpicked the men." William came up beside me. "They wouldn't be here if he didn't trust them. He even exchanged several."

Vladimir had probably trusted the soldiers in the throne room too. My jaw tightened. "Did your mother send you in her stead?"

William chuckled. "She forbade me to come."

I glanced sideways at him. William carried himself as someone who despised orders, yet always showed deference to his mother. Why had that changed now?

"She's afraid my safety will be compromised, but she's also going to need people she can trust while she's patching things up at the capital."

That still hadn't answered my question. It made sense the queen had not wanted him to leave. If anything happened to her, he was next in line for the throne, and if anything happened to him—

The thought ended as quickly as it had begun.

"Then why are you here?"

William's expression turned hard and angry, simmering like a billowing storm preparing to unleash its wrath. "I had friends in that room, Taryn."

It had been a bloodbath. I shivered at the memories of the lifeless bodies on the floor, the picture making me nauseous. When we'd passed back through the throne room, Queen Adamara had been distraught, beyond words. Her eyes were wide with unbelief at the realization that her most trusted advisor had turned against her.

"Zedekiah betrayed our country," William continued. "His threat to us is a direct threat to me, and I want to ensure he's prevented from doing any further damage."

Maybe William did have a heart.

I leaned into Stryder's warm mane, inhaling his scent in the hopes of clearing my mind. Zedekiah's words haunted me, and I couldn't forget the feel of the cold steel against my skin nor the perpetual fear that my life was about to end. Stryder's warmth helped combat the cold sensations and memories that continued to bombard me.

"How are you holding up?"

I threw my arm underneath Stryder's neck, pulling my face out of his mane. William gently stroked Stryder's side. The soldiers hadn't turned William's help away but embraced him as one of their own. Out here, it was as if he was no longer the crown prince.

I swallowed my fear and took solace once again in revenge. "Once Zedekiah is dead, I'll be fine."

I squeezed my eyes shut in frustration. We should have caught up with them today. I could only pray and hope that we would make faster time tomorrow, and Zedekiah could be done with for good, but that was only possible if we were following the right trail.

"Not exactly what I meant, but it works." William studied me. "He almost killed you today. There hasn't been much time to process that."

There hadn't been much time to process drowning in the river either. Today wasn't the first time I had tasted death, nor would it be the last. Every event had stacked upon one another like a wall of bricks. Misplace one stone, and the entire wall would crumble down into ruin.

"I'm still alive; what does it matter?"

Even if I had wanted to talk through events, it definitely wouldn't be happening with William. Or with anyone else in this camp. If I didn't need the safety in numbers, I would have gone after Zedekiah on my own.

Stryder snorted abruptly, lifting his head. My eyes shot up as his muscles instantly tensed beneath my hands. I searched the surrounding shadows for any movement, but no one was there.

Except—

The slightest movement caught my eye across the camp, so minuscule that I almost questioned if I had seen it. Something unseen shifted in the woods.

"What is it?" William asked.

Six arrows flew into the camp, each finding its mark in a Gharridan soldier. A gasp escaped my throat. Shouts broke out as our men scrambled for weapons, then another volley came in, taking out two more soldiers. William grabbed my waist and all but threw me onto Stryder.

"Go!"

His fist landed hard on Stryder's rump, and the horse

bolted at the contact. I grabbed handfuls of his mane, my legs tightly squeezing his sides, barely managing to keep my balance. Stryder barreled through the forest away from the massacre.

Dead.

They were all dead.

When I heard the hoofbeats, there was no time to stop Stryder. The other horse plowed into his shoulder. Suddenly I was flying through the air in dizzying darkness. The ground came soaring up to me, and I crashed, rolling into the fall. My head spun, unable to tell up from down as the world proceeded to reel. It felt like I was stuck on the spoke of a wagon wheel as it turned round and round. My legs were jelly as I struggled to stand. I couldn't find my balance, and the world pivoted on me again. My scrambling arms dug into the earth and grabbed at the fallen leaves as I crawled across the forest floor. When I managed to get my legs underneath me again, I stood, and then something hard struck me in the side of the head.

CHAPTER TWENTY-SEVEN

Taryn

THE PAIN WOKE me.

It felt like two barricades were drawing closer together, smashing my head between them as they struggled to become one. Everything was black except for the sparks of light that flew around my vision like shooting stars.

Something cold splattered my face. I coughed, my sight flickering, and took a deep breath as my mind tried to slip back into darkness. The substance splashed my face again—more of it this time. I moved my lips, my tongue trying to identify it.

I tried to touch my face but realized I couldn't move my arm. Coarse ropes cut into my wrists, securely fastening my hands behind my back. Another hand brushed up against mine, and I jerked away, my vision momentarily blacking out again at the sharp movement.

Laughter erupted around me, pounding inside my head. All I wanted to do was lie down, but my body was forced into this upright position. I felt my eyelids open, the world nothing but a blur around me.

"Taryn."

The soft voice was familiar, coming from someone close behind me. I tried to focus on my surroundings, but the effort caused my head to ache. Dark objects moved at the edges of my vision, lurking around me like shadowy monsters.

"Taryn."

William.

I opened my mouth to respond but instead ended up spitting out blood.

"What?" I managed.

"Are you okay?"

I felt the hand again, William's hand, brush against mine. I squeezed my eyes shut, trying to regain my lost vision. Slowly my clarity returned, and the dark shapes surrounding us shifted into men who circled the perimeter of our small campfire.

"I'm breathing. I think." Those few words took too much effort.

William shifted, and I realized our hands were tied together behind our backs. A form moved in front of me, and I lifted my head, attempting to focus without blacking out again. A man stood before me with arms folded tightly across a broad chest. His mouth was curved, not in a pleasant way, but in a sneer of authority. His condescending eyes studied me for a moment before he strode out of sight to stand before William.

"You two should be very grateful." His voice was as smooth as honey but deadly as a snake's bite. "If Zedekiah were here, you'd both be dead by now."

William shifted behind me. "How generous."

William wouldn't die in battle but from mouthing off at an inappropriate moment. Right now, that didn't seem like too horrible a way to go, but I pushed at his hands in warning anyway. The mention of Zedekiah's name, however, relit a fury in me, and I found myself responding in kind.

"If he couldn't finish the job back in Gharridan, what makes you think he could do it now?" I spat the words contemptuously.

Boots thudded behind me, and a scowling face was suddenly in mine. The stench emanating from him nearly made me gag. The dirty, greasy exterior indicated he hadn't bathed in months. He lifted something circular into my vision. It took me a minute to realize what it was, but when I did, my heart stopped.

"You must be Michael Gallows' daughter." The man smiled, twirling the ring between his fingers. "The greatest news I ever received was the news of his death."

A low chuckle escaped his throat as he stood back to full height and took us in. "I can't help but wonder about your great plan. Did you really think you'd ever get close enough to capture Zedekiah, let alone kill him?"

The rope on my hands pulled slightly, and I realized that William was fiddling with the knots. I kept my eyes riveted on the speaker in order to keep his attention from shifting to William.

"Well done, men!" The leader raised his fist, and a volley of cheers and laughter broke out among the surrounding soldiers. "The crown prince of Gharridan and the daughter of

Michael Gallows—I'm sure Zedekiah will have a handsome reward ready when we deliver them."

My eyes fell to the bodies littering the ground, arrows protruding from their chests and backs. These vagabonds had dragged us back to our own fire without respect for the dead men around them. Men who had given their life for their country. There had been no warning. They weren't even given the honor of defending themselves. This attack had been planned, but I didn't know if it had been planned for us. With the growing number of dead or missing Kavari, I wondered if they'd been hoping to capture Vladimir.

The man in charge snapped his fingers, grabbing my attention as he waved at his men. "Get them onto horses."

William's hands stilled as we were approached, his attempts unsuccessful. The rope that bound us together was loosed before I was jerked roughly to my feet. The world began spinning, and I stumbled forward drunkenly as they shoved me onto a horse. I clutched at the only comfort I had—they had put me on Stryder. Another rope fastened my hands to the saddle, and we immediately took off. Every ounce of strength that remained was used to keep me in the saddle. It was too soon for the rocking movement of a horse's back, and comprehension was slowly fading from my mind again. I prayed that when morning came, I would simply be alive.

I didn't know how long we rode. I don't even know if I was dreaming or awake, but my mind became alert as my body plummeted toward the ground and landed hard in the dirt. My head was still turning, the spinning sensation clouding all thoughts from my mind. Two hands dragged me backward and plopped me down, reversing the bonds to place my hands behind my back again and tying my feet. All I wanted to do was sleep, my eyes already sagging shut.

There was a thud close by as William's body fell next to mine. Out of the corner of my vision a fire came to life, illuminating William's face in dark shadows. I couldn't tell if the splotch covering his eye was shadow or bruise.

Our captors busied themselves making camp, but I couldn't care less about what was going on around me. If the pain would go away, then everything would be fine. There was only so much more I could take. My eyes slowly drifted closed. If I was to be a prisoner, I would at least be a sleeping one.

"Taryn?"

The voice cut through my swirling head, and I grunted in response, too tired for anything else. Could he not have spoken before I shut my eyes?

"I don't think you should go to sleep yet."

I peeked at him through the pain, irritated.

"Whyever not?" I snapped.

His gaze focused on my forehead, concern outlining his face.

"Because."

This must have something to do with my injury, but I couldn't understand or remember why.

"I'm going to need help staying awake, then." My eyelids were growing heavy again.

"Listen."

Struggling to keep my eyes open, I focused on the noise around me. I could hear the horses munching on grass, bedrolls rolling out, and armor chinking as the men moved about the camp. A few men were conversing, but I noticed two specific voices struggling to be quieter than the rest that caught my attention.

"We're changing course in the morning. I want this camp dismantled by daybreak."

That voice belonged to the man who had taunted William and me, the leader of the group.

"Are we transporting them to the prison with the other Kavari?" the other soldier asked.

"No. Once they get the information they need, he'll be disposed of. We'll take them across the border into Brenden where Zedekiah will meet us in a few weeks."

William's eyes met mine in the darkness.

"Do you think they captured Vladimir too?" I whispered.

Ever so slightly, he shook his head. "They must be talking about Marco, but I don't know which prison they're referring to."

"Why would they take us to Brenden?" Nothing in my head was working right, but I did know that Brenden didn't make sense.

He raised an eyebrow, making the answer seem obvious. "What did Zedekiah have to gain by murdering your father?"

Silence hung between us; my mind was blank. Power? He'd lost that when Mordakai had betrayed him in the throne room, and when he'd killed his brother, he'd condemned himself.

"Nothing," William finished. "Nothing unless another country offered him a substantial reward to weaken our country."

The implications of his words finally dawned on me. Killing Michael offered Zedekiah no advantage in Gharridan, but if he fed Gharridan's secrets to Brenden, as long as they continued to supply him with money, that provided him with power and gold.

Twigs snapped beneath a set of boots, and both of us closed our eyes, mocking sleep. The footsteps stopped a few feet from us, a sigh escaping his body as the guard sank to the ground. We'd been lucky to converse what little we'd managed. There would be no more discussion tonight.

CHAPTER TWENTY-EIGHT

Vladimir

I FELT THE heat of the eyes and the fierceness of the gaze that bore into me. A glance to the left revealed Katherine watching me, and I shifted uncomfortably before the small flames. The last thing I needed was another lecture or some hopeless encouragement. It had been four days, yet while the tracks remained fresh, we had not come any closer to Zedekiah and his men since the first day.

"They'll be fine, Vladimir." Katherine was still watching me.

"I didn't say they wouldn't be."

"Maybe not verbally, but it's written all over your face."

I ground my teeth together, irritated by the fact that Katherine always seemed to know what I was thinking. Something that must be expected when we'd grown up together. She was like a sister to me not only in guessing my thoughts but in annoyance as well.

"They had ten soldiers for protection."

"It's not the soldiers I'm worried about."

Katherine grew quiet at my words. "William may not be one to always make rational decisions, but Taryn knows how to think for herself. From the way she told you off back at the capital, she's not going to let anyone tell her what to do—just like someone else I know."

I met her eyes, a sorrow passing between us. Taryn was exactly like her father in that way. Though he had always remained respectful and subject to authority, he'd never held any fear about speaking his mind or taking matters into his own hands. I still didn't understand why he hadn't told me what he suspected before he died.

"Do you think they caught up to their group yet?"

At the rate we were progressing, I highly doubted it.

"I don't know."

There was an uneasiness about the whole situation that plagued me. Zedekiah knew Taryn was alive because we had been betrayed, but had he been planning on leaving the capital even if his true intentions hadn't been exposed? Had Zedekiah suspected that his brother knew of his treason before the ceremony? He had men, his men, prepared to defend him in the throne room as well as a definite way of escape with the horses outside the hidden tunnel. There was something I was missing.

"A lot of good men died in that throne room, Vladimir."

It was on Katherine's mind as well. I stared at the smoke billowing out of the flames, my jaw clenched.

"It was Jakob."

"I know. I watched as his blade turned against us."

Jakob was a newer recruit, but he'd never shown anything but loyalty. Trusting him had been a fatal mistake. I glanced at the men around me, running their names through my head. All of them had at least ten years' experience in the military. I'd made sure of it; made sure that I had proven actions to go off and not just professed loyalty.

Melvin sat across the fire with Cairo, talking quietly. Melvin was one of the only soldiers present that I trusted with my life. He'd been in the army for twenty-five years and helped me when I was learning strategy and Gharridan's military tactics. I held high respect for him, and so had Michael. After leaving the capital, I'd asked him to investigate each soldier with us to ensure we knew where their loyalties laid.

"What about the other soldiers who betrayed us?"

Captain Verone was looking into it. He had plenty to deal with, especially with tripling security on the queen in addition to her personal guard. Worry gnawed at my gut. Zedekiah's infiltration was deeper than I feared with his foothold in both the council and the military. Something told me he wouldn't have taken all his loyalists with him.

"We should have some answers by the time we get back," I said.

Who knew when that would be, or how we would meet up with Taryn and William. With no means of communication and no specified destination, there was no telling how long it would be before we crossed paths again.

It wasn't the soldiers I was worried about or necessarily even William, although one could never predict what he might do. I'd made a promise to Michael that I would protect his daughter and keep her safe. A promise that was growing quite difficult to keep. The desire for vengeance was consuming Taryn, and killing Zedekiah would not bring her the peace she hoped for—it would destroy her.

CHAPTER TWENTY-NINE

Taryn

I WAS NO longer on Stryder.

The gait of the brown horse beneath me was bumpy and unfamiliar as it jostled me around. My bound hands gripped his mane, the reins tied to the horse in front of me. One rider rode behind me while two others flanked each side. Escaping wasn't even within the realm of possibility. I didn't know how many days had passed since we'd been captured. The pounding in my head on the first day had been so intense that I wondered if I hadn't blacked out in the saddle as we were riding. I did remember vomiting from the pain and nausea, hanging over the side of the horse. At least I was able to sit up in the saddle now without feeling like I was about to die, but my head still ached.

My gaze whipped to the man at the head of the company,

who was setting the quick pace. His name was Silas. I'd learned that much. Fire burned across my skin as I watched him commandeer Stryder, but I kept my feelings hidden well to prevent them from attaining any leverage. Silas had quickly taken a liking to Stryder, claiming my horse for himself.

A shiver ran down my spine, and I lifted my hands, trying to reposition my cloak. I was thankful they hadn't confiscated it. There would be snow soon. I could sense it in the paleness of the sky and taste it in the frostiness of the air. Every day grew colder with the darkness of the evening.

William and I were only together at night, but even then, we were heavily watched. If either of us so much as rolled over or breathed irregularly, the guards responded with a reprimand or a kick. Talking was out of the question.

But to get out of here, we needed to talk.

My tongue was immobile, but my eyes were not. I watched each of the guards closely, observed their interactions, learned their routines, and listened to their conversations in search of any chink in their armor. Nothing had surfaced yet. The only bright side to our situation was that we were being taken exactly where we wanted—straight to Zedekiah. My concern was what would happen when we caught up to him. Our weapons were securely stored with the other riders, and there was never a moment when we were left alone. Taking Zedekiah down needed to be conducted in an ambush, not a captive situation.

If we didn't figure out something quickly, neither of us would get through this unscathed. With each passing day, my gut twisted a little tighter. Time was running shorter for me as the men's lingering gazes were becoming harder to ignore. I looked over and caught William's eye. His expression relayed my own message. We had to escape. He was acutely aware of the men's thoughts and knew the danger.

The horse flanking my left rode up beside Silas. I tilted my head slightly, trying to tune out the step of the horses' hooves around me and straining to hear their conversation, but it was lost in the creaking saddles and pounding hooves. Their voices were too low and far away. When they finished, Silas motioned to one of the other men to join them. After a moment of conversing, the two soldiers then left the group and rode out of sight.

I glanced over at William again. Our faces both asked the same question. Where were the men going?

"Eyes ahead!"

I jerked my gaze forward at the harsh voice, keeping them fixed on the rider in front of me as the day wore on. Woods still surrounded our company, the branches of the trees interweaving into a cage that hid us from the outside world, but their depths would aid our escape. I wondered if William knew where we were, and if he would have any idea where to go when we managed to escape—if and when we managed to escape.

After a while, Silas brought the company to a halt, and the men began to dismount. Daylight still slipped between the bare branches of the trees, and I glanced around nervously. We never stopped before sunset, and there was at least another hour of light left.

The man who removed me from the saddle jerked roughly on my arm, and I bit my tongue to keep a cry from escaping my lips. The coarse ropes had cut into the skin, leaving angry bands of red where they'd chafed my wrists completely raw. William's were no better than mine. I wished that nighttime would've granted relief for our tender skin, but our captors left them tied.

William's confused eyes connected with mine as they escorted us to our beds of leaves for the night. The two soldiers who'd separated from us earlier in the day had not returned, but the other men carried on setting up camp. I wished we were closer to the fire. I yearned for its warmth to envelop me and suck the cold from my bones.

A guard hovered over us, and little more than brief glances passed between William and me. The horses stood grazing several yards away, but even if we made a run for it, they would catch us before we reached the first horse. There were twelve men altogether, each heavily armed. I stared down at my hands, being careful not to move them and wishing the guard had left them just a slip looser.

The sun was nearly down when the hoofbeats approached. I lifted my head, hoping to see Vladimir, but it was the missing horsemen who broke out of the trees. They were quickly surrounded by the other men whose eyes gleamed with excitement. Even our guard strayed a few feet away to observe.

It took me a moment to understand what was going on, but then I understood. Food was being unloaded from the saddlebags and distributed among the men. My mouth watered at the sight of a fresh loaf of bread, a hunk of cheese. This was good news—it meant we were close to a town.

Hoots and hollers went around as several bottles of ale emerged from the saddlebags. My stomach dropped. The bottles were opened immediately and passed around, each man taking a long draught before passing it along. One of the men who never seemed to let his gaze wander far from me stared me down as he took a long swig from the bottle. Ale ran down his chin and dribbled into his braided beard, a malicious smile ghosting his lips. The hair on the back of my neck prickled, and sweat broke out on my forehead as I looked away. We had to escape tonight. There was no other option. Whatever morals had kept the men at bay would be lost to the alcohol.

I waited for our guard to join them, but he stayed put, and the minutes ticked by dreadfully slow as the world completely engulfed us in darkness. We were running out of time. Our guard suddenly took a step closer to his fellow soldiers. I held my breath, hoping he would leave. After a moment of deliberation, he cast us a leery eye before sauntering off to have a turn with the bottle. I looked back down at my hands. He had not yet reversed our bonds.

"William," I whispered, my voice tight.

"Roll over and face me."

I obeyed his command and moved to my side as adrenaline pumped through my veins. He began working at the knots in my hands, the movement rubbing the rope across my chafed hands. I bit my lip as a burst of pain erupted and closed my eyes.

"Keep your eyes on the men," William said. "Tell me if any of them look this way."

With my eyes fixed on the drinking men, he worked his fingers furiously to untie my knots. Time was continuing to quickly slip by as the ropes refused to loosen. The men had already finished the first few bottles, our guard having waited long enough to join them that the alcohol was beginning to take effect.

"Stop." My voice was quick, too loud.

Both of us froze as our guard's gaze passed over, but the shadows from the fire were dancing across us, making it unlikely for our motives to be seen from a distance. His attention returned to his comrades, and William set to work again. My heart pounded wildly within my chest, every fiber in my being telling me to run. The tension in the rope suddenly went slack, and my hands separated for the first time since they'd been bound. Stiffness permeated my arms, but it felt so good to be able to move again. My fingers fumbled for William's ropes, but he pulled away.

"Untie your feet first."

Ignoring his order, my hands reached for his wrists again. "I'm not going to leave you helpless. Watch the men."

Getting my hands loose had taken William a while, but nothing compared to how long it was taking me to get him free. Either they'd tied him harder, or William knew his way around knots. My hands began cramping, and I had no idea how he'd managed this with his hands still bound. Fear made my fingers clammy and slippery, and I could sense the nervousness growing in William as well.

Finally, the rope fell from his hands, and a quick sigh of relief escaped both of us.

"Inch your feet up slowly."

My eyes were riveted on the drinking men who seemed to have forgotten about us for the moment. Our feet weren't tied as tightly, and as soon as William loosened the ropes slightly, I slipped right out of them.

The talking and laughter continued to grow louder, making my heart pound harder within my chest. Once William's feet were free, he rose to a crouch, motioning for me to follow him. We crept through the shadowy darkness, darting behind trees as we moved toward the pack of horses. I fought the urge to break into a run to get out of here as quickly as I could. We would never make it out of here without a horse. They'd hunt us down within minutes.

Stryder gave a low whicker at my presence, and I glanced nervously behind me. Ever so quietly, I picked up a saddle and slipped it onto his back, tightening the latches and then throwing the bridle over his head. They would realize we were missing at any time. William had gotten a bridle on Othello, but the prince was now more interested in getting his hands on a weapon than his legs on a horse. He threw me a bow and my father's sword, belting his own sword on before strapping the saddle to Othello's back.

"Where do you think you're going?"

A scowling face and outstretched arm filled my vision as the soldier stumbled toward me. I jumped out of the way, and his gnarly fingers missed me by a hands breath only to clamp down on my wrist a few steps later. A muted cry escaped my lips as I turned to fight back. William slammed into him, the force throwing both of them against one of the horses and then falling beneath the frantic hooves.

"Get out of here!" William yelled.

It was chaos as the horses bolted away from the sudden commotion in a thunder of hooves and flying legs. I snatched Stryder's reins before he ran, and leapt into the saddle, trying to keep him steady in the sea of frightened horses. The men had realized what was going on and, with a shout, ran toward us, their weapons drawn.

William would be completely surrounded.

I aimed Stryder at the oncoming men and dug my heels into his sides. His massive frame plowed into the men, scattering them in every direction as they dove for cover. Stryder spun on his heels, charging through them a second time. William shoved the soldier off and took him down with a fist. All of the other horses had bolted, even Othello. Stryder's pounding hooves raced toward William, and I reached out my arm, leaning down to grasp his. He took it and clambered up into the saddle behind me. The extra weight bore down on Stryder, and he stumbled slightly, but I encouraged him to keep moving. His stride lengthened, and we surged into the night, leaving a barrage of shouts and curses behind us.

Terror still clung to me even though we'd escaped. I was afraid to look over my shoulder for fear they would be right behind us. William held onto me with one arm while the other was wound tightly into Stryder's mane. His finger pointed up ahead, and my heart nearly stopped, but I realized he had spotted Othello's grey coat gleaming in the moonlight.

"Take me up beside him!" William yelled in my ear.

Othello's pace was slowing along with the other horses running around him, and we easily maneuvered next to him. I could feel William slowly rising up behind me, using my shoulders for balance as he jumped from Stryder's back onto Othello's. The saddle slipped back, the sudden weight and shift of the tack causing the grey to buck. William barely managed to hold on, grabbing the reins and yanking him to a stop to bring him under control.

"They're going to catch the horses." William was winded. "It won't take them long, and when they do, they'll be on to us. We need to put as much distance between them and us as quickly as possible."

William snapped a branch off a tree and swung it through the air, smacking one of the horses' rumps and sending them scattering off again. I had already kicked Stryder forward, dashing ahead to avoid the hands of our captors that would soon be reaching for us. Quick glances over my shoulder proved we were still at an advantage, but my pounding heart reminded me it wouldn't last for long. The wind played with my hair as I hung low over Stryder's neck, clinging to him as he swerved among the trees.

When we broke out of the woods, both horses surged forward into a gallop, and we were nothing but a dark shadow and a silver streak racing across the countryside, the pounding hooves the only noise in the silence of the night.

CHAPTER THIRTY

Taryn

IT WAS UNCANNY, to be chased by an enemy we couldn't see. The road behind us held no sign of pursuit, but the knowledge that they were there unnerved me. As the biting wind blew across my cheeks, I kept imagining the sound of horse's hooves pounding the ground behind us like the beating of a death drum. I could almost feel their fingers reaching out for me, preparing to close around my shoulders and yank me from Stryder's back into unknown darkness. Death laughed at me, making a mockery of my feeble attempt at survival.

Our reckless pace didn't slow until the horses were incapable of running any farther. Stryder's thick coat dripped with sweat, the droplets falling to the ground like a light rain. His mane was plastered to his neck like drying pitch, and his nostrils flared wildly as he labored to catch his breath. I was struggling to catch my own breath, exhausted even though adrenaline continued to pump through my veins.

Above the labored breathing, I heard another noise. William noticed it too and guided a stumbling Othello toward it. The rushing river floated through our path, the sound making my chest constrict. I dismounted and let the horses drink heavily before kneeling to satisfy my own thirst. The icy water was a long-awaited relief. During our captivity, water had been scarce. Being able to drink from an endless supply was heavenly, a privilege I would never take for granted again. The coolness of the water was medicine to my burning wrists and the alleviation of pain a generous comfort.

"We need to cover our tracks."

Water dribbled down William's chin as he got back on Othello and ushered him into the shallow water.

An uneasiness churned in the pit of my stomach as I mounted. Dark memories flooded my mind of being sucked beneath the water, of the chilling numbness of my limbs, the hand shoving me beneath its glassy top, and an overwhelming sense of fear that each breath of air might be my last.

I swallowed hard as Stryder stepped in after Othello. He lifted his legs with each step, the icy water making him almost prance. It sprayed us, completely soaking everything below my knees. When the river deepened, occasional splashes reached my torso. I gathered my cloak up around me, trying to keep the hem from absorbing more water than it already had. The night air was frigid, the combination of elements producing shivers in Stryder and stiffness in my hands.

My eyes locked on the depths below us as we followed the

stream until it rose up nearly to the horse's shoulders. At that point, William quickly guided Othello out, and we emerged on the bank a dripping, shivering mess. Stryder stumbled on the slick rocks that lined the shore, but I was grateful for the stony beach that would obscure our tracks.

The land remained open here, dotted with small patches of trees and rolling hills. The landscape offered a feeling of freedom but also composed a sense of vulnerability. Our path was lit by the light of the moon as we pushed on through the exhaustion. Shadows chased us, changed shapes, and played with our minds.

Water that was dripping off Stryder's coat formed into icicles which I brushed away. The cloth of my dress was frozen as well, creating an ice palace in which my shivering legs could abide. Beneath me, Stryder trotted stiffly, his heavy breathing creating a fog that went before us.

Sleep was inevitable. Neither William nor I would make it much longer without it, and I'd nearly fallen out of the saddle twice already. A small stretch of trees came up on our right that looked like it would provide protection and shelter.

"It'll take them a while to pick up our trail after the river," William managed through chattering teeth. "We should be okay to rest for a little while."

I was too cold to even nod. Sliding off Stryder's back, I clumsily undid the buckles, slipping the saddle from his back.

William rolled out a blanket. "If you want to live through the night, we're going to have to keep each other warm."

Lighting a fire posed too great a risk. It would be a beacon to our captors, leading them exactly to where we were. Dawn was still hours from breaking, meaning that right now, darkness was our only ally.

Still shivering, I crawled under the blanket and curled up next to William, forgoing any propriety. The heat emanating from our bodies beneath the confines of the blanket helped combat the cold, but it would be a long, miserable night.

Light awakened me, dancing across my eyes and beckoning me to open them to its beauty. I jerked awake, fear pumping through my veins as I frantically tried to figure out where I was. A steadying breath left me as I saw William saddling the horses.

We were not captives anymore.

I dug through the saddlebags in search of even a trace of a crumb, but there was nothing. The only useful things buried in the bag were some flint and a pouch of coins. Flint would be great once it was safe to light a fire, and gold might be our savior in town, but it couldn't feed us out in the wilderness.

"We can try to catch something to eat tonight." William swung up into the saddle, and I followed suit. "I haven't seen any sign of them yet."

I shielded my eyes from the sunlight, looking beyond our small copse of trees. We were encircled by a countryside that winter had killed until spring. Everything from the highest hill to the shortest blade of grass was a shade of crackling brown.

"Do you know where we are?" I asked.

Hesitation wavered in William's eyes as he took in our surroundings. "There's no road, so I'm not certain, but I'm going to guess there's a town"—he pointed to the right—"about twenty miles in that direction."

For someone who hovered in uncertainty, his guess was

quite specific.

"How long will it take us to get there?"

"Well," William cocked his head, "considering that's the first place they'll look for us, we're actually going to go this way." He pointed left. "If we're where I think we are, there should be another town some fifty miles out."

"And you're sure?" I asked, uneasy. Hiding my skepticism of his coordinates failed horribly.

William laughed. "Absolutely not."

His attempt at humor wasn't received well, but I followed him anyway. He had a plan. At least it was something, even if it wasn't much. The habit of looking over my shoulder stayed with me, and even though there wasn't another human being in sight, the hair on the back of my neck still prickled.

They were coming for us.

We just couldn't see them yet.

"Where did Silas and his men come from?" I asked. "I thought we were trailing three rogue soldiers."

William clenched his jaw. "We were. They were with Silas' men."

My eyes shot to William. Without their Gharridan uniforms, I wouldn't have recognized them, but if William was familiar with their faces, he would've been able to pick them out.

"So Vladimir is on Zedekiah's trail."

William nodded.

"If Silas was waiting to meet with Zedekiah's men, that means—"

"Then that means that Zedekiah planned on leaving all along," William finished. "Something is off about this whole situation, and I don't know what it is."

Zedekiah must have already suspected that Mordakai was going to betray him. There was no other explanation for the horses outside the tunnel or meeting up with Silas and his men. I looked up at the sky. The golden, outstretched rays of sunshine penetrated my skin with a welcome warmth, but it did not give off enough heat to completely warm or dry me. I wondered if Vladimir had already captured Zedekiah. If he had already made him pay.

When we finally made camp that night, our limbs hung wearily, and our stomachs growled like a chorus of ravenous wolves. We were sitting across from each other, contemplating our current situation when we both heard it. Our necks jerked at the sound of the twig snapping and the rustle of a small animal too fast to hunt with a knife. Slowly, I lifted my bow, nocking an arrow to the string, and squinted, focusing on the elongated ears of the rabbit as it nibbled on a sprout of dead grass. The string was taut; my arm was steady, its head was in focus. When I released my hold, the bowstring catapulted the arrow away from the bow, striking the rabbit cleanly through the eye.

A smile broke out across my face, the first in days, as we both raced toward what would now be our dinner. William picked it up by its back feet, looking it up and down. My mouth was already watering.

"I'm not a fan of raw meat," he stated.

We both hesitated. Hopefully we had outrun our pursuers enough that they wouldn't see the smoke, but it was still a risk. I glanced over my shoulder, an action that had become second nature to me, but I came to the conclusion that we might not make it through another cold night without a fire.

"Neither am I," I said.

"I'll skin and gut it."

"I'll build a fire."

I scooped up any bits of dead leaves and small wood for kindling, and then with the flint, I began a small fire, grabbing the nearest sticks to throw into it as it got larger. William was making fast work of the rabbit, and we both watched anxiously as he began to turn the raw meat over the fire. It felt like we were children, watching an entertainer as he breathed fire from his mouth or juggled a dozen oranges in his hands.

"I'm surprised the crown prince knows how to skin and cook a rabbit," I spoke for lack of conversation. We'd barely spoken after escaping Silas and his men. Here we were, stuck with each other in the middle of the wilderness, and I hardly knew him.

"You'd be surprised about a lot of things." William's gaze was focused on our dinner. "But I trained in the army as well as in politics. Out in the field with the other soldiers, you're just like everyone else: no special treatment."

I shot him a funny look. "But what if something happened to you? Aren't you the only heir to the throne?"

"I think my father was more concerned with taming my arrogance." William pulled the rabbit out of the fire, preoccupied. "I'd say that's cooked good enough."

As long as it wasn't raw, there would be no argument from me. The meat was tantalizing, my senses exploding as its flavor reached my tongue. After nearly inhaling the first piece, I forced myself to slow down to savor it. This might be our last meal for a while. The meat was chewy and gamey. It didn't burst with as much flavor as I'd first thought, but in that moment, it was the most glorious food I had ever tasted.

The world seemed to grow dimmer once the meat was gone, but it wasn't as gloomy with food in my belly. I rolled the pouch of gold between my hands, and for lack of anything better to do, poured it out to count it. The firelight glinted off the gold, but an imposter was hidden within the treasure. Like a starving thief swiping a loaf of bread, I snatched it from the golden pile, cradling the familiar object in my hands. I quickly slipped my father's ring onto my hand, afraid it would vanish again if it left my sight. The circlet of gold brought a sense of comfort to me as I studied it. I hadn't expected to ever see it again.

"For someone who doesn't hold their father in very high regard, you seem quite attached to that ring."

I met William's observing look studying me from the other side of the fire and then took in the ring again. Why was I so attached to it? I twirled it around my finger, the firelight glinting off its golden exterior.

"It was the last thing he gave me."

I knew that wasn't the reason I kept it, but the statement was true. When my father had come to see me for the very last time, somber and travel-worn, I had refused to even make eye contact. As he'd left, he set his ring in the center of our table. For weeks I'd refused to touch it, to even look at it—until I learned of his death. That was when I had put it on and determined never to take it off. I suppose that was why I had held onto it so closely. When I had forsaken the ring, it was a picture of me forsaking him, but when I learned he was dead … the guilt of not looking him in the eye, of refusing to speak with him, it was as if keeping this ring was the only way to make amends. As if treasuring it would redeem me for not treasuring him.

"Gharridan adored your father." Curiosity welled in William's voice. "Why do you hate him so much?"

At his words, my arms folded in front of me protectively. This was not something I had ever spoken of. I'd merely let it fester in my mind for years. My mouth grew dry, my throat constricting to stop the words, but for whatever reason, they came flowing out.

"Because my father abandoned me."

I'd never said those words aloud, and it felt as if a heavy weight had been lifted from my chest, like I'd been drowning for years and just gulped in my first breath of air.

"As a child, I saw him very little, but when my—" My voice faltered. "After my mother died, I never saw him again until shortly before his death. Every few months, the money still came, but he never did. It planted a seed of doubt, making me wonder if my mother was the only reason he'd ever come at all."

My arms squeezed my legs tighter. Those days had been agony. I'd been reeling from my mother's death, alone in the world, with no one to comfort me. Lidia, the sweet widow next door, took me in, but my father had disappeared. I shifted uncomfortably, debating whether or not to go on.

"How did you feel when he died?" William asked.

I raised my head stubbornly. "It felt like a massive burden had been lifted from my shoulders."

No longer would I have to endure the pain of his abandonment, face the longing of wishing he was there or spending my days wondering and worrying if he would ever come home again. There would be no more constant tug on my emotions.

It was over.

"I told myself his passing was for the better; I could finally move on with my life. He always said that he only ever wished for my happiness. To me, his death was a release. I was ready to move on with my life, but then Vladimir found me." I paused, recalling his haunting words. "When he told me that my father had been murdered, guilt rushed over me. Before knowing that, I'd been ecstatic at his death. This news nearly made me sick; I didn't know if I could live with myself. But then Vladimir needed help to bring his killer to justice, and I convinced myself that avenging his death would appease the guilt."

We sat quietly for a moment.

"Why did your father never return after your mother's death?" William's voice was gentle.

"I don't know." I shrugged. "His words were dripping with apologies, but he never gave me an explanation, not even before his death. I never knew where he lived or what trade he practiced. Neither he nor my mother ever told me."

William's expression overflowed with surprise. "You were never aware of your father's position?"

I shook my head. "If my mother was aware, she never disclosed it to me. My father refused to tell."

When I was a child, I convinced myself the reason he didn't stay for very long was because he didn't love us enough, but now I wondered if the reason he stayed away was *because* he loved us so much. I was never able to decide what had hurt more: that my father was never around, or that he never told us why he wasn't around.

"Your parents," William asked slowly. "Were they, were they married?"

His question offended me at first, but then I realized how it must look with my father sneaking away to meet a woman in secret, and I nodded. My mother had not been a mistress. Whenever she was nervous, she would twirl the braided silver band around her finger and look out the window, waiting for my father to come home.

"What was her name?"

"Evelyn," I said softly. "Evelyn Gallows."

Stryder gave a low whicker, and I glanced at where he was grazing. "That's where I was headed when I left home. To find her family. She always spoke of Dalendria in the north."

William's brows knit together. "You asked about that place before, didn't you? In the library?"

"Yes," I said. "No one seems to know where it is."

The crackling fire filled the silence between us as I contemplated our conversation. I'd never spoken that openly with anyone before, and I wrapped my cloak tighter around me, feeling vulnerable. William and I were stuck in this together, but I wasn't sure how trustworthy he was.

"I just can't wrap my head around the fact that Michael was married, or that he kept it a secret."

William's words caught me off guard.

"Do the Kavari not marry?"

William shrugged. "There's no law that prevents it; it's just very unusual. The Kavari travel quite a bit and don't stay in one place for very long. That tends to put a lot of strain on any kind of relationship."

I knew my mother was lonely, but she had never spoken one unkind word about my father, even when it was months before he came to see us.

I cocked my head, realizing that William himself had also lost a parent.

"Were you close with your father?" I knew little about the king's death, other than it was unexpected. William would've been barely older than a boy at the time.

At my question, William's face became rigid, a myriad of emotions. Loss, anger, resentment, and pain flashed across his face simultaneously.

"Yes," he managed.

There was something more to his answer, but he looked so tormented I was afraid to say anything else. My gaze fell to the flames, avoiding his eyes. Did he resent his father too? Across the fire, William shifted to a different sitting position.

"I was very close with my father." He brought his eyes to mine. "And then Katherine killed him."

CHAPTER THIRTY-ONE

Taryn

WILLIAM'S WORDS SENT an icy shock through my system, freezing every limb in my body like a frosty winter morning. I shook my head, sure that I had misheard him. Katherine couldn't have killed the king of Gharridan.

"What do you mean she killed him?"

A bitter laugh escaped William's throat, and he looked up at me. "Even in the farthest corners of Gharridan, surely you would have heard about his death."

My confused expression prompted an explanation from William.

"I'm sure you know that Katherine is a Radonaya, a 'healer' as some used to call it, but you would know that because of her blood-red hair. You can spot a Radonaya a mile away."

I simply nodded, refraining from mentioning that the first time I'd heard of the Radonaya was when Katherine told me. Her words echoed in my head.

It's not magic, it—it's something else.

Why do they treat you with disdain, Katherine?

Because I wasn't able to save someone, and they never forgave me for it.

That must be what William was referring to. Katherine hadn't been able to save his father, and in his mind, that meant she had sealed his fate.

"Michael had just chosen Katherine as the next Kavari, which in and of itself caused major backlash. Neither the council nor the country was happy he'd chosen a woman."

"Let me guess—she was the first."

William nodded. "It took them a while to agree to it."

No one had welcomed me with open arms either, and I wondered if the council wouldn't have balked as much had I been born a son instead of a daughter.

"Several weeks before my father died, he fell very ill. I'd never seen him sick like that before, and it scared me. Despite everything the physician tried, the fever would not leave my father, and he was unable to even rise from his bed. Several more physicians were called upon, but no one could figure out what was wrong with him. Any treatment they tried only seemed to make his illness worse.

"Katherine was young and inexperienced at the time, but those she had healed fared well. After he failed to improve with all the traditional methods, she was called upon one evening to attend to my father. We all watched expectantly as she sat beside him on the bed, placing her hands on him in a healing manner.

Even Katherine looked doubtful at first, but when my father's eyes fully opened for the first time in days, it dared to give us hope.

"The following morning, he was sitting up in bed, having returned to his jovial self and feeling better than he had in weeks. Katherine was praised for her work, her favor growing with the council, but that night my father grew worse again, much worse than ever before. When she was called upon again, Katherine was very reluctant as she'd never had to lay hands on someone a second time, nor had we ever heard of someone requiring a Radonaya's healing twice. After initial contact, my father showed no signs of improvement, but Katherine assured us he would be fine. My mother stayed beside him that night and was awakened in the morning by the servants to find him dead."

As William spoke, the pain and grief in his voice slowly transformed until every word was festering with bitterness and malice. It stemmed from his hatred that was directed at Katherine. Looking at it from the outside, it appeared to me that William's father had simply been too far gone for Katherine to help, yet William was firm in the conviction that Katherine was guilty of murder. I chose my next words carefully.

"Could the illness simply have been too far gone for her to heal him?" I asked.

William looked at me seriously. "The thing about the Radonaya, Taryn, is they can't just haphazardly bestow healing—it has to be a deliberate choice. In order for her to heal someone, Katherine has to willingly choose to do so. Their life is in her hands. For reasons that are beyond me, Katherine did not want to heal my father. She wanted him to die."

I refused to believe it. The woman he described to me was not the Katherine I knew and had grown to respect. Though she kept her emotions under tight control, she was not without care. She was not a murderer.

Or was she?

Katherine had said herself the Radonaya were looked upon as either a sign of life or a symbol of death. She could've been referring to what William had just revealed, but something was missing here. It didn't make sense. Why would Katherine want the king to die? What would the motive be? Her job was to protect the Crown. She'd been chosen to be a Kavari. There was no reason for her to risk losing that. If it was merely a matter of her choice, then why had she chosen to heal me? She'd never seemed very happy about me joining the Kavari.

"Katherine was the reason my mother lost her respect for the Kavari. Michael swayed the council and brought Katherine into the Kavari against my mother's advisement, refusing to renounce her after she killed my father. While she still held respect for his position, my mother felt she could no longer trust Michael's judgment."

The queen sounded too emotional to have made a rational decision at that time, but I could see why she had fought so hard to place her choice of candidate in the Kavari this time. In her eyes, the Kavari were the ones who had brought death upon her family.

"If it was truly Katherine's fault, wouldn't she have been convicted?" I asked.

"The council merely brushed it off as an accidental tragedy due to her inexperience, arguing that she had healed him the first time and perhaps he was even beyond saving. Radonaya are known for healing flesh wounds, not internal ones."

William was convinced that what he spoke was truth, yet from what I knew of Katherine, she didn't seem capable of this. It was strange that neither Vladimir nor Katherine had ever mentioned it. I doubted they held the same beliefs as William.

"You don't believe me, do you?"

Reluctantly, I met William's eyes, unsure of how to answer. William was convincing, but there had to be another side to the story.

"I don't know what to believe anymore."

And I didn't.

William looked away from me in frustration. I settled down for the night, contemplating his words as I turned my back to the fire.

"Be careful of Katherine," he warned.

Both the royalty and the Kavari were firm in their beliefs, but one of them was wrong. The fear of ending up on the wrong side gripped me. For the first time since his death, I wished that my father were here, to hear his wisdom on the matter if only for a moment. He had a talent for finding the correct solution to a problem after careful evaluation of both sides of the argument. Surely he had known the truth about this. Katherine would not have been left in the Kavari if she were guilty. I feared this hatred for Katherine stemmed from the need to blame someone when the king had died. Perhaps there was a way to clear her name of this accusation once and for all. If anyone had known a way, it would have been my father, but I had already learned that my father had taken far too many secrets to the grave.

Strange dreams filled my sleep that night, dreams of captivity, of ropes that burned my skin and blinding light that healed the wounds. They shifted and changed until I knelt over William, a gaping wound in his side. Katherine stood over us, her eyes filled with disdain as I begged her to heal him. She turned and walked away as William lay dying in my arms.

I awoke with a start. My dress clung to my sweaty back even though it was freezing outside. William was already awake, dousing the fire and preparing the horses. The path behind us still lay barren, but the farther we got from here, the better.

Our conversation from the previous night was never mentioned as we rode throughout the day. I was relieved. William was sensitive to the subject, and as I didn't know where I stood on the matter, it was best to leave it alone.

There was still no sign of our captors, and our spirits lightened. The intensity and fear of the last few days slowly faded away into memory as we replaced the quietness with small conversations that sparked between us.

"Stryder is a very beautiful horse," William commented. "Where did he come from?"

I gazed down at Stryder's wavy black mane, his ears swiveling back as if listening to our conversation. "He comes from Adellaia."

William's eyebrows rose. "Only the finest horses come from Adellaia, and that's if you can convince an Adellaion to sell you one."

"What do you mean?" I looked up.

"The Adellaions are extremely possessive of their steeds. My father was given one as a gift, but yours is the only one besides Michael's that I've ever seen."

I peered back to Stryder. I'd always been aware that he was

more than the average horse, but I'd never taken his value into consideration. I blinked, wondering what my father had done to attain him.

"Do you know what happened to my father's horse?"

William thought for a moment and then shook his head. "I'm not sure that he was still there when—" William halted. "When he found your father. You'd have to ask Vladimir."

Zedekiah would've known his worth. The horse was probably sold long ago.

"Did you train him yourself?" William asked.

I nodded. "My father brought him to me eight years ago when he was just a yearling. Stryder possessed so much spirit that I didn't know if we were going to make it, but we worked through it, and he turned out better than I could've ever hoped."

"Impressive." William patted Othello's neck. "I also trained Othello myself. All it took was patience and several mouthfuls of dirt."

I cocked an eyebrow. "The crown prince doesn't have horse masters to train his steeds for him?"

William scoffed. "I can't have others do *everything* for me. I'd be a helpless wit."

I smiled. It felt odd. We had just been prisoners for days, and now we were wandering the wilderness unsure of where we were. He was the crown prince and I ... well, I wasn't quite sure what I was, but we talked, and we laughed. William went on without a care in the world, like we were going for an afternoon ride. It was funny, yet the reprieve of seriousness felt incredibly lovely. Our real circumstances might have been forgotten if it hadn't been for our growling stomachs.

"Are you sure this is the way?" I asked.

William looked off in the distance. "I've never been sure."

It had been three days with no food. Finally seeing civilization in the distance was like finding a pool of water in the middle of the desert. White flakes descended from the sky, carpeting the landscape in a sheet of endless white. Hunger grew in my belly as exhaustion threatened to overtake me. By the time we reached the village, the steady stream of flurries had slowed, but it rose past my ankles when I dropped from the saddle.

With chattering teeth, I pulled my cloak tightly around me. There wasn't much to the town or people. I had never seen such poverty before. Defeated faces paid no attention to us as they hurried by in layer upon layer of tattered clothes. The houses were no better. Most stood in shambles. Where entire planks of wood were missing, some had shoved blankets through or across the hole to keep out the cold. Roofs caved in with splintered wood jutting to the sky, yet smoke still rose from the chimneys.

Friendliness did not exist here, and our presence seemed to go completely unnoticed. William approached a man, and he ignored us as if we weren't even there. William and I exchanged confused glances as we moved on.

"At least no one will recognize you," I said. "They won't even look at you."

William searched up and down the street. "I'm more concerned about there not being any food to buy. These people won't have much to spare."

He handed his reins to me. "Wait here. If trouble stirs, get out."

Snow crunched beneath his boots as he strode away, leaving a trail of footprints behind. I glanced at the road behind us, ever afraid of hearing a thundering of hooves evidencing that Silas and his men had caught up with us. The road held no pursuers, yet a dark feeling that they were still chasing us hovered over me.

My eyes wandered, coming to rest on a woman sitting on a porch. Several shawls were wrapped around her shoulders, and grey hairs peeked out from underneath a tattered hat and shabby scarf. I found myself wishing I had something to spare. The beginnings of a blanket lay in her lap as she worked her needles, the yarn weaving together in between them.

I led the horses over to her and nodded my head in hello. She ignored me. No attention was to be spared from her knitting. Her eyes were dull, looking but not seeing. They paid no attention to the project before her, but she carried on without a mistake.

Farther down the street, William walked into a shop, and my stomach growled, hoping he would be able to find food. A strange contraption across the street caught my attention, drawing my eyes in. It appeared to be a basket, but upside down and larger than any I had ever seen. Something stirred within its confines, and my eyes widened in horror when the mass rolled over.

It was a man.

His body shook with tremors, the thin tunic barely covering him and not at all conducive to the weather. I felt for the knife at my side, taking a step forward to cut him free.

"Good day to you."

The voice startled me, and I turned, realizing it had come from the older woman. Her needles were still knitting together furiously in her hands.

"Good day," I managed, not quite sure how to respond. The horror of the man freezing to death in the snow haunted me.

"Not worth it," the woman croaked. "He's a murderer, that one."

I turned back to the helpless man.

"Murdered Binniker in his sleep, he did." The intonation in her voice distracted me.

Never once did her gaze leave her work as she spoke, yet I still felt as if her eyes were boring into me. The needles switched hands as she began the next row of yarn.

"No authority to bring justice to him here, so he must wait for justice. Eventually, they will come to take him to the prison. The prison in the north."

Her speech was halting as she stopped between phrases. I looked back at the caged man. He wouldn't last another night in there. That in itself might be justice. Whatever authorities this town was waiting on would only find a stiff, frozen body.

"The same prison they took one of your kind to. One that came through a few weeks ago."

I wondered if she meant another woman or if she had just gone mad. Her head shook back and forth.

"He was in rough shape when they dragged him through town. Passed right by here. Wouldn't have given him a second thought if it hadn't been for the ring."

My eyes shot up to meet hers, and I fought the urge to touch the ring encircling my finger. Her needles stilled as she stared at the ring, then returned to her work. She knew what I was—or what I appeared to be. My gaze flitted around nervously, but she did not betray my identity.

The ring.

There was only one person she could possibly be referring to.

Marco.

No one else would have come through this town. It couldn't have been Vladimir or Katherine. The timeline was off. It had to be Marco. I tightened my grip on Stryder's reins, and the woman gave me a stern look.

"They wanted something from him. Weren't very nice to him neither, but nothing any of us could do."

Marco was still alive.

"The prison in the north, where is it?" I asked urgently.

"Outside of Gapsvar." Her dull eyes flicked up to the sky. "A nasty storm is coming."

Footsteps crunched behind us in the snow, and the woman quickly gathered her work, shuffling stiffly into the house and bolting the door behind her. The approaching man surveyed the horses, his hungry gaze unsettling me, and I moved them farther down the street.

I threw one last look at the criminal freezing in the snow. Marco had been here. In that very spot. Marco, who possessed the document that was so critical to the country's survival. Zedekiah had killed my father and captured Marco. When he fled the throne room, he wasn't running away from the capital. He was running toward something. If I found Marco, I would find Zedekiah.

"We need to go."

William stuffed the food into our saddlebags and then threw something toward me that I quickly snatched. Gloves. I slipped them over my hands, grateful for the extra warmth.

"Do you know where we are?" My mind was still on the prison, but more importantly, on how to get there.

"Let's get out of here first." William swung up onto Othello and urged him toward the edge of town. Once we were a good way past the final houses, I pulled Stryder up beside him.

"We're not where I thought we were," William said, "but we're close to the border of Brenden. The merchant I spoke with said that if we headed straight southeast, we should come upon a trading route that will lead us back to the capital, getting us there in three, maybe four, weeks."

William urged Othello forward, and I hurried to keep up.

"But what about Zedekiah?" I asked.

"There's no way to track Zedekiah. We need to get back to the capital as quickly as possible and report what happened."

He was right. We had no way of tracking Zedekiah, but we did have a way to rescue Marco, and Marco could possibly lead us to him.

"Do you think Vladimir and Katherine were captured as well?" I asked.

"There's no way to know or find them."

I realized I would be doing this on my own. William wanted to get out of this countryside and with good reason, but I was not ready to give up yet.

"Where is Gapsvar?"

William threw a strange glance at me. "They wouldn't be in Gapsvar."

He wasn't going to escape the question. "Where is it,

William?"

"Why do you want to know?" William was catching on.

I said nothing but lifted my eyebrows, waiting for a response.

William jerked his head in the opposite direction. "I think it's that way. I've never been there but going there would do us no good. Now if we hurry, we might be able to find the road before nightfall."

I halted Stryder, Othello's hooves crunching several paces farther in the snow before William realized we'd stopped.

"I'm not going back to the capital," I stated.

His face clouded over as he turned Othello to face me. "What are you talking about?"

I watched closely for his reaction. "Marco is in a prison outside Gapsvar."

William shifted his grip on the reins. "How do you know?"

"The woman in the village." I lifted my chin. "She recognized my ring. Whoever captured Marco took him through here several weeks ago."

William shrugged. "That old woman? How do you know she was telling the truth?"

Heat rushed to my face. "That would be quite a specific and coincidental lie to weave. That *old woman* recognized my father's ring and linked it to the prisoner who was dragged through town. They abducted Marco because he knew something critical. Wherever he is, Zedekiah can't be far behind."

William's expression darkened as he realized where my thoughts were headed.

"Do you really believe Marco is still alive?" He brought Othello up to Stryder and got in my face, his voice low. "He was captured weeks ago; whatever information he held has already been tortured out. They killed him just like they killed your father. There's nothing you can do for him. I want Zedekiah dead too, but going after him with only two people and a pack of pursuers at our back is a fool's mission."

Anger surged within me. "They didn't capture my father, William; they murdered him."

I took a shuddering breath before continuing. "My father deserves as much justice as the men who died in the throne room and the ten soldiers that Silas and his men killed. There's no place for me in the capital, and I refuse to hide behind stone walls like a coward when I have the ability to do something about it."

"You think I'm a coward for returning to the capital?" William laughed in disbelief. "A coward for not embarking on a suicide mission into dangerous territory—with no hope of success—and only the daughter of a dead Kavari for protection?"

"I won't rest until Zedekiah is dead." My voice remained firm.

"What's your big plan?" He asked incredulously and threw his hands in the air. "Waltz into the prison and demand Marco's freedom? Gapsvar hates Gharridan, Taryn. You wouldn't make it past the outer gates!"

I didn't have a plan, but that didn't matter right now. All that mattered was getting to Gapsvar. Figuring out a way to get Marco out would come later. The stream of words flowing from William's mouth spoke reason, but I'd had enough of reason, and I knew what my gut was telling me. I had to at least try.

I looked past William, my mind made up. "I'm not asking you to come with me."

"I have a duty to my country!" William yelled. "And so do you!"

Fury lit within me. "I have no duty to anyone, William! I did not take the oath of the Kavari. The only oath I swore was to bring my father's murderer to justice!"

The world hushed around us, so quiet the sound of the snowflakes hitting the ground was almost audible. We stood there in the frozen landscape, two opposites facing each other. Stryder's dark coat stood out while Othello's blended in. Our eyes locked. Our desires, once intertwined in search of the same thing, were now unwinding and departing down separate roads. William was just as set in his decision as I, and I knew that neither of us would sway the other. This was not a task I wanted to carry out on my own, but I would.

I set my jaw, firm in my decision. William shook his head disapprovingly, recognizing the determination in me and turning Othello back toward the capital.

"This is a death sentence, Gallows."

I caught his gaze again, holding it as I turned Stryder around. "Good luck, William."

I kicked Stryder forward and refused to glance over my shoulder as we trotted away. This was something that I had to do. Finding both Zedekiah and Marco wasn't very likely, but dying for something was better than living for nothing.

The air was thick with snow, the flakes assaulting my eyes like tiny pins, the pure number of them making it difficult to see. I pulled my cloak tighter and my hood lower, grateful for the gloves that provided the extra warmth. For the first time since I'd left my home, I was completely alone in the world again.

Guilt lingered over me for leaving the crown prince to cross the wilderness on his own, but I owed nothing to Gharridan. The only promise I had made was to Vladimir. Seeking justice against Zedekiah was a way of fulfilling that promise. I was helping him find my father's killer, and if I didn't find Zedekiah with Marco, then I would hunt him down until I did.

CHAPTER THIRTY-TWO

Vladimir

AN ICY DRIZZLE descended from the black clouds, dripping misery onto our hopeless outlook. The world was a dreary sight, the weather promising that this evening would be a chilling and rather drenching affair. Water continued to slide off my cloak, but I could feel splotches of cold where it was slowly beginning to soak through the thick wool.

It must have been weeks, yet still no sign of Zedekiah. Day after day, we never grew one step closer but faithfully remained one step behind. Even tracking after dark was useless. Barely covering a mile had taken hours. It was like they knew exactly how far ahead to stay, because the tracks never grew fresher the next morning, as if some dark wind carried a message warning of our coming.

A water droplet slid down a leaf, its weight bending the petal until the liquid plopped onto my hand. I shook it off in irritation. What I wouldn't give for a warm place to sleep and a full meal. My gaze roved over the haggard traveling companions surrounding me. What we all wouldn't give. Dark circles hung below their vacant eyes, bodies slouched low in the saddle, and cloaks pulled tightly around their hungry bodies. Too many days had passed since the last decent meal, and there was no hope for when the next one might come.

I couldn't wait to get my hands on Zedekiah.

Melvin hadn't discovered anything from the soldiers accompanying them. So far, they all appeared to be trustworthy. The picture of Jakob's lifeless body splayed out before the steps of the dais flashed in my mind. He'd been young, and he'd been new. I shuffled my memories of the throne room together. I'd been so focused on Zedekiah and Taryn that I hadn't gotten a good look at the others who had betrayed Gharridan, but I recalled two others. Both young. Both new. I wondered if Captain Verone had found any connections yet and what kind of information he had uncovered.

I looked up from the faint trail, catching a visual distortion farther ahead. My lifted hand halted the company as I moved Dante to higher ground. The disturbance appeared to be a cloud of smoke worming its way up into the sky.

"What is it?" Katherine asked.

I ignored her, climbing higher until we finally made enough ground to see over the ridge. A rush of excitement beat through my chest. The plume of smoke multiplied into many, and the faint outline of a small village materialized through the hazy mist.

I loped back down the hill, my refreshed expression eliciting hope in the men's faces.

"Melvin," I said, "I want you and Bog to come with me. There's a small village where we should be able to get supplies. Katherine, you and the rest of the men continue tracking the trail. We'll catch up with you by nightfall."

I sat up straight in the saddle as we rode away, a welcome relief after hours of leaning forward to scour the ground for tracks. While the dimness of the world made it difficult to tell, I guessed we had maybe one or two hours of daylight left.

As we entered the town, suspicious eyes peeked out at us from underneath layers of fur, watching us as they made their way through the streets. The three of us split up, each with a different task and destination.

"Meet back here within the hour," I said.

Dante sloshed through the street, flinging up mud as I searched the buildings. I found the wooden sign, engraved with a loaf of bread and a trickle of steam, swinging in the wind. Fog coated the window from the frigid air colliding with the heat of the stoves inside. When I opened the door, the smell alone was enough to bring me to my knees, my mouth watering and stomach growling at the sight of the fresh bread lining the shelves.

I stepped inside and was plowed into by a man, the force knocking my hood back. His eyes met mine for a brief moment before he darted away.

"Excuse me, sir." He dipped his head, ducking out the door.

The wrinkles on the baker's face increased as he frowned at our collision, even though we were nowhere near the shelves of bread.

"Good afternoon," I said, moving forward to place my order. I glanced over my shoulder, watching through the foggy window as the man turned to the right. His face jogged something in my memory, but I couldn't place him. I leaned over the counter, replaying his face over and over in my mind, sure that I knew him. There was a familiarity in his rounded face and the way his eyebrows stuck out farther than the rest of his skull—

The realization hit me like a stone wall.

I rushed out of the store, the baker calling after me as I frantically searched the street for any sign of the man. Through the drizzling rain, I caught sight of a travel-worn cloak disappearing into an alley farther down the street. The freezing downpour soaked my hair as a mixture of water and tiny ice pellets beat against my head. Hot blood pumped furiously through every vein in my body like air into a furnace. The weather covered the sound of my footsteps as I came up behind him in the alley. The hooded figure slowly began to turn, and I grabbed him, shoving him up against the alley wall. His cry was lost in the downpour and cut off at the sight of me.

"I wouldn't do that if I were you, Randal."

The shadowed face paled in the darkness, his wild eyes filling with horror.

"Sir Vladimir, please, I don't want any trouble."

"Where's your brother?" I demanded.

He quickly shook his head. "I don't know. I swear I don't."

I clenched my jaw, my fists shaking as they gripped his shoulders. "You told Gavil you would speak to your brother."

"I did speak to him."

I raised an eyebrow, waiting for his answer. "And?"

He hesitated, then furiously shook his head, panic racing through him. "He won't come forward. Not after Michael was killed. It's too risky."

The leader of the Kavari had been murdered. Marco was taken. Mordakai was struck down—but Zedekiah had been discovered.

"Zedekiah murdered Michael. He betrayed our country and killed his brother Mordakai to hide it, but we're tracking him down now. He will be brought to justice. If your brother was afraid of Zedekiah, he'll be safe now. We can protect him."

Randal's eyes widened, and he tried to pull away from me. My anger and firm grip kept him in place.

"This had nothing to do with Zedekiah," he panted, "but Jarrod's never going to come forward if there's treason in the court."

My hold on him grew slack. Michael had been searching for Jarrod Lynch for years. When Mordakai was killed, I assumed Michael's obsession must have concerned Zedekiah's allegiance, but I began to wonder if I was wrong.

"If this isn't about Zedekiah's allegiance, then what is this about?"

Randal looked in both directions before pursing his lips in defiance.

Slowly I shook my head. "You don't even know, do you?"

I twisted his face into the wall, shoving his arm upward to only stop at the breaking point. He yelled out in pain, squirming beneath my grip.

"I've found you once," I growled through gritted teeth. "You won't be very happy when I find you again. Unless you want your country completely destroyed, you will find your brother, and you will convince him to come forward. If you don't, I will have both of your faces plastered across every city in Gharridan and in every surrounding country with orders to bring you to me either dead or alive."

Randal turned back to me. "Michael never wanted anyone to know he was looking for my brother, he—"

"I'm not Michael!" I yelled into the man's ear, rage emanating in my voice as he shook with fear. I took a deep breath in an attempt to calm myself.

"Find your brother and bring him to me." I let go of his arm and shoved him toward the other end of the alley.

Heat flooded my chest as I stormed back through the increasing downpour to retrieve the bread from the bakery. If Jarrod Lynch's testimony had nothing to do with Zedekiah, then we had another enemy that I was not yet privy to. Why hadn't Michael just told me why he was tracking Jarrod Lynch down? Even after Michael's death, he'd sent Gavil to inform Taryn and me about his discoveries. If Michael had ensured the information's survival without enlightening us, then Jarrod Lynch must still have a critical role to play.

CHAPTER THIRTY-THREE

Taryn

WITH TWO FINGERS, I spun my father's ring around and around, fixated on the shiny metal. What great trouble such a small thing had caused me. It symbolized what had stolen my father from me—the Kavari. If my father had never joined them, how different my life might be. I wondered what it would've been like to grow up without secrecy and never having to wonder whether or not your father was coming back.

"What if I hadn't gone with Vladimir?" I asked aloud into the darkness.

There was no one to answer me.

I could've walked away from Vladimir's offer and continued on my way. I never would've had to deal with any of this, but if I had walked away from Vladimir that day, I knew that I wouldn't have been able to live with myself. The mystery of my father's death would've haunted me for the rest of my life.

I scooted closer to the fire, and the smoke tickled my nose. Vladimir still owed me that clasp and my mother's family name.

If I live to see him again, I thought.

William was probably right about this being a suicide mission, but I didn't care. I would not let fear keep me from finding Zedekiah. I looked to my right, expecting William to be there, but he wasn't. I lay down, pulling my blanket up to my chin. It was strange without William. Angry as I was with him for choosing to go back to the capital, I still missed him. I'd gotten used to his presence out here in the wilderness.

Sleep did not come willingly that night. I tossed and turned, my eyes continually popping open, expecting Silas and his men to be standing at the outskirts of my fire. As soon as morning broke, I packed up camp. Dark thunderclouds billowed directly over where Stryder and I were headed, and I took a deep breath to calm my nerves. It was going to be a long day. I cast a final glance behind me for assurance that I was alone.

My breath caught.

I was not.

Fear seized me as I beheld a group of horsemen riding toward me from the fields below. The vantage point I held looking down from the crest of the hill was also a dead giveaway. Judging by the ferocity with which the horsemen rode, they had already spotted us.

I lurched onto Stryder's back and dug my heels into his side. We shot forward, snow flying around us as we charged toward the approaching blizzard, escaping the clutches of our captors and descending into the belly of the beast.

It was the fiercest wind I had ever experienced. Its hands found their way underneath my clothing, little icicles that stabbed at my skin and chilled me to the bone. My cloak whipped around me in every direction as the wind tore at it like a ravenous wolf, and Stryder and I were left to the mercy of the storm raging around us, a delicate flower in the midst of a raging tempest. We had to find shelter soon. It was no longer a desire but a necessity. If we continued into the night and were still out in this blizzard, I feared we wouldn't survive until morning. I'd seen the distant shadows of the forest when I set up camp last night, but now the snow was up to Stryder's knees, and I couldn't even see ten feet in front of me. I swallowed hard, my mind working quickly as I assessed our situation. I couldn't spot Silas and his men behind me, which meant they couldn't see me, but if they didn't kill me, this blizzard would.

Out of the blinding white suddenly rose a dark form, nearly upon us. My heart pounded hard within my chest, images of Silas filling my mind. The dark form materialized into a man, and he was—*floating* toward us. Above the ground. My stiff limbs couldn't hurry Stryder along fast enough, but it was too late. He was upon us, his white horse completely camouflaged by the blinding snow.

William.

Shock coursed through my veins, and I stared at him. What was he doing here? His mouth kept opening and closing, but no sound came out. A moment later, I realized he was yelling at me, but the wind had swept away all noise except for its own angry voice. My confused expression got through to him, and he waved his arms a little to the right. Part of me wanted to know why William had come back, but at the moment, I didn't care. All that mattered was he had, and I wouldn't have to die alone out here in this white wilderness. It didn't matter if he was leading me back to the capital as long as he knew how to get us out of this storm.

Stryder kept pace beside Othello as they pushed against the wind. William was covered in snow, his golden hair frozen as we kept each other in sight, knowing that if anything happened to either one of us, we wouldn't be able to hear it above the howling wind.

I could feel Stryder shivering beneath me, only continuing on because I pushed him. The severity of our situation was growing greater with every second, and anxiety rose within me. White was the only thing left to see as the biting wind fought against us, making it impossible to move the horses any faster. My teeth were chattering so hard that pain was beginning to shoot into my jaw.

We were going to die out here.

Heat flared in my chest at the helplessness of our situation. I did not come all this way, surviving attempted assassinations and escaping thieves and mercenaries, just to die in a snowstorm. Dying was supposed to mean something.

This meant nothing.

I cried out to God asking for help, asking for anything, and that was when I saw it. Another dark shape began to form in front of us, and hope rose in my chest. It was a tree trunk. I saw several more forms just within sight—which wasn't far. Excitement swelled in my heart as we entered the tree line. It deferred the wind slightly, offering a welcome reprieve from its icy fingers, but we still desperately needed shelter. The trees would not be enough.

Massive round objects came into the path several times, and I realized they were giant boulders. Occasional clusters of them offered a small space, but none were big enough for two people, let alone two horses.

A rather large boulder came up on our left, stacked with what appeared to be several other rocks. I placed a hand on William's arm, alerting him to its presence, and we moved over to it. Once we were in front of the grouping, I could see the dark space. The boulders blocked the wind, and the way in which the rocks were piled created a cave that nestled between the boulders and the hillside. It wasn't large, but it was tall enough for the horses and deep enough to get out of the wind. The cave was mostly devoid of snow except for a light dusting that the fierce wind had managed to blow in.

When I hopped off Stryder, such pain jolted up my legs that, for a moment, I thought I had broken them. They had gone completely numb. I clutched at Stryder for support as I led him to the back of the cave where he and Othello bunched together for warmth as I brushed the snow from their coats.

A few crisp leaves had blown into the dark corners, and I grabbed them, searching for any other pine needles or snapped twigs on the cave floor as William began breaking pieces from a dead tree that had fallen halfway into the cave. I nearly cried with relief when I saw the first flame of fire. It wouldn't last long, but I hoped it would at least keep us alive for another hour.

William and I huddled together in front of the fire, trying to absorb each other's warmth as well as the heat from the flames. The raging storm outside was lashing out like a venomous snake. This fire was our antidote.

"I thought," I began, but had to get my chattering teeth under control before continuing. "I thought you had a d-duty to your c-country."

"I do." William's teeth were chattering just as hard as mine.

I looked over at him. "W-why did you turn around?"

William was quiet for a moment, his silence worrying me. "When I reached the top of the hill, I looked back. You were no longer in sight, but the town was still barely outlined in the distance. I saw a group of horsemen leaving the town, and fast. I don't know how they managed, but they must have tracked us down."

My heart sank, realizing that if this storm didn't throw them off our trail, then nothing else would. "You could've kept going."

"Trust me, I thought about it."

That sounded more like William.

"But I don't think I could have lived with myself if I'd left you at their mercy."

"How did you get around Silas?" I asked.

"That's why it took so long. I was afraid if they saw me that they might split up. I stayed behind the group until there was enough foliage to hide behind in order to circle around them. I think they finally saw me before the snow grew too thick. I tried yelling for you, but the wind didn't blow in my favor. Once the storm picked up, I wasn't sure if I'd be able to find you."

"How did you find me?" I didn't understand how he had managed to find the one spot where I was. All I'd been able to see was white.

Next to me, I felt William shrug. "I prayed."

I rubbed my arms, surprised. William didn't trust in anyone but himself.

We leaned against each other, the chattering of our teeth fading. The wind howled outside the cave, an angry fury enraged that its victims had escaped. Exhaustion was threatening to take over, and I finally gave in, my eyes fluttering shut.

When I awoke, I was lying on the cold earth. The horses slowly came into focus, still huddled along the back wall. Our proximity was so close that if anything spooked them, William and I would most likely be trampled to death. I felt the empty space where William had been and found him leaning against the wall; his eyes focused on the storm outside. The wind had abated, but it was still howling. We were snowed into the cave. Only two feet of the outside world was still visible between the snow drift and ceiling.

While the storm was still terrifying, I felt safe within the security of our cave. Freezing to death was still a possibility, but the rate of survival was higher in here. The wall of snow trapped our body heat inside the cave, and with two horses and two humans, it wasn't near as cold as I'd expected. I was still gripped by fear, thinking about what would come after the storm passed. If the snow would be too deep to dig through. If our captors discovered us.

I looked over at William, who was so lost in thought that he hadn't noticed I was awake. His eyes stared bleakly into the sky. Within their depths, I sensed a vulnerability that had never been present before. William was a difficult person to read. He was hardly ever serious, hiding his true feelings beneath a layer of jokes and sarcasm. I'd never seen the unguarded expression that currently encompassed his face.

"What are you afraid of, William?" The question escaped my lips before I could stop it.

His fatigued gaze ripped to mine, eyebrows pulling low over his hazel eyes. "What do you mean?"

I knew what I had meant, but couldn't quite put my thoughts into words. "You go about life fearlessly as if you don't have a care in the world, but you do care."

A smile twitched at his lips before quickly disappearing as he turned away. "Why do you want to know?"

Because I wanted to figure him out. I wanted to know why he had forsaken the duty to his country by coming after me. Beneath all of the arrogance and indifference lurked something he refused to let out. I chewed on my lip, unable to formulate an answer.

William cast his eyes downward to the fire, staring into its flames. Time moved on, but he didn't speak. I shifted. He wasn't going to answer me.

"I'm afraid of failing my father."

He said it so bluntly. How old was William when his father died?

I proceeded with my next words cautiously. "How could you fail your father?"

William hugged his knees to his chest and rested his chin. I wondered if this was a protective stance or if he was just chilled. "My father was one of the greatest leaders our country has ever known. A kind, just, merciful king." He trailed off. "He cared about the people of Gharridan and did everything he could to protect them and to keep the peace. He possessed so much wisdom at a level I can't even begin to fathom. He always knew what to say and the best possible way of approaching it."

The same could be said about my father.

"The people's love for him was unmatched. When he died... ambassadors said they'd never seen a people mourn for their king as greatly as ours did. My father, he was just *good*. I don't see how I'm going to measure up."

At least I'd been given a choice, in a way, of whether or not I wanted to follow in my father's footsteps. Before William was born, his fate had already been decided. He didn't have a choice in the matter.

"You have the desire to do what is right," I said. "That's one of the greatest qualities you can possess. You sought justice for the men killed in the courtroom, and you came back for me when you saw Silas. From what I've seen, you have a passion for your people. I think you'll be an outstanding king."

William laughed, the seriousness fading from his voice. "That's the thing. You didn't know me before. If you had, you wouldn't have said that. People still judge me from when I was younger." William cocked his head slightly. "I was not the most, shall we say, 'well-behaved' prince."

My eyes rolled mockingly. "The William I know would *never* break protocol."

A smile crept up his face. "Obviously. I may or may not have nearly burned down the castle at one point."

I flew upright. "You what?"

William's laughter continued. "Mind you, I was ten, and quite bored with practicing archery on immobile objects. Flaming arrows made it much more interesting, especially when I made targets out of the birds flying overhead."

My mouth dropped. "Where was your teacher?"

"Not present." William smirked. "I was far from a skilled archer, and one of the arrows ended up flying through a castle window—straight into my mother's favorite tapestry. Thankfully, the servants were able to stifle the fire before it spread too far, but the tapestry and a large part of that hallway were destroyed."

"That's terrible!" I laughed and covered my mouth. The humor seemed inappropriate, but William was laughing with me.

"The worst part," he continued, "is that no questions were asked, and I was simply summoned to the courtroom because my mother already knew I was somehow involved."

A picture developed in my mind of a younger William walking into the throne room, attempting to hide the grin on his face, most likely covered in soot, as he stood before his scowling mother.

"She's still as disappointed with me now as she was back then."

"What does she have to be disappointed about?"

William chuckled nervously. "My existence."

I'd never heard William talk about his mother like this before, and I wasn't sure where he was headed.

"When my father died—" He hesitated. "I don't think she was ready to rule. She took his death very hard; we all did, but my father was her whole world. They first met when she came here seeking asylum after her kingdom was overthrown. My mother had no one left, but then my father became her family, and he was her rock. After he was gone, it took a while for her to adjust, but she managed and has turned into a wonderful queen. Her focus is now on grooming me for the throne, making sure I'm completely ready. Whenever I screw up, though, she's very short on patience. I messed up plenty as a child, and my father would set me straight. However, he was still encouraging and forgiving. With my mother, there's never any room for mistakes."

My parents had always been gracious with my mistakes as a child. I may have never burned down a castle, but I'd never felt like I was unable to meet the expectations they set before me.

"My mother will have my hide when I get back to the capital. She was adamant I not be a part of this mission."

We'd been gone for weeks. That would hopefully provide plenty of time for her emotions to simmer down. "Well, whatever she thinks, I'm glad you came. I probably wouldn't be alive right now if you hadn't."

"You wouldn't have made it past the first day."

I raised an eyebrow. "Thanks for the vote of confidence."

William scooted closer to the fire, eyeing me. "What about you, Gallows—what are you afraid of?"

My gaze drifted to Stryder before falling on my father's ring. What was I afraid of? I was afraid I would never find my mother's family, that I would wake one morning to realize I would forever be alone in the world. And still, I knew there was something scarier looming before me.

"That this guilt will haunt me for the rest of my life because I won't be able to bring my father's murderer to justice."

The crackle of the dying flames filled the quietness that followed, its death darkening the cave and elongating the shadows on the walls. I felt like the darkness was going to smother me, just like the guilt was beginning to choke the life out of me.

"Your father would forgive you, Taryn."

I met his eyes. He believed his words, but my father's forgiveness wasn't the issue.

"I would never be able to forgive myself."

It wasn't his forgiveness that I cared about. Everything I had recently learned about my father had challenged me to change my view of him, but even for all the good he had done, there was still no explanation for his abandonment of me. That was something I could never forgive. I didn't feel guilty for hating him; I felt guilty for pushing him out when he knew he was about to die.

"How long do you think the storm will last?" I asked.

William cast a glance at the wicked storm outside. "Hours. Days. There's not really any way to tell."

"If we make it out of this, do you think Silas will find us again?"

William leaned against the wall again and closed his eyes. "Let's just plan on them not making it out of it. That'll solve our problem."

CHAPTER THIRTY-FOUR

Taryn

WE RATIONED FOOD, eating the bare minimum even though our stomachs continued to growl. There was no way to know how long it would be before we would be able to get more, nor did I have any idea how long we were going to be in this cave. It felt like days. The only color seeping in from the outside world was different shades of white that grew dim in the night but brightened in the morning.

When the howling wind finally subsided, we had to dig our way out into a still and silent world coated in layers of deep snow. I hadn't realized how much I missed the fresh air, especially after the horse's dung had been piling up in our small quarters. There was no sound here. No birds singing, no squirrels chattering.

William emerged from the cave, taking in the world around us.

The snow had to be over three feet deep.

"We need to move forward and find the nearest village quickly."

Quickly wasn't something in the realm of possibility at the moment. The deep snow slowed the horses down, forcing us to keep the pace at a walk as they pushed through it. Their well-being concerned me. What little grass there had been was buried, and they needed forage to help them regain the weight they'd lost. It was a miracle we'd made it this far.

We passed the trees slowly, our surroundings never changing. I watched our backs closely, but there was no sign of Silas or his men. They couldn't track us after a storm like that. If they were unable to find shelter in that blizzard, they couldn't have survived it.

William and I talked little, although we both were aware that since it had taken us so long to find the first village, there was no telling how far out the next city could be—if we even came close enough to cross it. The thought of being within a few miles of civilization and missing it made my insides churn.

The woods grew progressively thicker, the horse's steps becoming rigid and stiff from the cold. There was a short break in the trees, wide enough for three horses to walk side by side through. William suddenly pulled Othello up in the gap, and I held Stryder back.

"What is it?" I asked.

William slowly looked one direction and then the other.

"The break," he said. "It's too convenient."

I strained to see what William had uncovered, noting that

the break stretched farther into the forest, and then the realization dawned on me.

It was a road.

We directed the horses northbound and urged them faster through the snow. If William's idea was right, and we were on a path, we may be closer to a village than we realized.

The road eventually opened up into a valley surrounded by mountains and revealed the ridgeline of a town on the opposite side. The horses picked up a trot. The snow wasn't as deep here, and we began to close the gap between us and the town. The sun peeked out from the clouds, promising warmth, but it was just an illusion. With every step, the village grew larger and spread out in either direction. This was a good thing. A large city would make it easier to hide from Silas and his men. The wind blowing across the plain knocked my teeth together and only abated once we made it past the first buildings, but its anger was still loudly proclaimed above the heights of the city.

"I vote we find an inn first thing," William said.

I agreed.

This village was in a better state than the last. Each building stood completely whole and devoid of any imperfections. The houses were all constructed of the same pale wood, stacked log upon log. Shredded banners hung across the street, commemorating a past celebration that the wild wind had since ravaged.

Not many people passed by, but the few who did gave us wary glances, and why wouldn't they? We were two frozen foreigners covered in snow and riding worn-out horses. William's usually fair skin was rosy, his short, sandy beard trailing a string of icicles. I could feel the sting of the icicles coating the outer edge of my hairline as well.

A man in fine clothes crossed the street directly in front of us.

"Sir," William called out. "The nearest inn, could you tell us where it is?"

The man's red face scrunched up as he scowled up and down at us. He spit at William's feet, harshly uttering a response in an unfamiliar tongue. As he stormed away, William rode up beside him and spoke in what I assumed was the man's native tongue. Frustration broke out on William's face as he hesitated between words, searching for the next, and coming out in short and jagged phrases. The man's disapproving gaze flicked from me to William, muttering low in his throat as he jabbed his finger to indicate farther up the road.

"He didn't look happy."

William scowled. "Nor will anyone else we meet."

"What do you mean?"

William sarcastically threw out his arm. "Welcome to Gapsvar."

I took in the city around us with wide eyes. "We're in Gapsvar?"

"I thought that's where you wanted to be."

"Well, yes, but—what's the deal?"

William sighed. "This city belongs to no country. Gapsvar is a mingling of various cultures, but if the people have anything in common here, it's that everyone hates Gharridan. I know enough of the language to get by, but it will be best to not use our own tongue when anyone else is near."

If I wasn't even allowed to speak, I had no idea how I would worm my way to Marco. I remembered William saying that Gapsvar hated Gharridans, but I didn't realize to what extent.

"Who rules the city, then?" I asked.

William shrugged. "Whoever happens to hold the most power. It's usually a family lord: the Bohannons, Graysons, Prathers. I don't know which family is currently ruling. They tend to kill each other off quite often."

Hardly anyone else passed us as we made our way farther into the city's depths. If they noticed us, we were paid no attention. None of the buildings so far were merchants, only homes with tightly drawn curtains and smoke pluming from the top. Did Gapsvar even have an inn? If they hated Gharridans that much, I doubted they were welcoming to other visitors. After a moment, I thought I saw a stable farther down another street. Upon closer inspection, I caught sight of the inn's sign swinging in the wind. The sight of it overwhelmed me, and we hurried toward it.

When my feet dropped into the snow, I nearly succumbed to the rigid stiffness of my limbs. Walking Stryder into the stable was agony, but I knew he had to be in a worse state than I was. It was warmer in the stable, but not by much. A young stable boy with scruffy hair approached, his eyes wary as he took in our frozen figures. His voice was haughty as he lifted his chin and spoke to us. William fumbled through a response, but it appeared to satisfy. The boy called for someone over his shoulder, waving us toward the inn and reaching for Othello's reins.

William quickly caught the boy's arm, speaking with a low voice as he placed two silver coins into the boy's hand, causing the boy's eyebrows to rise in awe. The boy nodded and quickly stuffed the coins into the pocket of his dirty trousers, his face growing serious again as a young girl approached.

She couldn't have been more than ten years old. Her large, dark eyes were framed with extremely thick hair pulled back tightly over her ruddy brown skin. I removed my gloves and quickly felt each of Stryder's legs for any sign of inflammation. While I did, the boy spoke harshly to the young girl, motioning with his hands toward the empty stalls before marching away with Othello.

I turned to see the girl's outstretched hand reaching for Stryder's reins, and I handed them to her with a small smile. As she took them, she glanced down at my hand, continuing to stare at it. Her gaze caused my own to fall as well, coming to rest on my father's ring that was out in the open for all to see. Her deep brown eyes caught mine. The expression etched on her face was unreadable, but she refused to break eye contact. I held my breath, fear crawling up my skin for what I had just done. She blinked twice, glanced at the ring again, then walked off with Stryder as he towered above her.

A chill ran down my spine as she disappeared. William hadn't noticed the encounter and was already waiting for me at the stable door.

"William—"

He leaned low to my ear and whispered, "Wait to speak until we are by ourselves."

My jaw tensed, irritated that I couldn't even talk. I doubted there was much harm a young girl could do. The chances of her knowing what the ring signified were very low. My ring might've been nothing more than an extravagance to her. That was what I continued to tell myself as we made our way to the inn, but it didn't keep a knot from forming in my stomach.

A wave of warmth enveloped me in a strong embrace as we stepped inside. The roaring fire on the far wall was the most welcoming sight I had ever beheld. My only wish was to lie in front of it and never rise again. The burning flames gave a life to the room that the inhabitants of the inn lacked. Most of the wooden tables sat empty, with only a few patrons occupying the benches.

At our arrival, the innkeeper turned, his bushy grey eyebrows lowering as he examined us. The man continued drying his tankard as William started a conversation. He shifted away slightly, making an obvious show that we meant very little to him. Seeing as his livelihood was mostly in the business of serving and befriending strangers, he didn't appear to be very good at it. He grunted as William spoke, looking over his nose at us. I had no idea what the two men were saying, but it was obvious that the man wished for us to spend our money elsewhere.

William crossed his arms and leaned on the counter, dismissing any thoughts of leaving. The man scowled and slammed the second dry tankard on the counter, stomping over to where several keys hung on the wall. After ripping one from its peg, he returned to William, his hand outstretched and waiting for payment. William placed several gold coins into the man's hand. The innkeeper stared at them, frowned, and then extended his hand again for more.

William cocked his head, face hardening. They stared at each other, neither willing to cave. Finally, William drew two more gold coins from his pouch and swapped them for the key. The innkeeper picked up another tankard with his greedy hands and waved dismissively toward the staircase when William asked another question.

"How accommodating," I mused as the door to our room shut firmly behind us.

"You don't even have to speak Gharridese to be hated," William explained. "You just have to look it."

"Why do they hate Gharridan so much?"

William knelt in front of the hearth to get a fire going, gently blowing into the kindling. "It began with Ananaia Prather, the governor at the time. He emancipated Gapsvar from Gharridan authority and started to claim part of Gharridan's land as his own, going as far as to bring two small villages under his command. When my grandfather got word of what was going on, he sent an army that quickly put a stop to their incursions. Lord Ananaia didn't react well to the humiliation of defeat. He infected the people's minds with lies and deceits about how this land was theirs, and the Gharridans had stolen it from them. Ananaia Prather knew that if he told the lie long enough and loud enough, people would start to believe it. Hatred for Gharridan has simply been ingrained and passed down from the generation before."

It reminded me of how much the Crown hated Katherine, and how that hatred had infected the people of Gharridan as well.

"Gapsvar never tried to take more land again?"

William laughed. "They're lucky my grandfather didn't obliterate them for disloyalty and treason. Gapsvar knows good and well that if they set their borders even a foot inside Gharridan territory, Gharridan will crush them before they can draw a sword."

It was insane to think his grandfather had allowed Gapsvar to remain its own estate, but if everyone in Gapsvar had been against Gharridan, reconquering them would've only brought a massacre.

My eyes took in the small room. All it contained was a sitting chair that looked like it would crumble to dust when sat upon, the small hearth, and a bed with a straw mattress so lumpy I almost thought the snowy ground would be more comfortable.

William noticed my surveillance. "I'll take the floor."

After sitting on the mattress, I was tempted to ask William to rescind his offer.

"I'm pretty sure you got the better deal," I mumbled.

"Hmm?"

"I said, what did you tell the innkeeper about us?" I could always transfer to the floor if it was too uncomfortable.

William threw a few larger pieces of wood into the kindling. "We're now brother and sister, just so you know, and we're traveling through on our way to Brenden."

"I'm sure he believed that."

William and I looked absolutely nothing alike. It was like saying Othello and Stryder were the same color.

William leaned back, turning his face up toward mine. "I meant to introduce myself as the crown prince of Gharridan and you as the daughter of Michael Gallows. Didn't seem like a good idea at the time, although it probably would've gotten us a better room." He looked back at the fire. "Until they came to either arrest or kill us that is."

Dinner in the tavern below was little more than warm water with meat and potatoes mixed in, but it filled our hungry bellies. We returned straight to the room afterward, and I looked out the window, unable to see anything farther than the closest house underneath the night sky.

I glanced down at my dress, its green color mottled with mud and dust from the past several weeks. William's appearance was worse than mine. He was equally weathered, and his unshaven beard looked haggard hanging off his chin. Blood still stained the front of his tunic, but from a distance, it was difficult to distinguish from all the dirt.

"How are we going to get into the prison?" I asked.

William was already lying down, his eyes closed. "You do remember that this was your idea. Surely you've come up with a plan by now."

I rolled my eyes. With the blizzard and our captors bearing down upon us, it hadn't exactly been in the forefront of my mind. Getting any strategy from William was going to be difficult. He hadn't wanted to do this in the first place and was now stuck here because of me. Any plan to sneak in or get Marco out would be of my own doing.

After weeks of sleeping outside, the bed felt completely foreign, and I rolled over and over, trying to invoke sleep to possess me. I'd forgotten to mention the stable girl to William, but since no one had come pounding on the door, we were safe. For now. The whole incident was plaguing my mind, though. She appeared in my vision like an aching headache that wouldn't go away. I tried to brush off the notion and forget it, but the truth refused to leave my mind.

She knew what the ring was.

She knew it was a sign of the Kavari, which didn't make any sense. Gapsvar hated Gharridan. That raised the question of why a young girl would know anything about a guild in the politics of Gharridan. She knew, but she didn't say anything.

The question was why.

CHAPTER THIRTY-FIVE

Vladimir

THE DOUBT WAS evident in everyone, even myself. We still had a trail to follow, but the distance between Zedekiah and us never changed. Not if we tracked farther into the night. Not if we moved at a reckless place. I had done everything in my power to keep this from happening, yet it hadn't been enough to stop it.

I finally faced the question I'd been avoiding—what if we didn't catch Zedekiah?

Losing Michael's murderer and Gharridan's betrayer was devastating in and of itself, but returning to the capital a failure with the same unanswered questions made the whole situation worse. I'd been leader of the Kavari for less than four months and had done nothing but cause division. I wasn't remorseful about it. I refused to agree with someone solely for the sake of unity, but it did make my job harder.

"Something troubling you?"

Melvin sat beside me, stretching his legs. Everyone else was already asleep for the night. Melvin should be too, but he didn't appear to sleep as well as he used to. I'd volunteered for the first watch of the night, but keeping my eyes open and alert was growing more challenging.

"Do you ever feel like everything you touch just falls apart?" I asked.

Melvin blew out a long breath and crossed his arms. "Honestly, I think everyone goes through phases like that, Vladimir. If they don't, then they're not human."

The failures I was experiencing didn't feel like a phase, though. They felt like a lifetime.

"I'm assuming this is stemming from the rapid changes that have occurred over the past few months."

I rubbed the back of my neck, unsure of how to answer.

"I don't much care for politics," Melvin said, "but I've learned a few things about them during my time in the military, and if everyone is against you, that either means you're an idiot, or you're doing something right. What you walked into when you took on the role as leader of the Kavari is a mess and a chore that I wouldn't wish on anyone, but you did it—and you did it well."

He looked over at me. "Young and inexperienced as you are, the queen and the council tried to walk all over you to get their way, but you stood your ground. You held your own and refused to be turned into a puppet. That takes integrity, and that takes guts."

I'd only been doing what I knew was right. What I knew

Michael would have done.

"When I first met you, you were a boy so full of anger that I didn't know if there was any hope for you, but Michael didn't give up. He saw something in you, and he wasn't going to let it go. You grew out of that anger and moved beyond your past, and Michael would be proud of the man you've become today."

His words meant more than he knew. It was reassuring to know that there was at least one person who had my back. Accepting this role hadn't been followed by much encouragement.

"You can criticize yourself and the choices you've made until you're blue in the face. Don't. Learn from them, then move on. If you did everything to the best of your ability, then there's nothing else you could have done."

I didn't know what else I could have done. I'd known there was a traitor in our midst, but I'd pegged the wrong one. That mistake had cost many lives, and nearly Taryn's and the queen's. I still struggled with that. Even as I went back and thought about it, all the evidence had pointed to Mordakai. If I had the chance to go back, I doubted I would have come to a different conclusion the second time.

"I think your age is showing through in your wisdom, Melvin."

His eyes narrowed. "Just because you outrank me doesn't mean you can slack on the respect."

I chuckled. "Point taken."

Melvin struggled to his feet with a groan. "But for a man of my age, I think it's time that I had some rest."

I looked up at the moon, calculating how long I had until waking the next watch. We couldn't continue this manhunt forever, but if we didn't catch him soon, I didn't know what we were going to do. I refused to return to the capital with nothing.

CHAPTER THIRTY-SIX

Taryn

IT WOULD TAKE an army just to get to Marco, let alone to get him out. This place was not a prison. It was a fortress. A fortress built within a mountain and surrounded by a forest that blinded us to whatever lay within. We would never have found it except for the road leading out of town. At the base of the mountain stood a small guard's shack where six armed guards patrolled the entrance.

"Even if we could fight our way in, with that many guards, there's bound to be others hiding in the trees waiting to pick us off with arrows." William crouched next to me in the bushes, hidden from the soldiers we were spying on. Two towers jutted from the trees, barely visible from their place on the hilltop.

"There's got to be another way in."

I scanned the surrounding area. The entire valley was wide

open until the tree line. Sneaking in would require circling around to the other side of the mountain, assuming there weren't soldiers positioned on that end as well.

The side of the mountain was basically a cliff. The base of it had been carved out. Roots jutted through the snowy drop-offs, but they were spread far apart with no promise of bearing our weight.

"I don't know if there's anywhere for us to reach level ground by climbing," I said.

Next to me, William assessed our options. "Definitely not here. Let's look farther on."

We crawled back to the horses, staying at the edge of the tree line and moving with shadows as we rode around searching for any type of opening.

"What about there?" I pointed to a small section of the valley where the ground sloped downward. It wasn't much, but it might be enough to hide us from the sight of the sentries.

"If it was night," William considered, "and we were able to sneak across, I think the horses may be able to get up that embankment because *if* we somehow manage to get in there, we would never outrun them on foot."

He glanced up at the sky. "Another whiteout would be helpful about now."

I peered through the trees, visually forming a path that would keep us well hidden, when the slightest movement caught my eye. The disturbance was faint, little more than a shadow waving in the wind. It was the slightest swish of a tail, the most minuscule shift that caused the sun to glint off the silver armor. I lifted my finger and pointed the guard out to William.

"We'd never make it," I said.

William's teeth ground together as he paced back and forth in our little hideout. He kicked a pebble and sent it flying into the forest. I crossed my arms, staring at the mountain and willing it to provide us with an answer. We were so close. There had to be a way.

"You do realize the only chance of getting up there is to either be incarcerated or storm it with an army. Neither of which is a good idea—just in case you were wondering."

My head shot up.

That might be our ticket in.

"If we got arrested, they would take us up there, wouldn't they?"

William rolled his eyes. "I wasn't being serious, Taryn."

"But I was."

William got in my face. "If you get arrested, you can kiss your life goodbye. These family lords aren't known for hospitality toward their prisoners; I wouldn't want to know what they'll do to a foreigner—let alone a Gharridan. Throwing you in a cell would be wasting their time. Most likely, you'd be hanged, and then have your head mounted on a pike for all to see. Any other brilliant ideas?"

I averted my gaze.

William didn't agree. He never did, but I wasn't leaving here until I'd tried.

Over the next few days, we continued to scope out the entrance, learning the guards' schedules and watching for any type of weakness in the system. Six men stood guard whether it was day or night. No one was excused from duty without first being replaced. If the fortress was just a prison, why was the entrance so heavily guarded? Something else was going on here. Something they were hiding.

The soldiers hidden in the trees were difficult to find. We'd been watching for days and hadn't calculated any rhyme or reason to their positions—it was completely random. When the sun began to fall, we made our way back to the inn with less hope than we'd started with that morning.

"We need to come back tonight."

William wasn't pleased with the prospect, but he didn't disagree. "We can pack our things and make our way back after dark."

I shivered, the thought of spending the night out in the elements unappealing, but if it meant getting us closer to Marco, then it would be worth it.

"How do you really think this is going to play out, Taryn?"

My jaw set. The lecture was on the tip of his tongue, waiting to be unleashed.

"*If* we somehow manage to get in, how are you planning on talking to Marco? And if Zedekiah isn't there, are you just going to sit around and wait for him to show up?"

I closed my eyes, hearing the sense in his words but refusing to listen. "We'll get in."

If the prison was half as guarded inside as it was without, then we didn't stand a chance. I knew this, but it was all part of a plan that I had not yet disclosed to William. When I snuck across the plain up the mountainside tonight, I didn't mean for him to follow me. William would never survive capture if they discovered his identity, but if I could convince the soldiers to take me alive, I might have a chance. I hoped that if I gave the guards my name, they would take me straight to Zedekiah. I didn't have to survive this. I just needed to get close enough to Zedekiah to take him out.

Dinner at the inn was worse than it usually was. I stirred the myriad of vegetables and mystery meat around in the bowl, my mind consumed with how tonight would play out. William wasn't speaking to me at the moment, his mind heavy from the ale he was drinking.

"Don't you think you'll need a clear head tonight?" I asked.

"I'll have one."

The rate at which the liquid in his tankard was disappearing suggested otherwise. I took a sip of my water and coughed. They might as well have melted dirty snow in a cup. The murkiness of the water couldn't even reflect my image, and I wondered if that was exactly what had been done.

The tavern door suddenly swung wide open, a group of soldiers spilling inside with drunken laughter on their lips and empty tankards hanging from their hands. They were heavily armored, with weapons fastened wherever there was a latch. I quickly looked away, glancing up at William. His face had grown tense as he chewed on the soup in his mouth and swallowed. I noticed his hand fell to his lap, no doubt coming to rest on the hilt of his sword.

The most important thing was to not draw attention to ourselves. Whether these soldiers were from the prison or the reigning family, they didn't like Gharridans, but at least it wasn't Silas and his men.

I kept my eyes glued to the table, listening unintelligibly to their loud voices as they slammed their tankards on the counter, refilling them again and again. My eyes flicked up to William. His stature was rigid as he briefly met my gaze, indicating the door to the tavern.

Slowly, I rose from my seat and made my way across the wooden floor like a rabbit trying to silently step around a sleeping wolf. I didn't want to get into any more trouble, especially now that the plan was within reach. William moved close behind me, shielding our back. I was reaching for the door handle when a soldier stepped in front of me. I tried to push around his drunken slouch, but his arm blocked the door. My heart thudded in my chest. He began to speak, the foul smell of alcohol wafting from his mouth like poison and making me nauseous. His glassy eyes roved over me as he spoke lazily in his native tongue.

William placed himself between the drunken man and me, conversing with him while I stood there helplessly. The guard scowled, his voice growing louder as he got into William's face.

A yell came from across the room, capturing the angry man's attention. He yelled back, and William's face paled, stark in comparison to his navy cloak.

"I heard rumors there were Gharridans in the city." The accent was so thick that for a moment, I didn't realize the voice had spoken in our tongue. I turned to see who the voice had come from. His grizzled beard hung halfway down his chest, his hair pulled back into a ponytail. Heavy boots thudded across the floor, a drum of impending malice as he swaggered over.

He stopped in front of us and scrunched his nose. "I should've smelled you the moment I walked in the door."

William shifted until he was slightly in front of me, his chin jutting. The man stared at us, waiting for an answer, but William did not oblige.

"What are you scum doing in *our* city?" Hatred emanated from his voice like heat from a fire, his blazing expression waiting for William's response.

I fastened my eyes on William's shoulder, too afraid to look in his face.

"Traveling through."

I swallowed. William's voice was low, but I could feel the restraint in it. Sweat broke out on my brow, the hair on the back of my neck rising. Tensions hung heavy in the air like an evil presence one could feel but not see.

"Gharridans are not welcome in Gapsvar. *Traveling through* shouldn't even ha' been a consideration."

William's throat constricted, the veins in his neck bulging. "Blizzard threw us off course."

The man chuckled darkly, calling something to the soldiers behind him, who then stepped forward. "I don't think you're catching my words, boy. Best to make sure you understand the message."

The soldier's fist slammed William's face so quickly that I never saw it coming. As soon as William hit the floor, he jumped to his feet and retaliated with his own blow, but by that time, the other soldiers had joined in, overtaking William and pulling him to the ground.

I fought my way into the tangle but was quickly pushed out by a fist to the head. Fear and anger surged through my body as I snatched up a bench, heaving it through the air to bring it crashing down over one of the soldier's heads. One of the men grabbed me around the waist, hauling me away from the fight as I kicked and clawed at his arms.

"Stop it!" I screamed, tears of frustration streaming down my face as blow after blow descended upon William's body. It was a blur of limbs and blood, the sickening sound of fist on flesh filling my ears. There were so many of them.

Suddenly I was thrown backward, my arms flailing in empty air until I landed in the snow outside the inn door, my breath coming in ragged gasps. I struggled to my feet, stumbling back to the door. It swung open again, and a body came flying toward me. William landed heavily in the snow, and I rolled him over, my hands hovering over his wounds. Deep red blood covered his face, his fair skin shifting to red and rising with the swelling.

The door opened a final time, the innkeeper angrily pointing at the stable and then gesturing us to leave with his other. He slammed the door behind him, locking us outside in the prison of wind and snow.

"William." I touched his face lightly, my voice trembling with fear.

His eyelids flickered as he slipped in and out of consciousness, a small groan escaping his lips.

"William!" My voice was louder this time and slipping into a panic.

He didn't move.

My eyes darted about the street frantically, but no one was out at this time of night. The soldiers wouldn't stay in the tavern forever, and if William was still here when they came back out—

I surveyed his body, lying motionless in the snow. He needed a healer and fast. He was too heavy to lift on a horse by myself. I stepped out into the distressed snow of the street; my gaze fixed on the one house with a light still burning inside. It was like a beacon, beckoning me toward it.

I pounded on the door as my heart raced wildly in my chest like an untamed horse. The floor creaked inside the house, but the door did not open. I pounded again, harder and faster than before, waiting a moment before beginning to pound again, nearly falling forward when the door abruptly swung inward.

I stared up at the man who had opened the door, his wife peeking around him and curious children hiding behind her back. Lowered brows hung over tired eyes with dark circles etched beneath as he looked me up and down.

I pulled my cloak tighter around me. "Please." My teeth chattered together. I pointed at William lying helpless in the snow. "He needs help."

The man glanced between William and me, then looked toward the inn door. He spoke several harsh words before slamming the door in my face. I stepped backward, the world seeming to close in on me as I looked at house after house that was shrouded in darkness. No one here was going to help me. I didn't speak their language. I was Gharridan. Even if they wanted to, I doubted their compassion would be greater than the fear of what their neighbors would think.

I reached underneath each of William's arms, attempting to drag him through the snow. If I could at least get him into the barn where it was warm, that would give me more time to figure out how to find help and get out of here. I pulled with all my strength. William might have moved half an inch, but I was almost sure it was a trick of the eyes procured by a mixture of hope and fear. I shook his shoulder, praying he would wake up. Tears threatened to spill over the edges of my eyes, but I fought them away. I would not leave us here to die.

I struggled to my feet, backing toward the stable as I kept an eye on William. Light slipped through the cracks of the stable wall and spilled out into the street as I opened the door. When I stepped into the soft light protruding from the lamp, no one else was in sight. I didn't know whether that was a blessing or a curse. Stryder and Othello's tack was stacked outside their stalls, and I quickly got both of them ready. If I could get Stryder to lie down next to William, I might be able to pull him over his back, but doubt hung heavy within me. It might not be possible for me to pull Stryder back to his feet and keep William from slipping off.

I led the horses forward, about to leave the barn when I heard something large scurrying in the shadows. Fear pricked my skin, every muscle on alert like a cornered animal waiting for the next blow. Someone slipped forward into the light with two dark, inquisitive eyes watching me. The girl who had noticed my ring looked around the horses, searching for someone else. Hope and fear mingled together in my chest as I wondered if I could convince her to help me.

"He's hurt," I mumbled.

Her mouth curved into a frown.

I shook my head at my own stupidity. She couldn't understand me.

I moved the horses out of the barn, and she followed closely behind. My eyes were pleading as I pointed at William. Suspicion plagued her face as she walked over to him, her features changing once she saw his wounded state.

I pointed to the tavern and then, making a fist with one hand, hit the open palm of my other. The soldier's drunken laughter could still be heard out in the street. She nodded her understanding, and I pointed from William to the horses, asking for help. I could see the fear in her eyes as she looked up and down the street. Indecision flickered across her face, but she was looking at my ring again. After taking a deep breath, she indicated the ring and then pointed to me, her eyes asking if I was what this ring said I was. I stared at her, aware that how I answered this question would determine both my own and William's fate. Slowly, I bobbed my head up and down. I was not officially a Kavari, but if it meant she would help me, I would say anything.

Slowly she began to nod and watched as I led Stryder over, asking him to lie down for me. He stamped the ground irritably; the motion throwing sprays of snow into the air.

"Shh," I murmured. "I know it's cold, but I need you to do this for me."

Reluctantly, Stryder knelt and heaved his body down to the ground with a great sigh. I rushed to William's side, and with the girl's added strength, we began to pull William toward Stryder's back and hang him over the saddle. We struggled with the weight, slipping in the snow, unable to find good footing. I glanced up at the tavern door, which was still closed. It would not stay that way for long. Somehow, we managed to get William partway over the saddle when Stryder stretched out one of his front legs.

"Not yet," I said with shaking breath as I placed a hand on his shoulder. With my shoving and the girl pulling, we maneuvered his body to where the center of his weight hung over the saddle. The girl quickly urged Stryder back to his feet while I held William steady. A sigh of relief rushed out of my lips, and

I grabbed Othello's reins, nodding my sincere thanks to the girl.

She shook her head, motioned down an alleyway, and pulled Stryder behind her. I rushed to William's side, keeping him from slipping off the saddle as she led us to who knows where. I swallowed hard, afraid to trust this girl, but knowing at this point, I had no other choice. All I could do was pray that she wasn't leading us into a trap.

Flurries began to fill the air around us. If enough fell, they would mask our tracks, something I was grateful for in the event that the soldiers decided to follow us. We made our way down several different alleys, the girl stopping before each street to check for anyone or anything that might be passing by. This elicited a few groans from William, but he still had not fully regained consciousness.

The snow fell heavier.

We'd left the heart of the city and entered the outskirts where the houses spread out farther, most of which had winterized gardens growing in front of them. The girl handed Stryder's reins back to me and ran inside one of the small houses. My teeth chattered, and I wondered whether we would be invited in or left to freeze in the cold.

William stirred beside me as a woman emerged from the house, her squinted eyes scrutinizing us in the dark. At the sight of William, she hurried toward us. She grabbed my hand, pointing at my ring and speaking. She raised an eyebrow in question.

My mouth slipped open, but my expression was blank as I didn't comprehend any of the words. Understanding dawned on her face, and she started to get William down from the saddle.

"Questions later, Kavari. We need to get him inside."

CHAPTER THIRTY-SEVEN

Taryn

It was a small wooden house composed of two bedrooms. Fire crackled in the hearth of the main room, flooding my senses with warmth as the girl laid out a mat in front of the fire. We quickly laid William on it, and the woman returned with a bowl of fresh water and a rag. As I knelt beside William and touched the first cut on his face, my stomach nearly turned at the gruesome sight. He winced, a small groan slipping from his mouth.

"Where am I?" he rasped.

My eyes flicked over my shoulder at the woman pulling several plants from various jars.

"Somewhere safe."

"I feel like—" He coughed, his body shuddering as he rolled on his side and spit out blood.

I dipped the rag back into the bowl, and the water turned red. "I know."

There was no telling how many of the blows had struck his head. I wondered how serious the damage was because even after these past few months, my head still bothered me from falling off Stryder, let alone from when Silas and his men captured us.

"I'm going to kill them." William spat the words.

I raised an eyebrow. "You and what army?"

He didn't have a retort, which was surprising. He must be worse than I thought. The woman squatted beside me and began applying a salve to his wounds. William cracked his eyes open, watching the woman suspiciously. The salve had an ugly yellow color and smelled as repulsive as a decomposing animal. My nose scrunched up as I helped her, wondering what was in it. Both of us ignored William's choice words about the smell and continued to apply it through his protests.

I continued to sit by him, forcing him to rest and asking questions to ensure his sentences remained coherent. Most of the damage appeared to be external, which was a huge relief. After a while, the woman went back to her cabinet and returned with a small cup that she raised to his mouth.

"Drink this. It will help you feel better."

William pursed his swollen lip, his brows lowering over red and puffy eyes.

I took the cup from her and forced it between his lips. "She said drink."

William glowered at me as he swallowed the liquid, his glare warning me that if anything went awry, it would be my fault. After a few minutes, his body relaxed, his eyes closing as his breathing evened out.

"It'll help with the pain and keep him asleep for a while," the woman explained, offering a hand and drawing me to my feet. She led me over to the table where I sat down while she poured us something to drink.

We sat in silence, slowly sipping from our glasses. The woman didn't look Gharridan, but she spoke the language fluently. Her brown dress was simple, her long hair pulled back from her work-lined face and dark brown eyes. She tapped the cup with her finger nervously, her eyes wandering the room before coming back to me.

"My name is Beva." She indicated my ring. "You are indeed a Kavari?"

I stared at the gold encircling my finger, the emblem of my father's house etched into the metal. Continuing to lie ensured our safety, but it would only take a few questions for her to figure out I wasn't telling the truth. Giving up the information willingly instead of surrendering it from being caught seemed a better way to earn her trust.

"Not—" I hesitated, licking my lips. "Not entirely."

The cup froze halfway to her mouth.

"I was about to be instated when …" I trailed off, not quite sure how to explain everything that had happened. "My father was a Kavari." I watched closely for her reaction. "Michael Gallows."

Beva slowly lowered her glass to the table, her bright face clouding over with sorrow. "So he is gone, then."

Even this far away from Gharridan, in a city of people who hated our country, Beva had known who my father was. I might never know just how far his influence had reached.

"You knew him?" I asked.

A small laugh escaped her lips. "No, but I knew of him. I am originally from Gharridan, but it has been many years since I've set foot there. Helvah, my daughter, was born here, which is why she doesn't know your tongue."

Yet she knew what I was, or rather, what I represented.

Helvah peeked around the corner, her dark, watchful gaze flitting over us like a wild animal afraid to approach. Her fingers curled around the edge of the door as she listened intently without understanding our conversation.

"How did she recognize my ring?"

Beva smiled. "I may not have shared the language of Gharridan with her, but I have been very forthcoming with its culture and history."

Not knowing our language may have been a safety barrier for her daughter. William had refused to speak it in Gapsvar except for the times when we were alone. I wondered what had caused Beva to leave Gharridan for Gapsvar.

The room grew quiet except for William's steady breathing, which was escalating into loud snores against the crackling of the fire.

"What are the two of you doing all the way out here in Gapsvar?"

My mouth grew dry, unsure of how to answer.

"We came here in search of someone."

Beva was watching me closely. "Who?"

She was digging for information. Even though she was helping us, I had known her for less than an hour. I wasn't willing to trust her with too much yet. Helvah had risked her life by bringing us here, but her mother might not feel the same way.

"Marco of the Kavari."

"Did you find him?"

I shook my head, my mind working. If William was incapacitated for a few days, that might give me a chance to come up with a plan and worm my way into the fortress.

"What does he look like?"

Her question caught me off guard. "I-I don't know."

Beva's expression grew contemplative as she leaned back in her chair. "Several weeks ago, the soldiers dragged a man up to the fortress. He had to have been half dead. There was a ring on his finger resembling the Kavari, but I never got close enough to confirm it. It's been weeks since I've seen him. I'm not sure whether or not he's still alive."

I leaned forward with eagerness, my mind already reeling with this new information.

"You've been up to the fortress?"

Beva shifted uncomfortably in her seat. "After my husband passed, I obtained a job in the kitchens at the fortress as head cook. It helps us survive on our own. Their schedule only requires me to work four days out of the week; I just returned this evening. I don't like leaving Helvah alone, but our neighbors are very good to watch out for her when I am gone."

Helvah raced to stand beside her mother, her gaze never leaving me as she placed her head on Beva's shoulder. In turn, her mother wrapped her arms around her, drawing her into an embrace. A flicker of jealousy sparked within me, a desire to have my mother's loving arms once again envelop me. I missed her, more than I would ever be able to explain. There was nothing like the tender loving embrace of a mother.

My eyes flicked to William on the floor, then back to Beva,

deliberating.

"Can you get us into the fortress?" The question escaped my lips before I could stop it or consider what I was saying.

Beva's brows drew together in understanding. "You intend to break him out."

I was more interested in searching for Zedekiah, but if Marco was indeed still alive, he was my second objective—if I lived that long. I lifted my chin, my determined eyes unwilling to back down from her obvious disapproval. I would find a way into that fortress whether she helped me or not.

Beva's eyes fell to William. "There's no way I could get him in, even after he's healed. They're very strict. Helvah is allowed inside; she goes up with me on occasion to help, but I don't like it."

The conversation halted as Beva stroked her daughter's hair. Ever so slowly, she brought her eyes back up to meet mine. "I can get you in, but if they discover who you really are, your life is out of my hands."

My life had been out of my hands from the moment I left home.

"How long do we have until you have to return?"

"Two days."

I leaned back in my chair.

Two days.

Two days to form a plan.

CHAPTER THIRTY-EIGHT

Vladimir

THE WAVING TREES manifested shadows that danced across the whitewashed landscape. Eight horsemen trotted across the tundra, leaving a trail behind them. My eyes lingered on them. Waiting. The horsemen came to a stop before the outpost, arranging themselves into a line. Cloaks fell backward, and nothing changed except one thing. The absence of the cloak revealed a head of white that reflected in the moonlight.

"That's him."

From behind me came the sound of an arrow being drawn and nocked, the string pulling tight.

"No." I reached up and firmly grabbed the bow in Katherine's grasp. "The shot is too far. We'll only alert them to our presence."

Katherine jerked the bow from my grasp but did not draw the string again; she shoved the arrow back into her quiver and trudged away.

Women.

I trusted Katherine with my life, but there was no denying that her emotions were in the way right now. Her heart was dead set on revenge. I walked after her and found her angrily fussing with the buckles on her saddle.

"If we had advanced on them when I'd suggested, Zedekiah would be in our possession right now," she hissed.

"If we had jumped them, as you suggested, we would never figure out where Zedekiah was going. He's more valuable to us alive right now."

"More valuable, or does it just ease your conscience for you not to kill him?" Katherine accused. "He killed Michael, Vladimir, and I know that he was as much a father to you as he was to me, so why are you so consumed with preserving his life?"

"Don't you dare for one second think that Michael's death doesn't matter to me." My voice held a warning tone. "You think I don't want to shove my sword through him, fire arrows into his eyes, make him suffer the way that he made Michael suffer? There is nothing more in this world that I would like to do than kill that man."

Katherine fiercely stared me down, waiting for my point.

"We are not killers, Katherine. Yes, Zedekiah deserves to die, but we both swore an oath to protect our country and uphold justice within it. Lashing out in revenge is not the way to bring justice. As the leader of the Kavari, I have a responsibility to act above what I myself would deem right."

Katherine turned away, irritated, but knowing I was right.

"My only goal is to lead the Kavari as well as Michael did, and you know that your way is not Michael's way." I paused, watching her. The next words lingered on the tip of my tongue, a thought that had haunted me, and a truth I had tried to deny. "You would have preferred Marco to be Michael's successor."

Katherine crossed her arms, scuffing her boot against the snow. I held my breath, afraid that my suspicions were correct, but after a moment, she shook her head.

"There was a time when I would have wished that, but the truth is that Marco has always been more invested in foreign affairs. Unlike you, he doesn't hesitate to act but asks for forgiveness later. His hastiness would've brought the Kavari down." Katherine met my eyes. "I don't say this lightly, but Michael knew from the first time he met you that you would become his successor. I didn't believe him, no one believed him, but he saw something in you that no one else could."

Those were almost Melvin's exact words.

"So you understand my decision about this?" I asked.

Katherine rolled her eyes. "Though I may not agree with all your decisions, I trust Michael's *judgment* of you, and I trust *you*. Don't doubt that, but I will not always agree with you. This would be one of those times."

She marched back to the soldiers, leaving me behind in frustration. Katherine was good at what she did, but she could be a real pain sometimes. I ran my fingers through my hair, studying the fortress and trying to find an answer where there was none. With a sigh, I rejoined the others, Katherine still irked by my decision.

"What's the plan?" she asked.

The other men turned their attention to me, waiting for my answer.

I frowned. "If our coordinates are right, that outpost belongs to Gapsvar. I don't want to start a war with them; it'll be best to wait them out. Zedekiah has to be running toward something. No doubt he's made an alliance with another country, and we need to figure out who it is. Brenden and Algarar are both easily accessible from here, and either one could be a potential enemy."

Katherine and the men nodded their agreement.

"Melvin, you have first watch," I ordered. "We'll alternate shifts throughout the night, and I want to know the second that anyone leaves that outpost. Keep an eye out for any sign of movement, and wake us at the slightest possibility of company."

We set up camp for the night, but I kept my eyes trained on the outpost. We would wait him out no matter how long it took.

CHAPTER THIRTY-NINE

Taryn

FLURRIES CONTINUED TO meander through the sky the following morning, drifting down to the snow already collected on the ground. Helvah walked in front of me, leading me out to the lean-to behind their house. Stryder and Othello stood head to tail huddled together against the cold wind along with Beva's cart horse. A low whicker issued from Stryder's throat at our approach.

Helvah flashed a shy smile back at me as she raced forward to the horses. Her little fingers reached out to stroke their soft muzzles, the adoration in her eyes like that of a mother holding her newborn babe for the first time. Helvah's voice murmured to the horses as she stroked their foreheads.

Her eyes met mine, and she pointed to Stryder, her voice rising in a question. I wasn't sure what she meant, but I placed my hand on his side. "Stryder." I spoke the word distinctly.

Her smile grew wider as she surveyed him and repeated "Stryder" in a heavy accent. I returned her smile and placed a hand on William's horse. "Othello." Her gentle voice repeated his name as well, but it was less intelligible than Stryder's.

Helvah eventually pulled herself away from the horses to show me the hay. She continued to rattle off in her own language as we carried the food to them, Stryder and Othello nearly attacking us before we reached them with the first load. I understood nothing of our conversation but smiled warmly at her, enjoying the pure joy that radiated from her face.

Even after the few nights at the inn's stable, the horses were still ravenous from their days without sufficient food. Stryder's frame was growing thinner from the excessive exercise and sparse forage. My smile faltered slightly as I ran my hand over his side, his ribs now discernable. I had never even seen them on him before.

After the horses were fed, Helvah flitted about them, jabbering away as she ran her hands over their warm fuzzy coats and wove braids in their manes and tails. Her innocence produced a contentment that swelled in my chest, renewing hope within my soul. The superstition and quietness her manner had displayed back at the inn was nothing more than a distant memory.

I jumped as Beva's voice rang across the snowy ground, my heartbeat quickening and then slowing again as I realized there was no danger. Helvah ran back through the snow, retracing her previous footsteps, and I worked my way back as well. When she reached her mother, Helvah stood on her tiptoes to plant a happy kiss on her cheek.

The intimate interaction struck me in the heart as I realized that asking Beva for help would surely place both of them in imminent danger. My steps faltered, my morals battling the desires in my heart as I saw the devotion that passed between them. I looked out toward the fortress. There was still a possibility I might be able to sneak in under nightfall, but Beva had the advantage of getting me inside without fear of getting caught. It would be fine. I would make sure that she stayed safe.

Beva cast a smile at me as Helvah threw a series of words at her. "She's curious about where your horse came from. He's one of the finest she's ever seen."

I fought to smile, a vision of her and Helvah being torn apart invading my thoughts. "He's an Adellaion steed."

As she translated my answer, Helvah's smile grew wider.

Beva ushered me to the table and set a bowl of warm porridge before me. "Caring for the horses at the stable has been a lifesaver for Helvah since her father died. I don't like sending her to work so young, but it keeps her mind off things, and the money does help."

I ate a spoonful of porridge, the flavor of it far better than the rubbish they'd been serving at the inn. Beva sat across from me, her thoughts distracted.

"If it's in your best interest not to help us, I understand."

She glanced up at my words, her eyes quickly falling back to the porridge in front of her.

"Do not worry about us, child. We will be fine."

Except she didn't know the entirety of my plan.

I chewed on my lip, sneaking a look at William before placing my spoon on the table and facing Beva. "There's something I need you to do for me."

William rolled onto his side with a groan, sitting up on his elbows. I knelt next to him with a bowl of porridge. "How are you feeling?"

"Never better." He rubbed his bruised eyes, face scrunched in pain. "Ever been trampled by a horse?"

I shook my head. "Can't say that I have."

William grunted as he moved into a sitting position.

I handed him the porridge, encouraging him to eat. The motion of opening his swollen lips looked painful. He surveyed his surroundings, his gaze landing on Helvah. "How long was I out?"

I applied more salve to the open cut on William's face, which rewarded me with an ugly glare from him. "The girl, Helvah, brought us here the night before last. You've been out ever since."

I could see thoughts turning in the back of William's mind as he took in everything around him, watching Beva and Helvah closely. His expression indicated he would like to talk, but their presence kept him silenced.

"Beva works in the fortress," I revealed, avoiding eye contact. "She can get us inside."

William choked on his food. "How?"

I chose my next words carefully. "She works in the kitchens. If we go with her, she can get us in as workers. She returns the day after tomorrow."

William laughed, spitting out porridge and angrily wiping it from his mouth. "I look about as much a Gapsvarian as I do a horse, and you can't even speak the language."

I knew he wouldn't be thrilled about this, because he hadn't been thrilled about anything since I'd told him I intended to find Marco. If there was a way, I was going to find it, but William would do everything in his power to avoid it.

"What's your great plan, then?" I asked. "We already got kicked out of the inn, and the soldiers are probably looking for us as we speak. Sneaking around the perimeter is no longer an option."

"And trusting a complete stranger is?" William's voice was mocking.

My voice was sharp. "I'll be fine."

William hesitated. "Taryn, you're walking into a prison camp with soldiers who don't have respect for anyone except their own kind."

"This is our only shot." I shrugged and refused to let his opinion bother me. "You're the one who chose to come with me. This is what I'm choosing to do."

William scowled, "Your choices haven't exactly put us in great positions lately."

Heat burned in my chest as anger bubbled to the top. "If we were riding on your choices, Marco wouldn't have had a chance. He's still alive, in case you were wondering."

"You don't really believe that, do you?" His condescending tone sliced through me.

I ripped the porridge from his hands and dropped the bowl of salve in his lap. "You can take care of yourself. I wouldn't want my choices to put you in a bad position."

I ignored Helvah's stare as I deposited the porridge on the table and stormed out the door. If it had been Vladimir with me instead of William, everything would have been different.

Vladimir could see sense and had no use for mindless arguing. I hated being angry, but the reason I was so angry was because deep down, I knew that William was partially right. I didn't know how I would get around speaking the language, but Beva and I would figure something out. I knew that he would never make it past the first set of guards—I wasn't a fool, but he had bought my lie. Now he just needed to keep buying it until it was too late. Deceiving William was not something I was proud of, but I didn't have any other choice.

Eventually, I slid back inside, William and I ignoring each other as we went about our day. Where I refused to help him, Beva came through. My irritation was strong enough that I wanted to leave him to fend for himself, but I felt guilty after realizing how much pain he was in. It was my fault he was in this state.

William and I didn't speak for the rest of the day, avoiding the topic of departure altogether even with Beva and Helvah. I'd told William we were leaving the day after tomorrow, but we were leaving in the morning. He needed to think he had more time to talk us out of this.

Beva cooked some soup and baked a loaf of bread for dinner, which we ate in silence. I watched my food closely while I ate, my leg nervously shaking beneath the table. Spoons scraped the bottom of the empty bowls, filling the empty silence. From my peripheral vision, I saw William raise the glass to his lips.

I held my breath, waiting for him to catch on.

He didn't.

William downed the same concoction as the first night without ever giving it a second thought.

CHAPTER FORTY

Taryn

THE MONOTONOUS CRUNCH of the snow beneath the horse's hooves and the wagon creaking along the road were the only sounds perforating the world around us. Orange and golden rays shot across the horizon, stretching farther and wider as the sun made its ascent, waking the earth from darkness to light. The brisk air abused the exposed skin on my face, sending a shiver racing down my spine. I stroked the nakedness of my finger. When the ring was absent, I felt like a part of my soul was absent as well.

"You'll need to take that off." Beva had advised me last night, slipping a long silver chain into my hand. "Someone might know what it represents."

That silver chain now hung around my neck with my father's ring strung through it. The unfamiliar weight was a burden on my chest. I glanced over my shoulder for what seemed like the hundredth time. William would still be sound asleep now, just like he had been at our departure this morning. He'd drunk enough to knock him out for two days. There was no reason for me to think he would suddenly come riding up behind us, but I continued to glance over my shoulder anyway. Guilt was a familiar friend, making me pay for deceiving William like I had.

The entrance to the fortress loomed before us, each step of the horses' hooves pulling us closer to what lay ahead. The guard's hands rested confidently on their swords as a warning. I swallowed hard, my hands fiddling in my lap.

"Do not appear nervous." Beva glanced sidelong at me as she steered the horse to the gate. "Whatever nerves you have, swallow them. Look as disinterested as possible. If you're asked a question, acknowledge me as your authority, and I will grant you permission. It is not custom for a young lady to speak without her elder's approval."

The guard's stances were square and rigid, their faces framed with suspicion and malice.

"I always come alone or with Helvah." The muscles in Beva's face were growing tighter. "Never with anyone else."

My heart began to pound within my chest like a galloping horse gaining speed, each beat accelerating faster than the beat before it, threatening to burst completely out of my chest. Cold air rushed into my lungs as I inhaled deeply, trying to calm my nerves. If I didn't act like I was a trespasser, then everything should go according to plan.

"Mind your gaze," Beva said. "It is very direct for a simple servant."

I quickly flicked my eyes downward, keeping them focused on my lap or on the snow-encrusted world—on anything except the possibility of death that lay before us.

The wagon rolled to a stop.

Our horse played with the bit in her mouth and stamped her hoof impatiently. Beva's expression was respectful as she bent her head to the soldiers, rattling off a stream of words I didn't understand.

One of the guard's boots crunched in the snow as he stepped forward, his face and voice welling with irritation. He thrust his arm at us in a sharp gesture and spoke harshly to Beva. He regarded me as a wolf might, deciding if its prey was worth the trouble. I sat perfectly still, keeping my gaze diverted from his. A cold sweat trickled on my brow, the heat of his gaze following me as he circled the wagon. With a snap of his fingers, another guard stepped forward and followed him to the back where I heard them rustling through the bags of food and supplies.

When they were finished, the guard came to my side of the wagon and pointed at the ground, indicating for me to get down. I looked to Beva for guidance. Suddenly I was yanked from the wagon. Snow flew around my feet as I fell and tried to regain balance, the guard's grip clamping down on my arm like iron. Beva's face was furious as she screamed at the guard, rising in her seat as he yelled back. He shoved me forward and inspected me as if looking for a hidden weapon, but I was in boots and a simple maid's dress. Fear pulsed through every vein in my body, the sound of my heartbeat deafening.

They weren't going to let me in.

If Beva couldn't get me in, then both of our lives would be

in grave danger. The guard lowered his voice, explaining something to Beva, who held no fear in her eyes, only blatant rebellion. The touch of his cold fingers on my bare neck made my spine stiffen. It took everything in me to keep the fear hidden as I felt him pull on the silver chain. The ring slipped up my chest, catching on the collar of my dress. I couldn't breathe. Seconds felt like hours. We'd failed.

Beva's voice startled me as she barked something at the man, nearly jumping out of the wagon. The man muttered under his breath, releasing the chain and shoving me back toward the wagon. I let out the breath I'd been holding as I clambered back into the seat. Beva sat down, rage still encompassing her face. The guards moved aside for our entrance, and we passed through. I could still feel their gazes boring into our backs.

"What was that about?" I asked once we were out of earshot.

Beva's face remained rigid. "They weren't going to let you through. Just be thankful they did."

Considering how heavily guarded the outside of the fortress was, I had expected that we would have to maneuver through another set of guards, but no one paid much attention to us when we arrived. Soldiers marched about, ignoring us as they fulfilled their various tasks.

The fortress contained five buildings. Two long ones appeared to be barracks. Horses walked in and out of the stable, and there was a smaller building that wasn't immediately identifiable. The largest building lay in the center of the compound. It rose two stories high and boasted a lookout tower even higher. It was stacked stone upon stone, giving it the appearance of a small castle. The wear on its outer walls evidenced that it had been built in an age long ago.

Beva pulled the carriage up beside the building, waving down two soldiers who began to unload the supplies and carry them in through a side door. I studied my surroundings.

The grounds seemed sparsely populated for such a large base. Several hundred men could reside up here, but it appeared that there were little more than a hundred. Beva's hard eyes warned me to keep my gaze down. I lowered them but continued to glance around as much as possible without arousing suspicion.

No fence encompassed the buildings, but they were encircled entirely by trees. Perimeter guards paced the edges of the forest, hands resting on the hilt of their swords. I swallowed. Once I found Zedekiah, there would be no escaping.

Beva's arm ushered me inside, leading me down a set of stone steps into what became a kitchen. She threw a wet rag at me and nodded to the spacious counter, which I began to wipe down. The soldiers continued to bring supplies down until the wagon was empty. Once we were alone, Beva still didn't speak but was already ordering the next job before I'd finished the last. Beva danced around me, completely in her element as she put everything perfectly in its place. I was the partner with two left feet who threw everything off, but her forgiveness was endless. She was never harsh, a bit firm at times, but she always offered another chance. However practiced her movements were, the glances toward the staircase and open doorway were still obvious.

The bowl thudded on the counter next to me, and Beva

leaned close to whisper in my ear. "We will stay very busy in the kitchens. It is uncommon for the kitchen help to leave this room, but I will try to find errands so that you can find what you are looking for. It will not be easy, and we must use extreme caution."

She stepped away and began the process of making what looked like dough.

"What are we making?" I asked.

Beva rolled up her sleeves and began kneading the dough, the counter and her apron already turning white from the loose flour flying out. "Cakes. They're having a celebration this week. Someone else is doing the cooking, but we are in charge of the bread. Our focus needs to be on getting our part of the work done."

My brows knit together as Beva tossed a hunk of dough at me. "What celebration?" A military fortress seemed an odd location for such a thing.

"I was never informed you spoke Gharridese, Beva."

I spun at the unexpected voice.

A figure hovered in the archway, his calculating eyes observing us. The uniform was different from the others, the insignia on his shoulder indicating a higher rank. The man's presence brought a chill to the room that sent a shiver down my spine.

Beva's mouth hung open, at a loss for words as he stepped farther in. "When I was told that you'd brought a young woman with you, I thought my informant had been mistaken. I do not believe your daughter has aged quite so quickly."

His deep voice resonated with authority, his commanding demeanor waiting for an answer.

Beva's expression was about to slip into a panic, her eyes wide as she met mine, seeking for what to say. "Helvah took ill, Captain," she finally managed. "My niece, Taryn, was able to help. She is not from Gapsvar and is unfamiliar with the language."

I held my breath as his condescending scrutiny focused on me. The gaze was so direct I felt that he might stare into my soul and discover our secret.

"Taryn." He chewed on the word like a new food, trying to decide whether the flavor was pleasant or sour. The man moved closer, his mustache twitching. The scent of metal and ink overpowered me. His discerning eyes reminded me of passing someone in a dark, damp alley and knowing it was best to avoid them.

"This should have been cleared with me first." He turned to Beva. "You know how I hate strangers within these walls."

Beva wavered beneath his glare. "I apologize, Captain. My girl just fell ill last night, and with the celebration, I feared I would not be able to complete everything alone. If my thoughtless actions have caused any trouble, I am truly sorry."

Beva was shifting the attention to herself, avoiding discussion of the actual problem, which was that I only spoke Gharridese.

He let the silence hang between us, displaying his control of the situation. If anyone was to discover my true intent for being here, it would be him. My fingernails dug into the counter to keep my hands from shaking, and I held my breath. After a moment, he turned to leave.

"I will overlook it this once because I am in a good mood for the celebration," he decided. "But be sure to not let her out of your sight lest she wanders where she shouldn't."

Beva dipped her head respectfully. "Thank you for your generosity, Captain Dugal."

His footsteps faded down the hallway as Beva shuddered, his absence warming the room once again. I leaned against the counter, nauseous.

"Is all well?" I barely spoke above a whisper, afraid his ears were still tuned to our conversation.

Beva did not answer.

CHAPTER FORTY-ONE

Taryn

THE UNEVEN MATTRESS poked me unmercifully on the third night, keeping me awake as I stared up at the ceiling. Soft snores drifted from Beva next to me. Stressed as she was, sleep was not difficult for her. Tomorrow was the banquet. The day after, I would be forced to return down the mountain with Beva. If I wasn't successful before then, I would have to sneak back in through the woods. At least I would know the layout, but knowing the layout wouldn't keep me from getting killed.

Zedekiah was not here. Of that, I was fairly certain, but by feigning ignorance and careful exploration, I had discovered a way to get to Marco—if he was still alive. The entrance to the dungeon rested on the floor above us, but guards stood stationed on either side of the heavy metal door. When I'd passed the guards earlier, I'd found no evidence of keys hanging from their belts or on any nails in the wall. There hadn't been enough time to study further because another guard quickly stopped me, and he wasn't very pleased about my presence in the corridor. His harsh words were meaningless grumblings, so I had simply pointed to the water pail with a confused expression.

He'd chewed on his mouth for a moment before growling and motioning for me to follow him. When Beva had sent me to fetch the water, I'd purposefully gone the wrong direction to find what I was looking for. I had taken my time at the well, the guard frowning and tapping his foot in impatience, but my mind had not been on the water pail. I needed to find a way to get through that door. Even if I managed to get close enough to the guards without suspicion, I would have to react quickly enough that neither man would have time to call out before my blade met them—and then there would be the bodies. No dark alcove was big enough to hide them. Dragging them to an empty room would leave a trail of blood and cost too much time and energy. My only hope was for there to be no guards on the other side of the door, allowing me to stash them there, but that was unlikely. If not, I had to pray I could get in and out of that dungeon before the sentry passed, because as soon as he discovered the messy scene I had left behind, he would raise the alarm.

Once I'd filled the water pail, my guard had escorted me back to the kitchen and spoken to Beva, while giving me a knowing eye. Beva had placed her tray on the table as he left.

"He's warning you to go the proper way next time."

I had nodded and focused on the dough before me, staying in line for the remainder of the day.

I now rose from the bed, slipping my cloak around my shoulders and silently padding out of the room. The air was damp and chilled my skin, the stone walls providing little warmth within the depths of the fortress. My fingers felt my way along the cool walls, a torch lighting the path every so often. My hair billowed behind me like a ghost in the night as I flitted from shadow to shadow, my heart racing within my chest until I finally reached the end of the hall where I snuck up the stairs to the main floor.

I waited at the archway, listening and watching for any sign of movement. I sidled around the corner where I could peek at the entrance to the dungeon. Two torches burned brightly on either side, glinting off the guard's armor. They couldn't detect me from where I stood in the shadows—I was little more than a shadow myself.

Footsteps echoed down the hall, and I disappeared deeper into the darkness, hiding in the lip of the archway. The steps grew louder, never slowing or quickening but staying perfectly in time. Suddenly they were right next to me, and I panicked, thinking they were going to come down the stairs, but they continued past. I released my breath and saw a guard from the corner of my eye as he continued his patrol down the corridor. Immediately I started counting, keeping my breaths slow and even to stay in rhythm. Two minutes. Five minutes. Ten minutes, twelve, fifteen.

The footsteps were again growing louder as the man made another round. Fifteen minutes. If I was to get Marco out, then I had fifteen minutes to find him and do so. I tilted my head back against the wall and fought tears of frustration as the weight of my situation came crashing down on me. That was not near enough time. It would take me fifteen minutes to hide the bodies and get through the door. If I took out the night patrol, no doubt there was an outside watch who would notice his disappearance. I stole one last glance at the door, trying to guess how many levels the dungeon had and how long it would take me to descend the stairs. Beva's space was not very far below the main level, but I had a feeling that this dungeon burrowed deeper. I took a deep breath, slipping back down the staircase.

It would take more than one person to breach that dungeon.

I couldn't do this by myself. If William were here, he'd have another idea. A swathe of guilt wrapped around me, knowing he was awake by now and probably angry as a hornet. A smile touched my lips, thinking of how furious he would be. Not just furious at me, but furious for his own carelessness in drinking the concoction. Even though Helvah wouldn't be able to explain anything, he would already know what had happened.

I carefully opened the door to our room and slipped inside, jumping at the sight of Beva sitting on the edge of the bed. The paleness of her face was illuminated in the darkness. Quietly, I shut the door and shifted to my side of the bed.

"You nearly scared me half to death, child. Where were you?"

Beva had introduced me as her niece, which meant she would also be responsible for my actions if I was suspected or caught.

"I found where the dungeon entrance is, but it's guarded at all hours, plus a patrol every fifteen minutes." This was hopeless. "I don't know how I'm going to get in, but I have to try."

Fear festered in Beva's eyes, and she bit her lip, her mind working. "If you must, it needs to be tomorrow night—during the feast. There will be fewer guards patrolling; most will be at the feast. That time will be your only hope."

I nodded, swallowing hard. It wasn't much of a chance, but I had to take it. I met Beva's gaze, and Helvah's face flashed before mine.

"I need you to do something for me, Beva."

Her expression grew cautious.

"Are you able to leave once the feast begins?"

She hesitated thoughtfully, as if considering her options, then nodded.

I took a deep breath, hating myself for the words I had to speak. "When I enter the dungeon, I need you to leave. Get Helvah as quickly as you can and get somewhere safe. If I don't make it out of there, they'll know you were involved. I don't want you and Helvah caught." My eyes were serious as they bore into her, willing her to understand.

Beva knew exactly what I was saying—I didn't hope to make it out of here alive, and I was worried about her safety too. She also knew what I was asking: that she and Helvah leave the only home Helvah had ever known. Because of me. Bringing Beva and her family into this was a terrible mistake, and whether or not I was successful in my endeavor, helping me would be a heavy price for them to pay.

All of this understanding reflected in her eyes as she slowly nodded. "We have idled in Gapsvar too long anyway. I will hope to meet you in Gharridan again one day, Kavari."

I nodded, hating myself for what I had done and what I

was doing to her family. She didn't deserve this, and neither did Helvah.

I lay back down on the mattress, the idea of what I was doing to Beva making me nauseous. If there was any other way, I would change to it in a heartbeat. Dark dreams haunted my sleep, sickly ghosts of guilt and regret that plagued my soul and screamed accusations in my ears. They chained me with their words, holding me hostage as I struggled to break free. When I did, I awoke, my clothes drenched with sweat.

CHAPTER FORTY-TWO

Taryn

THERE WAS AN excitement in the air that touched every part of the fortress, a spring in the step of each soldier who passed Beva and me as we set out the cakes for the feast. Serious faces had melted into soft features that carried occasional smiles. The sun was already beginning its descent, and the feast was set to start at dusk. I was thankful I would be operating under the cover of darkness. Shadows that stretched across corridors made it easier to slip by unnoticed.

My movements were clumsy, and my fingers fumbled as I helped Beva with her work. As soon as the feast began, my plan was to go inside and take out the guards first. If I was able to get close enough without them suspecting a threat, I would have the element of surprise, but once I was past them, it would be a race against time to work my way through the dungeon to

Marco.

"You look nervous," Beva warned. "Don't."

My eyes wandered to where Captain Dugal stood in the shadow of a pillar, his ever-present gaze fixed on us. He hadn't bought Beva's story when we first arrived. His suspicion sent my skin crawling, and I turned away, pretending not to have noticed him.

The grounds were quickly filling with soldiers as the sun dipped lower into the sky, the world darkening in the first sign of dusk. A rainbow of colors shot across the sky, morphing from one shade of sunset into the next until the absent light settled into a dull grey.

Beva grabbed my hand and squeezed it, whispering, "I'm sorry there wasn't more I could do for you."

I tightly squeezed her hand back. "You did everything you possibly could. I will not forget your kindness."

I moved from her to stand in the shadow of the building, casting a glance over my shoulder and watching to make sure she disappeared from the feast. My emotions struggled within me, watching as she casually moved out of sight, and then I looked up at the sky.

Dusk had descended.

Like a thief who slips from the market unnoticed, I slipped away from the merriment and shrank into the shadows. My eyes were peeled for any watchers as I darted between the groups of soldiers and searched for anything suspicious, but their attention had already been captivated by the food and wine as the world shifted completely into night.

My hand circled around the hilt of my dagger hidden beneath the folds of my skirt as I entered the main building and hid in an alcove, waiting to see if the patrol would come. No guards marched past me. The laughter outside was growing louder.

It was now or never.

I closed my eyes, took a deep breath, and strode forward, emerging from the shadows like a sinner repenting his sins. My knife was safely concealed at my side as I approached the two men standing guard at the prison door. They hadn't noticed me yet, but they would. I crept closer, building my plan of attack with each stride that I took. My hands were shaking and slick with sweat.

Thirty more steps.

One of the guards looked in my direction.

Twenty more steps.

My hand tightened again on the dagger.

"Taryn?"

The deep, accented voice stopped me in my tracks, and the hair rose on the back of my neck. This was not part of the plan. I pressed the dagger into the folds of my skirt as I turned. Captain Dugal stood behind me, his chin raised as he looked me up and down. He glanced at the soldiers standing guard before returning his steely eyes to search my soul.

"Yes?"

My voice was shaky, my fingers clutching at the dagger. I prayed he wouldn't notice my hand obscured within my dress. I had to get away from him. Time was quickly running away from me.

Suspicion was written all over his face. "What are you doing in here?"

I swallowed, looking at the two heavily armored soldiers

standing on either side of the captain. He wouldn't have to ask very many questions to figure out that I was lying.

"I was ..." Words left me, my unfinished answer hanging in the air.

"You know ..." He stepped closer to me, intertwining his hands in front of him. "I never had the chance to talk with you after you first arrived. Beva was always very insistent that you were kept busy."

The captain smiled. It was not the pleasant smile someone flashes when they behold the beauty of creation. It was the smile of a hunter watching a deer step into the sight of his arrow. He held the smile as he surveyed the empty hall.

"It appears you have time now."

He signaled, and his guards took their place on either side of me, eliminating any chance of escape. I glanced briefly at the dungeon door before stepping forward. The only choice left was to follow the captain.

Despite my attempts to keep them even, the beats of my heart were chaotic. Excuses raced through my mind, but none were viable. Every thought jumbled together and collided into one another, and I couldn't find a substantial claim to rest upon. Sweat dripped down my back in an icy trickle. My only hope was the dagger clutched at my side.

We entered what I assumed was Captain Dugal's office. A shelf of books lined the far left wall, while a massive oak desk sat in the center of the room. The soldiers led me before the desk, the captain circling behind it to face me. He gave the guards a command in his own tongue, and they stepped out of the room.

My senses tingled, my body on high alert. I felt my back

stiffen as he assessed me, his sharp face contemplating.

"You said your name was Taryn?" His words cut toward me through the tense air.

"Yes," I answered. My dress clung to the sweat on my back.

He nodded slightly, pacing. "Where is it that you're from, Taryn?"

My mind raced for an answer. "Navarre."

"Navarre." Captain Dugal spoke slowly, pondering the name. "I've never heard of it."

"It's a small village southeast of here."

"And you traveled all this way just to visit your aunt?"

"Of course." I filled my voice with confidence. "She's very dear to me."

He smiled in the same unpleasant way as before. "How is your family managing without you?"

I lifted my chin. "They are no longer alive."

Telling partial truths was the best way to keep the words believable.

"No family back home." His voice was smooth, calculating. "Have you any other relations?"

Where was he going with this?

"My aunt is the only I know of."

His gaze lowered, apparently noting my hands hidden behind my back. "Have we met before, Taryn? Your face seems familiar, yet I'm unable to place it. I doubt I would fail to remember a face as pretty as yours."

Heat rose to my cheeks, but my gaze remained steady as I firmly shook my head. His face almost seemed to fill with disappointment. "Not that I recall, Captain."

"Strange, because I never forget a face. Perhaps it is something in your eyes."

His gaze unnerved me, stealing into my soul, desperately searching for whatever he thought he was going to find. I didn't understand why I should look familiar to him. I'd never seen him before in my life, until the kitchen three days ago. Words echoed in my mind as I recalled Zedekiah's sword pressed against my throat, preparing to end the line of Gallows.

You have your father's eyes.

I could still feel Zedekiah's breath on my neck, the realization of everything slamming into my chest. If I looked familiar to Captain Dugal, he might have crossed paths with my father at some point in his life, but it couldn't be just the eyes. To think one might recognize me by them was foolish.

"Some people tend to carry a more familiar face than others."

The captain's shoulders shrugged indifferently, the matter appearing of no use to him, yet he watched my reactions closely. He stepped around the desk toward me, his mouth opening to ask another question.

An urgent knock came at the door.

Captain Dugal threw a glance at the door, irritated.

"Come in," he said with a rough voice.

The door flew open, two men stumbling through it. One looked rather scared while the other was vastly out of breath and panting.

The heavy breather rattled off in his own tongue, barely managing to gasp the words as he extended a parchment of leather into the captain's hands. It looked like a missive.

He frowned as he accepted the letter, opening it tiredly. Once he began reading, his entire demeanor changed, and he turned away from me as he devoured the words inside. I looked over his shoulder at the paper, surprised that I could understand it. His body obscured the bottom half, but I could easily read the top.

Captain Dugal,

The first conditions of the treaty have been accomplished, and your station in Gapsvar has been instrumental in our plight. Your cooperation in imprisoning the Kavari is greatly appreciated, but he is no longer needed. If Zedekiah has not reached you yet, Marco may be terminated before then.

Brenden is ready.

Inform King Dorjan that the second condition will be met shortly, erasing any enemies, and that the land that was promised will be given into the possession of—

The captain turned, blocking my view of the letter. I restrained myself from moving to follow him. My mind reeled at the missive. What treaty? Conditions? Land? Brenden was ready? But there was only one revelation I had eyes for.

Marco was still alive.

After a moment, the captain re-rolled the missive, placing it inside his leather jerkin. He dismissed the messenger and nodded quickly at the guards. They stepped aside as the captain escorted me from the room. I adjusted my grip on the knife, turning it like the thoughts in my head turned for a way to escape. The celebration was in full swing when we entered the porch of the house. Promptly, the captain poured me a glass of wine, raising his own to his lips. I stared at the dark liquid, raising it to my lips but keeping it from entering my mouth.

"What are you celebrating?" It was a dangerous question.

Captain Dugal ignored me, downing the rest of his glass and slamming it back onto the table.

A commotion came from the far end of the crowd, a minor tussle from the sound of it. Captain Dugal stepped forward, and I shrank slightly back, hoping this might provide me with an opportunity to escape. The sea of men parted, revealing two soldiers dragging someone behind them. They brought him before the steps of the dais and shoved their victim to the ground.

Captain Dugal barked at them, waving his hand out as he strode forward.

One of the soldiers ripped the man back by his hair, and a small gasp escaped my throat.

William.

Horror and anger sliced through me at the sight of him. What was he doing here?

The soldier spoke harshly, and I desperately wished I could understand. He indicated the woods beyond the fortress, and I assumed that's where they'd found William.

William was defiant as he stared up at the captain, the bruises from his last encounter still visible. When he saw me, a flash of fear lit his face, which he quickly obscured, but it had not escaped Captain Dugal's notice. He spun toward me, catching the recognition in my eyes before I could hide it.

Two guards suddenly grabbed me, dragging me down the steps to William's side. Captain Dugal brought his face close to mine, alcohol emanating from his breath. He pointed at William, keeping his eyes on me. "Do you know this man?"

I shook my head. He already knew the answer, but I refused to assure him. William was obviously Gharridan. Our simultaneous presence would have made a simpleton suspicious. The captain smiled, but it never reached his eyes.

"Of course you don't." His attention returned to William. "Who are you?"

William was watching me from the corner of his eye. I held my breath. He couldn't give up his identity, but he wouldn't be able to lie his way out of this. Blood seeped from his nose where his face had been slammed into the ground.

A fist smashed into William's stomach, and he lurched forward, spitting up blood. I cringed, itching to put a stop to this and dreading what would happen if I couldn't. Captain Dugal bent down, inches from William's face. "Here's how this is going to work. When I ask a question, you give an answer." He spoke clearly in Gharridese, making sure we didn't miss a single syllable.

A gargled cough escaped William's throat, and he slowly brought his eyes up to the captain's.

"Name's Will," he said dryly.

"Who sent you?"

A smirk tugged at William's mouth, but he remained tightlipped. I knew beneath that smirk was a smart remark fighting to get out.

It was the captain's turn to smirk now. "All right. We'll do it your way instead."

He marched toward me, yanking me against him. A cry escaped my lips, two soldiers securing me in place as the captain brought the tip of a knife just below my eye. A short, shallow breath escaped my throat.

"Start giving me answers, or she loses an eye."

Fear enveloped William's face as he met my gaze. I wanted to shake my head, to tell him not to give in, but I was too paralyzed with fear to move.

"If your answer doesn't suffice, we'll move to the next eye and keep removing appendages until it does."

I didn't doubt his threat.

The air was thick with tension, the company around us watching for what would take place next. I sucked in a shuddering breath, my eyes locking with William's.

"We were sent here to find Marco," William said.

The knife hovered, pressing against my skin. "By whom?"

"The Kavari."

He frowned. "The Kavari would send one of their own. You're not Vladimir."

The captain yanked my hands from my side, discovering the knife and twisting it from my grasp. He must have seen the necklace because he pulled the chain from beneath my dress, revealing my father's ring. Its appearance seemed to confound him. He grabbed a fistful of my hair, rubbing it between his fingers. "You're not the read-headed demon either."

He dropped the ring, bringing his eyes back to mine. "What's your name, girl?"

My heart hammered against my ribcage. Even if I didn't give him an answer, it wouldn't take him long to figure it out.

"Taryn," I managed. "Taryn Gallows."

I watched the realization flood through him, and he leaned back, a laugh beginning deep in his throat. He smiled that wicked smile, the laugh forcing its way out. "The eyes …"

He turned to his men, rattling off in their own language, and they joined in his laughter.

"Gallows."

His eager face neared mine, his reeking breath hot on my face. "Do you know what we do with a Gallows when we find one?"

He turned to his men, most likely relaying his words to them.

Shouts erupted from the crowd, followed by cheers that deafened me.

The captain was still laughing when he looked back at me. "We hang them on one!"

CHAPTER FORTY-THREE

Taryn

THE STONE FLOOR rose to meet my face as the metal door of the cell slammed shut behind us. Dampness hung heavy in the air, the thickness of it nearly suffocating me. A chill ran up my arms, the cool floor icy against my warm skin, and I stumbled to my feet, gripping the sides of the narrow eye slit in the door. The only light that spilled through the window and into our cell came from a torch burning in the hallway. I rattled the door, seeking some form of escape as the guards' footsteps faded back up the passageway.

Three of our surrounding walls were stone, the fourth an iron gate that separated us from an adjacent cell even darker than ours and cloaked in shadow. My fingers felt along the walls and the iron in the hope of finding a weakness. Moss covered the stones, as well as a variety of other substances of which I didn't care to know the origin. I felt hope leave me as my hand slipped from the wall.

Nothing. It had all been for nothing.

"What are you doing?" William coughed.

I pursed my lips, refusing to give up. "There has to be a way out."

The one thing I'd wanted for the past few days was a way into this dungeon. Now the only thing I wanted was a way out.

"I'm sure its last prisoner left a map somewhere."

I rolled my eyes at the ceiling, which also offered no escape.

William was struggling to stand, sweat beading his forehead. He grimaced, and even in the low light, the colorful bruises splayed across his face were visible. It was then that I noticed his shoulder. He was clutching at it, and something in the angle of it looked terribly off.

"What's wrong?" I knelt beside him, looking for the source of the problem.

"Where would you like me to start? It'll take a while to list everything."

"Your *arm*, William." My patience was thinning.

He looked sideways at his shoulder. "I think it's dislocated." He attempted to move it and let out a groan. "It's not the first time."

I recalled this happening to a young boy in Navarre once. He'd fallen out of a tree, screaming as his arm hung limp at his side. The town healer was able to reverse the damage, but I had only heard the boy's painful screams and not seen the mending.

"Do you know how to fix it?"

William's face scrunched in pain as he bent forward. "Yes."

His words were garbled. "But I can't do it myself. I need you to do it for me."

I shook my head in terror. "I'm not a healer, William."

"I'll show you what to do. Grab hold of my arm and slowly lift here."

I leaned away from him. "I'll end up making it worse."

William let out an exasperated sigh. "Taryn, if you screw it up, I'll only have to deal with it until morning anyway, but I'd rather not spend my final night writhing in agony."

He clenched his teeth as he accidentally moved his arm. His voice was low as he leaned toward me. "If you don't help me, I will never forgive you."

"I hadn't expected you to forgive me anyway."

He stretched his arm in front of me, and I bit my lower lip, tensing up.

William rolled his eyes. "Just relax, Taryn."

I could tell he was in a lot of pain, yet his expression had grown relatively calm.

"Okay." He let out a deep breath. "Grab my wrist and elbow firmly. Good, ok, now I need you to rotate it slowly—"

William yelled out, and I jumped in fright.

"Not that way!"

I clenched my teeth and slowly began rotating it in the opposite direction, following his instructions as I pulled his upper arm out and forward, then turned it back to where it had been. We both heard the pop, and William let out a shuddering breath, relief flooding his face.

"You didn't break it, so I guess you didn't do too horribly."

I scowled at him and stood, pacing the cell. "You wouldn't have hurt your shoulder if you hadn't come sneaking in through the woods."

William laughed. "Oh right, because it's not like I wasn't following the original plan that *you* came up with—that is, until you decided to drug me and form a new one."

"You would never have agreed to it, and it was our best shot of getting up here."

William tested his arm experimentally. "And it looked like your plan was going so nicely."

"Well, at least I wasn't locked in the dungeon," I shot back. "That didn't happen till you showed up!"

I wasn't about to tell him that Captain Dugal had foiled my plans. I was too angry. Angry at myself for how I'd deceived him, at his barging in here, and angry that I was selfish enough to even be angry about that. I don't know what I'd expected him to do after waking up to find us gone. If he'd been willing to come with me this far, he wasn't going to just walk away—and most frustrating of all, I knew he was right.

"You're the one who wanted to go after Marco, Taryn. Not me."

"I never asked you to come along."

"You'd be dead if I hadn't!"

My chest burned, and for a moment, I wished he hadn't found me in that blizzard. Maybe I could've found a way to survive it on my own, but my anger slowly abated at the absurdity of the thought, and I realized that if William hadn't known what little of the language he did, I never would've made it this far. No one in Gapsvar would've given a room to a girl who only spoke Gharridese.

I turned away from him, tears stinging my eyes as I buried my head in my hands, defeat rushing over me. I had no reason to be upset with him. This wasn't his fault. It was mine. I was the one who'd gotten us into this mess. I had embarked on this suicide mission with little thought for anyone else. The only thing I cared about was vengeance, and it didn't matter what I'd had to sacrifice to get it. Because of my actions, we were stuck here in this dungeon, facing death, with no hope of survival. I had foolishly dragged Beva and Helvah into this, and now I feared if they didn't get away that they would face the same fate.

If they died, it was on me.

The fault for everything that had happened rested solely with me.

I glanced over at William leaning against the back wall, clearly done talking with me and refusing to meet my gaze. He kept his injured arm tucked close to his side as he chugged out of the canteen that still hung around his neck. Water dripped down his chin as he turned it toward me.

"Thirsty?"

It was obvious the offer was out of obligation. I didn't say anything, too ashamed to even answer. He raised an eyebrow at my refusal and capped the canteen. I gazed at him sheepishly, unable to procure a way to fix everything I had messed up, and then I squinted. Now that my eyes had adjusted to the dim light, I noticed that what I initially thought were bruises covering his face was actually partially dried blood plastered to his head.

"Your face looks horrible," I said.

William sighed. "And?"

I untied my apron and squatted beside him.

"What are you doing?"

My fingers took the canteen from him, pouring water over the cloth. When I dabbed the cloth to his head, he flinched and drew away.

"Sorry." My next touch was gentler. "You might as well look like a royal when they parade you out."

William chuckled. "I'm sure a clean face, along with my charm, will completely remove their intentions of killing me."

"We're not dying tomorrow." Firmness radiated from my tone.

His eyes met mine. "But what if we do?"

My fingers stilled. What if we *didn't* make it out of here? I'd been robbed, nearly drowned, abducted twice, and almost frozen in a blizzard. Was this really how my story would end, with my body swinging from the gallows? We'd come so far but still had yet to avenge my father's murder. I was not afraid, yet I was not ready to face Death again. I could sense him in the shadows, waiting for me with a wicked smile. The sweetness that once permeated Death had rotted into a foul, nasty taste that clung to my mouth and suffocated me. The last few experiences with Death had been too brief, too full of terror to notice the savor in my mouth, but now it was the only thing that I could taste.

As death hung over me, another face filled my mind: my father's. My stomach twisted, knotting with uneasiness. I almost vomited, the torn demeanor of my soul nearly ripping me apart. If I was to leave this world, then the matter must be dealt with—but I was not ready for judgment day. Slowly, the bitterness began to grow within me, twisting around my heart until it was as hard as the stone floor beneath me.

I would not forgive.

Forcefully, I pushed the thought from my mind. Guilt intertwined with the bitterness, inseparable from one another, each element seeking a way to resolve, but in the end, the bitterness won out.

I sat next to William, hugging my knees to my chest, my heart as heavy as a mountain.

"I'm sorry, Taryn."

Those were the last words I ever expected to hear out of William's mouth. I scrunched my nose. "What are you sorry for? This isn't your fault. You're not the one who got us into this mess."

William stayed quiet for a moment. "That you ever got tangled up with this in the first place. It doesn't seem like a life you would have chosen."

No, I wouldn't have. I stretched my legs back out in front of me. "In the beginning, it was partially my choice. I made the decision to go with Vladimir, but once he announced my provenience to the council, I no longer had control of anything. Vladimir promised he would get me out of there once another Kavari was found."

I could hear the slow dripping of water, splattering somewhere on the floor of our cell and interrupting my thoughts.

"What do you mean 'once another Kavari was found'?"

My mouth suddenly went dry. William and I had spoken so freely with one another that I forgot there were matters to which he was not privy.

"Taryn?"

I swallowed. "Vladimir didn't intend for me to join the Kavari. I was simply a pawn in the game. He needed to stall for time so he could seek counsel from Marco and prevent your mother from instating Mordakai."

The realization slowly dawned on William's face, which

hardened. "Vladimir went behind the Crown's back."

Yes, he had, but he'd done it for the sake of Gharridan. "If he hadn't, then you might've never known that Zedekiah was a traitor—not until it was too late."

William's voice rose. "If Vladimir had let the Crown choose the next Kavari, all this bloodshed might have been avoided! Mordakai wasn't the traitor. Zedekiah was—cold-blooded enough to kill his own brother!"

"Zedekiah wanted to destroy the Kavari. If he was left in power, he would've done it one way or another."

William threw his good hand in the air. "It's just a blasted power struggle! Whether it's my mother or Vladimir or Zedekiah, all they're concerned about is how much power they possess, and they don't care what they have to do to get it." He leaned back against the wall, laughing out of helplessness. "What does it matter now? What's done is done. There's no undoing it. We're about to die anyway, and our country is headed for war."

"What do you mean?"

William jabbed his finger at the door. "Those are Algarian soldiers up there, Taryn. Gharridan's relations with Algarar have been precarious since the war, but we've managed to avoid any bloodshed. I bet you anything they've negotiated a deal with Gapsvar so they can use their land and attack us from two places at once."

The war had been fought decades ago. I'd learned about it while training to become a Kavari, but I didn't remember much other than that Gharridan had managed to emerge victorious thanks to Gabriel, the Kavari's leader at the time. If Algarar really was planning to attack Gharridan, then our country would be completely unprepared.

"Do you think Zedekiah was working with Algarar?" I asked. "When I was in Captain Dugal's office, he received a missive. Zedekiah was mentioned in it. It also talked about a treaty and King Dorjan."

William was still deep in thought. "King Dorjan is the ruler of Algarar. It wouldn't surprise me, but I don't know, because if he was, then why were Silas and his men taking us to Brenden?"

My eyes narrowed. "The missive mentioned that Brenden was ready, but nothing else."

William's expression soured. "If he was, then they've been trying to infiltrate our country for years. They would've had to buy Zedekiah, who managed to work his way up into the position of my mother's advisor. We already know he was responsible for your father's death. Killing Michael made my mother more vulnerable to his suggestions, which would've made room for Mordakai to join the Kavari and become his brother's personal puppet."

William's anger toward Vladimir seemed to have temporarily abated.

"We need to get this information to the queen," I said.

"Let me see if I can fit it in between breakfast and our execution tomorrow."

I crossed my arms, frustrated that we had crippling information and could not do anything with it. I was about to die knowing my father wouldn't be avenged, but William would die knowing that his country would quickly crumble after him.

I wondered if Vladimir and his company had ever captured Zedekiah. Even if they had, getting the information out of him wouldn't be an easy task, and that was if it was even possible. Zedekiah's weaknesses had yet to reveal themselves.

"If you don't like your father, then why in the world did you ever agree to Vladimir's plan in the first place?"

My eyes slid shut. Why had I? There were a thousand times I wished I would have simply walked away that day.

"Once Vladimir spoke my name in front of the council, my choices were either vie for the Kavari or die. I only originally came with Vladimir because he offered me information about my mother's family."

"Your mother's family?" William sounded perplexed.

I squirmed uncomfortably. I didn't really like to talk about it much because, despite the time that had passed, the memory of her was still fresh and painful. "My mother was a very quiet and closed person. She often spoke of her family in the north, telling me that if anything ever happened to her and my father, she hoped I could reunite with them."

"Why didn't you?"

I pursed my lips, still upset about what she had asked of me. "Before she died, my mother made me promise that I would never leave the valley without my father's blessing or that I wait until his death."

"And you kept your promise all those years?"

I nodded. "When I learned he was dead, that's when I finally left."

More than once, I'd been tempted to break it, but in those moments, I was never able to go through with it.

"This is a strange mess," I lamented.

"It definitely wasn't the way I expected to die."

Silence hung between us for a while, the dark cell eerily

quiet. It was funny how William and I could go from yelling at each other to laughing over the ridiculousness of our situation. We didn't agree on most things, but there was an openness with him that I hadn't experienced with anyone else in a long time.

"I'm sorry," I said.

I could sense William smirking beside me. "What are you sorry for? Oh, right, you're the one who got us into this predicament."

I stared at the ground as I blinked back tears.

"I mean it, William." My voice grew serious. "You risked your life helping me go after Marco. You didn't deserve the dishonesty."

When I turned to look at him, his roguish expression was gone. Sincerity hung in his eyes, offering forgiveness, and the heavy guilt of my trickery lightened. In that moment, I realized how close we were; I studied the bruises on his face where the soldiers had struck him, noticed the patchiness of the stubble on his chin, the way his eyes locked on mine. The air seemed to grow very thin, my heart quickening within me as the unknown lingered between us. I saw the look in his eyes as he leaned forward, mixed emotions racing through my mind and body.

"William."

The apprehension in my voice held him back. The name was not spoken tenderly as one might speak to a lover, but as a warning. It brought us back to the reality of the situation, two strangers thrown together under unprecedented circumstances. Clustered together down here, with the threat of death hovering, had almost diminished us to equals, but my mind would not let me forget how far apart in life our stations were.

William's lips hovered near mine, a flicker of hesitancy in

his gaze. Slowly he drew away, turning to the far wall. I kept completely still and shifted my attention to the door. There was no denying that something lingered between William and me. After everything we'd been through together, it only made sense. I'd had to trust him in ways I'd never trusted anyone before. I felt safer around him, and I'd slowly become aware of it, but there had always been too much disagreement between us to entertain the thought of what could be. I wondered if he had felt the same as I, but I pushed the notion away. Facing death was a frightening experience, one that might alter a person's logic.

A small cough echoed through the chamber. I froze and gripped William's arm, meeting his alarmed eyes. We stood as one, staring into the dark abyss of the cell next to us. I could still hear the dripping of the water, and there was a soft patter of what sounded like mouse feet scurrying around, but nothing moved within the cell next to us. Had I imagined it?

No. We couldn't have both imagined the same thing.

"Who's there?" I called out, my voice shaky. If someone was in the cell next to us, why had they waited so long to reveal themselves? Our argument would have woken them long ago.

"We know you're in there." I was more confident this time, stepping closer to the bars of the cell, beating down the hope that was daring to rise within me. Something shuffled along the floor. Both our gazes were riveted on the shadows, watching carefully as a figure emerged from the darkness.

The window on our cell door cast a dim light on the man before us. Wild eyes stared back as if from a fear-struck animal, pupils wide and unseeing. Mangled hair filtered into a beard smeared with an array of dirt and grime, the knots so large and vast that they could never be undone. Filthy clothes hung on him like tattered rags and were covered with slashes, burns, and blood. The man's fingers wrapped around the iron railing between us, his frightened eyes squinting in the dim light. The narrow beam glinted off a golden ring encircling his finger.

"Marco?"

At the sound of his name, a recognition stirred in his mind as he licked his chapped lips. "You know me?"

I stepped up to the bars, placing my hand next to his. "You knew my father, Michael Gallows."

His eyes flitted in their sockets, beginning to fill with hope, and then plummeted into grief. Torment raged in his eyes as he struggled to understand, and the confusion warred with his sanity. Marco covered his face with his hands, suddenly overcome with emotion, and began to weep. Tears slipped between his fingers, clearing a trail through the dirt covering his skin.

I turned to William helplessly, but his unnerved expression showed he was just as baffled as me.

"Dead," Marco mumbled between sobs. A cry of anguish burst from him as his hand pounded on the iron. "He's dead! They killed him!"

His cries echoed off the walls in a cascade of sounds that bounced around the room. These were the tears of a man who had lost everything, even himself. He clung to the iron as he sobbed, his shoulders shaking.

I slipped my hand over his in an attempt to express my empathy. "We know, Marco."

After a moment, he quieted, the chaos in his eyes beginning to calm. There was no telling what they had done to him. He'd been a prisoner for weeks, a slave to the will of his captors. Scars covered his face, and no doubt dozens more lay beneath his tattered clothes. I let him relax a little longer before asking my question.

"My father, he sent you something before he died. It was a letter of high importance."

I waited for recognition, and he very slowly began to nod. A small smile tinged my lips.

"Do you know where it is? What was in it?"

His eyes grew dark, and he eyed me with suspicion, releasing his grip on the iron and stepping back. "It's a trick. You're one of them."

I pressed against the bars. "Please, Marco, we're not here to hurt you."

He shook his head, slinking back into the shadows, the darkness wrapping itself around Marco and concealing him from our sight.

"One of them. That's what they wanted to know. Don't tell them. It's a trap."

"Marco!" I jerked on the cell bars, willing them to part before me as I lifted the chain from around my neck and brought attention to my father's ring. I called his name again and again until William placed a hand on my shoulder, drawing me away.

"His mind is gone, Taryn."

Tears slipped from my eyes as the dungeons quieted once again. William wrapped his arms around me, and I cried softly into his shoulder. This really was the end. No one was coming to save us. We'd finally found Marco, but he was beyond help. If he'd had the letter or knew what was inside it, he would never be able to tell us. We'd found out who the traitor was without the letter, but Vladimir suspected Zedekiah hadn't acted alone.

Whatever hope we'd had of bringing unity to the country was lost with it.

"I don't want to die, William."

His hands stroked my hair, fear emanating from him.

"Neither do I."

CHAPTER FORTY-FOUR

Vladimir

ZEDEKIAH WAS ON the move again.

He was heading toward Gapsvar.

I was certain of it.

We followed stealthily, hiding in the trees. It was difficult to stay hidden with the snow, but it made tracking him easier than breathing. Anxiety wrestled within each of us. It was nerve-wracking to be so close to Zedekiah yet have to refrain from capturing him. My hand subconsciously kept reaching for my sword, and I had to force myself to keep it sheathed. Katherine's bow lay in her lap as we rode along, one hand resting on the arch of the wood, prepared to fire an arrow at any moment. Her fierce eyes focused straight ahead, unwilling to let Zedekiah escape her grasp.

The day dragged on, falling into nightfall at a torturous

rate. The snow crunched softly beneath the horse's hooves as we continued to track them. My body stiffened from both cold and sitting in the saddle. I thought Zedekiah would've stopped for the night by now, but I began to realize that he intended to ride straight through.

Why was he traveling through the night? I wondered if that was how they'd managed to stay two steps ahead of us this entire time.

The night stretched on, but we never had to slow our pace. The moonlight shining brightly above us reflected on the snow and illuminated the tracks. Around us, the trees were growing thinner, and I saw lights flickering off in the distance. I motioned for the men to stop, staying safely hidden within the trees.

I could see smoke rising from the chimneys in the village as Zedekiah and his three men made their way across the white plain toward what must be Gapsvar. We managed to follow them parallel as we kept at the tree line to keep from exposing ourselves.

"We're going to lose him in the city if we don't follow him, Vladimir," Katherine warned.

I knew she was right.

She always was.

"We can't go in there," I stated to the men. They all understood why.

"Let me go in," Katherine said.

I glanced at her before looking at the city. She could speak some of the language, but her hair would draw unwanted attention, and I couldn't send my men in wearing their military uniforms. Our relationship with Gapsvar was precarious at best.

Gharridans were little more than a plague to the people of Gapsvar. The news of Gharridan soldiers in the city would spread like wildfire, and if Zedekiah had spies in Gapsvar, he would quickly learn about us.

"It's too risky." My eyes looked beyond the city to the base of a mountain that backed it. "Besides, I have an idea of where he plans on going."

CHAPTER FORTY-FIVE

Taryn

THE SQUEAKING HINGES startled me, and I flew upright as the cell door banged against the stone wall. The sudden light blinded me, and I shielded my eyes, disconcerted from the commotion as William and I were yanked upright and hauled out the door. I struggled along the slick floor, my stumbling feet trying to regain balance as well as my senses.

Marco yelled as they dragged him from his cell, an earth-piercing shriek that echoed through the chamber as we ascended from the dungeon. His cries of protest rattled my ribcage as my heart hammered against my chest.

We were going to die.

My breaths were growing deeper and setting into a panic when I noticed the daggers swinging from the guard's belts.

The number of stairs left to climb were quickly dwindling before me, and my eyes darted about, forming a plan. I took a deep breath—it was now or never.

I slammed the full force of my body into the guard on my left, smashing him against the wall as I swiped his knife and shoved him down the stairs. The other guard grabbed a fistful of my hair and yanked me away. I cried out, thrusting the knife backward where it met flesh. The grip on my hair released, and I turned to see him tumble down the stairs, clutching at his wound.

William had already disposed of his guards and was tugging a most unwilling Marco up the stairs. My boots pounded against the stone. I ignored the shouts behind me, reaching the iron door and flinging it open to freedom.

I took one step outside the dungeon and was immediately thrust to the floor. A heavy boot stomped on my hand, breaking my grip on the dagger. Blood dribbled out of my mouth, and my head spun in a swirl of flashes and stars. I zoned in on a single pair of leather boots surrounded by countless others. Roughly, the guards forced me to my feet until I was facing Captain Dugal's dark eyes.

William and Marco had already been detained, and Marco struggled against his captor's grip. I swayed wearily where I stood but tried to appear confident before the captain. A strange expression covered his face as if he held a secret I did not possess. He gloated over our helplessness, reveling in our despair.

His fingers snapped. "Take those two to the gallows."

William's gaze briefly met mine before they marched him down the corridor and out of sight. Fear rose within me, leery of why they were holding me back.

I cocked my head mockingly. "Afraid to hang me?"

The captain chuckled, turning toward his office. "Your time is coming, but first, you must meet our special guest."

They yanked me forward, my confusion obvious as we approached his office. What special guest could there possibly be? My stomach sank, afraid of who or what lay behind the door, scared he had found someone else to execute with us as well. His office door swung open, light spilling in from the windows that had only bled moonlight the night before. The light was still blinding, and I squinted at its fierceness. Someone stood behind the desk, gazing out the windows. It took a moment for my eyes to completely adjust. His stark white hair was the first thing I noticed, the paleness of his skin pleading for sunshine.

Zedekiah slowly turned to us, smiling.

Every emotion spreading through me was fire to my veins. It awoke the anger within me, igniting the vengeance I so desperately sought. There was no fear left in my body, only the thought that this man must die. He stepped forward, and I spit in his face, pouring every ounce of disgust I could into the gesture.

It earned me a sharp slap across the face, but my fury was too strong to notice the sting.

"Pathetic," he sneered. "Just like your father."

I jutted my chin in defiance.

Zedekiah laughed. It was a low, wicked sound that crept into my ears like poison. "You escaped my reach of death once. Why track me halfway across the continent only to fall right back into it?"

"I've survived every previous encounter with death," I

said. "I'd say the odds are in my favor."

He smiled again. "I see death is of no consequence to you. It wasn't to your father, either, but then I killed him. You see, Taryn, your father learned the hard way that death is not the end of suffering."

The door swung open again, and Captain Dugal hauled a struggling Beva inside. One hand maintained a death grip on her arm while the other held a dagger, prepared to strike. The scene slowed around me, the weight of a thousand worlds pressing against my chest. Beva wasn't supposed to be here. She should be far down the road with Helvah by now.

Helvah.

Beva's eyes were wide with fear, but I could tell she was trying to stay strong for my sake.

"I was curious as to how you managed to infiltrate the fortress." Zedekiah stepped closer to Beva. "But then Captain Dugal informed me about your *aunt*."

Fear hammered within my chest. "She had nothing to do with this. She doesn't know anything."

Zedekiah tilted his head. "My dear, she had to know something if she was willing to lie for you."

I shook my head. "You have me. Leave her out of this. She had no choice. I forced her to help."

My voice was growing desperate, my lies more transparent. I didn't know how to save her from this other than to plead. Beva wouldn't be here with Death hovering next to her if I hadn't involved her in this mess.

"It's okay, Taryn." Beva's words were fragile; the tears sliding down her face felt like a knife slicing through my heart. "Just remember what brought you to me."

Zedekiah drew his brows together in mock remorse. "I so hate it when people gloat as they die, when they believe that there is victory in death." Zedekiah took the knife from Captain Dugal, testing its weight in his hand. "Your father thought that because he intercepted that message, his death was not in vain, but my last words to him left him feeling anything but victorious." Zedekiah was watching me closely as I held my breath, the air in the room growing thinner and thinner. His pale face transformed into a dark expression. "When you swing from that gallows, I want this woman to be on your mind. I want you to know full and well that it was your hand of ignorance that killed her, not mine."

The yell ripped out of my lungs, begging for mercy as I threw myself against the hold of my captors, watching in utter helplessness as Zedekiah mercilessly slit Beva's throat. She fell from the captain's arms into a crumpled state on the floor. Her mouth moved soundlessly, then stilled, her vacant eyes open as her lifeless form bled out on the stone floor. Zedekiah crowed over her dead body, watching as I descended into shambles. Tears poured from my eyes as I struggled against the guard's grip, but they pulled me away from her. I kicked and screamed in agony as my sanity ripped at the seams.

"Beva!"

I tried to turn to go back to her. To help her. But I couldn't. One thought filled my mind, consumed it, tortured it, destroyed it.

Beva was dead, and it was my fault.

My writhing soul struggled to break free, but their hold on my hands was as strong as iron. Tears blurred my vision, pictures of Beva's lifeless eyes swarming my mind. Even in the end, Beva hadn't blamed me. She had only thought of her daughter. She knew what she was risking when she agreed to help me. I'd known what I was asking, and yet I had gone ahead with it anyway.

The sunlight accosted me as we stepped out onto the dais. The entirety of the fortress' inhabitants gathered around us, their fists pumping the air as they yelled out curses and spit at me. I lifted my eyes, blinking away the tears and focusing on the erected gallows with three circles of rope waiting for our necks. William and Marco already stood before their contrivances of death. One soldier held a flailing Marco in place while another fit the noose around William's throat.

What a horrible atrocity the world was, filled with vile and wicked people completely devoid of compassion. Nothing good was left. I heard the beating of the drum, marching me to my death as the sea of soldiers parted before me. The steps leading to the platform creaked beneath my weight, the infrastructure shifting. My eyes surveyed the crowd gathered before us, and I wondered: maybe I deserved to die.

Helvah's face flashed before my eyes—a girl I hardly knew, yet the sadness my heart felt for her in this moment was beyond compare. She was alone in this world. Her mother would never return, and she would never know why. All she would know is that her mother left with two strangers. Two strangers who were supposed to protect her. But instead, Helvah would never see her mother again.

Anger coursed through my veins like poison as my stare burned into Zedekiah and his black heart. He stood on the steps of the dais, watching. Gloating. Enough hatred burned within me to bury his soul a hundred feet within the ground. I felt the noose get snugly fitted around my neck, and Zedekiah smiled.

The rhythm of the drum doubled, beating intensity into the coming event. I didn't hold my breath. Each inhale was another second of life. The continuity of the drum filled my ears, and I counted each final breath, waiting for the sudden feeling of weightlessness before the rope caught me. My breath shuddered out of me, preparing for death.

The drums ceased.

And the world around me was suddenly consumed in an explosion of smoke and flames.

CHAPTER FORTY-SIX

Vladimir

DARKNESS WAS BOTH a friend and foe, concealing us from searching eyes yet also hiding our enemy from us. The trees were dense, the underbrush thick as it pushed and clawed at us, warning us with its prickly fingers that we weren't welcome here. The horses slowly plowed ahead, the thick foliage making it difficult to accelerate our pace.

We'd already encountered one guard, managing to incapacitate him before he sounded the alarm, but we kept our eyes peeled for any others. I rode in front, with Katherine flanking my right and Melvin on the left. Bog and the others spread out behind us in a line, far enough to sense trouble but close enough to alert us to its presence.

The night was gradually melting away into dawn. Shadows still shifted around us, but the woods were beginning to fill with light. Snow crunched beneath the horse's hooves. Moving through the forest silently was impossible. I was afraid that we would soon have to leave the horses behind and continue on foot. There was no way to know what lay ahead, but as heavily guarded as the road was, I assumed there would be more than a handful of soldiers to face.

Beside me, Katherine pursed her lips and refused to acknowledge my presence. I understood her thirst for vengeance, but something else was going on here. Unearthing what Zedekiah was up to would prove more beneficial in the long run. There would be plenty of time to kill him later.

Somewhere to the right, a horse nickered.

Our company froze, my eyes darting to where the sound had reached us through the darkness. Dante grunted beneath me, and I placed a hand on his neck, willing him to stay quiet.

Another nicker answered.

Katherine's bowstring was taut, an arrow aimed toward our attackers. My sword grew heavy in my hand as I anticipated their appearance, but there was no crunch of snow beneath a horse's hooves, no clink of armor as a soldier drew his sword or strung his bow. No movement permeated the ever-brightening woods. The nicker came again, exactly in the same spot it had come from before.

Quietly, I dropped from the saddle, motioning for Katherine to cover me. As I slipped through the trees, gliding from one trunk to another, my eyes swept the surroundings for any sign of danger. My boots dug into the snow as I crept higher over the rising incline, but once I was over the crest, there was nothing but trees and snow. My brows furrowed. The horse should've been in sight by now.

A horse gave a deep grunt and shifted restlessly in the snow. I ducked low, peeking back over the ridge. Hidden in the shadows of several large trees and dense underbrush stood two horses. My hand tightened on the hilt of my sword, ready for the riders when they appeared, and I held my breath. My body tensed as it waited for the moment of the attack.

But no one came.

Sunlight glinted off the buckles of the saddles still strapped to their backs and the reins tied to low hanging branches. The snow beneath the horse's feet was greatly distressed as if they'd been standing in the same spot for a significant amount of time. Dirt and dust plastered their coats, indicating that they'd been on the road for a while, but with one look at their conformation, there was no denying the beasts were more than simple cavalry horses. Sensing my presence, they'd turned to me, noses flaring in and out to catch my scent. One looked like a light grey, the other black as night—

I scurried down the hill for a closer look, not believing what my eyes were telling me, but the close proximity only confirmed my disbelief. Underneath all the dirt, the horse was white.

"William?" I barely spoke above a whisper, repeating the name louder as I scanned the woods around me. No answer followed. Stryder and Othello gave a low whicker as I approached them, weariness framing their eyes. The reins were wrapped tightly to the branches, implying a previous attempt to free themselves.

"What is it?" Katherine appeared at the top of the hill, her eyes questioning.

The snow concealed which direction William and Taryn

had left behind, but with the lay of the land, I suspected it was uphill. There was a reason they'd left the horses behind.

At the sight of the horses, Katherine couldn't form words.

"They've been gone for a while," I said.

The other men were filtering over the crest now, confused by the discovery as much as we were.

"Bog, with Katherine and me. The rest of you stay here."

The large trail our boots left in the snow would either lead them to us or send our enemies back to them. Noises drifted from farther up ahead, growing louder with each step we took: shouting, and lots of it. Whatever the commotion was, it involved a large crowd.

"How did William and Taryn get here?" Katherine asked.

"I don't know."

We hadn't passed any lookouts, but I refused to let my guard down. Our stumbling feet had shifted slightly to the right and up to an outcrop. I grabbed Katherine's shoulder, pulling her down before she revealed herself.

Her irritated look was brief as we both crawled through the snow until we could peek over the edge. The crowd drew my attention first. There were almost a hundred armed men meandering around what looked like an outpost. A gallows had been newly built with three nooses swinging from it. Considering their horses had been left behind, I was quite certain I knew who two of them were intended for. Several men were still hammering on it.

"We can't breach that," Katherine whispered.

It would be eight of us against an army.

I scanned the crowd but saw no sign of Zedekiah or William and Taryn. Suddenly four soldiers exited the largest building with two captives between them. One of them was William. My stomach twisted as I watched them be escorted to the gallows, where ropes were tightened around their necks. Katherine nocked an arrow, and my hand shot out, grabbing the shaft.

Her wild eyes met mine. "They have Marco!"

My gaze shot back to the other captive, squinting against the morning light at the filthy man. Underneath the crazed appearance, I began to see the man I once had known so well. Shoulders once squared with regal pride sagged beneath the weight of his head, which now seemed too large for his frail body.

Katherine jerked the arrow from my grasp. "They're going to hang them!"

My attention was still riveted on the ghost of a man about to fall to his death.

"Not yet." Two drums sat at the base of the gallows, their sticks still in the drummers' hands. "Not until the drums start beating."

No other prisoners descended from the dais. Taryn might already be dead, but the delaying of Marco and William's hanging gave me hope. I hurried back down the hill, Katherine matching my steps.

"We can't take them," I said. "If we halved the ropes with an arrow, the soldiers would just sling over new ones. We need a distraction."

One that would buy us enough time to get the three of them out of there and make the guards think that there were more of us. I stopped at the horses, my mind racing for a plan. We needed something big, and there was no time for strategic planning.

"How big of a distraction?"

Katherine was holding a black shafted arrow in her hand. Only once before had I seen it in action, and I'd hoped that I would never have to see it again. I hesitated, an unspoken conversation passing between Katherine and me. The shaft ran the same length of a regular arrow, but thicker, and the arrowhead was almost twice as large as any other. Katherine knew what I was asking.

"It's heavier, but as long as you're precise enough to hit it, it'll land where I intend it to."

My eyes flicked down to the arrow again. As far as I knew, the execution of the black-shafted arrow had never been successful, but it was the best option we had right now. I turned to Bog.

"Find me some pitch or tree sap."

Bog began digging through the saddlebags for any such item. I ripped a shred of cloth from a blanket and wound it tightly around an arrowhead, tying it securely. Bog returned with a small leather parcel with a bottle nestled inside. When I tipped it over, the liquid began to drizzle out from the cap and sink into the cloth. I issued the other men to take place on the ridge and prepare to fire, spreading out to make our defenses appear wider. The arrowhead rotated in my hands, absorbing as much of the liquid as it could. When I pulled it away, the rag wasn't completely soaked through, but there wasn't enough time for that.

The drums were beginning to beat.

Katherine and I clambered back up the hill, nocking our arrows and testing their weight uncertainly in our hands. Bog was attempting to get a flame with the flint, but any useful kindling was buried beneath the layer of snow and difficult to find.

Taryn emerged from the building, the guards all but dragging her up to the platform.

Her face held no light.

Something was terribly wrong.

"I need a flame, Bog!"

My heart was galloping. Katherine hunkered down, focusing on her mark.

"There's a discoloration on the wood of the stable."

My searching gaze found her intended target and took note of it.

"I'm not sure that I'll hit it." Our eyes met, but there was no confidence in her gaze. "Your arrow is lighter and will fly faster. You'll have to loose it after mine."

I nodded.

The black shaft of the arrow was hollow and filled with oil that, upon impact, would shoot into the thick substance packed inside the arrowhead. Combined with both force and fire, we should have a weapon powerful enough to create the distraction we needed—if our shots were accurate.

The noose was placed around Taryn's neck, the beating of the drums doubling.

Flames erupted from Bog's flint, and I moved behind it, dipping the arrowhead with the soaked rag into the blaze. The fire devoured it.

"Now."

I pulled my string taut, the flames licking at my left hand and burning my face as I zoned in on Katherine's arrow as she released her grip on the string. I saw the arrow falter slightly, dropping lower than any normal arrow would have. It would not be hitting its intended mark. The bow creaked beneath the tension as I calculated the wind and distance, releasing my arrow a second after Katherine's and praying it would reach its target.

CHAPTER FORTY-SEVEN

Taryn

THE GALLOWS SHUDDERED beneath me. The ringing in my ears was deafening, my vision blurry as I struggled to keep my feet planted on the stool. Slipping would be a guaranteed death sentence. I searched for the source of the explosion. Something had struck the stables. Flames shot upward, the inferno licking at the corners of the barn as smoke billowed up into the sky. The hay in the barn was already burning, the entire infrastructure about to turn into a raging inferno.

I blinked, still stunned, and as I did, I realized that everyone else was just as stunned as I was. Several soldiers had already rushed toward the barn, trying to save the horses trapped inside. Some stood staring at the flames in helplessness while others searched for the source of the fire. My eyes shot into the woods, calculating where the attack must have come from, but there was no movement.

I cried out as an arm wrapped around my waist and went for the rope around my neck. I quieted when I realized it was William. He inched the rope from my head and shoved me off the platform.

"Get down."

A soldier was waiting for me on the ground, his sword preparing to strike. Something whirred through the air, followed by a thud. The soldier faceplanted in the dirt with an arrow sticking out of his back. Arrows were suddenly flying in in volleys, seemingly from several different points along the ridge. The soldiers ran for cover. They were armed with swords, but swords were useless against an unseen archer.

My eyes fell to the fallen soldier's sword, his dying hand reaching for it in the snow. I quickly snatched it from his reach, my shaking hands tightening around the leather hilt. William was clambering down the gallows with a screaming Marco clawing at his ears. I knew his ears must be ringing like mine, but with all this commotion, he had reached the breaking point.

A flaming arrow shot through the air and found its mark in the barracks. No explosion followed this one, and soldiers quickly raced to put it out before it spread farther. Another soldier rushed at us, sword raised. My blade met his, and I pushed the man back. William kicked his knee, and the man's legs buckled beneath him. In one swift movement, William grabbed the knife sticking from the soldier's exposed boot and plunged it into his chest.

I whirled around, searching for an escape. The stables were now completely engulfed in flames, the snow surrounding the building melting from the raging inferno. Loose and terrified horses scattered wildly away from the barn and into the trees.

The number of fallen bodies was growing as they crumpled into the trampled snow. Arrows still flew in from the tree line, but bows had emerged from the armory, and the defense was quickly taken. The soldiers' first volley of arrows fired back into the forest.

William pulled on my arm, dragging me away from the madness and toward the safety of the woods. I stumbled along beside him, casting one final look over my shoulder at the volatile scene. A flash of white caught my attention, halting me in my tracks. Pain and anger coursed through me as I once again saw Beva's dying body fall before my eyes. Zedekiah was mounting a horse, fleeing the scene.

"Taryn, we need to go!"

I heard the sense in William's voice, knew that he spoke the truth, but vengeance forbade me to leave. He was getting away. Helvah flashed before my eyes, and I jerked my arm from William's grasp.

"Get Marco out of here!"

William yelled after me as I tore through the snow, kicking up the powder in a cascade of white dust that billowed around my feet. Anger pulsed through my veins, beating through my heart and pushing me to run faster. Smoke wound around me like a formless demon, invading my lungs and blurring my vision—but I could still see Zedekiah running away. Hands reached for me, but I dodged away, sidestepped as an arrow flew near my head. Survival was of no importance to me—only vengeance.

A horse bolted in front of me, and I extended my arms out

on either side, standing before him. His shuddering body skidded to swerve me, throwing up a wave of snow. The reins flew through the air, saddle half-attached, evidence of a failed escape. As my fingers clamped down on the reins, he backed away, trying to evade my grasp, eyes rolling white. I brought him firmly back to all fours and lurched into the saddle before he sidestepped away from me. Zedekiah was disappearing into the trees, and I pointed the unpredictable horse in his direction. My heels dug into his sides as I opened up the reins, letting him explode into a gallop beneath me.

The sound of his hooves striking against the ground pounded in my ears as we left the chaos and the smoke behind us and surged ahead into the shadows of the forest. Cold, brisk air whipped at my face, hair streaming behind me. The trees grew thicker around us, and the frightened horse beneath me slowed as he darted in and out of them, but I kept him moving. With each stride he took, the gap between Zedekiah and me dwindled.

It was down to a handful of yards between us. I kicked the horse faster, bringing us nearly upon him. I slipped my feet from the stirrups and moved up onto the horse's back, crouching, my fingers twisting into his mane for support as I balanced the sword in my other hand, barely managing to stay on. One sharp jerk and I would tumble. Zedekiah turned his head, hearing hoofbeats, and I dove at him with my sword.

At the same time, his horse abruptly swerved into mine, the world filling with limbs and horses and snow. Something struck my chest, knocking the air from my lungs. Everything was spinning like the wheel of a runaway wagon, imperceptible flashes of movement and color clouding my vision. Eventually,

I went still, unable to determine which way was up from down. I rolled onto my side, a ragged breath escaping my lungs as I struggled to my feet. The world tilted to the right, and I stumbled forward, trying to regain balance. A disconnection lay between my mind and feet.

Sun glinted off the blade of a sword, and my fingers curled around the hilt. From the corner of my vision came another flash of metal, and I rolled onto my back, bringing my blade up to block the blow. Zedekiah stood above me, a nasty look protruding beneath the blood running down his face.

"Gharridan invades, and you run away with your tail tucked?" I challenged.

His standing weight gave him the advantage as he pushed the crossed blades closer to my chest.

"Come to get your revenge, have you? I should've killed you the moment Vladimir brought you through the gates of the capital."

My arms shook, sweat breaking out on my brow even though I was lying in the snow. The spinning world shifted to a standstill, my feet once again connecting with my brain, and I kicked at his left leg. It bent beneath the force.

He stumbled backward with a yell, barely able to stay upright. Taking the advantage, I crawled to my feet, clenching the hilt possessively. Zedekiah turned back to me with murder in his eyes, veins bulging and arms shaking with pain and fury.

Emotions swelled within me. Agony. Anger. Vengeance. Hurt. Bitterness. Fear. Everything that had happened was because of him. He killed my father, betrayed his country, killed Beva. Tears burned behind my eyes. *He killed Beva.* His death was the only thing that would make this right. My heart hammered in my chest in anticipation, preparing to release the emotions that tormented me with one final blow. I had waited so long for this moment.

Zedekiah raised his sword mockingly and sidestepped. "If you'd died when you were supposed to, we wouldn't be here right now. Vladimir wasn't supposed to make it back when he went looking for Marco. You were supposed to drown in the river along with Katherine."

I ground my teeth together. "You murdered my father."

Zedekiah limped forward, smiling. "Yes," he said, blood coating his teeth. "And I would gladly do it again."

His blade came down, and mine rose to meet it. My arms were weak, chest screaming where the horse's hoof had struck it, but I did not give up. The clash of steel rang in my ears as blow after blow rained down upon me. Even with his injured leg and bloody forehead, Zedekiah fought as if uninjured. Behind each strike was a fury that hadn't been present in the throne room. I drove my fury to match his.

Every ounce of bitterness radiated into my blows; every pain struck out with a thrust of my sword. The vengeance I so craved guided me, dictating my moves, forbidding me to give up, and refusing to let him obtain the upper hand. It kept me going even as I felt him gaining ground, but I fought to reclaim every precious step he stole. He did not relinquish them easily. His movements gradually became clumsy, his blows messy, but he was just as determined not to lose.

I took a step back, and my boot slipped on a sheet of ice, sending my feet flying from underneath me. The world was suddenly spinning again, and my eyes began to lose focus. I knew I was falling, knew that I had lost. Triumph twinkled in

Zedekiah's eyes as his sword plummeted down with me, preparing to take the final blow, and then my vision shattered into a thousand pieces as my head smacked against the ice.

CHAPTER FORTY-EIGHT

Vladimir

IT WORKED. I hadn't expected it to, but it did, and now all three of them were at least off the platform. I fired off another arrow, and it quickly found its intended target. My fingers reached for another one. The supply was growing dangerously low. We needed to continue with the attack until the three of them were safely behind us, but we were running out of time. It wouldn't take the soldiers long to realize how few of us were hidden on the ridge. William broke the tree line, struggling as Marco lashed out like a madman.

Taryn wasn't with them.

My eyes scanned the outpost as arrows whizzed over our heads. A thundering horse broke out of the smoke, barreling into the trees in pursuit of another horse. Dark brown hair streamed from its rider. There was no need to guess who she was trailing.

"Fall back." My voice was quiet, barely carrying to the other men.

Taryn was so hell-bent on revenge that she'd walked out of one noose and into another.

Bog brought the horses up behind us, and as I turned to mount, one of my men suddenly cried out. I swung around and saw him fall forward over the ridge with two arrows in his chest. He rolled to the base of the hill, lying still at the bottom, and I kicked the ground in anguish as grief rushed through me. There was nothing we could do for him now. Dante came up beside me, and I jumped into his saddle, the other men following suit.

"Start riding. *Now.*"

William helped Marco into the saddle with Bog and then mounted Othello one-handed, turning to me.

"She—"

"I saw," I said, aiming Dante in Taryn's direction.

My feet kicked him forward, and I felt his stride lengthen beneath me. The two horses were no longer in sight, but their tracks were freshly indented in the snow. The wind whistled in my ears as we followed the hoofprints, and I heard the clang of steel off in the distance, gradually growing louder as we approached.

My stomach dropped.

When I came upon them, I saw deep ruts gouging the snow down to the dirt, and one limping horse tottered after the other. Taryn and Zedekiah were on foot, their swords locked in combat. Zedekiah was gaining ground. Too much ground. Taryn slipped on an ice patch, her feet flying out from underneath her, and Zedekiah prepared to plunge his blade down upon her. Dread clawed at me like a ferocious beast. With uncanny speed, I unsheathed my sword as I slipped from the saddle, my blade outstretched to meet his.

The squeal of metal rang in the clearing as I caught his blade before it broke her skin. The strike jolted my arm, and I forcefully drove him back until he staggered away from me, raising his hand for a respite. Everything in me wanted to kill him. My sword ached to take him from this earth one piece at a time until there was nothing left but ash, but I lowered my weapon. Striking him down in anger would not give me what I wanted.

Zedekiah's chest rose with each labored breath he took, blood ran down his forehead, and his left leg was awkwardly bent.

"Come to finish the job, mighty warrior?" he asked. "It wouldn't be the first time."

I gripped the hilt of my sword harder, but my gaze remained steady. Whenever Zedekiah lost the advantage of brute force, he always resorted to verbal abuse, weaving words into vicious mind games.

"I never understood why Michael chose you as his successor." Zedekiah's voice mocked bewilderment. "You obviously had a thirst for blood, and certain skills with a sword, but you never held much promise for leadership. Michael refused to admit it, but the fact has proven itself since the hour you took his place. Disappearing for weeks, returning with 'the daughter of Michael Gallows,' digging a rift between the Crown and the Kavari. Gharridan is ripping at the seams, and you're cutting each string at a time."

My clenched knuckles paled to bone white, my eyes riveted on Zedekiah as we circled each other like vultures in the snow. The only thing coming from his mouth was lies, his seething voice trying to gut me with words, twisting them until the blame for everything came to rest upon me.

"Mordakai was ready. If Gallows had trained him from the beginning like I wanted, all of this could have been avoided. All you had to do was follow orders, but even that was too menial a task for someone of your *importance*."

None of it was true. Zedekiah had frowned upon me from the moment I stepped foot in the capital. He'd protested when Michael declared me his successor, advised against it for years, and spewed his discontent into the queen's susceptible ears. His hatred of me had been no secret. I loathed myself for not discovering his treason sooner.

"You would've destroyed Gharridan one way or another."

His sword whistled through the air in answer, and a resounding clang echoed in the silence of the forest as my weapon stopped his. The blades quickly rushed together again and again, striking out like a viper, blocking each other in rapid succession. I spun in a circle, his blade parrying mine as I swung back, but with each swing, his movements grew slower. Our feet slipped across the forest floor, snow spraying our faces.

Zedekiah sidestepped. I moved left to compensate and slid to the ground, my sword falling just out of reach. Zedekiah's blade pressed firmly against my neck. One movement and he would impale me.

"You always forget to watch where you're stepping, Vladimir."

Sweat broke out on my brow, and I laughed, Zedekiah's

blade ice against my skin.

"And you always let your guard down too quickly."

I thrust the dagger into Zedekiah's injured leg. He jerked back with a howl, and I wrenched it back out only to sit up and burrow it into his abdomen. His sword dropped soundlessly into the snow as he fell to his knees, a gurgled cry of pain screeching from his throat like a wild animal. I kicked his sword away, grabbing mine and touching the tip against the traitor's throat, our swapped positions ironic.

Death hovered over my hand as I prepared to take the final blow.

"Your death will provide Michael Gallows the proper justice he deserves."

Under other circumstances, Zedekiah would have been brought before the council and confronted with a public trial and execution. The suffering he warranted didn't compare to what he faced now. The people of Gharridan deserved to see him destroyed for his crimes, but from the moment we set after him, I knew the only way we could transport him back to Gharridan was as a dead body.

The point of my sword held steady and unwavering, yet I didn't strike. I found myself waiting for a confession, giving him one last chance to redeem himself, but his eyes remained cold and unrelenting.

"You know, I really thought you had it in you." Zedekiah's face strangled with pain. "Michael was too soft on you. Must've wanted to try a different method than that of your old man."

I took a step forward, my hands shaking as I pushed the tip farther into his skin, drawing a trickle of blood. Death hung in his eyes, the dark blood from his injury staining the trampled snow. Every breath grew more ragged than the last. He knew he was about to go.

He laughed, a strange, gurgled sound. "Michael was so close to the truth. They wanted him dead for it."

My brows lowered. "Who wanted him dead?"

Zedekiah's hand disappeared into a pocket, returning with a slim silver object that slid into the snow. His desperate eyes met mine, ever calculating.

"I have information." He was wheezing now. "We can make a deal."

"I don't negotiate with traitors."

His eyes were growing distant. "Information on why they killed him."

My sword faltered, lowering slightly.

"Tell me, and I might consider ending your suffering."

His gaze focused on something beyond me, a crazed smile touching his lips. "You don't know who she is, do you?"

The arrow flew beneath my arm and struck Zedekiah in the chest. A gasp escaped his throat, and he swayed on his knees. The light left his eyes as he fell forward into the snow, obscuring his face from the world forever.

I turned. Taryn stood behind me, staring at a lone figure beyond her, the string of the bow still vibrating. Katherine's eyes met mine, the vengeance in them finalized.

"I always knew I would have to do it for you," she said.

I sheathed my sword. "He had information."

"Every dying man has information."

The small silver object he'd pulled from his pocket lay half-buried in the snow. I knelt to examine it, pricking my finger on its sharp edge. It was paper-thin and curved in the shape of a crescent moon, no bigger than the palm of my hand.

Hoofbeats thundered up behind us. Bog, Melvin, and the rest of the men took note of the blood seeping away from Zedekiah's dead body in the snow.

"They're right behind us."

Taryn's expression was haunted as she swung into Stryder's saddle. Katherine peered curiously at the object in my hand, and I quickly wrapped it, shoving it into my pocket.

"Let's go."

CHAPTER FORTY-NINE

Taryn

THE WORLD BECAME a blur of trees and wind and cold. We thundered through the forest recklessly like a herd of spooked horses, the rhythm of the hooves pounding in my ears as I steered Stryder around tree trunks and ducked to avoid low-hanging branches. I threw a glance over my shoulder, comforted by the fact that I could no longer see our pursuers.

We were gaining ground.

The sunlight shone brighter up ahead, indicating that we were approaching the tree line. William suddenly pulled Othello up, swerving to the left; startled, I quickly did the same. We barely managed to turn before falling over the drop-off that marked the edge of the forest. The men behind us yelled as the horses dug their heels into the snow, trying to alter their course.

"This way!" William yelled over his shoulder as he galloped along the edge.

We continued curving around the forest until the cliff began to slant. Stryder charged down the slope after Othello, and I gave him his head, leaning back until I was nearly lying down. A barrage of snow attacked my face as Stryder's hooves kicked it up into the air.

We reached the plain, and my eyes caught sight of Gapsvar in the distance. Everything stopped around me. My chest constricted as I swallowed the lump in my throat, tears welling in my eyes.

Helvah.

I turned Stryder to the left, kicking him forward toward the town. William jumped in front of me and yanked on Stryder's reins.

"What are you doing?" he yelled in bewilderment. "We can't go back to Gapsvar!"

"Helvah is in the village!" I cried. "We can't leave her!"

William released my reins. "Beva will take care of her."

I sucked in a shuddering breath.

He didn't know.

He hadn't seen it.

"Beva's dead." My voice broke. "Zedekiah killed her."

I watched William's eyes transform into agony as he came to realize the situation. Helvah was alone in the world. She was now an orphan. An orphan whose mother was killed for assisting the enemy.

William ran his fingers through his hair, staring back at the town.

"What's going on?" Vladimir rode up beside us. "We can't

stay exposed like this."

Tears threatened to spill from William's eyes as he threw another look at Gapsvar, and then turned Othello in the opposite direction. "There's nothing we can do, Taryn. If you try to go back for her, it'll only end with a noose around your neck again."

I looked where his eyes had been and saw a line of soldiers streaming toward the town. My heart broke. Their straight shot down the mountain gave them the opportunity of reaching it first.

"She doesn't have anyone left," I whispered.

William gripped my shoulder. "I don't like it either, but she's beyond our help. The best thing for Helvah right now is for us to have nothing to do with her. She's smart, and she's quick. She'll either hide or find a way to escape if she needs to."

The sound of horses crashing through the trees drifted from the top of the embankment.

"We need to go." Vladimir urged Dante ahead of us.

Desperate tears fell from my eyes as I stared back at Gapsvar, but in my heart, I knew William was right. The soldiers were already entering the village. We would never be able to find her in time. Everything within me told me not to turn away, told me not to follow the others, but I did. I turned Stryder around, and the tears streamed across my cheeks as he burst into a gallop and carried me away from Helvah. I felt my soul splitting, aching for a girl that I hardly knew. A girl who had lost everything because of me. A girl I would never see again.

The heat of the flames seared my skin, but I barely even

noticed. They danced before my eyes in a series of leaps that wound into one another, making it impossible to determine where one ended and another began. No doubt, my body ached from the intense days of riding, but I couldn't feel anything. I was completely numb.

Confusion swept over me in waves. Zedekiah was dead. I should've felt better. When his lifeless body fell to the snow, I'd stared at it. I'd watched the blood drain from his body, waiting for myself to change, but I didn't.

Someone sat down next to me, but I couldn't take my eyes from the fire. It felt like I was in a trance, incapable of feeling or moving. Beva's pleading face hung before my eyes, her final words echoing in my ears.

Remember what brought you to me.

Beva had given up her life for me, and I hadn't even been able to grant her dying wish.

"William caught me up on most of what happened." Vladimir's voice was calm but radiated exhaustion. After several days of hard riding, we still didn't know if we'd lost our pursuers.

"Then there's nothing more to talk about," I said.

I didn't want any more discussion or deliberation. I just wanted peace, wanted to stop running from enemies, and stop constantly looking over my shoulder. Ever since my father's death, that's what my life had felt like.

"I'm sorry you couldn't save the girl."

I blinked back tears, my lip quivering.

Vladimir pulled something from his pocket, carefully rolling it around in his hands. It was the strange object that Zedekiah had thrown him, a small, elongated crescent with the sharpness of a dagger, unlike any weapon I had ever seen before.

"What is it?" I asked, studying its small structure.

Vladimir turned it over in his hands as if trying to decide whether he actually knew the answer. "I wasn't sure at first. I knew I'd seen it before, but it took me a while to place it." He held it out to me. "It's called a ricochet."

It was thinner than expected as I pressed the cold metal between my fingers.

"Choice weapon of the assassins of Brenden."

Brenden.

The country that appeared to be involved in my father's death.

"Captain Dugal received a missive while I was in the fortress," I said. "I couldn't see all of it, but one part said that Brenden was ready."

Vladimir grew quiet. "Zedekiah was definitely headed there before he changed course; I just don't understand why he was willing to give up the information, or why Algarian soldiers were in Gapsvar."

I chewed on my lip, not sure what to make of the information. "What are you going to do?"

"I don't know."

Vladimir shifted uncomfortably, and I returned my gaze to the flames, my emotions spent.

"You completed what you set out to do," he said. "I thought you'd be happy."

His words cut straight to the heart, clawing their way to where it hurt most. My arms curled around my knees, tears stinging my eyes. "I just, I thought that if I could kill Zedekiah, that if he was dead ..." I trailed off, looking to Vladimir for an explanation. "Why do I still feel this way?"

His serious yet empathetic pale blue eyes searched mine with hesitation, waiting to find the right words. "Because the war you're fighting inside did not end with Zedekiah's death. That's a battle you will have to face yourself."

The war between bitterness and forgiveness once again rose within me, but I shoved it back down, unprepared to fight.

Vladimir reached into his pocket and extended something to me. "I should have given this to you already."

It was my mother's clasp.

My fingers curled tightly around it, holding it close to my heart. The touch of it brought a comfort that had been lost to me for so long.

"Her family name," I asked. "What was it?"

He paused before speaking, "Illdalorre."

My brows lowered. "What part of the country does that come from?"

Vladimir turned to me. "It doesn't. I don't know where your mother was from, but it wasn't Gharridan."

CHAPTER FIFTY

Taryn

EVEN THOUGH THE men from Gapsvar were no longer hunting us, it was still difficult to relax. The men indulged in conversation each night, but I stayed out of it. I felt out of place. William remained close by, a welcome comfort after we'd been through so much together, but I struggled to even speak with him. He was always within sight, watching me, words hanging on the tip of his tongue, but as the distance grew between us, I could tell that he no longer knew how to approach me.

Vladimir occasionally sat with me by the fire, sometimes to ask questions, and other times just to sit in silence with me. There was no explanation for it, but somehow, I felt as if he knew what I was going through. Everything seemed so pointless now, like there was no way to move forward.

Helvah's face haunted me in dreams, her desperate cries and angry questions piercing my soul. Sometimes, I thought I saw her, standing at the edge of our fire, her curious eyes searching, waiting for a goodbye she would never get. I wanted to run to her, hold her close, and tell her how sorry I was. Tell her that her mother hadn't abandoned her. But then I would blink, and she was gone. She had never been there.

After the first day, Marco's hysterics had died out. Vladimir's presence seemed to calm him, but he remained mute except for a few mutterings here and there. Any attempts to coax anything more out of him were unsuccessful.

Vladimir was whispering with Bog, throwing a glance between Marco and me. I tuned them out, indifferent to the conversation. I wasn't even sure why I was still traveling with them. Zedekiah was dead. Mordakai was no longer able to vie for the Kavari. Freedom spread out before me like an open field.

Vladimir sidled his horse up next to mine, speaking in a low voice. "There's something I want to show you."

Whatever it was, it held no importance to me, but I urged Stryder after him. At this point, I would have followed Death himself had he asked. I could feel William's eyes on us as we rode away from the group, but I refrained from meeting his gaze.

Trees flew by us as we rode deeper into the woods, and the sun drooped lower in the sky, the shadows of the wood stretching out before us.

"Where are we going?" I asked.

Vladimir didn't answer but pushed on ahead, his rigid back betraying the tension he felt. The hills grew higher, and I felt the ground rise and fall beneath us as we meandered over them.

Vladimir's face was strained. Pain hovered behind his eyes, but still, he did not speak. The elusiveness of the situation made me sit up higher in my saddle, watch the woods a little closer. He had my attention now.

We reached the top of an incline and looked down into a small dip in the forest completely devoid of trees. Vladimir stopped, staring down into the small valley with a haunted expression. He made no move to go any farther. Nothing lay in the valley below.

"What is it?" I asked.

He nudged Dante forward, moving toward lower ground. A prickle of fear crept up my spine as I failed to understand what was happening. We stopped at the bottom of the valley, where snow still resided. Vladimir's eyes were transfixed on one solitary spot that seemed to hold nothing special.

"That was where I found him."

My mouth parted in confusion, but then he turned, sorrow etching the lines of his face.

I understood.

I tore my gaze back to the spot I had at first thought so meaningless.

"He lay there, pierced with his own sword, surrounded by seven bodies burned beyond recognition. Michael willingly sacrificed himself for the good of the country for a letter that we'll never see."

I'd known that Vladimir had found his body, but I'd never once considered what that had been like for him, what he must have gone through. My eyes were riveted on the spot as images formed in my mind. Images of my father bravely defending himself and his country, taking down seven enemies on his own before succumbing to defeat. I pictured his lifeless body lying in the snow.

"I don't know what his reasons for hiding you away were, Taryn, but as well as I knew your father, he did it for your protection. You can continue hating him for the rest of your life, but I promise it will never give you the peace or closure that you're looking for."

Vladimir's voice was cautious, like a friend warning another about a dangerous ledge they'd already decided to jump off. I dismounted, my emotions all over the place, threatening to destroy me. Vladimir took Stryder's reins from me, nodding toward the top of the hill.

"I laid him to rest just on the other side."

My heartbeat quickened within my chest, my soul a writhing, wavering ocean of uncertainty and indecision. My mind rebelled against me. I didn't want to see it. Yet I felt that I had to. I needed to.

My feet began moving without my consent, carrying my body toward the unknown. The incline was steep, the half-melted snow making the route slick. The top of the ridge loomed before me, a mystery yet to be solved, and I climbed higher. I stepped out of Vladimir's sight, searching the woods.

I saw it.

My breath caught in my throat as my pace slowed. With each step I took, the anger rose within me, continuing to build until I stopped before his grave. An assembly of stones covered the place where his body lay, the head of the grave marked by a roughly constructed wooden cross.

The guilt was still there. I could feel it—the hurt, the pain—then anger. We'd brought my father's murderer to justice, yet my feelings had only intensified. Bitterness seeped through my veins, infecting every part of my body until I realized I was crying. Hot tears poured down my cheeks in a swirling pool mixed of sorrow and anger. The hatred clung to me like a disease, unwilling to part with my body.

"Why?"

My voice broke.

"Why?"

The shout reverberated through the woods, a question that had gone unanswered for far too long. Now it could never be answered. Fresh tears streamed down my face as I collapsed to my knees, sobbing on the forest floor. I grabbed a rock and hurled it at the nearest tree. My arms grew too weak to reach for another one, and I crawled up to the grave, my fingers gently touching the rough wooden fibers of the cross.

"Why did you never come back for me?"

The hurt welled in my voice as I gave life to the question that had haunted me so fiercely. All the brief days I'd spent with him growing up were filled with nothing but love and adoration, but when he left, those feelings were replaced with a sense of pain and longing. I knew he had loved my mother, but his abandonment after her death made me question whether his love for me had been real—even if I knew that it was.

I buried my face in my hands. The torture of sitting in an empty house, unable to leave and not being able to tell anyone why, of never knowing if my father would return for me—it was agony. Money delivered but no letter. Not even so much as an "I miss you."

And then five years later, he had shown up unannounced on my doorstep, fear and guilt in his eyes as he tried to apologize, tried to explain, but how do you explain five years of absence? I'd asked him why, demanded an answer, but he could give none. Why would he now when he never had before?

I'd offered him no warm welcome. I didn't want to see him, didn't want to speak with him, wanted nothing to do with him. I just wanted him out of my life forever. Even though there were so many things I had wanted to say, so many questions I'd needed to ask, five years of lonely confusion and bitterness had stolen the words from me and drained me of any forgiveness.

He'd set his ring on the table, his green eyes asking for something I could not give. The realization of what he'd done, of what he'd put me through, had reflected in his eyes. He wanted to ask for my forgiveness, but he knew that he had no right to.

After he left, I refused to touch the ring on the table. Every evening I stared at it, resenting it, figuring that accepting it would mean accepting everything he had done to me.

When the messenger came, it was not to deliver the expected bag of coins to get me through the winter. It was to inform me of his death. The first emotion I felt was happiness. I was finally free, and that was why I'd felt so guilty.

"I'm sorry," I managed through sobs, releasing the guilt with my words.

Joy over his death had never been the action I intended, but after so much pain, it was the only thing that brought relief. I touched the stones covering his grave, struggling to understand why he had never just been honest with me. I didn't know why my father never told me he was a Kavari, didn't know why he never told me the truth about my mother, or why he chose to forget me for five years. I didn't even know if he loved me, but the fact was, even if he had never loved me, I had still loved him. I would never know his reasons, but I did know I could let it continue to destroy me, or I could let it go.

My fingers curled into the earth beneath me, dirt clustering under my nails.

"I forgive you."

With those words, I released all the anger and bitterness. The weight of a thousand worlds lifted from my shoulders. He would never hear those words, never know that I chose to forgive him, but it was almost like he knew. I only wished I'd been able to say them when he was still alive.

I smiled sadly, remembering my father as he ought to be remembered: long visits filled with laughter, running through the field at sunset, the smell of blueberry pie permeating the house. My father's soothing voice reading me stories each night from my favorite book. Soft brown hair, warm green eyes. Strong arms that wound around me. He was a man who loved his wife and daughter, a man who had made the ultimate sacrifice for the people and the country he loved.

I stood to my feet, holding back tears as I left my bitterness behind. One final longing look was lent to the grave as I whispered sorrowfully:

"Goodbye."

Vladimir stood waiting for me at the bottom of the hill, the horses grazing quietly beside him. I wiped the tears from my face, rubbing my damp hand on my skirt, and studied the ground, noting the patches in the earth devoid of any vegetation.

"Why would they burn the bodies?"

Vladimir's mind was calculating as he twirled the unusual weapon in his hands.

"His attackers didn't expect to lose that many men. I always assumed they were burned to destroy any trace of their identity left behind." He flipped the crescent, a streak of sunlight catching it for a moment. "Until I saw this." He rubbed his thumb over the top of the metal. "And I remembered that Brenden doesn't bury their dead. They burn them."

My hands clenched into fists at my sides, and I felt the cold metal of my father's ring on my finger, felt my mother's clasp poking against my skin from the pocket where it lay.

Brenden is ready.

The seven patches of scarred earth stared back at me, twisting in a dizzying circle before my eyes and igniting the vengeance that still burned within me—but the vengeance reigned purer now.

I looked up and found Death watching me from the shadows. He cocked his head, waiting for my next move. He hadn't come to claim me. I sensed it, sensed the change in him, and the question hovering in his eyes.

He had come to see if I would wield him.

I lifted my chin and stared Death in the face, remembering a time not so long ago when I had begged him for my life as he dragged me into the unknown.

Not yet, I whispered.

END OF BOOK 1

EPILOGUE

THE DISGRUNTLED SOLDIERS bowed their heads, parting before the approaching man like wheat bowing to the wind and bending to its will. The man's lifted gaze radiated confidence, his head held regally as he maneuvered his way through the men. A slight limp disturbed his stride, giving a lilt to his otherwise commanding gait. Blood seeped through a bandage wound tightly around his upper thigh, and though the injury appeared brutal, no pain marked the man's face. A thick hand rested on the pommel of his longsword. Soot clung to the sheath, and the man's dirty clothes reeked of smoke.

His dark eyes focused straight ahead, riveted on a lone canvas tent with the outer flaps tied securely shut. Five sentries guarded the entrance. Nervousness encompassed their faces like a hunted animal's. Always waiting for an enemy to appear.

"Unfasten the door." The man's voice was rough and authoritative.

Hesitation slithered through the men. The youngest one stepped forward, concern lacing his face as he began to undo the knots. The man frowned as he waited, fingers tapping against the hilt of his weapon. The entrance fluttered before him, canvas now loose. It took his eyes a moment to adjust as he stepped into the dim light, but the interior began to unfold before him.

"Sir?" Four guards stood, one at each corner of the tent, with their swords held protectively in front of them.

A soldier lay on the ground at the center of the large tent, his lifeless eyes staring into the beyond. His limbs were not twisted. No blood stained the man's uniform. No visible wound or broken bone. He lay as if he had crumpled to the earth exactly where he stood.

The authoritative man frowned again, eyes wandering beyond the body. A small form cowered on the ground before the dead soldier, arms clutched possessively around her knees, long braids falling down her back. Her dark eyes rose to meet the newcomer. A trail of tears stained her cheeks.

The man glanced up to the guards around him. They showed no fear of the dead man. It was the child they feared. She curled in on herself, yet stared up at the man defiantly.

"Captain Du—" One of the soldiers cleared his throat.

"They informed me of what happened." The captain interrupted him, stepping around the body to get closer to the girl. His advancement made the soldiers grip their swords tighter, wide eyes pleading for their commander to be careful. His injured leg wobbled as he knelt just out of reach of the frightened child.

"I must say," he began, "I am so very sorry for everything that has happened to you."

Suspicion pooled in the young girl's eyes, waiting for a trap.

"Tearing you away from your home like that was not my intention, but I needed to make sure you were safe. Make sure that the others didn't reach you first."

The girl said nothing. The captain hadn't expected her to speak. In fact, he found it better this way.

"We're not going to hurt you," he continued. "We want to help you. After all that your mother did for us, she would have wanted me to take care of you."

Her dark eyes narrowed to slits, glittering with distrust.

The captain's eyes fell to the dead soldier, eyes roving over the carcass. "I'm not angry about this. You were just trying to survive, but I'm glad that I know what you really are now. It explains why your mother tried to hide you in Gapsvar."

Her lower lip trembled as fear flashed across her features.

He half-smiled. "I had a daughter once, about your age. I loved her more than anything."

The girl loosened the death grip on her knees.

"What happened to her?" she asked quietly.

The captain let out a sigh tinged with sadness. "I'm afraid this world is full of evil people, and just like that man and woman tricked your mother and took her from you, someone also took my daughter from me."

"They were good people." Her voice grew softer.

The captain dipped his head. "So were the people who killed my daughter—or so they said."

He looked back to the man on the ground, pulling his

words together carefully. "Those evil people are out there running free, and I could really use your help in bringing them to justice. I can't bring your mother back any more than I can bring my daughter back, but together, I think we can afford them the justice they deserve." He watched her closely, gauging her response. "Is that something you would like?"

She stared at him, a girl who had been conditioned all her life to not trust anyone. Now the one person she had been able to trust was gone. He saw the workings of her mind reflected in her eyes. She would have to learn to trust someone else now.

"You won't have to hide anymore," the captain promised, and then he reached out his gloved hand, offering to take hers.

Each of the guards held their breath, shocked at the captain's recklessness. The girl considered his hand, mind warring over every option, but then she decided, placed her frail hand in his.

The captain smiled and pulled her to her feet. They stepped around the body, and the soldiers watched in shock as the two strolled out of the tent, brittle grass crunching beneath their feet.

"What shall I call you?" the captain asked, looking down at her.

"Helvah."

ACKNOWLEDGMENTS

I don't even know where to begin on the acknowledgments for this book. It seems surreal that *The Blood Vier* is even out in the world, that readers are holding a tangible copy within their hands.

Enough thanks could never be given to my mom who is my biggest supporter. I love you. You're always encouraging, always cheerleading, and always asking to read the first draft even though you know no one besides me is allowed to lay eyes on it. Thank you so much for always being excited about my books and wanting to read them (multiple times at your request). Not everyone has that stable rock in their lives that they can turn to, and I'm so thankful for you.

To my Aunt Debbie, this book would not be what it is without you. You spent countless hours of your own personal time reading and editing this book, trudging through my stupid grammar mistakes, putting up with my character's immaturity, and giving me all of the right pointers, plot development, and book changes that I needed. Your guidance made me feel like this book actually had a chance. You are a compassionate friend to everyone you meet, and the love of Jesus Christ shines through you. I don't know if you will ever know the depths of my gratefulness for all that you have contributed to my writing. Thank you.

To my sister Donna, thank you for reading my book (more than once) and giving me feedback, as well as enduring my never-ending texts and phone calls with blurb revisions and ideas. Thank you for your support and always being there if I needed someone to talk to.

An angel sent from heaven above, my Instagram writing buddy, Caitlan, you are a magician with words, and I can't wait to read your published book one day. You took the disaster of what I was trying to accomplish with the blurb and created a smooth and seamless masterpiece. Thank you for always being there to offer encouragement (and to help me through my book's identity crisis right before its publication announcement.)

To all the friends and family who read my book or listened to countless drafts of query letters and blurb revisions, thank you for always having my back and believing in me. This book wouldn't exist without you amazing people in my life.

I want to thank God for everything He has done for me, for allowing this publishing journey to be possible, for my salvation through His Son and for never turning His back on me.

And finally, to you, reader, thank you.

Thank you for taking a chance on this book, and on me.

CPSIA information can be obtained
at www.ICGtesting.com
Printed in the USA
BVHW092351020922
646137BV00018B/601/J